PIANO DAYS

Other Books by Don Reid

Heroes and Outlaws of the Bible

Sunday Morning Memories

You Know It's Christmas When…
(with Debo Reid and Langdon Reid)

Random Memories (with Harold Reid)

O Little Town

One Lane Bridge

The Mulligans of Mt. Jefferson

Half and Half

The Music of the Statler Brothers: An Anthology

Life Lessons

donreid.net
thestatlerbrothers.com

Piano Days

A Novel

DON REID

A story of three boys growing up once upon a beautiful time

MERCER UNIVERSITY PRESS
Macon, Georgia

MUP/ H1023

© 2022 by Mercer University Press
Published by Mercer University Press
1501 Mercer University Drive
Macon, Georgia 31207
All rights reserved

26 25 24 23 22   5 4 3 2 1

Books published by Mercer University Press are printed on acid-free paper that meets the requirements of the American National Standard for Information Sciences—Permanence of Paper for Printed Library Materials.

Printed and bound in Canada.

This book is set in Adobe Garamond Pro.

Cover/jacket design by Burt&Burt.

| ISBN | Print | 978-0-88146-840-3 |
| ISBN | eBook | 978-0-88146-841-0 |

Cataloging-in-Publication Data is available from the Library of Congress

To Harold

Maybe this is the place to say it. We were young and imperfect. Worse than some. Not as bad as others. Looking back on those wonderful and tender years, I can see some things we did were crude, even rude, and yes, we bent some rules but never broke any laws. We walked up to the line more than once, but we seldom crossed it. We were boys, red-blooded and green. Adventurous and curious. We liked girls and girls liked us. Some decisions we had to make on the spur of the moment; some we fretted over for days. But everything we finally did, we lived with for a lifetime to come, and to be honest, we had more good times than we had regrets. I don't know of any surviving adult who will admit to everything that has gone through their minds, or will confess to all the things they did and said when they were teenagers, or will own, without reservation, everything they wish they'd never done. Would I not change a thing? I won't go that far, but reflecting on all those sweet and youthful memories, there's some I wish I'd never done but a few I wish I'd done more. To intentionally repeat myself, we were young and imperfect, but we had fun.

Chapter One

August 1959

The first time I saw Lannie Mae Kiser the way I still remember her after all these years was by the candy shelf in the concession stand at the softball diamond behind the First Faith Presbyterian Church. I had seen her at school many times and a few Saturday mornings at the Empire Theater, but never in the light and manner that I saw her on that memorable, long-ago summer day. My eyes were full of the most beautiful suntanned face I had ever been that close to, and I admit I was a little short of breath at the things going through my mind. You see, as many times as I had glanced at Lannie Mae—and I'd even spoken to her a couple of times—this was a first I was not really prepared for. This was the first time she and I were totally alone in an enclosed room and her attention was fully and only on me. Fourteen years old. That was me. Lannie Mae was fifteen and it was August 17, 1959. And how do I remember the actual date? The better question is how could I ever forget it.

There were games four nights a week at the Church Softball League and I was there every night. Our team, the First Faith Presbyterians, played two games each week and this was my first summer in uniform on the adult team. Sort of a milestone toward manhood. I hadn't missed being at a game since I was six and had dreamed about playing on the field all those years. The season started in May and I had actually been in only a few games—hey, let's be honest, I had been in *one* game. June 10th, sixth inning, right field. No balls came my way, and when I got to bat in the top of the seventh, I got the bunt signal. I could always bunt and run fast. But not always fast enough because I got thrown out.

Do you know how awkward it is when you give it all you have but the ball beats you to the base and you have to turn and walk back to the bench? You never know where to look. You're out and you know it and so does everyone else within a hundred miles of the diamond. All of everyone's attention is on you and you just look at your feet as you walk that furlong back to the first seat you find available. Some guys kick the dust to show the spectators and coach and their fellow players that they're disappointed and angry, as if they need to prove to someone they didn't mean to get thrown out. I always just pulled at my pants and tugged at my belt and breathed really hard so I'd look like I had given 200 percent. (Don't you hate people who say 200%?) Parents, coaches, and some fans will all buy this sometime or another, but the other players, who didn't like you to start with, will stare you down with a look that says, "Quit acting, you little twerp and run faster the next time."

I was the youngest and newest member on First Faith. As the shiny new rookie, it was my honor to serve as the concession manager for all the games. This had been the tradition since the establishment of the league a decade ago. Well, at least that's one way of looking at it. Everyone has their own interpretation of things that happen, and I guess if someone had said they made me stock the shelves with candy bars and the drink boxes with Pepsi and Dr. Pepper twice a week because I was the youngest member on the team, I really couldn't have said they were lying. I mean, if someone even went as far as strongly suggesting they let me on the team just to keep the shelves and drink box full, I couldn't take a lot of issue with them. Oh, at fourteen, I might have walked away, pulled my cap off with one hand and pushed my hair back with the other and sighed really big, but I wouldn't have called them a liar or

August 1959

anything. Okay, truth be known, I was the concession manager because no one else wanted to be.

The softball field lay just behind the church parking lot and I spent most of my growing-up summers and a good part of my life on those premises. My family and I went to the church every Sunday morning. Preaching. Sunday school. Bible school. Picnics. Easter Sunrise Services. Christmas programs. Social suppers. Youth meetings. Halloween parties. Weddings. Funerals. Boy Scout meetings in the basement. In the winter we brought sleds, old tires, and trash can lids and flew down the embankment by the Sunday school rooms, ending up in a snowy left field every evening after supper for as long as the ice and snow would last.

By April, when the wildflowers began blooming again and the days got a little longer, the ball team would start their practices. I lived from spring to spring for that. I had practiced with them from the time I was nine years old but this was my first legal year. Fourteen to forty-five was pretty much the age of the team. It was an unwritten league rule. They figured anybody over or under those ages could get hurt out there. Fast-pitch softball was not a child's game. It has come to be a girls' game, but in those days of the '50s and '60s it was all men. The bases were closer than in baseball and the pitcher was closer to the batter than in baseball, and if you weren't careful you could take a line drive in the gullet before you knew what hit you.

The ballfield was the meeting place every June, July, and August weekday for about a half dozen of us in the neighborhood. The team colors were green and white, so if you wore a green felt ballcap and were ten to fourteen years old, you were likely to be there about ten a.m. We'd play pickup games, tell lies and make plans. But this summer was not my summer for telling lies because I was coming of age and doing many of the things I had been lying about for years—like being a present uniform-wearing member of the adult softball team. Another new thing that summer was the Key. I had the Key. The cherished and prestigious Key. The magic Key we all had fantasized about for so many summers past. The Key to the concession stand. We could open the door and go into the dark, cinder-block building and actually go behind the counter. We could swing out the heavy wooden shutter door that let in the sunlight and said, "We're Open" to the crowd each night. Of course, we weren't supposed to do that during the day. We, make that I, was only to open the door when the truck from Crown Groceries came on Monday and Thursday mornings at eleven a.m. They brought soft drinks, which Billy and Jayo always called pop, in glass returnable bottles: Pepsi, Dr. Pepper, Royal Crown Cola, and Pal. They brought four kinds of candy bars, too—Clark, Hershey, Milky Way, and Mounds—along with Cracker Jacks with prizes in the bottom and little bags of peanuts for pouring in your Pepsi. I promised the league president, Mr. C. M. Wester, who Daddy and everybody else called Sim, that I would not allow anyone else in the stand. Ever. That I would not lend the Key to anyone and that I would not steal anything. Ever. And that I would have the stand open at six thirty on every game night. And as good as my word, I always had the stand open at six thirty on every game night.

Without fail, Billy Hudlow and his little brother Jayo were waiting on me at ten o'clock on Monday mornings, usually riding their bikes around the bases or hitting pop-ups to each other. They knew the truck was coming and they knew the Key was coming, too. Now, of course, the Key was a luxury and a novelty, but by about twelve thirty when the sun was right above us, it became a necessity. When we opened the door and went inside that old eight-by-eight-foot cement-floored building, it was certainly a welcome comfort and refuge from the midday heat. We would stretch out on the floor and just lie there and pant and giggle and tell each other wishes and not-too-well-thought-out plans for the not-too-near or too-far future.

I rode my bike to the side door of the concession stand, kicked the kickstand in place, got off, took the Key out of my dungarees pocket and opened the door. I had no reason to go in yet but I liked exercising my authority in front of Billy and Jayo, who liked watching me exercise it. This particular morning, they were not riding the bases or playing ball. They were looking for change in the dirt near the stand that customers may have dropped. Two summers ago, Bennie Shipe accidently found a quarter and ever since, we looked for money like it was a promised treasure just waiting to jump in our pockets. To my knowledge, and I would have known, that quarter was the only piece of currency ever found on the grounds, but it kept us in suspense for years just looking and anticipating the possibility.

"I found a cigar."

"Whatcha gonna do with it, Jayo?"

"It's half-smoked."

"Watcha gonna do with the other half?"

"Eat it."

Jayo was six years old and it wasn't the first cigar he had eaten. Jayo ate cigars, pennies, postage stamps, and candy wrappers, and he chewed any gum he could find—stick or wad. He didn't do it for attention because he knew how sick it made us and how disgusting we thought he was for doing it. So he'd sneak off and do it, hiding under the bleachers eating a cheroot. He wouldn't touch a cigarette, though. He said they were nasty.

"Watcha doin'?" asked his big brother, Billy. He was my age.

"Opening up for the Crown truck," I said. "Where's Toby and the Spinners?"

In spite of the name, Toby and the Spinners weren't a current rock 'n' roll singing group. Toby was the typical chubby member of every group of young boys who ever hung out together. He was loud around a few and shy around many. He was overbearing to people who didn't like him and forgivable to his friends. Girls thought he was a jerk and didn't see a thing funny about him. We *knew* he was a jerk and thought he was hilarious. The Spinners were twins. All the twins I have ever known have had cutesy first names that rhymed. Larry and Gary. Donnie and Ronnie. Teddy and Freddy. Not the Spinners. They were called Howard and Bud. Whenever they were asked why they didn't have rhyming names, they would say, "One of us was named after our father and the other was named after our mother." That's all I know. If I knew more, I'd tell you. I swear I would. The Spinners were my age, thin and blond-haired. They were always polite to adults and had the trust and admiration of every mother in the neighborhood. They were viewed as the ideal companions every parent desired for their son or daughter. If you said, "I'm going with the Spinners," you were asked nothing else.

In reality, Howard and Bud had collectively smoked a pack of cigarettes every day since they were seven years old. They could cuss as bad or as good, however you want to look at it, as my Uncle Carl. And brother, he could stop a crap game. They loved picking fights even though Toby could whip both of them at the same time, and they would lie gloriously about any subject that came up.

August 1959

"This is the week Toby was going to camp," Billy said.

"That's right," I said. "I forgot about that."

Billy walked around and checked all the merchandise on the shelves, then finally said, "I want a drink."

"Not yet. Wait till we get hot." I was in charge.

Billy sat up on the drink box while I counted candy bars in stock and wrote down the numbers for the delivery truck.

"What about Howard and Bud?" I asked between numbers.

"Well, you ain't gonna believe this. They've gone on vacation!"

I lost count and stopped and looked at him. In 1959, in our circles, very few families went anywhere on vacation. Only white-collar families did that and then it was only a long weekend at the beach. I can count on half a hand the number of times my family got in a car and went anyplace to stay overnight. It just wasn't common. And it wasn't common for the Spinners either.

"Where'd they go?"

"To the zoo in Washington. And then they're goin' to a ballgame in Baltimore. Don't Jimmy Piersall play for Baltimore?"

"No. Cleveland now. When they get back, we won't know what to believe. They'll lie about everything they didn't see."

Billy jumped down and went to the door and yelled, "Jayo, get out of that trash can, you little idiot."

I started counting the Clark bars again. I couldn't hear Billy behind me and I thought he'd gone outside. But when he said something, I realized he was standing in the doorway looking up toward the road.

"Here she comes," he said.

"Crown Groceries truck?" I asked, because it was about

time for it.

"No. Her."

I turned around and walked to the door, but I knew before I looked who Her was. Her was the month of August wrapped in pink and soaked in a river of sweetness that made her skin soft and her hair smell like Christmas candy. Her was a picture I carried in my billfold that I looked at in my room on summer nights imagining she was doing something wonderful and exciting somewhere. Her was my first love and I knew it then. Some way, I knew how important she would always be in my memories. Her made me weak. And I loved it.

Lannie Mae stopped and said something to Jayo, who offered her something that looked like a small piece of wood. Then she came toward the door of the stand. I noticed the way she didn't speak to me first. I liked that, too.

"Hi, Billy. Where did Jayo get that taffy? He's got it all over himself."

"Taffy? I didn't know he had any taffy. Jayo! Where did you find taffy?"

Billy was gone and Jayo was running. I don't think Billy was all that worried about the taffy because Jayo had eaten a lot worse things than other people's candy. I think he was giving Lannie and me some privacy. Or maybe he was leaving because he felt uncomfortable. Or jealous. Or pushed out. Or maybe he thought Jayo was going to choke or something. You really never know why some people do things.

Lannie Mae had on white shorts and a blue shirt. She also had tan legs and pink lips. She wore glasses the way most people wore jewelry, like an ornament instead of a necessity. She made everything else in the world seem unimportant.

"Was it okay that I came down here?" she asked quietly.

Was it okay that Columbus discovered America? That we

won the Revolutionary War? That Jesus died for our sins so that I might go to heaven in spite of what I was thinking that very minute?

"Yeah, it's okay."

We stood and looked at one another for what must have been an awkward length of time but seems just the right amount in my memory. We were both wondering who was going to make the first move. She was a year older, but I was more in love and that made up for the difference. We had come close but we had never kissed before. I knew at that moment this would be the day. I reached and touched her arm. I could smell her skin. Not her perfume because she was wearing none. But I could smell her skin. And I still can.

I heard the roar about the same time I saw the dust, and I knew the Crown Groceries truck was on its way. I had no more time. I kissed her as hard and as sincerely as I've ever kissed anyone since. For the first time in my life, I felt a body pressed against mine from knee to nose. But nothing good lasts forever, for within seconds after Lannie Mae Kiser opened her mouth, the Crown Groceries man opened the door.

All the time he and I counted candy bars and peanut bags and figured return deposits on the drink bottles, he grinned. I know I moved around too fast and talked too much while Lannie drifted outside and talked with Billy and Jayo. It seemed to be taking a lot longer than usual to settle up with him, but I guess that was it. It just *seemed* to be taking longer. When he finally closed the back of his truck and climbed up to the driver's seat, I could see Lannie walking slowly up the hill toward the highway. I trotted past where Billy and Jayo were sitting on the grass to try and catch her.

"I found a tick," Jayo said.

"Way to go, buddy. I'll give you an RC to go with it when

I come back," I said over my shoulder.

I caught Lannie and said, "I'm sorry about that. I didn't realize he was that close on us."

"That's okay. It's just that he knows my daddy. But it's all right."

"Are you coming back?" I asked. Inquired. Pleaded. Begged.

"I can't right now. I've got a piano lesson at one."

"It's only a quarter to twelve."

"Yes, but I've got to practice before I go. She can tell when I don't practice and I haven't touched it since last Monday's lesson."

"I'll help you," I said quickly.

"Do you really play?" she asked. "People say you do, but I've never heard you play."

"I took from Miss Moyers for six years. Ever since I was eight."

"Did you really? Why'd you quit?"

"I got better than her."

Lannie Mae and I both laughed at this and I'm glad because I loved making Lannie Mae laugh. But it wasn't that big of a joke. Miss Kathleen Moyers was the leading piano virtuoso in the town. (There apparently weren't many other piano players in the area.) She had taught generations and was still going strong. She taught in the front parlor of her house, which looked haunted even on the brightest spring day of the year. She was always dressed the way most women dressed only once a week: high heels, pearls, and a tight home perm that made her white/blonde (I never could distinguish which) hair lay to her head like a Buick Roadmaster to a mountain road. She smelled, no, make that reeked of every scent Avon had on the open market. Everyone marveled at how she had not aged in

August 1959

the past thirty years. My belief was that she had, but no one could see it under all the makeup. She was a walking disguise for a stout, aging woman with an ostensive sweat gland problem. And she could smoke with the best of them. She made Howard and Bud look like the novices they were. She kept a pack of Pall Mall and a Zippo lighter on the ledge of the piano and had one lit at all times. She had a grown son no one ever saw who lived on the second floor of her old and spooky house. Rumor had it there was something not quite right about him mentally or emotionally. Others said he was an AWOL from WWII and still in hiding. Although no one can ever recall seeing him, you could hear him playing the piano if you walked past the house on summer nights when all the windows were open. We knew it was him even though all the lights were off inside because Miss Moyers would always be sitting on the front porch smoking. And there he was, playing music in the dark house like you hear in an old horror movie when the heroine sits down to play after dinner just before the scream. We climbed up the rose trestle one night and looked in the window, but then that's another story I'll tell you later because it doesn't have squat to do with Lannie Mae and her piano lesson.

After the laugh was over, Lannie Mae and I stood there just looking at each other. Really looking at each other. We could both feel the mood change and deepen. It felt like something was going to happen. I didn't know what, but then I didn't care what. I was just ready for it. I think I learned an adult lesson there on the dirt lane leading up to the highway in the near-noon August sun. I learned that you have to *make* things happen sometimes. You have to move at the right time and say the right thing. They say nothing happens until someone sells something. And sometimes you have to sell before you even know what you're selling. I made that move not knowing where it was going to take me. Instead of asking again, "Are you coming back?" I looked straight in her evergreen eyes and said, "Come back."

Lannie Mae said, "When?"

And I knew I'd made the sale.

When I got back to the stand, Billy and Jayo were inside digging through the big blue Pepsi drink box.

"I gave Jayo an RC and I got him some peanuts, too," Billy said.

"That's all right," I said. "I'll tell Mr. Wester the Crown man miscounted. Hand me a Dr. Pepper."

Billy handed me the drink and then playfully went through the motions of closing the drink box lid on Jayo's head. "Come on, Jayo. Get your head out of there. You're letting all the cold out."

Jayo slid down and headed for the door with his RC cradled in one hand and the other guiding peanuts into his mouth. He mumbled something about going out behind center field and looking for wild onions. Billy waited for his little brother to clear the door.

"Well, what happened?" he asked.

"Nothin' really."

"Come on. Did you kiss her?"

"Oh, yeah."

"What'd she say?"

"Nothin' really."

"Come on, man. You ain't tellin' me nothin'."

"I'm tryin'," I said, a little annoyed. "I mean, can you imagine what it would be like to kiss Debbie Reynolds?"

Billy didn't answer. He was waiting for more.

August 1959

"She's comin' back at five thirty," I finally said. "Nobody will be down here except her and me."

"Old man Wester," Billy offered.

"Naw, he never comes till six forty-five anyway."

"You gonna tell me about it tonight?" Billy asked, grinning.

"Sure. Yeah."

"You nervous?"

I thought about this for a minute. But Billy was too good a friend to lie to. And anyway, he would have known I was lying as soon as I said it. So I threw it back to him. "Wouldn't you be?"

"Yeah," he said. "If I was gonna kiss Debbie Reynolds I would be."

If Debbie Reynolds ever did to Donald O'Conner in one of their movies together what Lannie Mae was doing to me, I don't know how he tap-danced as gracefully as he did. I was scrubbed and dressed in my ball uniform and sitting on the edge of the bed at four thirty. My mother was puzzled as to why I washed my hair and took a bath *before* a ballgame. I told her I was kind of sleepy and was just trying to get awake. It's funny, but she grinned at me the same way the Crown Groceries man had.

I killed as much time as I possibly could. As I was going through the house on the way to the back door, the living room piano caught my eye. All of a sudden it was a symbol of Her and I was drawn to it. I sat down and played, and I wish I could remember exactly what it was I played. But no matter how hard I try I just can't say for sure. For some reason I feel it would be important if I could remember. It could have been anything from "Heart and Soul" to "Theme from Picnic." Lannie asked earlier if I really played. Well, yeah, I really play. I just can't remember what I played on one of the most important and memorable days of my life.

Later, I opened the side door of the concession stand and stood inside in the dark, watching for Lannie to round the church and start down the hill. I wanted to be prepared for her, but I wasn't. There's no way to prepare for the unknown. It's like fighting evil spirits; you don't know they're coming until they're on you and you have no earthly defense. I had no earthly defense for what rounded that Presbyterian corner. To this day, after all this passing time, that image is as clear to me as the eastern sun that blinded me through my bedroom window this morning. Her hair hung straight below her shoulders. Her yellow blouse was tucked tightly in the waistband of a baby blue skirt. Her suntan burned a memory in my mind that hasn't faded one shade with the years.

This time we didn't talk. Words were of no value now. When she walked through the door, she stopped and pushed it shut behind her. Then she made the move that nearly buckled my knees. She leaned her back against it like Dorothy Malone in *Written on the Wind* and just stared at me. Sunlight streamed through the cracks of the wooden shutter and the side door. Just enough light to see her outline and her eyes—so close to me I couldn't focus. Fourteen can't stand much more than this. I went to her and we kissed and clung to each other. I can't recall all the things that went through my heart and my body as I held this dream and this teenage vision against me. I do remember thinking about Billy and knowing that he was going to ask me to tell him everything. I also knew I never would. And out of respect for Lannie, I never did. I only knew that nothing had ever mattered as much to me as this perfect,

August 1959

sweetest moment of my life. And nothing in my future could ever matter as much. Nothing could pull me away from her soft young body and her warm angelic face. Nothing but the whine of a Ford pickup truck pulling up beside the stand.

I didn't have to look out, and it's a good thing because I didn't have time to. I knew it was old Sim Wester. How could I forget! He always came early to drag the field before the game on Monday evenings. The next thirty seconds were like a scene from one of those movies where the room is in turmoil and someone walks up the outside steps and puts a key in the lock. Then, when he opens the door, everything in the room is in perfect order. I don't know how, but when Mr. Wester made his untimely entrance, Lannie was sitting on the drink box and I was counting Clark bars again.

"Oh, hello Mr. Wester. This is Lannie Mae Kiser. She's gonna work the stand for me tonight during our game in case I play. I've been going over the prices of everything with her. Showin' her how to restock the drink box. In case I'm on the bench tonight, I'll be here to help her if she has any problem. She's really good at makin' change and everything. I'll help you drag the field if you need any help or anything." The words kept coming and I couldn't slow down.

C. M. "Sim" Wester said he could manage by himself, and just as he walked out he grinned at me. For a fleeting second, the old man reminded me of the Crown Groceries guy and a little bit of my mother.

There was a big crowd at the game that night because we were into the playoffs. We were also into the heart of vacation season, and those few who always went to the beach were gone. We had exactly ten players and one more game to lose, and then we were out of it. I was on the bench. Come to think of it, I was the *only* one on the bench. I walked up to the stand and sort of stood around with Lannie when our team was in the field. We didn't have much to say and she didn't need much help with candy bars and drinks. I was standing up there looking at her instead of the game when our shortstop took one in the mouth in the fifth inning. He cut his lip and knocked out a tooth and they took him straight to the hospital. The game had been halted for about fifteen minutes when the coach called for me, and I started going the other way. I mean, I wanted to get in the game, but I didn't want to play short where a guy just got his tooth knocked out. I tried to think of a way of telling the coach this and at the same time suppress the smile that was fighting to control my face. I was thinking, "I hope Jayo doesn't find that tooth tomorrow!"

As it turned out, the coach had no intention of putting me at shortstop. He moved the second baseman over, brought the center fielder up to second, the right fielder over to center and yes, sent me to right field. I never got a ball but I did get to bat in the sixth inning. Two men were on and two outs were gone. We were one run behind. I could save the game and keep us in the playoffs. The count was 2–2, and I was *almost* as nervous as I had been an hour and a half before in the concession stand. (Some things do take precedence over softball.) I swung at the next pitch with the force most men save for national enemies. I discovered my second revelation of the day: that it's a longer walk from the plate to the bench than from first base to the bench.

In the seventh inning, they got us three up and three down, so I didn't have the misfortune of making the last out of the season. I only blew the last opportunity to score runs with men in scoring position. There was a lot of consoling and handshaking after the game, and my mom and dad were particularly concerned that I might be upset. They waited on me in the car while Lannie Mae and I locked up. Her dad was waiting on her, too. She was putting empties in the cases.

"Leave those," I said. "I'll get 'em in the morning. Will you be here in the morning?"

She looked at me and then at the floor. She held my hand and said, "Are you mad at me?"

"Why would I be mad at you?" I asked in all sincerity.

"Well...you know."

I really didn't know because I was anything but mad. How could letting me kiss her and hold her make me mad? I don't think she meant to say that. She didn't know what to say and she was just looking for some sort of reaction from me. Some sort of approval of us. I didn't know what words to use to let her know everything was alright. That everything was great! So I did what was natural, and what I found out years later always works when you're confronted by a crying or saddened woman and your mind can't deliver the proper solace your tongue should be delivering.

I kissed her.

And then came the words. It was like a speech you learn in a school play that you can still recite twenty years later. It was like it was written for me and I had memorized each word and practiced each phrase. There were thoughts and combinations of words I didn't even know I knew. And I'm not adding to them now. I remember them exactly as I spoke them.

"Lannie Mae, what happened here this evening is the most beautiful thing that has ever happened to me. Just being close to you takes my breath away. Touching your hand makes me feel faint, like I'm walking in my own dream. If I never touch another girl's hand or kiss another pair of lips, my life is complete. What we felt and had here today is sacred. It's between us forever and always. I would never breathe a word of it to anyone. Even if I live to be fifty years old and they torture me with knives and hot needles, I'd never tell a soul. This moment belongs to you and me alone."

As I crawled in the backseat of the car, my mother reached over from the front and patted my knee. She smiled her smile of comfort for the lost ballgame. My dad looked over his shoulder at me as he started the engine and said, "Cheer up, son. Every day won't be this bad."

Lannie Mae's dad drove by us as they were pulling out of the parking lot. From her window she turned and threw me a kiss. I caught it. And I've never let it go.

Chapter Two

October 1959

It was a time when DJs were called radio announcers and considered celebrities in small towns. A time when the Jackson High basketball game was the biggest social event of the week for the whole city. A time of hair tonic, ponytails, and twenty-five-cent school lunches. Of record hops, Ajax, and Fluid Drive. A time when teachers were feared, preachers were respected, and the Friday night fights were on television and only occasionally on the parking lot at Jackson High. Occasionally meant about once every five years.

Every time the subject of great fights came up, the one five years before was still talked about and exaggerated about and added to. Tommy Barr hit Lloyd Showker so hard he knocked his left eyeball out of its socket and it was hanging on his cheek. Coach Lambert put it back in place and Lloyd never even had to wear glasses. At least, that was the word around school by the time Billy and Toby and the Spinners and I got there. We were charmed and awed by all the inaccurate details that go with any school legend. This is the way we heard it and pieced it together:

It was January 1954, about two weeks after the first of the year. A senior, Tommy was a guard on the football team whose season had been something short of brag worthy. Having a losing record his last year, Tommy missed the glory he felt the years before had earned him. He had played varsity even as a freshman, always first string and always most feared. He had a shoulder span a good-sized crow couldn't fly across and a haircut it definitely couldn't make a nest in. Tommy had trusted old Mr. Toliver to give him a flattop and Mr. Toliver thought a flattop was something on table legs. He had been a barber for forty-two years and resented anyone who told him how to cut their hair. He cut everyone's hair the way *he* wanted to, therefore, he cut everyone's hair the same. What Tommy's request got him was a near shave with a little dab hanging down in the front. A crew cut. A skeeball. A teddy bear. A summer buzz cut. Except Tommy's was year-round. He looked like that trumpet player, Rocky Rockwell, on *The Lawrence Welk Show*. His head was the shape and approximate weight of a medicine ball and looked like it sat on an oak stump that stretched a nineteen-and-a-half-inch collar to its limit. He had steel-hard arms that hung precariously close to his knees, and when he swayed, the seat of his pants came dangerously close to the ground. Tommy was not a whisper over five feet six.

Lloyd Showker was a different animal.

He stood a full six feet, topped off with a well-Vaselined head of black hair that you could always see the comb tracks in. It was parted cleanly, if not severely, on the left side of his head. He wore long-sleeved sport shirts buttoned tightly to the neck, Cordovan shoes in search of a shine, and dungarees rolled up twice at the bottom. He had a face that defied his few years on earth. At eighteen, he looked like he was sixty years old. He walked with his fingers and arms bowed at the same degree, kind of like he was carrying a bucket of something in each hand. He stooped slightly for what he must have thought gave off a manly effect and was never seen carrying a book or books his entire four years of high school. He carried a constant air, or should that be aroma, of Chesterfield cigarettes and some sort of grain. Wheat? Barley? Alfalfa? Whatever that smell was, it seemed to be in his pores. Or maybe just in his clothes. Or

October 1959

maybe in his blood. And maybe it was something he rolled around in out in the fields, kind of like our old dog, Willie, who couldn't pass up a good rolling opportunity. It was rather offensive and not something you'd want to cuddle up to. But be that as it may, it didn't seem that Lloyd was ever in need of female companionship. He always had a girlfriend. They walked the halls arm in arm and she was always a good-looking girl.

Lloyd did not excel in sports, nor was he academically inclined. He participated in no extracurricular school activities of any kind and would have been one of many who passed through the halls and the years undistinguished if not for The Fight. I've never understood the connection, but whenever anyone told this story, they always pointed out that the guy had a real fear of red worms. Do with that whatever you like. It means nothing to me.

Statistics tell us that most murders and crimes of any nature are committed for love or money. This doesn't apply to snipers, terrorists, and schoolkids flushing cherry bombs down toilets to watch the pipes blow out of the wall, but it's safe to say most. Therefore, therewith, thereby, and even thereupon, you won't be surprised to learn there was a young lady involved in, if not totally the cause for, The Fight.

Scarlett O'Hara was not beautiful, but Betty Jo Phelps was an absolute doll. She had short black hair that curled forward around her ears and a face as clean and smooth as a Monday morning gym floor. She had what many people often described as "the body of a much older woman," but in all reality, much older women seldom looked like this. She had the body of a beautiful seventeen-year-old girl, and it looked its best in bobby socks, saddle oxfords, wool skirts, and short-sleeved sweaters with a scarf around the neck. Betty Jo was not a cheerleader as so many popular, pretty girls were. Her only claim to school eminence was being Vice President of the Senior Class and a perennial teachers' pet. She was voted most likely something or other every year, but her most famous attributes were the wool skirts and short-sleeved sweaters. Or at least that was the opinion most heard in the lunchroom each day. Somebody was always asking, "Did you see that sweater Betty Jo Phelps has on today?" The boys loved her sweaters and Betty Jo loved them loving them. She was the only girl in school who didn't carry her books cradled in her arms in front of her. She carried them at her side like the guys all did so she wouldn't spoil her lines. She teased a little and flirted a little without having the reputation of being a flirt or a tease. Girls and teachers liked her as much as the boys did, and they were all equally shocked and bewildered when she started dating Lloyd "Paw-Paw" Showker.

She and Tommy Barr had broken up their two-year courtship over the Christmas holidays. No one ever knew exactly why. All anyone at Jackson High knew was that come the first day of school, 1954, Betty Jo and Lloyd were walking the halls, arms encircled. The part was combed out of Lloyd's well-oiled hair and he was wearing it brushed straight back, more like Eddie Fisher's. This was believed to be Betty Jo's influence.

There were stories of Lloyd and Tommy staring one another down as they passed in the hallways. Of bumping one another. Of making comments over their shoulders. Things like, "What are you looking at?" or "Don't give me no lip or I'll bust it for you." Real cerebral and clever things like that. Rumor even had it Lloyd gave Tommy the finger one day in English class and Tommy shot back immediately with, "You built it, you climb it." That sort of thing. Clever and intellectual humor abound. Thus it went for days and into a couple of

October 1959

weeks. But on January 15, the Friday night of Jackson versus Bulvane, at eight fifteen during halftime of the basketball game, these two lovers of the same woman, these two defenders of teenage honor, these two masters of the English language took fate in their clenched fists and beat the hell out of one another.

Betty Jo stood with her girlfriends, watching through her fingers. She watched Coach Lambert break it up after about a dozen hard-landing punches. She watched the coach put Lloyd's eye back in, and then she left and spent the night with Janet Stokely, who was having a pajama party for the girls in the Latin Club. She never dated either one of them again until prom night. She went with Tommy because they were to be named king and queen. Two years after high school she married a med student and moved to Macon, Georgia.

Tommy Barr is still around town. I see him from time to time but I don't know what he does and he really doesn't know me. I'd like to tell you Lloyd became a renowned eye surgeon, but you could check with just about anyone and find out he runs an auto parts store out near the mall. Whenever I see them, I always think about The Fight and wonder what they remember. I wonder if they speak to each other today. If maybe they're friends now. If either of them knows where Betty Jo is. I hope at least one of them does.

But this was Our Fight, one we could pass down to future freshmen and embellish as we saw fit. Ours was also a Friday night fight, which is better than any other night's fight. Friday night has an excitement about it that no other night can come close to. Friday night gives birth to Saturday morning, which spells freedom and leisure and adventure. Friday night gives voice to the meek and provides social opportunities even Saturday night doesn't offer. Friday nights were the best and I miss them the most.

It was the next-to-last home game for the Jackson Riders' football team. It was cold and every bleacher seat was filled. Allen Welcher was walking the length of the field, back and forth, back and forth, looking for Howard Spinner. Allen was a senior and six-foot-one. But more important than this, he was mad. I assure you his anger was justified, though not based on total fact. He was angry because Howard Spinner, one of the Spinner twins, had walked into the girls' bathroom between fourth and fifth periods that day while Allen's girlfriend, Kitty Huntley, was inappropriately exposed. She screamed, "Get out of here you little creep!" and threw an algebra book at him and began to cry.

Howard ducked the book and said, "I just came in to tell you we're having a fire drill and I think it's the real thing."

This was why Allen was mad. Furious. Kitty had told him about this on the school bus on the way home, and he had promised her he would take care of things before the day was over. He consoled her and even got off the bus at her house, walked her to her door, and then walked a mile home. Allen had already asked his dad for the car that night to take Kitty to the football game, but when he came to pick her up she was still too upset and embarrassed to show her face, as she was sure the entire school knew about it by now. I don't think the *entire* school knew about it. There were at least two people out that day with the flu who hadn't got wind of it yet.

The part that Allen was not aware of, and only a few of us were, was that Howard's intrusion into Kitty's private world was not personal, even though it was intentional. Howard had no idea who would be sitting there when he opened the door and walked in. He did it on a dare and a bet. He was already wearing the dare with pride just in retelling the story, which he had done about fifty times in the past few hours. He would collect and eat the bet on Monday because, as Billy, Bud, Howard, and I were walking down the corridor together that day, a senior Charles Batton came up behind Howard and said to him, "Hey, Spinner. I'll buy you an extra lunch Monday if you just open that door and walk into the girls' bathroom."

Batton apparently knew the Spinners' penchant for a dare. They just couldn't refuse one. Howard never flinched, gave an answer, or broke stride. He just took a sharp left, pushed the door open, and walked in. When he disappeared through the doorway, we all froze in the hall, looking at one another. That's when we heard the scream. Howard came out no faster than he went in, and we all fell in step beside him asking, "What happened? Who screamed?" Howard just grinned, shook his head, and refused to say anything. We all began to laugh and then Howard did, too. He was the first to turn off at Miss Dugan's math class. We were twenty feet down the hallway when we heard Howard come back out of the math class and mockingly holler loud enough for all the floor to hear, "*Get out of here you little creep!* It was Kitty Huntley on the toilet!"

As an adult, I know there's nothing humorous about what happened that day. But when you're fourteen and in a group of laughing boys, it's funny. Not for poor Kitty, but hey, we were fourteen and everything was funny then. Bud fell up against the lockers laughing and Toby fell on the floor, beating it with both fists while tears ran down his cheeks. Billy was hitting his thighs hard with open palms. People were going by and staring, and some began to laugh out of contagiousness. I knew we were going to be late for class, so I had just about rounded the three of them up and was guiding them down the hall when Bud said, "Hold it. I wanna see her when she comes out!"

We lost it again. We were beating the walls and crying and howling. Only the sound of the bell brought us to our good senses and we ran, still laughing, to class.

Because I was fourteen and because I was still laughing about the incident when I got home that evening, I told my mom and dad about it at the dinner table. When I finished, I didn't get the reaction I expected. Mom squinted at me and contorted her face a little and said, "And you thought that was funny?"

"Well, yeah. Kinda."

Her next words hurt. "I'm a little ashamed of you."

"I didn't do it. I just laughed. Howard did it."

"And I'm surprised at Howard. I thought those boys had better manners than that."

"Well, we only..." I began, but she interrupted me.

"No. I want you to consider this girl's situation. What if that had been your sister? Or a girl you cared about? Would it still have been funny?"

I always knew when my mother had me and she had me good this time. And I was always smart enough not to argue when I didn't have anything to say that I really believed in. It's a lesson I've carried all my life. When you know you can't win, the simple thing is to just shut up. It has worked for me so many times, and it truly began that evening at the dinner table. To this day I still remember verbatim what my retort to her was: "Can I have some more potatoes?"

So, without question, Allen Welcher had a right to be angry. After dinner I called Billy, my confidant and best buddy among all of us who palled around together. We both were concerned that Howard might be in some serious trouble when Allen found out about it all. This somber thought caused me to hang up and call Howard and suggest he might not want to come to the game tonight. He was still laughing when he answered the phone, and there was only one thing I could get out of skinny little Howard between guffaws—"I don't care what Allen Welcher thinks."

From where I was standing on the thirty-yard line, I started to care what Allen thought. He was coming toward Billy and me by the fence, and I could see the school colors in his eyes. I conceded that he had a right to be angry, but I was concerned that he also felt he had a right to be drunk. Not staggering-falling-down drunk but mean drunk. Just enough to lose any inhibitions about hurting Howard really, really bad. Just as I turned to punch Billy to warn him of approaching danger, I saw Howard leaving the portable food stand with a hot dog in his hand. The two met not eight feet from us. The tall senior with just enough beers in him to tear someone's head off and the freshman pipsqueak casually eating a hot dog with mustard dripping off his wrist.

"I wanna see you behind the bleachers." Allen's lips were tight and his breathing made him sound scared even though I knew it was all anger.

"What for?" Howard never quit chewing.

"You know what for, little man. You know what for." Allen choked on his words through clenched teeth. His breath came out frosty, and his nose was just beginning to run. He took his gloves off and stuffed them in his coat pockets, readying himself for battle.

"Allen, I don't know what you're talkin' about. Your nose is runnin'." Howard took another bite of hot dog.

Oh, man! How could he be so cool? Billy and I looked at each other with our mouths open. If he was scared, he had us both fooled. And, trust me, he had every reason to be scared. Allen Welcher could have changed the shape of Howard's thin blond head for life with just one punch. But he kept chewing and looking Allen calmly in the eye.

Allen wiped his nose and shifted his feet, and I could see that Howard had him emotionally off balance. I could see his adrenaline slow down, and for a flashing second I could read in his face that maybe this was the wrong guy. That maybe Kitty made a mistake about who saw her on the toilet. Or that maybe she even lied to him. Because this guy was not scared and he should be. He really should be.

Allen stuck his finger in Howard's face and spit out, "I'm talkin' about you in the girls' bathroom today."

"Allen, you've got the wrong boy."

"You're Howard ain't you?" It was half statement and half question.

"I'm Bud. Howard is the one who saw Kitty almost naked in the bathroom."

"You shut up!" Allen yelled, sounding near tears.

What Judas did to Jesus, Howard had just done to his brother, Bud. I don't suppose there's ever been a set of identical twins who didn't switch classes and confound teachers and try to pull jokes on girlfriends and all the typical twin pranks. But this was a new one to me, and I didn't know whether to laugh or get angry. This could become really serious, really quick. So Billy and I just stood quietly and watched. Howard was having no trouble and seemed to be enjoying himself.

"Okay, then where *is* that stupid look-alike brother of yours?" Allen was shaking and almost slurring his words.

Howard motioned with his head and said, "He's around

there on the bleachers somewhere. And I don't blame you, Allen, for being mad. I told him today I didn't see anything funny about him seeing Kitty like that with her—"

"You shut up!" Allen was hollering louder now and his nose was running again. He took off around the bleachers, rubbing his hands and wiping his nose.

Howard walked over to us and looked first at me and then at Billy, and then he dropped his head in mock shame and broke out laughing harder than he had on the phone. I wasn't sure what he was laughing at, but I knew things were getting more dangerous by the minute. I could feel it in the cold night air.

"You guys follow Welcher and see what happens," Howard said. "I'll stay right here."

We did just that, Billy and I, and what we saw and heard was more intriguing than any trick I have ever seen played on such an unsuspecting, angry drunk. Allen stopped in front of the bleacher section where Bud was sitting and motioned for him to come down. Bud, pointing to himself, said, "Me?"

"Yeah, you," Allen said. "Come down here."

As Bud stepped his way down the crowded bleacher seats, I felt overcome by the revelation of what was happening. Billy and I had known the Spinners since the first grade. We had seen most of their routines dozens of times. What we hadn't seen since about the fifth grade was the two of them dressed alike. Not until tonight. Watching Bud climb down and around teachers, parents, and students, I realized he was wearing a Washington Senators ballcap, a pea jacket, and khakis. Howard, now standing at the fence by the thirty-yard line, was wearing the same thing. Bud reached the ground and followed Allen behind the bleachers. Billy and I joined them. As they cleared the corner, Allen turned and grabbed Bud by the coat collar.

"I'm gonna stomp your face in." Same red eyes. Same blue lips he had confronted Howard with.

"Hold it. Hold it. Hold it. You got the wrong boy." Bud was holding his hands in the air. "That was Howard in the bathroom. I'm Bud."

"I just saw Bud. He said you're Howard," Allen snapped back.

"That *was* Howard. I'm Bud, and I don't blame you for being mad. I'd be mad, too."

"Wait just a cowboy minute here," Allen shouted at the top of his voice. He turned and looked at Billy and me as if he had known we were standing there all the time. He never let go of Bud's collar as he talked to us. "You two jerks are friends of these little towheads. Which one is this?"

I, in all honesty, said, "That's Bud."

"Then where is Howard?" Allen asked with a little less volume and a little more confusion.

Bud pulled away from Allen's grip and answered this one. "I don't know but I ain't Howard."

"Well...well," Allen stammered, "you tell him I'm looking for him. And I'll find him." Then he left, flustered and confused and quite a bit more unsure of his mission than when he had left home.

Bud went back to the bleachers, and Billy and I went back to the fence at the thirty-yard line where Howard was nowhere to be found. I told Billy this whole thing reminded me of a story my granddaddy used to tell. He knew this old man who would sit on his front porch all day and just rock and call his dogs. The old man could throw his voice like a ventriloquist, so when the dogs came to him, he would throw his voice and call the dogs down to the far end of the lane. When they got there, he'd call them back in his natural voice and do it all over again. He had a lot of fun, but it nearly ran the old dogs to death. I wondered how long Allen could keep up this pace.

After about two plays, Billy and I realized the bloodhound was standing not far behind us. I guess he figured the Spinners would eventually show up next to us before the night was over. We just kept watching the game and he kept watching us. Ten, fifteen minutes into the second half, Howard appeared, eating another hot dog.

"You better watch out. Allen's been watchin' us," Billy warned.

We all three searched the crowd from our vantage point but could not spot Allen anywhere.

"Maybe he went home," I offered. "I hope so anyway."

A forty-yard run brought our attention back to the field and held it there for the next few minutes. We watched as three players and a local doctor carried Leland Perry off the field. He'd been tackled, attacked, and left for sod by four farm-boy linemen from Archer County High. When he was carried past us, I noticed that they had cracked his helmet, which gave me some insight into what they may have done to his head and ribs. I didn't want to look, so I turned my head and stared straight into the ever-scarlet face of Allen Welcher. His knuckles were white from gripping the back of Howard's peacoat collar. He was nearly lifting him off the ground and talking into the back of his head.

"Okay, you little whistle pig, which one are you?"

"Allen, I'm the one you talked to a while ago," Howard said as his arms dangled helplessly at his sides.

"I ain't lettin' you go this time. I'm keepin' you with me till we find the other one."

The game had changed. Allen was a smarter breed of dog

than we had figured, and at this point, even with Billy and me pleading with him, I didn't see a good way out of this one. I think Howard shared my feelings at the time because he had no quick comeback as Allen dragged him toward the back of the bleachers with one hand. Billy and I followed, intermittently sayings things like, "Come on, Allen. Let him go," and the even bolder, "Come on, Allen. This is enough." But the angrier and drunker Allen Welcher gave no ear to our pleas and no slack to Howard's collar. His lone and determined goal was to find that "look-alike brother" while still holding on to the one he had. It didn't take long. Bud was standing behind the bleachers with two girls, smoking. Suddenly, from out of the night without warning, Kitty the Commode Girl came running in front of us, screaming and pointing at Bud.

"There he is! There he is! That's him, Allen. That's the one!"

We found out later that Allen had gone to Kitty's house during the time we couldn't find him in the crowd. Apparently, he'd convinced her to come to the game after all to support her story and help identify the perpetrator. She was currently doing this, though rather poorly and inaccurately. It was obvious to the growing crowd that neither she nor her boyfriend could tell Howard and Bud apart, and if they found a miraculous way to do so in the next few minutes or years, they had no way of proving which one was actually the Bathroom Phantom. As the gathering continued to enjoy the Howard and Bud Show, I realized that only four people in the entire crowd knew which was which. Five, really, but at the time I didn't know he was there. The four I was sure of were Billy and me and the twins themselves.

"Grab him. Hold him," Allen commanded Kitty. And she probably could have handled Bud by herself. The Spinners were small and wiry and not big enough to act the way they did, but they always got by with it. They were a lot of things, but they were never scared. Always together and never scared.

Allen still had Howard by the coat collar and now he was reaching for Bud. At one point, he had one Spinner in each hand and wasn't sure what to do with them. He turned them around and pushed them against the back of the bleachers. He stood centered in front of them, and even crouched over in rage he was two heads taller than each of them. But they weren't afraid. Howard still had his hot dog and Bud still had his cigarette. Allen slapped each out of their respective hands.

"Alright, I gotcha both now. Which one of you did it?"

"Allen, your nose is running again," Howard said without expression. "Here's a tissue."

This was awfully funny to me later, but at the time I was in no mood to laugh. I could see a messy climax coming and I didn't understand why Howard couldn't.

"Should we jump in?" Billy whispered to me.

"I'm not sure," I said. I mean, when two guys are beating up on one, you jump in and help the one. But here was one guy beating up on two, and I wasn't sure what the protocol on this one was. No punches had been thrown yet, only questions and verbal threats. But then it got worse.

Allen reached into his coat pocket and pulled out a knife, already opened. Everyone gasped. "You tell me which is which and which one was in the toilet, or I'm gonna make mincemeat of both of you right now and I mean it." Allen meant it.

"That wouldn't be fair."

This voice came from behind us, and every head whose eyes had been watching these proceedings turned to see who belonged to these words.

Remember that our friend Toby was chubby and

obnoxious to most everyone who knew him. He was a little immature at times and some folks made fun of him and girls didn't like him much, but he was part of us. The five of us. And we understood him and overlooked some traits because he was our friend and that's what friends do. A song I used to hear on the radio said *you can't judge a book by its cover.* I thought about that a lot. Like when I'd see school bullies at the grocery store with their moms on Saturdays. They always looked and acted differently than they did during the week. Sometimes they'd even speak to me, which they never did at school. I learned early that no one is exactly like they first look to you and they seldom say and do exactly what you expect even when you think you know them really well. People are surprises, and unless you had been with him almost daily since he was seven years old, Toby was full of surprises. For Billy and me, this was not one of them. But for Allen and Miss Porcelain 1959, here was a surprise party wrapped in baggy pants, his daddy's old overcoat, and a sailor cap.

"What did you say, fat boy?" Allen's talent for turning a clever phrase under pressure was beginning to show again.

"I said it wouldn't be fair to beat up both of them just because you don't know which one of them did it." Toby walked toward the center of the scene and stood close to Allen.

Toby wasn't much taller than the twins, and I think Allen's confidence was shaken for about the third time that night. I could read his face. Why was this sophomore walking up to him like this? What exactly was going on here tonight? Why was no one afraid of him? He looked for a quick second to Kitty, who took the cue and began a tirade that could have started another world war.

"You just shut up, blubber boy. You don't have nothin' in this. You just get out of here or Allen will whup your butt. Tell him, Allen. Tell him you'll whup him."

I was to observe women like Kitty through the years. If she had a drink or two over par, such a woman would stir up trouble through flirtatious or insulting actions and then announce to her opponent that her husband or boyfriend would settle the score. She would proceed to instigate revenge on the spot, much to the dismay of her mate, who was remiss if he didn't defend her honor that she had forced upon him. Kitty was frustrating Allen even more than Toby was, but he had no place to go if he meant to save face and avenge and protect her right to pee in private.

Reaching his boiling point, Allen made the ultimate mistake when he ripped off his coat and threw it to the ground along with his knife. He yelled for Kitty to "shut your big mouth" and told her he was taking control of the situation. He then looked Toby directly in the eye and said, "Maybe you think it would be fair if I just stomped you."

"Yeah, that would be fair but it wouldn't be possible." Toby had returned the serve and it was clearly Allen's move.

He hesitated for just a moment and only reacted when Kitty said, "Hit him, Allen. Take him out now."

Allen threw everything he had in a roundhouse right that landed, strangely enough, in the center of Toby's chest. It made almost no sound at all, but it rocked Toby back on his heels. He reminded me of one of those bottom-heavy clowns you blow up and punch, and it rocks back and forth till it comes to a stop. Jayo had one I always hit whenever I walked into his and Billy's bedroom. Toby rocked only once. He never staggered and he never raised his hands until Allen threw the second swing. While his fist was still in flight, searching for a target, Toby hit him as hard as he could with an overcoat on, right in the armpit. Until later that night when I tested my own sensitivity by pressing my armpit, I never knew just how tender a spot that is. Allen doubled over and yelped in pain. While this was happening, Toby took the pugilistic opportunity to hit him squarely in the side of the head with a cold, hard fist that probably hurt Toby as much as Allen. This sat Allen firmly in the dirt, and Kitty started crying and screaming threats again. She pulled her boyfriend to his feet, all the time saying, "Get him, Allen. Get him!"

"Okay. Okay. I'll get him." He was looking for him but he couldn't find or focus on him.

This is when Toby went for the nose. That usually does it, and this Friday night was no exception. Allen wound up on his knees with a puddle of blood in front of him. Kitty was holding his head and crying. I took Toby by the arm and said, "Come on. Let's go."

He stood there for a few moments to make sure Allen didn't get up and give Kitty a reason to say Toby had hit and run. Billy and I got on each side of him and walked him through the crowd. We were scanning the faces for teachers and parents, but there were none to be seen. We knew if we got him to the gate, he'd be out of trouble until at least Monday morning. Howard and Bud were right behind us. I glanced back a couple of times and assumed they wanted to stay close to their protector in case Allen regained his sea legs and came after them. But there I go again thinking I know someone well enough to anticipate their actions. When we got to the gate and looked back one last time, we saw they had both stopped at the food stand and were buying hot dogs and drinks. We all three laughed and went home.

October 1959

Billy and Toby and I spent a nervous weekend wondering when the sky would fall. Every time the phone rang in our individual homes, we just knew it was the principal or the police or, worse yet, Allen. We talked a lot about Monday morning, and dreaded it even more. If we didn't get called to the office from homeroom, Billy and I to be questioned and Toby to be punished, we knew it could happen anytime during the day. And then there were the dangers in the halls. The lunchroom. The bus parking lot. Any number of places we might see Allen, who we were sure would be raving mad and hard to stop. Toby really wasn't scared, but Billy and I were worried for him. The Spinners barely mentioned it. Bud did say at lunchtime on Monday, "Good fight, Toby. That's the last he'll mess with *us*." But neither one of them ever thanked him or made a big ado about it at all. The school, however, was full of it. Everyone was talking about the sophomore who whipped Allen Welcher. Toby was a hero, and most of them didn't even know his name. Everyone was talking about "that fat kid" but only behind his back. For his remaining high school tenure, no one ever called him "fat boy" to his face again. The girls didn't like him much better, but he took on a new respect in the eyes of all the guys. Guys have more respect for blood than girls do.

And so did Allen, I guess. Monday came and went, as did Tuesday, and nothing out of the ordinary happened. Billy was the only one who saw Allen, and that was from a distance. They didn't even exchange glances. By Wednesday we began to rest a little easier, and by Friday we had all seen Allen in the hallways and discovered he wouldn't even look at us, much less fight us. It may have been more embarrassment than fear. But the more I thought about that armpit punch, maybe it was fear after all. And pain. And the desire not to have it done to him again.

By Friday night, things were back to normal. It was the last home game. The Spinners were eating hot dogs, two at a time this week, Kitty was sitting quietly on the bleachers with a group of girls, and Allen Welcher had decided not to come at all. Billy and I were keeping our thirty-yard-line vigil by the fence, watching the crowd more than the game. And Toby…well, Toby was somewhere being Toby. He didn't show up until the third quarter. He was wearing the same overcoat and sailor cap as the week before. He stood with us and we laughed and talked about the usual things. He stopped talking at one point as a group of girls walked by. He stepped toward them, almost in their path, and said, "Hi, Kitty. How's Allen?"

He was genuinely sincere. And Kitty must have sensed this because she slowed her pace and said, "He's okay," in a very soft and concerned voice.

"Tell him I'm sorry. I didn't mean to hurt him."

"I'll tell him. Thank you." Kitty was either scared or touched but either way, she was just right. Toby needed to say what he said and he needed understanding ears to hear it. She and the girls walked on, and he stood for a moment with his hands in his daddy's coat pockets, looking but not really seeing anything.

"I'm gonna walk around for a little bit," he said. "I'll be back."

He walked slowly toward the crowd. Billy and I fell in beside him and walked with him, in silence, because he was our friend and that's what friends do.

Chapter Three

May/June 1960

Songs are the wings of time. With the right song playing through your head and bouncing off your heart, you can sail back to almost any place you want to go. You can revisit old friends who haven't aged a bit; you can go in and walk through the house you grew up in; you can recover feelings and thoughts you lost years ago; and you can give tenderness to a bittersweet memory that will let you peacefully cry yourself to sleep.

There are a few old songs I turn up loud and just let them carry me away. And there are a few I can't listen to at all. I haven't heard them in years. Not all the way through, anyway. They start to play and I switch them off and turn on the news. Even bad news is not as bad as the cloud some old songs can leave you in. The happiest times can make the saddest memories.

Saturday night was Hop night. Now, whenever you say Hop to someone, they always say, "Oh, yeah! A Sock Hop." No. Listen to me. Not a Sock Hop. I've never been to a Sock Hop in my life. That's where you have to take your shoes off and leave them at the door and dance in your sock feet. We would never have gone to one of those. What we went to was just a Hop. Like Danny and the Juniors' "At the Hop."

Girls and guys, teenagers from thirteen to eighteen, lined the walls and sat at tables along the sides and danced in the middle of the green-tiled floor at the National Guard Armory on a Saturday night. Guys danced with girls, girls danced with girls, but guys never danced with guys. Girls without dates would enjoy a fast dance together while guys without dates walked the perimeter of the dance floor trying to catch the eye of the girls without dates. It was a hormone jungle just waiting to sparkle and crackle and explode.

In those dating days I found it interesting and sometimes funny that a pretty girl almost always had a "not-so-pretty girl friend" with her. A Jekyll and Hyde, side by side. Billy and I thought this was probably socially and emotionally planned. It was a great advantage for both girls. The "Not-So" girl got attention and was invited to places she may have been excluded from if not for her friendship with Miss Teen Angel. Miss Teen Angel, on the other hand, enjoyed the inevitable comparisons and the unchallenged reign of always being the prettiest and most sought after of the two.

Before anyone takes me to task over this, stop and think, as we did many times, how often you see two very pretty girls together. We looked for years, sometimes all night long, and we never found them. Many times, though, after we got our driver's licenses, we found this sweet/sour combination and Miss Teen Angel would always say to one of us, "We'd love to ride around with you. 'Not-So' can go with him. She has a real nice personality and she loves music." And without fail, Billy or I, whichever one had made the connection with the Teenage Queen, would try to talk the other one of us into going with Miss Personality.

"You know, she really don't look all that bad."

"Then you take her and I'll take the one with the teeth."

"No. Really now. She's got a pretty good figure."

"Look, I took that skinny one with the bad breath we met

at the Dairy Queen that night. It's your turn. You owe me."

"Hey, I'm tellin' you, I don't care. I think one's just as pretty as the other one. But I've already been talking to Teen Angel and I think she likes me. If it wasn't for that, I'd be happy to take Not-So."

"Tell the Angel to take her home. Then you can take me home and meet her someplace."

"She won't do that. She says if her friend can't go, she won't go. She don't wanna make her feel bad."

"Then our theory *is* right. They plan it this way. They won't split up because then it would go against their *deal*."

"Come on, man. Just for an hour. We'll go get something to eat. Curb service. We won't even get out of the car. We won't stay but an hour."

"Do guys do this kind of deal, too? Are these girls thinking one of us is Romeo and one of us is Goofy?"

"Probably. So come on, Goofy. It'll all be over within an hour."

And so it would go. Through the years we met lots of pretty girls and their friends. The Jekyll/Hyde pair we saw dancing at the Hop one night was no exception. Billy and I had walked the circle of the floor fifty times, stopping at tables, talking, looking, hoping. Then, out of the romantic night like a summer beach breeze, she blew by us. Billy spotted her heart-melting face and fell quickly and hopelessly in love.

"Did you see that?"

"I could see that in my sleep," I said. "As a matter of fact, I probably will."

"Let's follow her." Billy was already picking up his Coke.

"You follow her. She's by herself."

"Come on. Go with me," he coaxed.

I walked a few steps behind him. It was his play and I

didn't want to interfere. Just as we got to her table, Rockin' Raymond, the star radio announcer from the local rock 'n' roll station, played "Stagger Lee" by Lloyd Price. Miss Dream Face got up from her table and danced with her girl friend. Not her girlfriend, understand, but her girl friend. So I knew she was there alone—a good sign for Billy. But Billy turned immediately on his heel and walked quickly back toward me.

"Forget that," he said.

"Forget what? What happened?"

"I got a closer look at her. I know who she is now," he said disgustedly.

"Yeah? Who is she?"

"Sylvia something. She used to go with Wayne Trumbull."

"And? What do you mean?" My question was sincere.

"I don't like him. He's a crud."

"So what?" I asked, completely puzzled. "You're not going to ask *him* to dance. You're going to ask *her*."

"Yeah, but if she's danced with him and kissed on him, I don't want anything to do with her."

"Really!"

"I don't know," he said honestly. "I just don't think I'm interested now."

Billy was like that. He made quick decisions on quick impressions. Something really bothered him about this guy Wayne Trumbull and his beautiful ex-girl. I never understood what it was, and I'm not sure Billy did either. At the time, though, for just a fleeting moment I started to say, "Well, if you don't want her, I'll go talk to her." But it was his Dream Face. He saw her first, and if he never wanted to see her again, then neither did I.

May/June 1960

Did I mention Rockin' Raymond?

Rockin' Raymond Savoy gave birth to rock 'n' roll in our hometown. He had a quiet, soft-spoken voice, and until 1955 he played Perry Como and Patti Page every morning while I ate breakfast and got dressed for school. Then he switched from Tony Bennett to Bill Haley so fast it made dials spin all over town. Some spun away from it, but more spun over to the "Rockin' Rhythms of the Yellin' Youth." "We're ravin' and behavin' like a rock 'n' roll maven." "We're thumpin', bumpin', and jumpin'." Raymond was a major local star. It was his idea to start the Saturday night Hops. He'd been to Harrisburg and Richmond and even Philadelphia and seen what some of the big cities were doing, so he'd come back and convinced the owner of the local pop station that this would be a money-making and promotional venture he could handle. And he did, with the help of his beautiful wife Roma.

Roma and Raymond came down from Hagerstown, where Raymond landed the job as station manager, and the two of them were pretty much the top echelon when it came to local celebrities. When people saw Roma in the grocery store in skin-tight pedal pushers, high heels, and sunglasses, looking not unlike a motor oil calendar girl, they would whisper and say, "That's Roma Savoy." And they really felt like they'd seen somebody. Roma didn't speak to a lot of people. She carried her star-by-association status to the fullest. I won't say she wasn't attractive, because she certainly could attract attention and that's all the word attractive really means. I won't say she wasn't exciting, because she could excite and arouse just on the strength of being different from the other women in the grocery stores. And I won't say she wasn't desirable, because she was. She had that strange, sexy air that women found hard to compete with so they called her cheap. That slightly scarlet appeal that men laughed at with other men but sought out when they were by themselves. Roma was not loved by her public, but then it was not her public. She never wanted to be loved by them all—only by about two or three hundred of them, so the legend goes.

Raymond, that's Rockin' Raymond to you, was round of face, round of body and 'round about forty years old. He had long, straight, Johnny Weissmuller hair (think Tarzan). He greased it and combed it into a perfect duck's tail in the back. He wore large black-framed glasses (think Buddy Holly), and at the Hop, he always had on a bright red sport coat (think Jerry Lewis in *Cinderfella*). He finished the look with a pencil-thin black tie, black gaberdine pants, and pointed-toe shoes he had to order from Philadelphia. He sincerely thought he was hot stuff, and to tell you the truth, we did, too. However, Billy, Toby, and I were a little more sarcastic in our thinking of "hot stuff" than the way Raymond thought of himself.

At the Hop, Raymond sat on a little stand at the end of the dimly lit armory. In front of him were two turntables for back-to-back play and over his head was an arch of cardboard with the words ROCK AND ROLL THRONE painted in crimson-sport-coat red. The only thing lacking was a gold crown on his Vitalised head. From here he reigned every Saturday night from eight till eleven. Raymond spun the records and Roma sold the tickets and the Saturday Night Hop was on the air.

"This is Rock 'n' Roll Raymond, the Old Highwayman, stealin' hearts and playin' the charts. Takin' requests and spinnin' the best. From eight to eleven from rock 'n' roll heaven." And then he'd play the number-one record of that week. This is how it all started every Saturday night. Sometimes we'd sit in the car and listen on the radio before we went inside. It was better on the radio where you couldn't see Raymond. Then we'd go through the front door, give our money to Roma, and let her stamp our hands. She flirted with every boy who bought a ticket and seemed to take a certain pleasure in stamping each hand. The stamp meant if you went outside, you could get back in without paying again. Some of the older guys got stamped for free and never had to pay. But they knew Roma better than we did.

Once inside, we'd walk the circle looking at girls because no one hardly ever brought a date to the Hop. We met people there and sat and talked and danced, but those who had dates went to the movies. Never the Hop. And this is how Billy met Patsy. He and Toby and I were walking the circle, and Billy saw her and went immediately to her and asked her to dance. He never came back. I don't mean just that night. I mean he never came back from that dance the same person he'd been before. From the first few months of our turning fifteen years old, Patsy was a part of him. A part of us. Even when she wasn't around, she was practically all of his conversation. His life changed, and so did ours. We were still close but we had a partner. When she wanted Billy, she had him. When she didn't, we had him. Sometimes we had him together, and that was fun, but only when it pleased her. We doubled dated until she decided she didn't like my girlfriend so she and Billy wouldn't go out with us until I dated someone else. But all of this developed over the years. That night at the Hop was a little different.

"Did you get a look at her?" Billy asked as he joined Toby and me at the table where we were waiting.

"She's alright," I said. "Who is she?" I had never seen her before.

"Patsy Shriner. She goes to Bulvane."

"She ain't all that pretty, I don't think." Toby was being

honest, the only way Toby knew to be.

"It's dark in here. You can't see her all that well. Wait till you see her in the daylight."

Billy's first brick in a long wall of defense was met once again by Toby's logic. "Have you seen her in the daylight?"

"Well, no, Toby, I haven't," Billy shot back with more anger than he realized. "But I've seen her up close so just shut up!"

I'd never seen Billy kick a dog before, and Toby didn't deserve this kind of attitude.

"You want to walk some more?" I asked, the peacemaker one has to be when three friends begin to have words.

"No," Billy said quickly. "I'm gonna wait here and ask her to dance soon as they play another slow one."

And he did. They danced to every slow song that night. Toby and I sat with some guys from school and then a couple of girls who were also walking the circle. I danced a few times but mostly drank Cokes and went to the bathroom. I swear Roma placed her chair behind the card table in the lobby, where she kept the tickets and ink pad and stamper, so she could look in the boys' restroom every time the door opened. Once when I came out, I think she winked at me.

Raymond always played a final song to show it was eleven o'clock and time to clear the building: "The End," a beautiful slow song that put everyone in a dreamy mood and left them with only the good memories of the night. We waited at the door for Billy. Being a couple months older than Toby or me, he was the only one who could legally drive. He talked about Patsy all the way home. All Sunday afternoon. During P.E. on Monday. Then he came bursting in my bedroom Monday evening with something in his hand. I knew what it was before he showed me.

"I found it, buddy. Here!" He pushed it under my eyes.

It was the sheet music to "The End." A picture of Earl Grant, the singer, on the cover. Written by Sid Jacobson and Jimmy Krondes in the key of C. I smiled because I had a stack of sheet music in the piano bench Billy had bought me. Every time he heard a song he liked, he'd buy the music instead of the record and get me to play it for him on the piano. I had some pretty good stuff because of him. "It's Only Make Believe," "Love Me Tender," "Theme from a Summer Place." He'd been doing this for years. Billy was always somewhat of a romantic. He liked the eighth notes in "Theme from 'A Summer Place.'" We liked the movie, and whenever he wanted me to play that style, he'd say, "Play that Sandra Dee piano." I knew what he meant and even tried a few times to teach him to play it himself. But he wasn't musical. He only loved it.

I played for him in our living room while he sat on the piano stool with me and talked about Patsy. I played all the songs that night. Every one he'd ever bought me.

The next Saturday night, it was just Billy and me. He found Patsy shortly after we arrived at the armory and I was left pretty much alone. This was really no great problem, as I knew most everyone from our school who was sitting or dancing. The Spinners were there. Their big project that night, and they always had one, was sneaking aspirin in everyone's Coke to see if they could get anybody drunk. I never knew if this combination really worked, and frankly I don't think the twins did either. But it was the kind of folklore the two of them latched on to and treated as firm fact and eternal truth. All it proved to me was that Howard and Bud would probably never be pharmacists. (I could suddenly see both of them in little white coats and glasses and realized I could never picture them separately. I wondered if they would truly become the same things in life.) Billy looked me up about ten o'clock.

"What's happenin'?" he asked as he sat down at the table and took a long swig of my Coke.

"I've been dancin' with Sue Jane Wimer for the past hour," I said. "How's it goin' with you?"

"I'm ready to get out of here," he said, scanning the floor.

"You wanna leave now? Somethin' happen with you and Patsy?"

He looked at me like he had just noticed I was sitting there. "No," he said. "Everything's cool. Great, as a matter of fact. I'm gonna take her home. What about you and Sue Jane?"

"What about us?"

"You wanna go along? We'll take them both home."

"Sure. I'll ask her."

"If not," Billy smiled and pointed across the floor, "Lannie Mae is over there in the corner dancin' with Roger Smiley."

Lannie Mae, being a year older and having her own set of friends now, didn't see much of me lately.

"I'll ask Sue Jane. Be back in just a sec."

"Hey," he said, putting his hand on my arm, "before you do, here's what I got in mind. Let's go up on the Knoll and park. Patsy don't have to be home until eleven thirty. Okay with you?"

"Sure, it's okay with me. I don't care if she doesn't get home till one o'clock."

He hit me on the shoulder and laughed. "You know what I mean."

"Yeah, I know what you mean. I'll ask Sue Jane."

May/June 1960

The Knoll was a large, wooded, undeveloped hilltop between two other partially developed hilltops in our town. It was a parkers' paradise. Ronnie Burns used to make jokes on *The Burns and Allen Show* about Mulholland Drive. I guess the Knoll was to us what Mulholland Drive was to the Hollywood Hills. There were all kinds of tales about what went on up there through the years. We'd heard a girl was once kidnapped out of the front seat of a car through an open window. Legend was that a man jumped off a fifty-foot ledge to his death, sort of a lover's leap story except this guy wasn't running from his lover but from his lover's boyfriend. It was said that people went up there to fight and settle scores or to consummate extramarital affairs in broad daylight. One story even suggested a man buried his mistress up there after killing her with a croquet mallet. This added up to a command on the part of our mothers to stay away from the Knoll and never go up that winding dirt road for any reason under God's sun. And we never did because it was one long walk and simply too far to tackle. But two days after Billy got his driver's permit (we could get one as soon as we turned fifteen), the first night he got his mother's car he and Toby and I headed for the Knoll.

When the three of us first topped the crest of the rough and washed-out trail that was hardly wide enough for two cars to pass—one coming up, one going down—we saw the clearing in the woods and spied three cars parked in secluded locations. We agreed later that something caught in all three of our stomachs. In the first car we drove past, a big, rough, dirty-looking guy pulled himself up to peer out the window and watch us intently as we rode around the well-tracked circle carved in the soft ground from years of vehicles following the same path. The next car looked empty, but when we crept by the third one the front door flew open and a facsimile of old "rough and dirty" from car number one jumped out, his belly hanging over low-slung khaki pants, no shirt, and a whiskey bottle in his hand. He hit the hood of our car with his open hand and growled, "Whatta you snivelin' little boys want up here?" I was on his side, and I reached for the handle to roll up the window, but before I could, Toby, sitting in the middle in the front seat, leaned over me and yelled out the window, "What's it to you, grandpa?" At this point, Billy kicked it and left Mr. Wonderful standing in a haze of dust. This should have been a perfect deterrent to ever going back, but like oil and water, youth and good sense don't always mix. Because of this incident, I always had an uneasy feeling every time I started up that long, crooked road. My heart approached one hundred twenty beats a minute when I reached the top and could first see the clearing, but I still went. Sometimes with a girl, sometimes with another couple, sometimes with a carload of guys. And to be honest, in all the years, in all the trips, I never had a real bad experience. But I had a few good ones. A few nice memories. And I guess that's why I kept going back.

This Saturday night after we left the Hop, there were no cars at all. More would come later, but we had the hill to ourselves for now. Sue Jane and I got out of the back seat and walked around. We finally sat and eventually lay on the wild grass by a fallen tree. Billy and Patsy disappeared in the front seat with the Hop blasting on the radio.

"They're going to run the battery down, aren't they?" Sue Jane thought of everything.

"It'll be alright for a while," I said.

"What if they run the battery down and we can't get the car started? I'll get skinned."

"Turn the radio off!" I yelled. I wasn't heard because, duh, the radio was on. So I didn't bother to yell again. I admired

Sue Jane's foresight but was not particularly pleased with it at the time. At this point, I was willing to take my chances on drift-starting if necessary.

We could easily hear the final song, then the national news and the local weather and sports. Sue Jane was getting edgier by the second and whispered she had to be home in fifteen minutes. We walked toward the car and urged the new lovers to get moving. Billy and I got both girls home just in time and had a half hour to ride around before *our* curfew. Billy couldn't wait to start.

"We were layin' there and I had her face in both hands and they started playin' that song."

"Which song?" Billy liked so many I didn't know which one was his favorite tonight.

"The End," he said emphatically. "Last week I was just dancin' with her when they played it. This week I was kissin' her. Ah, man, she's something!"

"Sue Jane was afraid your battery was goin' to run down."

"I'm gonna call her tomorrow."

"I think I got pine needles down the back of my shirt."

"She wants to go out again next Saturday night."

"Pull in here and let's get a shake."

"That song should be called 'The Beginning.' I think I'll take her to the drive-in next week."

"You just passed the Dairy Queen."

"She said she had never parked before."

"Stop at this filling station. I'll just get a Coke."

"Ah, man, she's somethin'!"

Billy was in love and couldn't help it. And neither could I.

Piano Days

Sometimes Rockin' Raymond would book guests at the Hop. Once he had a famous, all-night disc jockey from Buffalo who sat in and talked between records and told stories about singers he knew. Nobody was favorably impressed by all this. We just wanted the lights turned back down and the records spinning again. Once Jimmy Clanton or Buddy Knox was there. I can't remember which, and I'm not sure I knew the difference at the time. He stood by the Rock and Roll Throne and pantomimed his latest hit and then signed autographs for twenty minutes. Raymond thought these events were going to put him on the star route. He talked on the air about how his special guests would be a regular feature, but nothing more ever came of it. And we were glad. We went to the Hop to see and be seen and dance and talk and drink Cokes and go to the bathroom. We didn't care who the guest of the week was. Only Raymond and Roma cared. It raised their star a little in the local heavens each time they referred to the guest as their "close friend." Raymond even got to introducing records this way on the air. Bobby Darin, Little Anthony, Johnny Horton, The Drifters. They were all close, personal friends he had known before landing in our little town. He had a story about each one of them and himself in the days before they made it big. Some, he said, he grew up with and went to school with. Some, he helped to get in "the business." And then he started getting letters from some of them, which he read in detail on the air. Raymond's past was getting bigger than his present. Even his gullible teenaged fans were beginning to doubt his validity, but his audience continued to multiply. The adults were now tuning in to hear his latest tall tale. He became a big joke and an even bigger asset to the station. Raymond was more famous than ever because lies seldom hurt show business figures. It's the truth that usually does them in. If not for the prevailing truth, he may still be "rantin' and pantin' and chantin'" and filling the air with rock 'n' roll in our unsuspecting, unforgiving little hometown.

Strange as it may seem, none of Raymond's on-the-air antics were offensive to the listening public. The bizarre fascinates and entertains. One does not have to be talented to be famous. Only different. Raymond was to different what Marilyn Monroe was to sexy. He worked at it. Planned it and was proud of it. So with him it was all show business. He enjoyed the stares and whispers and was hurt when he didn't get them. He was harmless, but what finally brought him down off his Rock and Roll Throne was Roma. They became members of the local country club, and it seems Roma was spending more time in the men's locker room than in the women's. They were finally asked to leave the club and eventually the town. Raymond announced one night at the Hop that he was leaving the local station to take a position at a 50,000-watt radio giant somewhere in Florida. He was heading for the big time. We heard later that he and Roma split a few months after their mysterious departure. Word was that he wound up selling advertising for a local TV listing magazine in the Sarasota area, and Roma moved back north with her family. I cannot verify exactly what became of Rockin' Raymond, because I never saw him or heard his name again. Hence, I have to assume he never reached the big time he so desperately reached for. It was about six years later, maybe more, that I confirmed what happened to Roma. I was traveling in the Midwest and spending a not-too-happy Sunday morning in a hotel room. I was switching the TV channels and suddenly saw, staring at me, the same eyes that had winked at me as I came out of the boys' bathroom so many years before, back at the old armory. There she was. A few years older and a few pounds heavier, but only a few. Brother Ansel and Miss Roma. She had married a preacher and they had a syndicated television show. He healed and hollered, and she prayed and played the piano. I sat fixed to the screen, thinking I should call somebody because I had the strangest feeling the Saturday Night Hop was on the air again.

Some people come and go in your life so quickly you forget you ever knew them. Some outstay their welcome. Sometimes it takes years to know the difference.

All that summer we went to the Hop. We laughingly mourned the Savoys' demise and speculated on the types of characters who might replace them. Joe Gaylord was the new man. He, along with his mousy wife, took over the glorious duties in a quiet and unglamourous way. We were disappointed. We missed the circus, but the music was the same. And that's really where the memories were anyway.

It was unlike Toby to be quiet or serious. He was usually in a state of constant movement of both body and mouth. From his vantage point of life, there were few sacred cows. He loved practical jokes, and I could fill pages with pranks he pulled through the years. Some were cruel but funny. Some were dirty but funny. Some were harmful but funny. Toby brought out the worst in people and loved every minute of it in his own innocent way. Age played no role in his evaluation of who should be his victim. He had no fear and little respect for elders or authority. One of my favorite Toby stories falls in the cruel but funny category.

It was our first day of high school, our first homeroom. Strange faces from other grade schools sat all around us. A male teacher presided at the front of the room We had never had a male teacher in our elementary school. This in itself was enough to make most of us freeze at attention. I looked around the room and saw only four people I knew. There were about twenty-five others staring back that I had never laid eyes on. Toby, thank God, was one of the four I knew. He and I were sitting next to one another.

"My name is Mr. Vaughan. This is your homeroom. You will be here for fifteen minutes every morning and five minutes every afternoon. Do not be late either time." Skinny and tall, with a five o'clock shadow even at eight thirty in the morning, Mr. Vaughan had a deep and hypnotic voice, and his overgrown Adam's apple bounced vigorously with every syllable he spoke. He was a frightful sight. His first ritual was the calling of the roll. He did it slowly and deliberately as to pronounce each new name correctly. As each student answered, "Present," he looked up from his book, memorizing their face and name together. We all sat patiently as he took his time and ours. And then he got to the Rs.

"Edward Ramsey."

No answer.

"Edward Ramsey."

Still no answer. We all looked around the room, along with Mr. Vaughan. He squinted at everyone, never taking his finger from his roll book.

"Mr. Ramsey is apparently not here. Does anyone know anything about Mr. Ramsey?"

This is where it happened. This question started Toby's high school career and reputation. His image was formed at this very moment. No single event, with the exception of the The Fight, would shape his character more for the next four years. When he looked around at the puzzled faces and saw that none of them seemed to know the elusive Edward Ramsey, and then looked back at the face of the teacher waiting for an answer, hungry for an answer, eager to have an answer, Toby couldn't resist the opportunity to provide one.

"Does anyone know anything about Edward Ramsey?" Mr. V. asked one final time.

Toby's hand shot up. Mr. Vaughan acknowledged him. "All right, young man, what was your name again?"

"Toby Painter."

"Toby Painter," the teacher repeated. "And do you know Edward Ramsey?"

"Yes sir, I do," Toby lied.

No one in the room was enjoying this but me, because I was the only one there who knew he was lying from the word go.

"Do you know where Edward Ramsey is?"

"No sir, I don't."

Mr. Vaughan looked irritated. "Do you know why he's not here today?"

"Yes sir. He's dead."

An after-the-battle silence engulfed the whole room. The gangly Mr. Vaughan actually gulped. "Are you sure of this, Toby?"

"Yes sir. He got killed this summer in a gunfight."

"In a gunfight? My God!" Vaughan was moved and the class was stunned. Toby was on a roll.

"Yes sir. He and some other boys were playin' cowboys and Indians or somethin' in their backyard. And they were shootin' cap pistols at each other and everything, and his little brother went in the house and got his daddy's real gun out of the dresser drawer and came out in the yard and wanted to play, too. So all of them were chasin' Edward and he went runnin' down through their backyard, shootin' back, you know, and he got down to the river, the river runs right along their backyard, and as they were shootin', Edward tripped and fell in the river, hit his head on a rock and it killed him."

"Oh, my Lord! That's horrible!" Mr. Vaughan was rubbing both sides of his neck.

"Yes sir."

"But what happened with the little boy who had his father's real gun?"

"Nothin', I don't reckon," Toby said earnestly.

"But what did the real gun have to do with what happened to Edward?" The teacher was equally sympathetic and confused.

"I don't know," Toby said. "I wasn't there."

Rubbing his forehead, perplexed and bewildered and obviously saddened, Mr. Vaughan said, "Well, I'll take his name off roll. I don't know how it was overlooked and left on here. Oh, my Lord! That's horrible."

I *shall* not look at Toby. I *will* not look at Toby. I *can*not look at Toby. I did not look at Toby.

About two minutes before the bell rang to send us to our first first-period class, a redheaded boy with freckles on his cheeks and fear in his eyes rushed in and stopped at Mr. Vaughan's desk. "I'm sorry I'm late," he said nervously. "I got lost and couldn't find the right room."

Mr. Vaughan was very understanding as he opened his roll book again and asked, "What's your name, son?"

Of course, you're way ahead of me. I could stop right here and you'd know what he said. But if I stopped right here, you wouldn't know that when he said, "Edward Ramsey," twenty-eight kids jerked and gasped, one girl in the back screamed, and Vaughan spilled his coffee all over his roll book.

The seething Mr. Vaughan pointed Edward, who by this time was visibly shaken if not scared half to death at the reaction his name had gotten from everyone present, toward an empty seat. While wiping up coffee, he found Toby's eye and motioned him with his index finger to come to his desk.

Vaughan was not subtle. In a suppressed voice, through clenched teeth, he spit out, "What were you talking about, boy?"

Neither was Toby subtle or apologetic. "I must have been thinkin' about somebody else."

The bell rang and high school began.

That's what we expected of Toby. If his mood or attitude was ever any other way, we knew something was seriously wrong. And something was seriously wrong when Billy and I walked in the Hop that particular Saturday night in June. We were late because we had softball practice. We had told Toby we'd see him there about nine p.m. Billy had told Patsy the same thing. We went home after practice, showered, and put on our sharpest summer-night clothes. We'd each bought a pack of Cloves chewing gum and had just got our hands stamped by Mrs. Mousy Gaylord when Toby met us in the lobby and said, "Nothin' is happenin' in there. Let's go to the show or somethin'."

"Are you crazy?" Billy said half seriously. "We just got here."

"Yeah, but there's nobody here. Things are dead. Let's go somewhere."

"Have you walked around?" I asked, trying to figure out what was running Toby off so quickly.

"Yeah, I been around a dozen times. Nothin' is happenin'."

Billy pushed on past him. "Is Patsy here yet?"

Toby looked particularly at me and said in a rare tone for

him, "Let's just get outta here, okay?"

Billy caught it the same time I did. Before I could say anything, he looked Toby in the eye with a defying squint. "What's goin' on, Toby?"

Toby looked to me. I hesitated because I couldn't ask questions without Billy hearing the answers and I could tell he didn't want Billy to hear.

"Is Patsy in there?" Billy's question was leveled squarely at Toby.

"Yeah. She's in there. Dancin'."

"With who?"

Toby took a deep breath. "She came with Roger Smiley. She's been dancin' with Roger Smiley. She's been slobberin' all over him and gigglin' and...come on, Billy. Don't even go in there. Let's go to the show or somethin'."

And certainly, we should have. Elvis was at the drive-in in *King Creole*, but Patsy Shriner was at the Hop. So in we went and sat at a table and watched Patsy and Roger Smiley dance. They were no Marge and Gower Champion, but they held their own as if we had paid just to see them. Billy was miserable. At one point, Patsy came to the table and talked to him for a few minutes and then hit the floor with Roger when the next slow song played. They left together about ten o'clock, and Billy said, "Let's follow them." Toby and I tried to talk him out of this, but he was hurt and mad and didn't want to hear anything reasonable from us.

We lost them, and after circling town a few times Billy said, "Let's try the Knoll." Toby and I had run out of persuasive words by this time, so we just lay back in the seat and listened to the radio and rode where Billy took us. As we crested the Knoll, there was Roger Smiley's blue '55 Chevy along with four or five other parked cars. Billy stopped and shined his headlights on the car for what seemed like twenty minutes, although it was probably only one. Nothing and nobody moved. No heads appeared. No one yelled. Nothing. He sat there staring out at it until we heard Joe Gaylord's voice say from the dashboard, "Goodnight young lovers, wherever you are," and then Earl Grant sang "The End." Billy put the car in gear and drove slowly around the dirt circle and down the rocky lane that took us back to the lights of town. All the time Earl Grant kept singing, and all the time tears kept running down Billy's cheeks.

This would not be the last time we followed Patsy. She would come and go in Billy's life like a summer thunderstorm. Fierce and intense and all-powerful and then gone just as quickly, leaving everything in her wake quiet and weak. She, like those memories of the Hop, would never completely leave us. Whether we were dancing with someone we loved or loving to dance with someone we couldn't, we only remembered the sweet times. The bad we bury immediately; the good we hold on to and smile and reminisce over a thousand times. At least we try to do it this way. Some things, though, you just can't force out of your mind. Whenever I think of the Hop and the Knoll, and Roma and Raymond, and the essence of those wonderful and painful years, I always hear Earl Grant singing and then I always see those tears running down Billy's face. The song finally ended, but I don't think those tears ever did for Billy.

May/June 1960

My uncle wrote these accounts about his young life, recording not just a personal history but one that reflects what so many experienced in that particular time period. I heard all of these stories and more as a youngster. I'd heard my uncle tell them, heard my mother repeat them, and, of course, read what he wrote so many years ago. Mom said he was a "chronicler of an era." A historian of a time cherished and past. Not important history but cultural history. Everyday memories of friendships and how America looked and was in the years he was given to grow up in. And the older I got and the more I reread them, I think my mother was on to something. She loved talking about him and his stories because I think it helped her understand who he was; a little more about the condition of his heart and mind; and a little more about the people who influenced him and shaped him.

You see, Mom was twelve years older than her only brother, and by the time he was growing up and stretching his boundaries and senses, she was out of college, married, and had started a family. She missed the years he wrote about, and her absence in his life during these times actually drew her closer to him in the years to come. She's the one who kept the "chapters" (Mom's term for his memoirs) in a bottom drawer of her vanity in a walk-in closet in her and Dad's bedroom. It was always locked, and even as a very young boy I knew something special was in there that I was not to see or touch. On occasion, she would take a key from someplace and open the drawer and read the pages again. Sometimes she would add to their number, and I never knew at the time what was on the new pages or where they were coming from. But how those chapters grew and came to her through the years, and how they came finally to me, is a story and process I revere and have committed myself to share.

As you'll detect, my uncle didn't always write his stories chronologically. He wrote them as they popped in his mind. Some were random. Sporadic. Even casual and unorganized. Mom insisted I put them in sequence and some sort of order, but I resisted her marshaling his creative freedom. I could tell he said things when he wanted to say them, and to move his chapters around would have been changing his wishes. And his wishes and words were something I never touched or tried to improve.

(The only time I relented was when my mother stood firm on removing a paragraph from the eighth chapter and placing it at the beginning of the book. It's the first thing you read. It's the one about how "they were young and imperfect. Worse than some. Not as bad as others." And even then, I compromised with her. I put it at the front but also left it in the eighth chapter as he originally wrote it.)

My uncle (my brothers and I always just called him Uncle Be-Bop) had an ear and a nose for the preservation of the times. He knew the music, the clothes, the lingo, the feel of the late '50s and early '60s, and he had a sincere way of telling us what it was like in "his day." The music was his favorite part, and I know this from the stories the family has told me all my life. They said from the time he was nine years old he would play piano every year for the church Christmas pageants and school cantatas. He played with a local dance band made up of older, semi-professional musicians when he was in high school. He played for weddings and funerals and birthday parties all through his teen years and made enough money to buy his first car. I always loved when Grandma told us how she could just walk into the house any time of the day when he was growing up and there he was at the piano, maybe romping an old pop ditty like "Alley Cat" or playing a beautiful, impromptu rendition of "Beyond the Sunset" that would just bring tears to your eyes. If he had the sheet music, fine. If he didn't, even better. His ear was as good as his fingers. Whenever he would stop by our house, after he got out of the hospital, my brothers and I, still *annoying little kids in our pajamas, used to beg him to play for us. He would just laugh and say, "Get your mamma to play for you. She's just as good as I am." Which would cause Mom to holler from the kitchen, "Now, you know that's not true. Play something for those boys." And we all three would yell, "Yeah! Yeah! Play something for us." But he never did.*

I clearly recall one night when I was about seven or eight years old, saying to him, "Uncle Be-Bop, play your favorite song." He stared down at me for a long while and just rubbed his chin. I thought he hadn't heard what I said to him. I said it again and this time he did a strange thing. He rubbed his hands together as if they hurt and said, "I don't have a favorite song." And I thought how sad. Everybody should have a favorite song. Then, without saying anything more, he just picked up his canes and went to the kitchen, and my brothers and I went to bed.

Chapter Four

September 1959

Autumn meant Halloween and Thanksgiving were coming soon. Short, cold, winter evenings, when it got dark even before supper was on the table, meant Christmas was coming. Spring flowers meant ball practice, Easter, and the end of school were coming. Even the end of summer, the saddest time of any year, promised something good. The dreaded start of school always had the proverbial silver lining if we took the time to look for it. About eight days after school started, around the second week in September, we could mark our calendar in red. The Annual Fall Hallston County Agriculture and Industrial Fair and Redmond Brothers Carnival was coming to town! And I was waiting for it.

Our fair was always in September, maybe because our town was small and we couldn't get the carnival there in the summer—the height of their season. We always got them when they were on their way back to Florida or wherever bearded ladies and pickpockets spend their winters. Posters would spring up all over town in August, announcing the Monday through Saturday dates and creating excitement for everyone.

Nothing can satisfy such a motley crowd as does a carnival/fair. The farmers, who never ventured to town except on Saturday mornings, would come and spend the week. The wives would bring exhibits for competition. Sons and daughters would bring livestock and sleep in the barns with them every night for the run of the show. Townspeople came by the families—the children to ride the rides, the older kids to play the games and ogle the shows and get cotton candy all over their clothes and eat horrible hot dogs, the grandparents to see who won the prizes and to hold their ears during the fireworks, and the moms and dads to carry the purse and watch everyone have a good time. There were always guys with sideburns and turned-up collars, one eye half closed from the smoke coming off the cigarettes dangling from the corners of their mouths, with girlfriends named Peggy and Shirley who had sweaters thrown over their shoulders and their arms folded underneath, tight to their bodies. Smokey never showed fear of the rides no matter how high or fast they went, and Peggy and Shirley always screamed at the right times. Groups of teenaged girls giggled and squealed decibels above the roar of the Ferris wheel engine, and game players stayed at one stand for hours, spending tens of dollars trying to win a sixty-nine-cent purple dog. Everyone was there for the same reasons, the same prices, and to have the same fun. It was, without a doubt, the trashiest and most colorful good time any of us could have without getting into trouble.

"You goin' to the circus?" Bud asked as we stood in the school lunch line.

"It ain't no circus," Toby answered, looking for his lunch ticket in all his pockets.

"It is, too." Howard took it up. "It starts Monday night."

"Yeah, but it ain't no circus." Toby found his ticket in his billfold.

"It is, too, Toby. They got rides and ever'thing." This was Bud again.

"Yeah, Bud, but what Toby means is that's not a circus,"

September 1959

I jumped in, maybe because I knew Toby would never tell them why it wasn't a circus. He'd just keep denying it to watch them boil.

"Then what is it if it's not a circus?" This was one of them. It really doesn't matter which.

"A circus has animals. You know, like elephants and all. Just rides is a carnival." This was as simple as I knew how to make it.

"There won't be any elephants there," Toby said, helping me now. "The only animals there will be you two and your family."

"Are you callin' our mother an elephant?" Bud squared off.

"Just shut up and get back in line." Toby turned him around and headed him toward the milk stand.

Billy was already at a table eating when the four of us set our trays down.

"Did you find all the answers on that history paper last night?" Bud asked before we even got seated.

"Yeah, I got 'em," Billy said.

"Can I have 'em?" Bud begged.

Billy looked at me and laughed, then shook his head and looked back to his plate. He resumed eating before he answered Bud.

"Sure, you can have them. For a price."

"How much?" Bud was eager.

"Get me a free pass to the fair."

"I can't get you no free pass, and anyway it ain't no fair. It's a carnival." Bud and Howard got a real bang out of this one.

"I never said it wasn't a fair," I inserted, protecting myself. "I said it wasn't a circus. A circus has animals. A carnival has rides. That's all I said."

"Then why does ever'body say they're goin' to the fair?" Howard demanded.

"Because it *is* a fair." Toby had quit eating to say this.

"He says it ain't a circus, it's a carnival. You say it's a fair. What do you want *me* to say?" Bud was getting hot.

"I don't want you to say nothin'. I want you to shut up and eat your beans." Toby was getting hot, too.

I took a minute to explain, sincerely trying to be helpful. "The fair, Bud, is the exhibits and the animal part of it."

"I thought there were no animals. If there's animals, then it's a circus, and you said so yourself." Howard hit Bud on the arm, showing solidarity in their self-proclaimed win.

I went back to eating without saying another word, and the twins did the same in full confidence that they had taught us all a lesson.

"So, you gonna get me that pass?" Billy prodded.

"I can't get you no pass to the circus," Bud said.

"Your uncle is on the Fair Board. He can get all the passes you want."

"Him and my daddy don't even speak to each other."

"Then forget the history questions."

"Come on, Billy. That ain't fair. I mean, I don't know if…okay, I'll try. But I don't know if I can or not."

"Get us three free passes"—Billy pointed to himself, to Toby, and to me—"and you've got the answers for the rest of this six weeks."

"All right!" Bud was sailing. "I'll call you tonight."

Bud and Howard gathered their trays and left the three of us at the table.

"What night do you want to go?" Billy asked.

Toby shrugged and I said, "Wednesday night is family night. I'm goin' with my mom and dad. If we're goin' one night, let's make it Friday or Saturday."

"Friday night is a football game, but it's away so we probably won't go anyhow," Billy offered.

"Let's go Saturday night. That's the best night. They all strip down to nothin' in the hoochie-coochie show at midnight," Toby said.

"Naw they don't, and anyway we can't get in those shows." I didn't say we didn't want to. I said we couldn't.

Toby looked from one of us to the other and leaned across the table as if he had a government secret to share. "We can sneak in."

"Hey, that's a good idea." Billy was excited. "Let's sneak in the whole place if we don't get the passes."

"How?" Toby was ready.

"Well, we can jump the fence," Billy said. "I know a lot of people who did that last year."

"If we wait till ten o'clock," I said, "they open the gate and you can just walk in." I'd seen this happen or heard about it happening or thought I'd seen it happen or dreamed I'd heard about it happening. Either way, it sounded like something that might happen.

Toby turned up his nose. "By ten o'clock it's half over."

"What's half over?" I asked.

"I don't know," Toby said, laughing. "Whatever goes on in there."

"Let's do this," Billy said. "I'll give the twins till next Friday to come up with the passes, and if they don't we jump the fence. Okay?"

"Okay."

"Okay."

Piano Days

Howard and Bud's uncle, Simon Lee, was the hinge that swung the door of our fate between legal and illegal entry to the fair. He was the twins' paternal uncle, and he and their dad hadn't been on good terms for nearly ten years. Simon Lee and brother Big Bud were legends, glorious hell-raisers since their teens, and had left notorious tracks throughout three counties and municipalities. Somewhere along the way, Simon Lee found what he believed to be the Lord and joined the Shepherds of Peace Holiness Church. Big Bud cussed him unmercifully for this. They hadn't spoken since and only saw one another at family funerals and weddings. Big Bud loved to tell people how the church had tricked Simon Lee and was making a fool of him. Simon Lee, on the other hand, seemed to enjoy telling everyone who would listen how Big Bud was headed for eternal hell, forever and ever, amen. Simon Lee went to church three nights a week and twice on Sundays. He became a lay preacher and gave up his job driving a beer truck. But that's the only thing he gave up, according to Big Bud, who said Simon Lee could still drink a fleet of Saturday night sailors under the ship and did so as often as he went to "preachin'." Only Bud and Simon knew whether all of this was really true. What we saw and knew was that Simon Lee Spinner got active in that particular church and then formed a local men's gospel singing group. They were called the Shepherds of Peace Trio, and there were five of them. A sixth member played the piano. Her name was Vital Sheets, and she only played in two keys, C and F#. Big Bud said the group was called a trio because Simon Lee couldn't spell quartet and didn't know the word for five. Thus, the Trio.

    The group offered an experience in sound that few listeners sat all the way through. They sang at a fundraising talent show in our grade school gym once when we were in the Boy

Scouts. The Scouts sold tickets and ushered and stood in the back and laughed while the Shepherds of Peace wailed unmusically through such standards as "Canaan's Land" and "Do Lord." Wyler Pratt was their baritone and Toby's mailman, and as we stood in the back against the brick wall under the basketball net, stifling giggles, Toby said, "That ole geezer is deaf."

"Tone deaf?" I snorted.

"Stone deaf," Toby corrected. "He's been our mailman all my life, and I'm tellin' you he can't hear jack."

Billy held his Boy Scout cap over his mouth to keep from laughing louder than the music.

"Toby, he couldn't sing if he couldn't hear," I said.

"Well, you can tell for yourself he can't sing, and I'm tellin' you he can't hear. My mama writes him notes when she wants to tell him somethin'. My dog's been bitin' him in the ankle every other day for the past five years 'cause he can't hear him comin' or hear him barkin'. I'm tellin' you, he can't hear wind in a tunnel."

Billy and I ran for the door looking for refuge and relief in the great open spaces of the schoolyard. We howled and then listened through an open window while Wyler Pratt, U.S. Mail, cut down on a solo that did nothing but support Toby's theory. After half an hour, we decided that for once, Toby may have not only been right but also kind. After those long and belabored thirty minutes, we decided the whole trio was deaf. All five of them.

So it wasn't his musical talent that made Simon Lee a near respected figure in the community; it was his dedication and sincerity, his good nature and willingness to serve. He was on special PTA committees, served as a Ruritan Club officer, headed up regional church meetings, and, of course, was a member of the Fair Board. We never knew exactly what procedure Bud used in trying to obtain free entry for us through the near-holy gates of the Hallston County Fair from his Uncle Simon Lee. All we ever knew was that he was not successful. Bud said he called his uncle, and Simon Lee hung up on him three times. Howard said he never asked him because he knew his daddy would beat him if he ever found out he had asked Simon Lee for a favor. As always, the truth of the matter lay somewhere just outside the reach of the Spinner twins. They would rather walk a mile in the rain and lie than stay in bed and tell the truth, so we didn't bother ourselves with the Why. Our only concern now was the How.

    Before I go any further and cast any more aspersions on the abilities of my parents to be good and loving providers, let me insert here a note of respectability to be ever pinned to the character of my mother and father. They would have given me the money to go to the fair, and in all honesty they did. My father would hand me money with the warning to bring some of it back with me, knowing I wouldn't but not feeling fatherly unless he said this and maintained his parental integrity. My mother's warnings were always concerning my safety. She had probably heard all the money warnings herself and had no desire to repeat them in earshot of my dad. So I was "jumping the fence" out of adventure and not out of necessity. Toby's situation was almost identical to mine, and Billy's was even better. He always had twice as much money in his pockets as the rest of us. His mother would give him five dollars for Saturday-morning movies when we were little kids. It only cost twenty cents to get in and fifteen cents for popcorn, so Billy was always well heeled. That Friday night at the fair, he had twenty dollars in his jeans' pocket. Toby had ten and I had twelve. Forty-two dollars, Friday night, the Hallston County

Fair, girls in shorts riding the Tilt-A-Whirl. We were in the best years of our lives and knew it.

A chain-link fence, seven feet tall, enclosed the lights and action of the carnival next to the three-acre parking lot. This was no problem. Any healthy boy of fourteen or fifteen can climb a seven-foot fence. It was the two strands of barbed wire at the top that had us a little concerned. We found a dark corner in the far end of the parking lot and stood there for ten minutes, deliberating exactly when and in what order we would go over. Toby wanted to go first.

"Just help hold me when I get up there till I get one leg over the barbwire," he said.

"What're you gonna do then?"

"When I get one leg over, then I'll jump."

"Be careful so that...look out!" I yelled in a whisper. "Here comes a guard."

Members of local civic clubs volunteered to walk the fence each night with flashlights and arm bands that read GUARD in orange letters. If they saw anyone jumping the fence, they blew a whistle that signaled German shepherd dogs and policemen. At least, this is what we had always heard. I can't say any of us had actually seen that happen or even knew of anyone who had, but we were afraid we were about to experience it firsthand. Toby jumped back off the fence, and we hid behind a group of trees until the guard's walking vigil took him out of sight.

"Now go," Billy urged.

"I've got a cramp in my leg. I can't go yet."

Toby had a lot of leg to cramp and wasn't in as good a shape as Billy and me. I know now he had pulled a muscle when he tried to lift his leg over the barbed wire, but at the time we figured he would be alright in a few minutes.

"I'll go first." Who said that? Somebody was in my head talking through my mouth. I didn't know who he was, but I was about half scared of him so I didn't talk back. I just took a running leap and scaled the fence. I placed my hands carefully between the sprigs of sharp wire and lifted one leg over. Now I was astraddle the legendary fence I had heard so much about all these years. I froze and reflected for…what? seconds? minutes? an hour and a half? I'm sure it was only seconds. Here I was atop the fence that separated my childhood from the adventures of whatever lay ahead. If I brought my leg back over to safety, I might never try it again. If I brought the other one over to Adventureland, I would fall at least seven feet, maybe land flat on my back. What I didn't know then was that seven feet was no fall at all in Adventureland. Or maybe I did know then, because there I went, headfirst into the unknown. I was bruised but not broken. Scared but still laughing. Unsure but ready.

Billy was next. It took him longer because all three of us were laughing. He almost fell a couple of times. He would get right to the top and make the straddle move and then get tickled and have to take his leg back and start over. Once he got right on top of the barbed wire, he tried to get stern and serious. He said, "Alright, you guys. Shut up, and I mean it." This only made Toby snort louder, and Billy nearly fell off laughing. He did finally fall off and landed on my side of the fence. This put Billy and me in and Toby still on the outside.

"How's your leg?" I asked through the fence.

"It still hurts but I'm comin' over. Do you see anybody?"

We looked quickly, scanning the fence line for as far as we could see, and gave Toby the go-ahead. It was not an easy sight to watch. With Toby's weight, compounded by the pulled muscle and his natural unathletic ability, we stifled laughter

September 1959

mercifully in our throats until he reached the dangerous peak. There he stood on the fence top, not able to go either way, sharp wire less than a quarter of an inch away from him being in the girls' P.E. class next week. He looked down and saw our strained, contorted faces trying to withhold the laughter and said, "I'm gonna kick some butt if I ever get down from here." That's when we all three lost it and broke into a fit of laughing that drowned out the distant sounds of the carnival night.

We were giggling so hard that we saw him beside us before we heard him. He just stood there looking from Toby to us and back again. Simon Lee Spinner's head came almost to where the barbed wire started on top of the fence. At least it looked that way to me. He stood between us and Toby and shook his big ole beefy head.

"Boys, don't you each have a dollar in your pocket?"

"Yes sir," I said. Billy chimed in affirmatively.

Simon Lee looked up at Toby, still astride the barbed wire and holding on with both hands.

"And you, son. Don't you have a dollar in your pocket?"

Toby, never completely scared and never completely tasteful, looked down on Simon Lee's head and said, "I don't know. I can't get in there right now to look."

In a swift move, Simon Lee put one hand on Toby's leg and one on his upper arm, lifted him off the fence, and stood him gently in the grass beside us. I was getting ready for the whistle and the police dogs. I started looking for a tree to climb.

"I think I know all three of you boys, don't I?"

I spoke for the group. "Yes sir."

"Well, go on to the fair and have a good time and behave yourselves."

"Do we have to pay?" Toby asked.

"Not here," Simon Lee said with a smile. "But you'll have

to pay someplace."

"What do you mean?" Billy asked.

Simon Lee Spinner met our eyes with a friendly gaze and exhaled a heavy sigh through his nose. "Tomorrow night I want you three boys to come to church. You know where it is. If you're not there, I'll know where to find you. Do you hear me?"

"Yes sir."

"Yes sir."

"Yes sir."

"Now go on to the fair and stay out of trouble."

We started down over the hill, and Simon Lee stood watching us. I turned and said, "Thank you." Not because I was more scared than the others but maybe because I was more grateful. I hated being in any kind of trouble. Billy did, too, but wasn't as quick to admit it as I was. And Toby, well, I knew Toby wasn't planning on going to church anyway.

"Did you see how big he was up close?" Toby whispered.

"He lifted you off that fence like you were a balloon or somethin'," Billy whispered back.

"Is he still behind us?"

"I don't see him anywhere," I said, looking over my shoulder.

"Was he serious about us goin' to church?" Billy wondered.

"He was serious," I assured them both.

"I ain't goin'," Toby said emphatically.

"I am," Billy said unashamedly.

"Tomorrow night is Saturday night. They got church on Saturday night?" Toby asked.

"They got church every night," I said as if I knew what I was talking about.

"Well, I ain't goin'."

"We gotta go, Toby," Billy said directly to him. "He'll come to our houses and get us if we don't. He said he knew who all three of us were."

"But Saturday night?" Toby was getting louder. "We were comin' back to the fair Saturday night."

"We can come afterwards," I reasoned.

"Well, I ain't goin'."

"After he let us go like that, we have to go."

"What time does it start?"

"Seven thirty, probably."

"We'll be out of there by eight thirty," I said, based on absolutely nothing. "We can still come to the fair."

"Saturday night is when they take ever'thing off in the hoochie-coochie shows. We gotta come tomorrow night." Toby just couldn't get those hoochie-coochie shows off his mind even though he didn't really know for sure what they were.

"And we'll have to pay tomorrow night," Billy said.

"Why?" Toby said. "We can jump the fence again."

"After what happened tonight?" Billy was getting fed up.

"Well, I ain't payin', I'll tell you that for sure."

We walked in silence for the rest of the way before we hit the bright lights of the midway. We stood there and watched some people pass by before we joined the crowd. Trying to salvage the night and have a good time after getting caught, Billy shook his head and said, "I can't believe it. Church on a Saturday night."

"I ain't goin'," Toby said for the fourth time.

"Shut up, Toby," I said. "We're all goin'."

A carnival is bright and fun and scary and dirty and exciting and smelly and crowded and loud and dangerous and funny and, best of all, annual. It wouldn't be as good if it happened once a week or even once a month. Once a year is enough. We breathed in and soaked up everything our senses could hold and enjoyed as much as we could stand. We saw strangers and friends and enemies and teachers and families with dirty little kids with runny noses. We saw pretty girls who we followed around and who followed us around. We saw dogs running loose and even some husbands running loose, sneaking into side shows. We saw ice cream eaters, snow cone lickers, cherry Coke sippers, cigar smokers, and tobacco chewers who spit over the side rail just before they got on the Whip. We saw babies riding hobby horses—some crying, some laughing, and some just scared in a frozen state of up and down animation. We heard screams from rides and invitations from amplified speakers to "Come in and see it for yourself." We smelled undistinguished and unrecognizable food and sweet perfumes and body odors and overflowing trash cans. We tasted dust and atmosphere on our tongues that we would never find duplicated anywhere else in the normal world. We felt bodies pressed against us and warm night air in our faces as we spun round and round on various rides of thrills. We ate cheap, cold food and drank watery sodas and bought trinkets we thought we would cherish but, in reality, could not lay our hands on by Monday morning. We spent dollars trying to win prizes we could have bought for cents. We paid to see the freaks and then felt guilty for staring at them. We stepped in mud puddles and over cables and butted in lines and got pushed out of lines. We watched people and were aware of people watching us. We went to the carnival and were no better or worse for it. We were simply having the time of our lives.

September 1959

Later, as we walked home, Toby asked, "What're you goin' to do tomorrow?"

"I've got to mow Mr. Farley's yard before noon," Billy answered.

"I'm goin' to a sale with my dad," I said. Saturday morning sales were a weekly ritual at our house. We'd go to these household sales at country farms and come home with antiques and old books and useless items that lined the walls of the basement. But we always went back for more. For some reason I loved them as much as my dad did.

"What about tomorrow night?" Billy fished.

"I ain't goin'." Toby was not as firm as he wanted to sound.

I ignored Toby's statement and directed my next one to Billy. "I'll go by that church tomorrow and see what their sign out front says. It'll tell us what time the service starts tomorrow night."

"They're holy rollers, ain't they?" Toby said.

"What's it matter to you? You ain't goin'," Billy said, cutting him off.

"I'm scared of them holy rollers. My mama's sister used to be one and they're crazy. They jump all over the place and holler and moan." Toby was downright serious.

"We don't have to do that even if they do," I said, trying to play down the fact that I was a little apprehensive of the whole situation, too.

"What if they want us to testify or somethin'?" Toby pleaded.

"Then testify!" Billy commanded. "Tell them you jumped the fence and you're sorry and you'll never do it again till next year."

We laughed, Billy and I, but Toby wasn't smiling. "I'm

serious, guys. They get crazy. Why do we have to go?"

"Well, Simon Lee didn't turn us in to the police or even kick us out of the fair. The only thing he asked was that we come to church. That ain't bad for gettin' caught. It'll all be over in an hour. We won't even have to tell our parents where we're goin' or anything about it." I thought my reasoning was sound until I heard Billy cackling. "What's so funny about that?" I asked, an edge of anger in my voice.

"We're gonna lie to our parents and tell them we're goin' to the fair but really we're goin' to church. Now that's funny!"

That *was* funny. Almost as funny as what was about to happen to us and our spiritual well-being.

I left home that evening in my fair-go-to-meeting best—tennis shoes, dungarees, and a white dress shirt with the sleeves rolled to the elbows. I carried a brown paper bag and as I went out the back door I told my mother I was taking some clothes back to Toby that he'd left the last time he spent the night with me. After that, I told her, we'd go to the fair. She said to be careful, come home by eleven, and why didn't I tell her about the clothes so she could have washed them instead of me taking them back dirty. I hated lying to my mother, but sometimes it was necessary and this was one of those times.

It was September of '59, months before Billy got his driver's license, nearly a year before I got mine. Our main mode of transportation was still walking or biking. If we'd had a car, this part of the evening would have been much easier. But we were still fourteen and hoofing, so we met behind Dinkel's Grocery at seven fifteen, each with a brown paper bag we had told the same story about, except for the name of the owner of the alleged contents. We all three hurriedly pulled a tie, dress shoes, and dress pants out of our respective bags and dressed behind the trash bin with the fancy Dinkel's lettering.

"Somebody's gonna have to tie my tie," Toby said unashamedly.

"I'll get it," I said. I was dressed first.

"Aw man! I forgot a belt," Billy said.

"Here, I got two," I offered. "Take the one off my dungarees."

We put our bags, stuffed with our everyday clothes, under the Dinkel's delivery truck. The store was already closed, and we knew the truck wouldn't be moved until Monday morning. Then we started off, the Three Stooges in shirts and ties on a Saturday night, walking down the street, going to church. The first car that went by, the very first car that went by, was the Spinner family. Big Bud and Big Wife in the front and Howard and Bud in the back. You'd think they would be at the window laughing and pointing, but they just stared, dumbfounded and apparently puzzled. We found out later that the reason they weren't laughing was because they thought we were "going to a funeral." Whose, I don't know, and I don't think I've ever been to one on a Saturday night, but we never told them any different. We told them Billy's cousin had died and not to ask any more about it because Billy was pretty upset. They bought that premise and we never had to add to the story.

There was a short walkway from the city sidewalk to the open door of the Shepherds of Peace Holiness Church. We could hear piano music coming out the doorway. I couldn't tell if it was inviting us in or warning us away, but we took deep breaths and walked toward the music. I was pushed to lead the way up the steps. As we crossed the threshold, we saw a serene gathering of normal-looking people, not the ogres we expected, sitting quietly in wooden pews, heads bowed, listening

Piano Days

prayerfully to the piano, which was playing what almost sounded like "Are You Washed in the Blood of the Lamb." My first thought was to sit as close to the back as possible, but due to our late arrival, what was possible meant about four rows from the front. It was a small church of only about twelve total rows, but they were all nearly filled. I turned into what looked like the least full pew and sat next to an elderly woman with a black sweater around her shoulders and a scarf around her head. She smiled at me and moved a few inches to her left. As I sat down, Billy sat beside me. This is when we discovered there was no more room on the bench for a third newcomer. Toby panicked when he couldn't squeeze between Billy and the arm of the pew. I motioned for him to go across the aisle. He did, reluctantly, and sat next to a short, fat man who had no teeth and wore a railroad engineer's cap. That's when I noticed we were overdressed. The Three Stooges were the only ones in ties. All I could see were plaid shirts, old sweaters, print housedresses, work shoes, and open collars. It looked more like we were at a union meeting than a church service. No one seemed to notice us, though, as every eye was closed in meditation. The piano piece soon ended, proving to me they believed in a merciful God even if other points of their religion differed from my Presbyterian upbringing.

Heavy silence mixed with the shuffling and coughing permeated the late summer night between the ending of the song and the opening statements of the reigning speaker. A breeze blew through the open windows, and I heard an occasional horn blow and tires cry from the street. The speaker ambled slowly down the aisle toward the pulpit and took his time fumbling with his notes before he ever spoke a word. Billy watched him and grinned. Toby watched Billy and me, red-faced and anxious. I stopped scanning the faces and backs of heads around me and centered my focus on the man standing, still silent, in the pulpit. That man, clad in matching gray khaki work shirt and pants with his Christian name over his left shirt pocket in green, was Mr. Simon Lee Spinner. He began at last.

"Friends and neighbors and fellow brothers in the bosom of our Lord and Savior, I welcome you to tonight's meeting. I'm gonna ask everyone to turn to page ninety-eight in the Hymns of Revival hymnbook and sing in loud praise and thanksgiving the words of the beautiful song, 'Let the Lower Lights Keep Burning.' Sister Vital, lead us into song."

Vital stumbled her way through the last two lines of the hymn as an introduction on the piano, and then the voices of the congregation drowned her out as if she were not playing at all. I was ready for a horrid storm of off-key droning but was served a beautiful chorale of harmony one would expect coming from the clouds. The old woman beside me sang a perfect alto, and from behind me I could hear tenors and sopranos and basses. I was serenaded by a groundswell of sweet singing that I thought was being saved for heaven. Billy looked at me with his mouth open. I knew he was wondering where he could get the sheet music to this song. Of course, it was right in front of us, and everyone was using it. I glanced across the aisle at Toby. He was still staring back, red-faced and worried and unfazed by the dulcet and honied tones surrounding him. "The Lower Lights" never burned prettier.

I sat back down at the end of this rendition with a new outlook on the evening. I wasn't looking forward to any sermon, as most fourteen-year-olds don't, but then I began to hold on to the hope and chance that there might not be one. Maybe it was just a song festival or hymn sing or something of that nature. Maybe the sermon was only for Sunday morning. Then, right in the middle of my dream, a strange and unexpected thing happened. Men started getting up in the side aisles and closing the windows. A hot night like this, and they were closing the windows while Simon Lee introduced someone named Brother Carlisle.

When he said, "The flock is all yours, Brother Carlisle," Carlisle hit the aisle running and never stopped until he had circled the inside of the church three times. Toby grabbed the back of the pew in front of him and started to stand up. I gave him a scolding look across the center of the church and shook my head. Billy, his hands in his lap, looked straight ahead as Carlisle stopped on the third pass and latched on to the pulpit with both hands and hollered, "Praise the Lord, I'm on fire!" Then he started to run again. Three more times he went around the inside walls of the church, up and down the center and side aisles, full speed and gaining. Murmurs and groans and unintelligible utterings began to build from the throats of the parishioners, which only made Carlisle run faster. When he grabbed the pulpit this time, he stopped. He was out of breath and so was I. "My soul's on fire! My heart's on fire! My feet's on fire!" And he was off again.

People began standing up in the pews and reaching for the sky, clutching the air as if they were trying to climb an invisible ladder to heaven. They chanted and cried and called out for people I had never heard of. When they all stood up, Toby stood up again and pointed to the back of the church and mimed to Billy and me the words, "I'm gone!"

Billy said, "Sit down. Let's see what's gonna happen."

I realized he was talking out loud to Toby across the aisle. No one noticed because everyone else was talking out loud too. Toby picked up on this immediately and said at normal conversational volume, "If we're stayin', I'm comin' over there."

"There's no room over here," Billy said back to him.

September 1959

"Make room!" Toby was not funning. Toby was on his way.

When Brother Carlisle made his final pass and final pause at the altar, he leaned on the pulpit, exhausted, until his breath came back and the fire left his face. The congregation took this as their cue to quiet down and sit down. When those in our pew sat, we had a serious squeeze because of our new seat partner. The old woman in the scarf looked irritated and jerked the tail of her sweater out from under me. I had to sit forward on the edge of the seat to make room for everyone, as if it weren't already uncomfortable enough.

It was now seven fifty, and it would not be the last time I looked at my watch that evening. The one hour I had speculated on was fast becoming a fantasy. At eight fifty, Brother C. was still going strong. He had started at a steam most dedicated ministers never reach in a lifetime and had crescendoed to a peak of frenzy that would test the faith of Abraham himself. It was long, and it was hot in there with the windows closed tightly, but I was never close to getting sleepy. I was afraid to go to sleep. Brother Carlisle had begun his sermon/performance with a prayer. "Let us all stand and worship the Lamb of God in holy prayer," he had said. And we did, but not like anything I had ever witnessed. We all stood up, and when Carlisle started to pray out loud, so did everyone else, all of them praying their own individual prayer at full and exuberant volume. It was an eerie sound that at first sent chills across the back and then, after eye contact with a couple of good friends, sent giggles up from the stomach. It wasn't enough to hear everyone praying and trying to contain ourselves, but Toby, who was beginning to loosen up now that he was on our side of the aisle, put his hand over his heart and began to say the Pledge of Allegiance. Billy and I controlled ourselves by staring at the hardwood floor directly beneath our feet. As soon as this was over, Brother C. got into the meat of his show.

The good Brother yelled, whispered, cried, beat his chest, walked on his knees, walked on the little wooden rail around the pulpit, walked up and down the center aisle, screamed, shook his fist, shook his finger, shook his head. And finally laid himself out flat on the floor and hollered at the ceiling. This brought a barrage of amens that could stop any normal show. But not this one. He went on. He called for sinners to come forward and be saved, and at least a dozen did. Toby's old friend with the engineer's cap was the first one up. Men, women, children, teenagers. One was a girl about our age. She was plain and simple but also very beautiful. She had long brown hair and sparkling eyes, smooth skin, a lovely face, and was a professed sinner. As she went past our pew toward the front, Toby leaned over and said, "I'm goin' up." We laughed and put our heads down, and it wasn't until I looked up again and saw his blue gaberdine pants stepping out in the aisle that I knew he was serious. He was not only serious; he was gone. Billy's eyes grew wider and his mouth fell farther open. I watched in complete disbelief as Toby took his place in line at the front of the church beside the Brown-haired Angel.

They were all in a perfect line, with their backs to us and their eyes on Carlisle, when the spirit of what this was all about came down on us. Brother started circling the dozen, a little faster with each round, and then started what I had heard of all my life but had never witnessed. He began speaking in tongues. The audience, I mean congregation, began to join in. A little eight-year-old boy stood up in the seat just in front of us and kicked it off. "Kala ma pu toka ta ka palama." In seconds everybody was doing it. Billy and I locked eyes. Then we both looked to the front and at the back of Toby's head. Slowly,

September 1959

Toby turned and looked at us. He was red-faced and worried again, but a mischievous smile was leaking through. I didn't even want to know what was on his mind.

Brother Carlisle stopped suddenly at one end of the line and stuck his arm out, stone stiff in the air. It was something akin to Leland Perry's fifty-yard runs at any given Friday night football game. Suddenly, he roughly and deliberately smacked the first person hard on the forehead with his open palm, and that person hit the floor in a dead lump faster than Jerry Lewis ever dropped for comic effect. Number two did the same thing. Brother C. was coming down the line fast and wiping out sin as he went. Each person he smacked seemed to pass out, fall and lie unconscious at his feet. Number three slumped. Then number four.

"What's goin' on?" Billy asked out of the corner of his mouth.

I didn't offer an answer because I didn't have one. Right at that moment I was busy counting. Toby was number eleven in the line of twelve, and number five had just bit the dust.

"What's he gonna do?" Billy asked.

At this moment, as if he'd heard Billy's question, Toby turned around and looked at us. He smiled and shrugged and rolled his eyes toward the Brown-haired Angel who was number ten. Billy and I, who would laugh at almost anything he did, laughed at this too. Number six hit the floor hard. We could hear her head bounce off the pine wood. This got us going even more. Then number seven. Bang! We were completely destroyed by this time. I was beginning to be embarrassed and ashamed but also helpless to do anything about it. I was saying under my breath, "God, please forgive me if this is on the level, and please forgive them if it ain't."

Carlisle was talking faster, sweat dripping off his chin like a faulty spigot. His voice was raspy and giving out but his energy was at an all-time Wheaties high. He hit number eight in the head so hard the man's feet were knocked out from under him and he landed on the floor sprawled flat on his back. When his legs shot forward, they kicked Carlisle in the shins and knocked him off balance and he dropped to his knees. Toby clapped his hands and threw his head back and laughed out loud. Misreading this as part of the spirit of the moment, no one even noticed it but Billy and me. Number nine went down easy. She was in her sixties, and I think I caught her catching herself with one hand when she fell. The crowd was hot now. There was a constant and enthusiastic din no basketball game could compete with. A roar of excitement. A fever. Everyone chanting their own chant and waving their arms and feeling the spirit. If not the spirit of the Lord, at least the spirit of whatever was going on here.

Miss Angel's number was up. Brother Carlisle placed his hand gently on her forehead, mumbled some special intonement that took a little longer than the others, and then quickly shoved her as she crumbled at his feet. Toby was next, and we had no idea what to expect. Brother raised both hands, gave one loud blast that almost totally wiped out his voice, and then hit Toby solidly on top of the head. Toby's eyes rolled around in their sockets like John Wayne's in *North to Alaska* when he got hit on the head in a barroom fight. He held this position long enough to be sure we both saw him, and then he dropped. Right on top of the Brown-haired Angel. And there they both lay, together in the front of the church, Toby with his face next to hers and his arm across her shoulder. Brother Carlisle went to number twelve, hit him hard and fast, and then went back to Toby. With the toe of his work boot, he caught Toby under the chin and rolled him off the Angel, stepping, deliberately

September 1959

I'm pretty sure, on his fingers as he walked away.

While Brother C. led his flock in a final prayer, half a dozen men came from the back of the church and helped revive the reposed and prone. They pulled them up and guided them back to their seats. At this point, Carlisle turned the service back over to Simon Lee, who thanked him for such a moving experience. Simon Lee went on to explain that Brother Carlisle was from over in Wickersville and worked for the telephone company there as a lineman. He was not even a minister! It was announced that the church's regular preacher would be back from vacation next week. Simon Lee ended with, "Then we'll have a *real* Holy Spirit service."

The same deacons who had closed the windows got up and opened them. Everyone stood and sang "When the Roll Is Called Up Yonder," and the flock was released into the late summer night.

It was nearly ten o'clock when we got back to Dinkel's Grocery and felt under the truck for our bags of clothes. We had not said a word for the two blocks because people from the church were walking in front of and behind us most of the way. We got our paper sacks and just sat on the loading dock for a few minutes, reflecting on what had happened to us.

Billy was the first to laugh. Then me. Then Toby. And we laughed for ten minutes without stopping. My throat hurt and my stomach muscles ached from it, and when we finally calmed down, we were lying on the cement dock with the rubber bumper around the edge, looking up at the stars.

"What made you go up front, Toby?"

"Oh, I don't know. Just to see what was gonna happen."

"How did you know what to do?"

"I just did what the rest of them did. I fell down. Except I had a girl and they didn't."

"Were they fakin'?"

"Sure, they were fakin'."

"Do you know that for sure?"

"Yeah. I've seen them do it a lot."

Billy and I sat up. "You've been there before?"

"No, not there. But I've seen 'em. I've seen 'em on television."

"Where have you ever seen anything like that on television?"

"Well, not exactly like that. But close. My granddaddy used to only watch two things on television when he lived with us. Oral Roberts and rasslin'. Oral used to hit 'em on the head just like Brother Carlisle, to heal 'em. And the fall. I learned to fall from Gorgeous George. If you watch enough Oral Roberts and rasslin', you can learn to fake almost anything."

"Then you think rasslin' is all fake?"

"Most of it. Sometimes there's blood and you can't fake that. But yeah, most of it. My granddaddy didn't think so, though. He believed everything he saw on television. Oral Roberts. Rasslin'. He even thought Howdy Doody was Buffalo Bob's little boy."

We rolled and howled at this until my voice felt like Brother Carlisle's must have felt at that very moment.

"But you know what?" Billy said, sitting up quickly and wide-eyed. "They could really sing."

"Yeah, that was pretty. I was really surprised at that," I said.

"Me, too, considering that the Shepherds of Peace Trio comes out of the same church and they couldn't carry a tune in a bucket with six handles." This was the first time I knew

September 1959

Toby had paid any attention to the music. "Wonder why that is?" he asked.

"I don't know."

"I don't either. Strange ain't it?"

"Anybody still wanna go to the fair?"

"We won't have long to stay. I gotta be home at eleven."

"Me, too. That gives us less than an hour."

"We payin' or jumpin' the fence?"

"Are you kiddin' me, brother? We're payin'. I can't afford to jump the fence anymore."

We walked around the carnival a few times and were surprised at such a slim crowd on a Saturday night. A couple of rides and a couple of stands were already starting to tear down, getting ready for tomorrow's trip south. By nine o'clock in the morning, they would all be gone. They always were, so the legend goes. Only a few tons of trash scattered over the grounds would be evidence that there were ever strangers in town.

We rode the Tubs once and threw pennies at glass plates and vases and shot rifles at tin ducks. That's what Billy and I were doing when Toby ran to get us.

"Come here. You gotta come here."

"What's wrong?"

"Just come here." He had us both by the arm. We walked halfway around the square and he stopped and pointed ahead. "Up there. Look up there in that booth."

About twenty feet away, in a booth where you threw baseballs at wooden milk bottles, sat the Brown-haired Angel, reading a magazine.

"That's her!" I said.

"What's she doin' here?" Billy asked.

"I don't know. I was just walkin' around while you all were shootin' and I looked up and there she was working in that booth."

"She must be with the carnival," I reasoned. "They don't hire local people when they come to town."

"Then what was she doin' at church?'

"Want me to ask her?" Toby volunteered.

"Yeah, ask her." Billy urged.

"Wait a minute," I said. "For some reason I don't know if we should."

"What could it hurt?"

"I'm not sure, but…"

"Come on. Let's do it."

Toby led the way. As we started toward the stand, a tall, scraggly man of about forty-five came in the back of it. He was dirty from the skin in. He had on black pants and a black shirt, with the collar turned up into greasy, matted hair. He had a tattoo of a snake running down his left arm and an anchor on his right. He was smoking a tiny, thin cigar. He said something to the girl just before we walked up. She answered him and went back to her magazine. He saw us first.

"Step right up here, fellows. Three balls for a quarter."

Toby ignored him and looked straight at the Angel and said, "Hi."

She looked up and caught her breath as if she had seen a ghost from another life. The magazine slid off her lap as she jumped off her stool. She looked quickly at Mr. Tattoo, whom I hastily took to be her father. He frowned at her and then at Toby.

"I've got to go to the trailer," she said hurriedly. And she was gone.

Tattoo's attention and glare was now solely on Toby.

September 1959

"You wanna play the game, boy?"

Toby looked him squarely in the eye and said, "Is that your daughter?"

"Three throws for two bits. Play it or move it."

"Come on, Toby. Let's go home."

We moved it.

The mystery of the Brown-haired Angel dominated us the rest of the week. We talked about her whenever we were together and thought about her whenever we were alone. Toby thought she really *wasn't* the Tattoo Man's daughter.

"Probably a child bride or whatever they call it," he said. "She wasn't a day over sixteen. I'll bet he met her somewhere out in California or somewhere like that and she ran off with the carnival and he married her."

Billy thought it really *was* his daughter. "Simon Lee probably caught her stealin' or somethin' or in somebody's trailer and made her go to church on a Saturday night just like he did us."

I had my own thoughts. I thought she was the man's daughter, too. And I thought she was just getting old enough to be ashamed of her father and her life and had sneaked off and subsequently found a church along the street. Sort of like us, she had sneaked off from her parents and gone to church. But she was serious and we were laughing about it. This didn't make me proud, and I always got a little hot with embarrassment behind my face when I thought about it. If she was looking for something, I hope she found it. And I hope we didn't get her in any trouble.

For two or three years after that, we went to the fair in anticipation of maybe seeing the Brown-haired Angel again, just to help solve the mystery or prolong it. One year Billy thought he saw the Tattoo Man working the Ferris wheel, but by the time he came and got Toby and me, we couldn't find anyone who looked anything like him. For all those years we went to the fair, up until the time we left home and town and went our separate ways after high school, but we never saw the Angel again. We never jumped the fence again. And we never went back to the Shepherds of Peace Holiness Church again. Although a week later, Wyler Pratt did knock on Toby's front door one evening after supper and ask if Toby was home. When he went to the door, Mr. Pratt, in his mailman suit, handed him some religious literature and a pamphlet titled ARE YOU READY? and invited him to come to church the next Sunday morning. Toby thanked him but told him he wouldn't be able to attend, as he was leaving in two days for India to join his uncle who was a missionary there. Wyler Pratt wished him well, said he hoped his uncle caught a lot of fish, and walked off the porch, where Sparky, Toby's bulldog, bit him in the seat of the pants, hanging on for dear life while ole Mr. Pratt kept walking down the street trying to shake him loose.

    Toby could have called him off but he didn't. He was having too much fun watching.

September 1959

It was always a mystery to me, and I think to my mother, too, just when my uncle started writing these stories about his youth, his school days. I distinctly remember her telling me once that he wrote many of them as they were happening. But then, on closer inspection as I got older and more interested in the things he had to say, I questioned if a fourteen-year-old boy could have written with the insight and empathy I saw in some of these early "chapters." I questioned Mom on the subject a couple of different times later on and found her to be unsure of just when he might have started writing. She conceded that the first time she was actually aware of them was when she went home to help my grandparents redecorate and paint some rooms while Uncle Be-Bop was away at college. That's when she came across a box of files he had stored in his bedroom closet. Not hidden but simply stored. She said that before she inspected what was in the box or read anything at all, she called him at his dorm at the University of North Carolina and asked if it was okay with him if she looked through them. He was nonchalant about the contents and told her she could read them and do anything she wanted with them. He even suggested she could throw them all away if she didn't want to go to the trouble of moving them. This attitude doesn't surprise me one bit. It is so him. Never taking himself seriously and never thinking anyone else should either.

But the tenor and tone of what my mother found in that box changed immediately once she began to read the pages. She was entranced by what he had set down of his young life. She saw something in his observations and preservation of the times that he didn't see himself. Or maybe he didn't care anymore. My uncle did not always have a good and carefree life. Some of the things he went through changed his views, and as he grew older I think it became harder for him to write about what I heard him on many occasions refer to as the "fluff years."

The twelve-year gap between Mom and her brother closed quickly for her after she found the chapters in that cardboard box at the back of his closet in the winter of 1963. She realized she had missed out on really knowing her little brother and understanding how he was growing up. And if she hadn't found the box, I think she would still have found a reason to call him and connect in ways she had neglected all their lives. She loved what she read and encouraged him to add to his stories. She would say that she pushed *him to add to them. Years later, she confessed to me that he didn't so much resist her as simply ignore her pleadings. She saw him as a promising writer and he saw her as a nagging sister. I asked my grandparents once who was right in all this, but they never offered an opinion. I think it was just one of those things they saw as none of my business and didn't deem it important to talk to me about it. Of course, they were right, but every time I read a new chapter my interest grew and I became more curious and fascinated with the times, with the stories, with my uncle in particular.*

My uncle was at college for nearly four years. That story alone becomes important in time and adds extensively to who he was and who he became. He once told my mother that he sometimes found a great joy in writing about his young days but sometimes found it very painful.

"Why would it be painful?" she asked. "It sounds like so much fun."

"Yes, and it was. While it was happening. But then looking back—I guess that's the painful part."

"You mean regrets? Immaturity? That sort of thing? That shouldn't be an issue. We all have those cringeworthy moments. Shed the inhibitions and just be honest. You have such a knack for that."

"Sis, you amaze me sometimes."

"Really? In what way?"

September 1959

"You're just always smarter than I think you are."

They laughed together about this for years, and that's the kind of thing that brought them closer. Every time I read and reread his pages, I feel a little closer to him, too.

Chapter Five

June 1959

For all the growing up I wanted to achieve—getting a drivers' license, having a parttime job, dating regularly, buying my own clothes with my own money, not having to be home until midnight—I still look back on the summer of '59 with great tenderness and a sadness that makes me smile. It was, as I have said, our last biking summer. It was the last summer I actually bought a tube patch or raised a three-cornered seat or lowered extra-long handlebars or traded rubber handle grips because of the color of the streamer hanging from them. It was the last summer I rode my twenty-six-inch with chrome fenders to the ballgame and the last summer we would gather on my front lawn after supper, sit and talk till near dark, and then decide to walk to Dinkel's and get ice cream. Dinkel's was open until nine p.m. every weekday, and we closed him down just about every night. It was the last summer we were all interested in the same things. The last summer for being kids and doing kid things and not being ashamed of them. The last summer for exploring the mysteries of life without having to solve them. The last summer of counting blue cars and red cars, making telephone pranks, sneaking cigarettes, and discovering new sex terms. It was a wonderful summer, and maybe the last one I can look back on with absolutely no regrets except that it is gone forever, taking the people and the time with it and leaving only my sentimental memory as a witness that it was ever there at all.

I was on my back in the grass, throwing a softball in the air with one hand and catching it in my glove. Supper was over and the sun was looking for a place to recline just like I was doing. It was still hot even though it was six thirty, and very little wind was blowing through the maple trees in our front yard. I was noticing the half moon and trying to remember if it meant anything when you could see the moon in the daylight. Daddy always said if the sun was shining while it was raining, it meant the devil was beating his wife. He also said if there was a circle around the moon, I should count the stars inside the circle, and that would be the number of days until it rained. I'm sure he had one about the moon in daylight, and I was trying to remember what it was when a piece of gravel hit the sole of my sneaker. I looked up and saw Jayo about ten feet away, grinning. His big brother Billy was a few steps behind him. I threw my ball glove at Jayo and started to chase him. He loved it. He was about eight years younger than Billy, and he was our pet.

"Help! Help! You're hurtin' my arm," he squealed.

"I'm not hurtin' you." I kept tickling him.

"I give. I give."

"Not yet," I said.

"I give up. Help! I give up."

I rolled off him and we lay in the grass and panted, out of breath. Billy picked up my softball and tossed it from one hand to the other. Then Jayo said it for the first time that I was aware of.

"Get off of Freddy. You'll mash him."

"You talkin' to me?" I asked, puzzled.

"You're layin' on his head. Get off," Jayo whined.

I jumped up and looked at Billy. He just shook his head and kept tossing the ball.

June 1959

"Freddy wants something to drink," Jayo said to me.

I looked at Billy again. I was needing some help here.

"Can he go in your house and get Freddy somethin' to drink?" Billy asked.

"Sure," I said.

Jayo headed for the back door, and Billy and I sat in the grass.

"What's that all about?" I didn't know if something was wrong with me or with Jayo.

"He's got an imaginary friend. Just go along with him."

"When did that start?"

"Within the past week. My mom noticed it first. Freddy sleeps with him and eats with him now."

"It scared me," I joked. "I thought I was losin' my mind or somethin'."

"Mom says just humor him. Being a nurse and all, she says it's normal. Not to worry about it."

"Yeah," I said. "He'll probably just stop it one day."

"That's what she says. Just play along with him and he'll stop on his own."

"Who named him Freddy?"

"What? He did. Who do you think named him? Me? He's not *my* friend." Billy was a little edgier than the question called for.

"All right," I explained. "I didn't really mean who. I meant why."

"I don't know." And then he went quiet and I knew he knew.

Billy tossed me the ball and I tossed it back, and then he just held it and looked down the road. He was silent for nearly a minute before simply saying, "I'm scared."

"Hey, it don't mean anything."

Fred was Billy and Jayo's father's name. Billy remembered him. Jayo didn't. He was killed in Korea during the last week of the war. The Battle of Kumsong in July of '53. My mother said it was the last day of the war and that some of his family think maybe it was even after the war had officially ended. Either way, he was no less dead. He died a month before Jayo was born.

There were pictures of him in uniform at their house. One always sat on their piano. He was standing in front of a long white building that I always took to be part of the Army barracks. His hat was on a tilt on the side of his head, and he was grinning. I always looked at that picture whenever I walked through their living room. I was drawn to it. You know that game. You try to make yourself walk by something without looking, but you get pulled back as if you're afraid something dreadful will happen to someone in your family if you don't finally look at it. That's the kind of relationship I had with that picture. And I played with it for years until one day I stopped and really looked at it and saw something I had never seen before. Cupped in his right hand, hanging by his side, was a cigarette. "Did your dad smoke?" I asked Billy at the time. "Yeah, I think so," he said and, as always, changed the subject. Billy couldn't talk about him. His mother tried, but he wouldn't talk or listen. As close as we were, I could recall easily the number of times he had ever mentioned his father. Maybe twice at the most.

Billy was still looking down the road and holding the ball. I felt like it was time to say something, I just wasn't sure what. So I stumbled into it without knowing what point I was going to make or how much solace it would be for him in that moment.

"Jayo's heard your mother and your grandparents talk

about your dad. He's picked up on the fact that his name was Fred, so when he came up with this imaginary friend, it was just natural for him to call him Freddy. That's all there is to it. Don't that make sense?"

Billy turned and looked at me for a long, uncomfortable time and then shook his head. "No, that don't make sense."

"Why not? They called your dad Fred. Jayo calls his friend Freddy. Makes sense to me."

"They didn't call him Fred and still don't. His name was Thomas Fredrick Hudlow. They called him Tom. They still do. All the time. Always talkin' about him and callin' him Tom. Jayo can't even read yet. He don't know his name was Fredrick. No way could he know that."

"Your mother told him." I was getting desperate for a good answer.

"I asked her. She didn't tell him. She said only people he went to school with ever called him Fred. Nobody in our family ever called him that."

"Your grandmother? Grandfather?"

"No."

"It could happen."

"No. He had no way of knowing. And that's what scares me."

I had no idea what this was all about or what it meant for me, but I lay there in the grass in the evening June sun and felt chills run up my back. I like a mystery as well as anyone, but not this close. Billy wouldn't look at me and I was glad.

By the time Jayo came back out of the house, Toby had joined us in the front yard and I suggested we pitch ball awhile and then go to Dinkel's.

"No. I gotta go home," Jayo answered quickly.

"Whatta you gotta go home for, boy? Don't you want some ice cream?" Toby asked playfully.

"Freddy don't like ice cream," Jayo reported as he got up off the lawn and headed down the street.

"Freddy who?" Toby quizzed everyone with a genuine look of bewilderment.

I jumped in like always, trying to smooth something over that may not have needed it. "Jayo's got an imaginary friend named Freddy. Just let it go."

"Oh, yeah. I used to have one of those. His name was Davy. Hey, Jayo!" Toby yelled after him. "Don't Freddy eat ice cream?"

Jayo never looked back but yelled over his shoulder, "No. He only likes beer."

Toby and I laughed while Billy just bounced the ball from hand to hand and smiled. Then he said, "Let's go to Dinkel's and get some beer ice cream."

Things were coming back to normal. I tossed the ball and glove on the front porch and we headed for the store.

To get to Dinkel's from my house, you had to walk right by Miss Kathleen Moyers's haunted house. The huge old Victorian frame house looked as foreboding as Miss Moyers, with her Avon smells and her croquignole curls. And as usual, that day she was dressed in heels and pearls and a blue summer dress, sitting on her porch glider, smoking. As if on cue, we always got quiet when we got to her property line, to listen for the piano playing upstairs. Tonight we heard nothing. The rumor was that she had a grown son. He lived on the second floor, and no one had ever seen him. Some believed he was not

June 1959

of sound mind, and some believed he was an AWOL from World War II, still in hiding from the government. But whatever he was, he was a piano player of the first order. She, of course, had taught everyone in town, and she was still teaching daily from her front parlor, so it was not strange to imagine that he, whoever he was, had also been subject to her teaching. And the front parlor was as far into the house as anyone had ever been. Even once when Miss Moyers had an operation on her toes and was laid up for a couple of weeks and my mother and other women from the church took her supper every other evening, Miss Kathleen, as they called her, met them at the door in her robe and took them no farther than the public parlor.

"Hello, Miss Moyers," Toby called and waved. "How's that crazy weirdo son of yours?" he said in a much, much lower voice.

"Shut up, Toby. Hi, Miss Moyers!" I was trying to cover again.

"He's not playin' tonight," Toby noted. "Guess it's not dark enough yet. He likes it spooky in there before he starts on all that long-hair music. Man! I'd give anything to see him."

"Go up there and ask her if you can go in and see him," Billy taunted.

"Come on, fellows, let's not do that." I was getting a little scared that someone might.

"Hey, you've done worse, Toby." Billy was ginning now. "Go on up there on the porch and ask her where her son is and if you can see him."

"You want me to?" Toby was getting ready now.

"No. I don't want you to," I said. "Let's just keep walkin'."

"Does anybody even know what his name is supposed to be?" Billy asked.

"They always just say 'her son' or 'her boy,' like that. I never heard any name."

"Sonny. I've heard people refer to him as Sonny. But I don't know for sure either."

"What do you think he is really? I mean, this is serious now." Billy frowned toward the house.

"Maybe it's not even a him. Maybe it's a her. Nobody's ever seen it." Toby was trying to be serious, too. But with him, it never came out totally serious.

Billy looked at me. "You're not saying anything. What do you think?"

"I don't know. Maybe he's a criminal. Maybe it's John Dillinger or Hitler or the real Jesse James. They say all of those people might still be alive. Or maybe she kidnapped a baby twenty years ago and raised him into some kind of monster who eats plants and plays scary music on the piano and can only survive where it's dark and can't stand the sight of sunlight. And his name is something like…Kruger. And he has a hump and he dances in the nude upstairs and is probably looking down at us right now from that side window."

Toby looked up immediately at the window and said, "Oh, crap! Don't say that." Billy laughed and we continued on to Dinkel's.

Lannie Mae Kiser worked the checkout counter three nights a week at Dinkel's, so ice cream wasn't the only attraction at the grocery store. Billy got a Dixie cup of chocolate; Toby got a grape Popsicle with two sticks and broke it in half so he could eat them one at a time; and I got a real good look at Lannie Mae's legs. She had shorts on under her white grocery apron. The apron had no back in it and gave the impression of being

June 1959

a revealing dress when she walked away from you. We were back on the sidewalk before I realized I hadn't bought any ice cream. Toby gave me his other Popsicle half and we started back home.

There was no ballgame that night, and all the television shows were in reruns or had summer replacement shows no one wanted to see. We had nothing to do and nowhere to go and were open for any suggestions. When the idle look for trouble, they usually find it and find very little reason to avoid it. They invite it. Embrace it. Welcome it. It fills up the time and makes funny memories for all the tomorrows to come. So why not? Why not wait till dark and climb up Miss Kathleen Moyers's rose trellis and look in the window and find out once and for all just who this mystery son is and why he hides and what he looks like. Find out what the big secret is. There's plenty of time and who's going to be hurt? It can only be fun. We won't get caught. We won't be seen. No harm will be done, and in the morning we'll still be laughing and just might know something no one else in town knows. We'll know the Secret of the Upstairs Room. The Identity of the Masked Pianist. And we'll be the only three who do.

It was ten minutes till nine, just dark enough to move across the yard without being easily seen. We had sat under a tree in a vacant lot waiting for the cover of night and planning exactly what we would do and how we would do it. As we talked, minor piano chords broke the otherwise silence of the evening, and we could hear the first nightly strands of music emitting from the second floor of the Moyers house, which was pitch dark. The only light on the property was the occasional red flicker of Miss Kathleen's perennial cigarette from the left side of the front porch. The song coming from the open upstairs window was not familiar, even to me. Vincent Price would have known it, but we didn't. We ran quietly through the side yard and stopped by an old smokehouse in the backyard.

"We need a ladder," Toby said.

"Where we gonna get a ladder?" Billy asked.

There was an open porch at the back of the house on both the first and second floors. They ran the width of the house, and each had a door leading inside. The door downstairs apparently led into the kitchen. The one upstairs, maybe into a bedroom? Maybe his! I could hear the music louder now and clearer than I ever had. And I could tell for sure something else that I had only assumed before. He was really good. Better than me by far and better than anyone I knew in town. I used to watch Liberace and his brother, George, on their fifteen-minute television show each week. I don't reckon the Moyers boy was that good, but he was better than Jerry Lee Lewis and that guy who played "Alley Cat." But then, of course, so was I. What *was* that guy's name? Oh, yeah, Bent Fabric.

The climb to the upstairs porch wasn't going to be any problem. Stand on the balustrade on the downstairs porch and grip the edge of the one upstairs. Lift one foot and step in a rung of the rose trestle, and push up so your left knee will be where your fingers were and your fingers are gripping the balustrade on the top porch. Then pull yourself up. It looked simple and it was. I was up in about three quick moves. Toby was right behind me, and all I had to do was grab his arm and help him over. We were both on the outside porch of the second floor, looking down at Billy whose attention was somewhere down in the lower backyard.

"Come on," I coaxed him.

He waved me off and said in a whisper, "Get down.

June 1959

Somebody's comin' up through the yard."

Toby and I pressed ourselves on the porch floor while Billy ducked behind the smokehouse. What I saw coming up through the garden in the back was not the scary sight I was prepared for, but it was certainly a surprise. It was Rosemary Herb carrying a paper bag and humming softly to herself. She walked under us, onto the back porch, and into the kitchen without knocking. It was as if she was expected and had done this a thousand times.

Let me take a few minutes to explain exactly who she was. The Herbs were a Negro family, what we called a Colored family in the fifties. Never Black. That was a fighting word then and didn't become the acceptable, preferred word until some years later. No derogatory words of that nature were ever allowed in our family. I've heard my mother say on many occasions, "We're from the Respectable South. We hold dignity for all of God's creations." Russell and Beta Herb were man and wife and also janitors at our church and our grade school, and in the spring they plowed gardens and mowed lawns. By anyone's standards they were nice people and neighbors and very well thought of in the community. They had a couple of kids who might have strained their reputation, but kids do that to their parents, don't they? (Says the guy who was trespassing and hiding on someone else's property with his two friends.) Russell and Beta had taken great pride and showed a sense of creativity in choosing their offspring's Christian names. The two girls were Rosemary and Ginger, and their younger brother was Basil.

Rosemary, the eldest, who must have been near thirty, was now in the house underneath us, and the music was still playing behind us. As soon as the kitchen door closed, Billy darted up the trestle. We tried the second-floor door but it was locked.

We tried looking in the windows but the rooms were dark. The music kept playing.

"What is Rosemary Herb doing here?" Toby asked.

"Maybe she works for Miss Moyers."

"Nine thirty at night?"

"Shh. I can hear somebody talkin'."

"No, you can't. That's just the cars goin' by."

"I heard a screen door slam down front."

"Maybe she heard us up here."

"Look! There's some kind of light in that room. Look through this window right here."

Suddenly, without warning and out of nowhere, Rosemary Herb's face materialized in front of us on the other side of the windowpane. We jumped and she screamed!

"What are you white boys doin' out there? You get down from there. You hear me?"

Before we could run, while we were still frozen in our current footprints, lights went on all through the upstairs. You could almost see the electricity flying from room to room, bringing each one to life as it went. And that's when we saw Basil Herb, Rosemary's brother, standing in the middle of the room in full formal dress. Tuxedo, black tie, and patent leather shoes. All six feet and three inches of him.

That's when we ran!

True, Rosemary scared us, but Basil unfroze our feet in a mere second. We wanted none of him, and the only way of having none was to get off the top porch and out of the yard before he got down the steps and out the door. We did, and we never stopped running till we hit *my* front porch. There we felt safe. I didn't know if tomorrow would be safe, but for now we were home, out of breath, and flat on our backs. Then I heard the phone ring in our living room, and I heard my dad answer it.

June 1959

"What was Basil Herb doing up there in a tuxedo?" Billy asked, and we all used what breath we had left to laugh ourselves silly until the front door opened and my dad came out on the porch.

"What's so funny out here, boys?"

"Aw, nothin'," I said. "Billy's just tellin' jokes."

He sat down in the wooden rocker and said, "Where you boys been?"

"Dinkel's. Gettin' ice cream."

"Dinkel's has been closed nearly an hour," Dad said without expression.

"Yeah, well, we were just foolin' around."

"Peepin' in windows?"

I had thought my feet were frozen a few minutes ago, but now my heart was frozen. I stopped breathing. I glanced at Toby and Billy and then delivered an ad lib even Uncle Miltie wouldn't have stolen, and he was famous for stealing everybody's one-liners. I said, "What?"

"You know what."

We all three were quiet. We didn't know how much he knew, so therefore we didn't know how much we could lie—a situation we all are destined to experience time after time in life in other circumstances. I, always the one to jump in with a quick explanation to get everyone off the hook, did not jump. I held my ground and my breath. Dad, merciful Dad, spoke next.

"All right, I won't make you lie to me by askin' you questions. I'll tell you what I know and you just tell me why. That phone call in there just now was Kathleen Moyers. She said all three of you were on her upstairs porch looking in the window tonight. Can I assume Kathleen is not lyin'?"

"Yes sir."

"Can I assume you were there out of curiosity and not tryin' to see Kathleen naked? I hope none of you boys are that foolish."

We looked at each other and snickered. "Yes sir," we all said in near unison. The ice was broken. My heart was coming back to almost two beats a minute now. Dad had made sort of a joke and was smiling.

"Did you find what you were lookin' for?" he asked.

"I don't know," I said honestly. "I'm not sure what we saw."

"Let me tell you what you saw. You saw Basil Herb playin' the piano in the dark."

"That's right! How did you know?"

"I've always known."

"You never told me," I said in bewilderment and almost hurt.

"You never asked me, son. There may be a lot of things I can tell you that you don't think I know."

"But everybody's always talked about her having a son up there that no one had ever seen and how he was hidin' out and maybe crazy and all that stuff. Is all that true?"

"Some of it." He reached in his shirt pocket and pulled out a pack of Camels, put one in his mouth, and then did the most surprising thing I had ever seen him do. He offered each of us one. He simply held the pack out to us, one at a time, without saying a word. Billy was the first to say, "No, thank you," very uncomfortably. Next was Toby with, "No sir." Then me. I just shook my head.

"Now I know you boys have tried them. If you want one, take it."

I sheepishly shook my head again and Billy reiterated, "No, thank you," but Toby, feeling encouraged by that last

June 1959

statement, said, "Yes sir. I think I will," and fired one up. So there the four of us sat on our front porch, Dad and Toby smoking and Billy and me watching. What a night this was turning out to be.

"You boys are at a funny age. In the next few years, you're goin' to see more things and learn more things than you ever thought existed. And you're goin' to learn that everything you have is not necessarily yours. And everything you know is not necessarily yours. You're goin' to see things and hear things that are none of your business, and you're goin' to have to learn what does and what doesn't concern you. All of this is called 'growin' up.' You already know right from wrong. Now you're goin' to have to decide how right and how wrong. You're goin' to have to learn what matters and what doesn't matter. What you can live with and what you can't. What you can help and what you can't. Life is not goin' to get simpler. But it's goin' to be up to you, as it is to all of us, just how tolerable we make it.

"Now I'm goin' to tell you what you saw tonight. And when I do, you're not goin' to tell another soul just to spread gossip. You're goin' to accept it as learning, and you won't talk about it to other people who may not understand. And I want all three of you to listen real close so that you'll never do another blasted fool thing like you did tonight.

"Years ago, Russell Herb had a brother, Ernest. He used to do yardwork for people all over town. A hard worker. Everybody liked Ernest and knew him to be a good and honest man. He used to do Kathleen Moyers's yard for years. When the war broke out in '41, he got drafted and was killed overseas. A few months after he left, Miss Moyers had a baby. She was all alone and didn't know what to do with it. Russell offered to take it and raise it as his own, and he did. Now, right or wrong, or whatever you may think about Miss Kathleen and how wrong you might think she was, it was still her son. And she wanted to pass on to him the one thing she could give him. Her music. And since he was able to walk, he's come up through her backyard at nights and she's taught him and made him practice. And right or wrong, she lives with the pain of not having him as a son even though he really is. That's a pain I hope none of you will ever have to know."

I felt an unreal sensation for the first time in my life, but it was one I'd feel in confused and emotional moments later on. I didn't want to speak or even move. I wanted to think and try to imagine and understand what had just been revealed to me in confidence. I went over everything Dad had said, and strangely the words that hung heaviest were the ones about life not getting simpler and that it's up to us how tolerable we make it.

Toby was rubbing the sides of his tennis shoes and looking at them as if he'd never seen them before. Billy was still staring into Dad's face. I didn't know the question I was going to ask until I heard it myself.

"Does Basil know?"

"It doesn't matter if Basil knows or not. You're not goin' to tell him or anyone else. You're not goin' to act or be any different toward anyone, so who knows is not important. The only thing important to you is that you know. And that's enough for you to handle."

"Does Mom know?"

His first look at me was one of irritation, and then love took over and he smiled and shook his head ever so slightly. He took the pack of Camels from his pocket and again went through the ritual of lighting up and said, "I can't think of anything your mother doesn't know. There's been a couple of things I thought she didn't know, but I was wrong, and I'll

June 1959

never make that mistake again." Then he chuckled to himself, and I think that's when I began to understand that part about how wrong and how right and about learning what doesn't concern you.

Before he put the Camels back in his pocket, Dad looked at Toby and said, "You want another one?"

"Yeah, I think I do," Toby said, reaching.

"Then buy your own. That's your second lesson tonight."

Dad went in the house and the screen door closed behind him.

My friends went home shortly and I went to bed quietly, but I didn't go to sleep for a long, long time. I was thinking about Kathleen and Basil and Mom and Dad and Ernest and everything Dad had said that did and didn't pertain to the situation at hand. I never dreamed much and still don't, and if I do, I never remember it. But I remember the dream I had that night. I was playing the piano in a place unfamiliar to me. I think it was some sort of bar, with pink and green lights all around me. I played harder and louder and better than I ever had, and when I'd finish a song, the people there would just keep talking and never look at me and never clap. I was crushed. Embarrassed. After a while, my mother came running into the bar and hollered at all the people and told them they should appreciate me and applaud when I finished a song. They just stared at her, and when I finished my next song, they just stared at both of us.

I woke up crying.

Billy's mom called me the next morning while I was still eating cereal and asked me to come over. She said Billy had just left to mow his grandfather's yard, and she wanted to talk to me while he was gone. That didn't make the cereal digest very well, but I told her I'd be right there. To this day I can't stand for someone to say "I need to talk to you as soon as possible" or "We have to talk right away" or any phrase in those urgent, personal tones people love to use to let you know something bad is in the air. Just tell me right now. Don't make me wait. Let's get it over with. My young stomach couldn't take it. Or maybe it was a guilty conscience. Maybe my imagination has always been worse than the reality I was about to face.

Billy's mom was making something at the stove when I went in. She was smiling and in great spirits, and I was relieved.

"Billy came home last night and was in a very unusual mood. He came up and sat on the side of my bed and we talked till after midnight. He told me all about your adventure last night and about the talk your father gave all of you. And, oh yes, he talked about Jayo and his imaginary friend and where he got the name and…well, he talked about everything I ever wanted to talk to him about. Something happened to him last night that opened a door. Do you want a piece of hot bread with butter on it?"

"No ma'am. No, thank you."

"Sure, you do. Get yourself a dish over there. You know where they are."

I got the dish and she continued.

"Billy wanted to know all the details about how Tom died and when, and then he wanted to talk about the funeral and the flag that's still folded on the shelf in the living room. Things he has never asked about before. Then he wanted to look at pictures last night. He wanted to know if his daddy was drafted or had he enlisted. You want something to drink? Iced tea? Pepsi?"

"Pepsi," I said. "I'll get it."

June 1959

"I think it all had to do with what your father told him about Ernest Herb and how he had died in a battle, too."

"Yes ma'am." My mouth was full of homemade bread and melted butter.

"How in the world did you ever get on the subject of Ernest Herb?"

I nearly choked on homemade bread and melted butter. What was she asking? Something was missing from this story, and I was beginning to wish I was missing from this kitchen.

"Ma'am?" I asked.

"How did you get to talking about Ernest Herb? I'm glad you did, understand, but I just wondered what got you on that subject."

"Didn't Billy tell you?" When in doubt, go with the obvious.

"He just told me you all climbed up the back porch at Miss Kathleen's—and you all ought to be ashamed of yourselves—and peeped in the window looking for her Sonny. And that she saw you and chased you off and called your father and told him. And that Frank scolded you, but not real bad, and sat on the porch and talked for a long time. And that he got to telling stories about different people in town, and one of them was Ernest Herb. You must have covered a lot of people."

"Yeah, I guess so," I said, a little dumbfounded.

"Well, I just wanted to tell you about Billy and thank your father. If ever Billy wants to talk about it all, please let him talk and tell me so I can encourage him even more. I feel like the barrier has been broken now, and I'll need you to help me keep it open."

I assured her I would. When I got up to leave, I stopped at the kitchen door and asked, "How's Jayo? His friend and all?"

"Oh, Jayo's just fine. He's over at his grandfather's, too. When he got up this morning, his imaginary friend had turned into a little girl. He was calling her Nancy. By tomorrow he'll probably have a whole gang running with him. Here, take another piece of bread with you while it's hot."

I went up the street eating my bread and stepping over the cracks and thinking about how Billy had not told his mother the whole truth because we were told not to, and how he had respected that, and how he had stared into my dad's face the whole time and had never taken his eyes off him. I finished the bread and wiped the butter off my fingers onto my pants and remembered that Sunday was Father's Day. I didn't know what I was going to get my dad, but I knew it wouldn't be near enough.

Chapter Six

July 1960

The human mind is a mystery, a conundrum, an enigma—all those crazy things. And the memories that stick to it and the ones that don't never fail to amaze me. You can study and memorize and learn and recite and pray and still forget what date the first shot was fired on Fort Sumter by Monday morning history class. You can search and fret and look up and tear up and whine and still not find your favorite ballcap just as you're walking out the door. You can easily forget things that you know are going to get you in serious trouble. Phone messages for your dad from his boss. Practicing two pages of music for your piano lesson. Being home at six for supper. No matter how important, some things just won't stick. Later in life, you forget anniversaries, birthdays, bread and milk as you're coming from work. And being home at six for supper.

It's usually the simple, unimportant things that stick firmly for so many years to the cluttered and taxed human brain. I can clearly recall sitting in the third grade and the windows were up and it was May, and the birds were drowning out the droning voice of Miss Celia Fay Hutton. More of us were listening to the traffic go by and watching the flag blow outside on the pole in the middle of the playground than were trying to decipher the monotone facts given us in earnest by our oft-despised and sometimes-beloved teacher. She finally sensed she was no match for spring and laid her book open on the desk, smiled, and asked a simple and poignant question. "Class, what are some of the things that let us know it's spring?"

Sharon Duffy's arm shot up first, as always, and she said with a plea of acceptance in her voice, "The robins sing."

"Very good, Sharon. Who else?"

"The flowers bloom," Sharon's gooey voice added.

"That's right, Sharon. Someone else now." Even dusty old Miss Hutton was fed up with eight months of Sharon.

No one else said anything, so after a long period of silence of about three seconds, Sharon enthusiastically exclaimed, "The grass turns green."

This was completely ignored by Miss Hutton, who began to eye each student in search of participation and, I'm sure, to wish she had never begun this impromptu discussion. Finally, she settled on someone. Why Clifton Snyder, I could not imagine then or now. But she must have sensed something in her desperation that she felt she could draw from him.

"Clifton, what is something that lets you know that spring is here?"

Clifton, proud to be called on, wasted no time giving his answer and getting to the core of the question. Without hesitation and with a smile as bright as the afternoon sun making squares across the floor in the front of the room, he said, "The Drive-In opens."

Clifton was right. As sure as the birds sang and the flowers bloomed and the grass turned green, the Twilight Drive-In Theater on Route 250 opened on May Day and closed on Labor Day. And I think Fort Sumter was fired on around April 9, 1861, but I'm not real sure.

My earliest recollection of the Twilight Drive-In happened in preschool. The whole family used to go, and it was a major trip. In miles from the house, it was only three. But in attitude and

July 1960

planning it was like a mini vacation. My dad would insist on my mother fixing food and taking it along in the back seat instead of spending money on popcorn at the concession stand. So, while everyone else had to get by on Cracker Jack and hot dogs and Red Dots, we were feasting on fried chicken, potato salad, and ham sandwiches. The only things Dad would go to the snack bar to get before the movie started were milkshakes, and I think that was because he loved them as much as I did. And those shakes and the large cardboard cups they came in are the key to my first memory of the outdoor culture of going to the movies.

I remember it was a *Blondie* movie, and somewhere about three-quarters of the way through, after eating a picnic lunch an hour and a half after supper that would have choked a team of horses, I, being severely five years old, had to go to the bathroom. My dad, not wanting to leave Dagwood in the predicament he was in with Mr. Dithers at the time, asked what I had to do. I assured him I only had to pee. He looked back at the screen and told me to pee in one of the empty disposable milkshake cups, that he would take it and empty it later. I did, and that's what I remember most about my first trip to the Twilight Drive-In. Anytime you pee in a cup other than in a doctor's office, you remember it for a long, long time. Especially if it took two large cups. And it did. The Twilight would hold other memories for me over the years. Some of those memories were not always as easy to relieve, but some of them were certainly more wonderful to relive.

The driver's license I had dreamed about and prayed for was about to be tucked firmly and proudly in my hip pocket in a new leather billfold my aunt had given me for my fifteenth birthday. The next day, I put my pictures in the plastic covers, slipped the twenty dollars my uncle gave me in the money slot, and saved a special place for that cherished piece of state-issued paper I would undoubtedly get first thing Monday morning. I was confident as only fifteen can be confident about something it knows absolutely nothing about. As the hours drew closer, though, I began to have doubts about the written exam. Was there a set speed limit in a hospital zone, or did you just have to be quiet? At a four-way stop intersection, how did you know who was on the right? Then I worried about the driving and what if I scraped gears. What if I gave the slowdown/stop signal out the window with my left hand and the policeman sitting in the car with me couldn't see it? What if someone ran into me and it wasn't my fault? Would they not give me my permit? What if I didn't park close enough to the curb? Would he give me another chance?

I didn't sleep for two nights, and come Monday morning I was up and sitting in the car at eight thirty waiting for my dad to take me. He didn't say much. He did ask if I was wide awake. I said yes. And that's about all I remember until the policeman filled out my permit to drive and operate a moving vehicle and handed it to me. Nothing before that and very little since has so affected my life. I was a new and different person. I had been to the river and I didn't get a drop on me. I was soaring somewhere inside my head that I had never been before, and when Dad handed me the keys and went around the car and got in on the passenger side, I almost cried.

I was driving, and more importantly, I was driving my dad. His life and well-being were, for the first time ever, my responsibility. I had never been in such a situation before. I had always worried when I was little about how I would know where to put my feet. It was like watching the organist in

July 1960

church playing the foot pedals. How was I to know where to put each foot without looking down at the floor and wrecking and killing myself? The steering, I knew, would be no problem. It looked easy and even fun. And of course, when I started to drive around parking lots and dirt roads a few years before with my dad sitting close beside me, I learned I had been worrying about the wrong things as usual. The feet came easy. The steering almost killed me more than once. But now, driving on a real honest-to-God highway and doing it legally, I found myself with a new problem. I kept glancing at the speedometer. Dad saw me doing this and chuckled.

I said, with my eyes darting from the windshield to the dashboard, "You never look at the speedometer every two seconds. How do you know how fast you're goin'?"

"You just learn how fast you're goin' without lookin' all the time. Don't worry. You'll learn."

"Do you know how fast I'm goin' right now?" I asked him as sort of a challenge and also as sort of a search for proof that I would learn it someday.

"Aw, you're goin' about forty-five," he said, looking straight ahead.

I looked down and found new hope for my future. I was doing exactly forty-five miles per hour.

Someone passed me, and I gripped the wheel and tensed. And then Dad offered the advice I remembered forever and applied to everything I've done in life. He leaned back and lit up a Camel and said, "There are only two people you ever have to look out for, son. Yourself and every other fool on the road."

He was right, but he never prepared me for how many there would be. I'm still looking out for them and the count is staggering.

It was mid-summer, and I'd had my license about a month

and a half and had the family car more nights than I thought I would. Mom and Dad trusted me more than I would have trusted me, so I always made an effort to deserve it. It was psychology most people are fooled by until they have children of their own. Then they see behind the curtain and realize they, too, were tricked into being better people than they really were. A big night with the car was usually circling Hamburger Hatch about thirty times and ordering French fries and shakes as often as the money held out. It was usually Billy and Toby and I on those nights. When it was just Billy and I and our dates, we would often head for the Twilight Drive-In. Some nights he had his mother's car, some nights I had mine. This particular time, I was driving Dad's '57 Chevy with Sue Jane Wimer by my side and Billy and Patsy in the back seat. John Wayne and Dean Martin were on the movie screen, and my face was buried deep in the soft part of Sue Jane's neck. Billy and Patsy were out of sight and uncommonly quiet. The first hint I had of anything out of the ordinary was a shriek and jerk from Sue Jane and an abrupt movement of the car. She tensed her whole body as she jumped up, erect in the seat. My head was swimming from the suddenness of the moment, and I asked, scared and stunned, "What's wrong?"

She merely looked straight ahead while I followed her gaze and saw the broad side of Toby's back sitting heavily on the front fender.

"What's he doing?" she asked, as if I were responsible for Toby's actions. I mean, even Toby wasn't responsible for most of his actions.

"What's wrong?" This was Billy from the back.

"Is that Toby?" Patsy asked.

"Yeah," I said disgustedly, with the knowledge that it would be me who would have to get out of the car and find out

July 1960

what he was doing there. I opened the door and closed it quickly so the light wouldn't disturb other people around us but mainly so people couldn't get a glimpse of the wrinkled clothes. I tucked my shirttail in tighter as I walked around to the front of the car.

"What are you up to, buddy?" I asked him.

"Man, I'm sorry to bother you. Mama and Daddy and my little sister are over there. I came with them. I didn't want to bother you all, but I had to talk to you tonight."

I could see he was worried, and I was getting concerned too. "What is it?"

"I went to the pool today. That's where I've been all afternoon, and I saw..."

Billy came around the other side of the car and interrupted us. "Hey, buddy. What're you doin' here?"

"My folks are over there in the car. I knew you all were here somewhere. I didn't want to come and knock on the car door or anything. You know, maybe embarrass somebody or somethin'. So I just sat out here till you all saw me."

"That's okay. Come on, let's go to the bathroom." Billy looked at the girls in the car and said, "We'll be back in a minute."

We walked through the rows of cars to the squatty little building that housed the projector, the food, and the restrooms. A loud blast of gunfire from the window speakers made all three of us look toward the movie simultaneously. We walked on through the screen door and toward the men's room.

"I've been at the pool at the park most of the day," Toby said again.

"They're havin' somethin' special there Monday night, I heard on the radio today," Billy offered.

"Yeah, that's what I've got to talk to you all about," Toby said, as if we were all in some dire trouble with the law.

"What happened at the pool today?" Sometimes it took a direct, stern question from me to get Toby started when he was as troubled as he seemed now.

Toby was standing in front of the urinal, staring dead into a cinder block that was at eye level, and he slowly began to grin a silly and all-encompassing grin that exploded into a growling laugh.

"Come on, Toby. Just tell us what happened at the pool today." I was thinking of Sue Jane out there in the car, and I didn't really want to be standing in the toilet with Toby laughing at the wall.

"They're havin' a dance at the pool Monday night. They're gonna play records and all. Just like the Hop, 'cept you wear your swimmin' suit and dance by the pool and swim and all."

"Okay. I just said I heard about it on the radio." Billy looked at me and raised his eyebrows.

Toby looked from me to Billy and back again. Then he dropped it on us the way he must have rehearsed it all evening. "I'm goin', and I've got a date."

Billy just looked at him. I used all the diplomacy, to the extent of my understanding of the word, that I could find. I didn't want to act surprised and embarrass him, and I didn't want to downplay it and rob him of the moment. This was Toby's first date, and I knew he was jumping inside.

"That's great!" I said. "Who is she?"

"You'll never believe it if I tell you."

"Try us," Billy said. "And we'll try to believe you."

"I'll tell you, but first let me tell you what I need you to do," Toby said excitedly.

"Need who to do?" Billy asked.

"Need both of you to do. You need to teach me to dance."

"By Monday night?" I said without thinking.

"That's why I had to come find you tonight. We gotta start tomorrow as soon as church is over. Then we'll have all day Monday. I mean, I wanna be Dan Dailey by Monday night."

"We can show you, but whether you can do it is up to you." Billy was being honest. "You've never even slowed danced, have you?"

"That's what I wanna learn most. Slow and close. You wanna meet me at my house or where?"

"Come to my house," I suggested. "My record player is in my room. It'll be private."

"Okay. Thanks, guys. Tomorrow 'bout one?"

"Okay by me," Billy said as we were going out the door. "Now will you tell us who?"

"You won't believe me. The prettiest girl in school. Nobody's gonna believe it. And *she* asked *me*. I didn't say nothin'. She asked *me*."

"All right! Who?" Billy was tired of the game.

"You ain't gonna believe it. Lannie Mae Kiser."

Toby walked back to the car with us, so Billy and I only had the opportunity to exchange glances. When we got in the car, we found the girls a little more subdued than when we left them. Sue Jane was merely distant, but Patsy was about to simmer.

"Why'd you have to go with him?"

"Well, he just wanted to talk to us," Billy said.

"What about? What did he have to talk about that he had

to do it right now? Doesn't he see you often enough to talk to you about whatever it was that was so important?"

"Well, he didn't have to do it right now. But we went to the bathroom and all." Whenever Billy started all his sentences with "Well," Patsy had him on the run. I could only look out the windshield and take it. But I didn't want to. I wanted to tell her it was none of her business.

"So." Patsy paused. "What did he want?"

I was thinking to myself, *If he tells her, I'm going to bust one of them right in the mouth. Both of them deserve it.*

"Well." Now Billy paused. "Should I tell her?"

I couldn't believe it. This last question was directed at me. He was dumping the responsibility on me to get Patsy off his back. I looked at Sue Jane, who was staring hard into my face and waiting for an answer. The cold silence from the back seat told me Billy and Patsy were waiting, too. Maybe I was threatening to bust the wrong person in the mouth. Maybe I should start on myself.

"Yeah, you can tell her," I heard myself saying. It was really no big deal, I rationalized in my head. I mean, Toby was happy and proud and would want us to tell the girls. Certainly, it would stop at that. Certainly, Billy wasn't going to let Patsy force us into telling her more. I was hoping he would only tell her Toby had a date. But with Patsy and Billy you could never be sure.

"You tell 'em," Billy urged. It was always my fate to get to do all the talking.

"Well," I said (now I was doing it), "there's really not a lot to it. Toby has a date Monday night for the pool party. That's all."

"Toby?" Patsy laughed. "Toby has got a date?" She began to snicker.

July 1960

I changed my mind again on who should get the first bust in the mouth. Sue Jane looked at me and slightly grinned. She didn't want to agitate me, but she also didn't want to completely go against Patsy. I looked quickly in the rearview mirror to see Billy's reaction. He was caught in the same web as Sue Jane.

"Who's he going with?" Patsy asked between snorts.

Nobody answered. I saw Billy say something quiet to her that must have been the answer because her reaction was definite. Her laughter stopped abruptly and she said, "I hate her guts."

Sue Jane looked at me and said, "Who?"

"Lannie Mae Kiser," I said softly.

Sue Jane just nodded and looked back at the screen.

There were no more sounds inside my dad's green, four-door 1957 Chevrolet until after John Wayne and Dean Martin had totally annihilated a storehouse with dynamite and Walter Brennan had delivered the final comedy line and the swelling music had faded into a snack bar cartoon. From all I could gather and assume from each individual silence, Patsy was riled, Billy was worried, Sue Jane was hurt, and I was mad. I was in no mood to stay for the second feature. I didn't even ask what everyone wanted to do. I just put the speaker back on its stand and started the engine.

"Are we leaving?" Patsy asked.

"Unless you want to lean against the pole and hold the speaker in your hand, you're leavin'," I said. I knew Billy and I would have to have it out later, but at the moment I didn't care.

After eating foot-long hot dogs in the car at Hamburger Hatch, I took Sue Jane home first. I thought I could tell by her mood that she might know something about Lannie Mae and me, but it could have just been my imagination or my guilty conscience. We kissed good night on her front porch and she held me extra tight and long. She was sad and I was afraid to ask why, so I just held her and patted her and promised I'd call tomorrow. When she turned to go in the door, she had tears in her eyes. Sue Jane was gentle and quiet and pretty in such an innocent way. She was so easy to love and even easier to hurt. She was no match for my moods because hers never changed unless it was forced upon her. She was born sweet and deserved the best of every moment. I knew even then she was too good for me, but I certainly wasn't about to settle for what I deserved. I walked off the porch a little ashamed and a lot relieved. I just wanted to get this night over with.

The next stop was Patsy's house. When she and Billy got out, there were no exchanges of good nights between us. I waited for about ten minutes for him to come down her walk. I dreaded what I felt was sure to come. He and I were going to have an argument about the way I had treated Patsy. I didn't want to fight with Billy, but I would have to tell him the truth about how I felt about her. He should have stood up for Toby when she started making fun of him. He was the one who should have said something.

I was playing with the radio dial when the car door opened and Billy got in. I drove off, waiting for him to start.

"Well, buddy, we got us a problem, don't we?"

"You mean about Patsy?" I stiffened.

"Naw, not about Patsy. Don't worry about her. She'll be alright in the morning."

I was relieved but confused. He could be so offhanded

July 1960

about her when she wasn't around and so controlled by her when she was. I wondered what he really felt for her. Who was actually in control? Should I ask? No, I had a more immediate problem at hand.

"You mean about Toby?" I asked.

"Of course, I mean about Toby. What are we gonna do?" Billy really was my friend.

No one but Billy and I knew anything about last summer's adventure at the concession stand behind the First Faith Presbyterian Church. Toby had been away at camp, and Billy and I had never shared the intimate goings-on with him when he came back. I hadn't seen Lannie Mae again except at school or at the Hop dancing with other guys, and I had learned to accept what happened as something that was wonderful and gone. I still dreamed about her and knew that I would, but she was older and had her own friends, and while she didn't ignore me in the halls at school, she didn't embrace me either.

"First off," Billy started, "why did she ask Toby to the pool dance?"

"Because she wanted to go with him," I offered half-heartedly.

"Come on. Get serious. Toby's my friend, too. But you know Lannie Mae Kiser does not want to go to no dance with Toby Painter in a bathin' suit."

We both allowed ourselves a laugh at this. It was okay for us to laugh. We knew what we meant by it.

"She could be doin' it to make you jealous." Billy was trying to bring in Buffalo, New York, on the radio.

"That's crazy. She couldn't care less about me."

"How do you know? Have you ever asked her out?"

"I've tried to talk to her. She cares nothin' about me."

"You don't know that," Billy said. "I mean, you've never

called her and really tried to get somethin' goin'."

"Hey, we had somethin' goin'. Believe me. Then when I saw her at school it was like we were strangers."

"Then you got to call her."

"Call her? I'm not goin' to call her."

"You have to." Billy's mind was made up. "That's the only way we can find out why she's askin' Toby to the dance. You call her and ask her to the dance like you don't know that she's already asked Toby. That'll get you all talkin' and maybe you'll find out why she's doin' it. I mean, we can't just throw Toby to the dogs and let him go out with her and make a fool of himself."

"Why can't we?" I wanted to help Toby but could feel myself getting deeper in this situation than I had the stomach for.

"Because he'll be the laughin' stock of that whole crowd of hers. It'll probably wind up in a fight. You've got to find out what's goin' on."

I drove around for a while and neither of us said anything. Billy found WKBW, Buffalo, and the Dick Biondi show that we always listened to while circling the town. They were playing "Alley Oop" as the static faded. We rode around Hamburger Hatch one more time, turned left, and headed home.

"Well, whatever we do," I said, "there's one thing for sure we have to do."

"What's that? Go back and watch that second feature at the Drive-In?" Billy laughed.

"No. Teach Toby to dance like Dan Dailey tomorrow at one o'clock."

"All right, let's start with the box step. You just go in a square."

July 1960

"What kind of a song will I do this to?" Toby was anxious to begin.

"You don't really do it to any song. It's just sort of an exercise. Just a way of learning how to move your feet."

Toby didn't like this. "Don't waste time with somethin' I won't use. Let's get to that close stuff."

"Just try this first." I turned to Billy and said, "Find 'Personality' in that record stack over there. If he can't feel the rhythm to that one, he'll never dance to anything."

"Just tell me where to start." Toby was standing in the middle of the room and ready to go.

"Just watch me," I said. "On one, when they say *walk*, that's the downbeat. The one count. *Talk* is on the one. *Charm* is on the one. Every time he says *Personality*, that's the two-three-four."

"You ready?" Billy asked with his head dipped, lining up the needle.

"Not yet. Wait a minute," I said. "Start with your left foot on one. Put your right foot down beside it on three. Move your right foot over, like this, on one, and bring your left foot over beside it on three. Then left over on one. Then right…that's it. Now up with the left. No, I mean step up. Forward. Then right…that's it. You've made a square. A box. Just do this in time with the music. All right, Billy, go ahead and play it."

From here it was between Lloyd Price and Toby. Lloyd belted out the song while Toby counted.

"Don't count out loud, Toby," Billy said with a frown. "Count to yourself. Here, hold this." He laughed as he threw him a pillow.

Toby swung the pillow and squeezed it and began to move his body along with his feet. He was laughing at himself and doing a pretty good job of staying with the beat. When Lloyd was all sung out, Toby was ready to move on to more serious things.

"I got that. Let's do a slow one," he demanded.

"Okay," I conceded. "Billy, the man wants a slow one. He's ready for the big time. What's it gonna be?"

"All right, ladies and gentlemen," Billy mocked as he pulled a 45 RPM single out of my green record box and placed it on the turntable, "up next, for your dancing pleasure, is the smash hit that has all the girls dreamin' and screamin'. Here's a record that's a real dilly dilly. 'Lavender Blue' by Sammy Turner."

Toby and the pillow took the floor. Billy and I continued to coach.

"Don't look at your feet."

"Don't count out loud or move your lips."

"Always start on your left foot."

"Go forward and kind of around in circles. She'll go backwards."

"Let your shoulders move with your feet."

"Your lips are movin'."

"Shut up, Billy. I'm singin' to her." And then Toby threw the pillow and hit Billy upside the head. We all wound up on the bed laughing and hitting each other with pillows. Everything was going to be all right after all.

Billy coaxed me all Sunday evening, whenever Toby wasn't in earshot, to call Lannie Mae. I refused and finally said, "Maybe tomorrow." By noon Monday I had agreed, and he sat down on the floor in front of me while I dialed her number.

"Want me to look it up?" he asked, trying to be helpful.

"No. That's okay. I know it."

July 1960

I let it ring my customary five times. I've always felt that five times was long enough for someone to get to the phone if they were home and wanted to answer it, and certainly long enough for me to have to wait on my end. I put the phone back in the cradle.

"We'll call every half hour till we get her," Billy said.

I loved Billy's use of the collective pronoun. I called three more times that day and never did find her. I never did have it real clear in my mind what I was going to say if I had found her. But fate saved me from that dilemma.

Four o'clock was the last dance class. After an hour of "Smoke Gets in Your Eyes" by the Platters and "Sleep Walk" by Santo and Johnny, we had our boy as close to ready as he was going to get. As he was leaving the house, Toby stopped on the porch and asked, "What are you guys doin' tonight?"

"We've got a softball game at six thirty," I said. "After that, nothin' I guess."

"My mom's goin' to drop me off at the pool. It starts at six thirty, too. I was just wonderin' if maybe you guys could pick me up at ten when it's over. You know, I don't want my mom there waitin' on me after a date and all. I don't know who might be standin' around and all."

Toby couldn't get his driver's permit until mid-August. Even then it wouldn't seem right for Toby to be driving. I'd heard all those comments from my aunts and uncles: "I just can't believe you're driving" and "Time just flies." I sort of felt the same about Toby. Flying time had nothing to do with it, but I couldn't imagine him behind the wheel and in control of a moving vehicle. I wasn't even sure how much he had driven before. His mom and dad were pretty strict about things like that.

"Yeah, we'll get you. Billy or I one will get the car," I said, hoping I could live up to the promise.

"Don't come until right at ten. I wanna stay as long as possible," Toby said as he danced down our front steps and onto the sidewalk. In the late July afternoon, with the day's long shadows just beginning to form behind him, I think I did see a hint of Dan Dailey as he double-tapped off that last step. Tennis shoes on concrete is no burden to a hoofer in love. He danced all the way home, I'm sure.

The game was over by eight. We won. We each went home and took a quick bath and changed clothes. I told Dad I needed the car around nine to pick up Toby at ten. I had already found it was more effective to say I *need* the car than may I *have* the car. It was an early experiment in language that I found useful in other phases of my life. For instance, after a fight with a girlfriend, if you say, "I *have* to talk to you," they may say no to show their power in the matter. To show you they don't *have* to talk if they don't want to. But if you say I *need* to talk to you, there is not a feminine heart out there who will turn you away. She feels the sincerity of *need*. The sympathy. The tenderness. She wants you to *need* her. Also, "May I have the car?" requires an answer, and "I need the car" leaves less room for a no. It'll work with almost anything. Try it.

The pool was huge. It had two large bathhouses at one end and a food and drink stand at the other. A jukebox and shuffleboard sat in the center area. We all had spent many summer hours there since we were babies. It was the only place to swim in our town, and tonight would have been a perfect night to hit the water. But we didn't want to crash Toby's party, so we rode

July 1960

around and got something to eat until ten p.m. as he had asked. Few cars were left when we pulled up, and we saw Toby immediately. My headlights caught him sitting on the curb by the turnstile at the main entrance. He didn't look happy. He got in the back seat and never said a word. As I turned out into the traffic, Billy quit playing with the radio and turned in the seat and looked at him.

"Well, how did it go?"

"She never showed up." Toby was crushed.

"What!" Billy looked mad.

"She never showed up."

Billy and I fixed our stares out the front windshield because we didn't want to see Toby's face. He didn't need anyone looking at him right now.

"I've been sittin' in there since six fifteen. Just sittin' and standin' around for three hours and forty-five minutes. If she didn't want to go with me, why'd she ask me? I didn't ask her. Why'd she even ask me in the first place? I know I'm fat and she's the prettiest girl in school and none of that is a secret. But why'd she have to ask me? Her friends were all there. They kept lookin' at me. I know they were laughin' behind my back. She had to do it on purpose. I know she did. But why? Why'd she ever have to ask me?"

I could hear the tears in his voice and I knew they'd soon be on his cheeks and I couldn't bear looking at him. We were at a stoplight, and I would have turned and said something but I didn't. Should I comfort him or try to reason out the why? Billy spoke before the answer came to me.

"Maybe she's out of town. You know, somethin' came up and she couldn't make it."

"I thought about all that," Toby said. "We can find out for sure. Ride by her house and see if anybody's home."

I threw Billy a quick look. Way to go, pardner. Don't make suggestions that can be checked out. We've got a hurt man here. He needs lying to. He does not need something that can be proved or disproved. Although it did cross my mind that the family may be gone, as I had been unable to reach Lannie Mae all day. But I certainly couldn't tell Toby this. Maybe this is what Billy was trying to check out. So to 324 Hardin Road we went.

There were lights on all over the house. Whether Lannie Mae was in there or not was an impossible fact to obtain from where we were sitting. But Toby had a solution.

"Let's call her and see if she's home."

"Why didn't you do that from the pool?" I asked logically.

"I don't know. I kept thinkin' she'd come walkin' in any minute and, well, I guess I didn't want to know for sure. Will you call?"

"Yeah, he'll call," Billy answered.

I stared at Billy but he wouldn't look at me, so I finally pulled off the road to look for a pay phone.

I called. She wasn't at home and her mother was not forthcoming in revealing to me where she was. Her tone of voice seemed to indicate she felt it was none of my business where Lannie Mae had gone or when she would return. My persuasive powers failed me, and I came away from the phone booth and back to the car in defeat. We rode around for another hour and talked and had Toby laughing about other things, and then we decided it was time to go home.

I didn't sleep well that night. I was feeling what Toby was feeling and also what I was feeling, and the latter was no easier to cope with. I knew Lannie Mae was the villain in this thing.

July 1960

I knew she had hurt Toby very much. She had also hurt me pretty badly the past year by ignoring me the way she had. I knew I should hate her for what she had done to both of us, but I just couldn't. First loves die hard.

I woke up early with the past night as fresh on my mind as if I had never slept. I lay there with the glaring realization of what I was going to do. I had to do it because I was the only one who could do it. There was no one else in my position. No one with the opportunity. No one with the means. Except me.

From nine to noon, I sat on the living room floor with the telephone between my legs. I had dialed four digits of her number ten different times before hanging up. Then five digits of her number six different times. I had yet to complete the number and let it ring, but I was getting closer. I would talk to her before the day was over. Maybe after lunch. Yes, maybe I should eat first. Maybe I'll try at one o'clock. That would be a good time. I'll just put it up now and call at...

The ringing of the phone doubled my heartbeat! I let it ring three times in my lap just to regain my composure before I said, "Hello." There was a pause at the other end long enough to entice me to say "Hello" a second time.

Then a voice said in a quiet, unsure tone, "Do you know who this is?"

As sure as there is a cowgirl in Texas, I knew who it was. There went the old heart rate again. After this, I reasoned, I wouldn't have to do jumping jack exercises for six months.

"Lannie?"

"That's right. I didn't know if you would recognize my voice or not."

"Yeah, I knew it was you. The strange thing is I was sittin' here just gettin' ready to call *you*."

"You were? Why?"

"Oh, I don't know. Just to see what you were doin'."
"Did you call me last night?"
"Ah, I did. That was me. I'm sorry it was so late."
"Oh, that's alright. My mother thought it was you."
"Yeah, it was me."

There was a pause here that could have accommodated three TV commercials and a station identification break.

"Well," she said, trying to recapture the flow, "what have you been doing this summer?"

"Oh, nothin' much really. You know, playin' ball and swimmin' and that kind of stuff."

"Are you going with anybody in particular?"

"Yeah. Sort of. Not steady or anything like that."

"Who? Sue Jane?"

"Yeah."

"I thought maybe that was why you were calling last night. I thought maybe you and Sue Jane had broken up."

"No. No, we still go together."

"Oh. I thought maybe that was why you were calling me."

"What if it had been?" I was feeling surer of myself now. The initial shock of Lannie Mae Kiser actually calling me on the phone was settling in my pores, and I was beginning to think like a near-human being again.

"What do you mean?" She seemed taken aback at my sudden control of this intellectual banter.

"I mean, what if I had been callin' to see what you were doin' because Sue Jane and I had broken up?"

"Have you?"

I felt the control shifting. "No. But I said what if we had? Would it make any difference?"

Time now for her pause. Her commercials and station IDs. When she resumed, she was tender and sincere and the

July 1960

clocks all started going back a year in time. "You never called me after last summer. I waited for days and weeks and you just never called. I never heard a word. When school started, I saw you in the halls and you spoke to me like I was just anybody else you might meet in the halls. I cried so many nights thinking I had done something wrong. I was so ashamed and felt bad because you treated me so different. I didn't know what to say to you and was afraid to look you in the eye. I felt like you were avoiding me and I didn't want to embarrass you by calling you or talking to you at school. I didn't know what to do."

Time out, team, for my side. Commercials. Station IDs. News flashes. A ballgame. Political convention coverage. As much time as possible. I needed all I could get to recoup from this. Was she actually telling me we had not continued our relationship because of *me*? That *I* was the reason we had not talked or gone out for almost a year now? Was *I* to blame for this time-wasting, irrevocable sin? I knew I may not be able to bounce back from this one. I couldn't stand such a burden. I could live blaming her, but I couldn't bear thinking *I* had spoiled such a beautiful slice of life. Could she ever forgive me? Could I ever forgive myself? Not unless I could get things back like they had been. When a good and convincing lie is not at hand, speak the truth. I don't know who said that, but someone should have.

So that's what I did.

"I don't know what to say."

"It's okay." Her voice was sweeter than I had ever heard it.

"No, I never meant for you to feel that because that's not the way it is. And that's not the reason I called last night. I don't know what to say."

The NETWORK TROUBLE sign shot on the screen but just for a few seconds. Someone found the problem before the announcement, "We have temporarily lost the sound portion of this program. The trouble is not in your set but in our studio," ended. Mercifully, after this extended silence, Lannie changed channels on me.

"I need to talk to you." There it was. That word. *Need.* And it works on guys, too. She sounded so sympathetic. So helpless. So in *need* of me. She continued, "My father's coming home for lunch and I've got to get off the phone. Where can I see you? I really do need to talk to you."

"Gee. I don't know. Anywhere." I was a hard man to break.

"Do you still work in that candy store at the ball diamond?"

"No, I don't do that this year. But there's never anybody down there this time of day. I can meet you there in fifteen minutes."

"Bye."

I was sitting in my mother's car beside the concession stand, playing the radio and chewing Chicklets, when I saw her top the hill and come down the gravel driveway in her sister's Plymouth coupe. She parked beside me and got out of hers and into mine with one fluid motion. Here we were, almost on the same playing field again. And like before, she had the advantage. I'd always been a sucker for suntans and pink lips.

"To start with," she started with, "I've got to tell you something. I've done something really stupid and mean. You probably know already what I'm going to say, don't you?"

"Maybe," I said. It was no time to go soft.

"Do you know about Toby Painter last night?"

"Yeah. I know some of it. Not all of it I don't guess."

July 1960

"Well, that's what I need to talk to you about. You must think I'm a real jerk. And I guess I am but I didn't want to be."

It was my turn to talk but I had nothing to say, so I just waited for her to pick up her cue.

"I was concerned about what you must be thinking of me," she said with her head down, "so I wanted to tell you exactly what happened and how it happened, okay?"

"Okay." I was on a conversational roll.

"I've been dating Roger Smiley, you know. And he's a good friend of Allen Welcher's. I don't really like his girlfriend, Kitty Huntly, all that much, but I've sort of been thrown with her and well, I guess she's alright sometimes. And you know about the big fight at the football game back in October, I think it was, between Allen and Toby. Anyway, Allen and Kitty and Roger and I and a bunch of others were at the pool the other day, and your friend Toby was there. Allen and Roger and Kitty and some of the others were all laughing at him saying they were going over to throw him in the pool and pull his trunks off of him and all kinds of stuff. They never did anything, understand, but they were planning to. They kept talking about it. It was all because of that fight. That's why they were going to throw him in the pool and all. Of course, they never actually tried. They never really said anything directly to him. Looking back now, I think they were all scared. I know Allen was. But together, I guess they felt brave. Anyway, about the time they were ready to go get him, Kitty said she had a better idea. That's when she came up with the idea of me asking him for a date, knowing I wasn't going to show up. Just to make a fool of him. I really didn't want to do it, but they kept riding me and, well, I did it. And I'm ashamed that I did. And I guess you really hate me now."

The villain was at hand. I had captured the culprit and

justice was in sight. I could cuff her and arrest her and send her to jail. Or I could reprimand her and release her on her own recognizance. I could look the other way and let her go off into a new land to find a new life and a fresh start. Or I could pull her toward me and kiss the pink off her lips and hold her next to me until her tan faded.

Decisions. Decisions. Decisions.

As she pulled out of the parking lot, I checked my face one more time in the rearview mirror. It was clean now and so would be my conscience, soon.

I didn't tell Billy anything about it until Friday.

"What are you doin' tomorrow night?" I asked him.

"Patsy and I are goin' to the show, I reckon. You and Sue Jane goin' with us?"

"Where you goin'?"

"Twilight."

"What's on?"

"I don't know," Billy said, shrugging.

"Yeah, I'll be there. I've got the car so I'll just see you there."

"I'll park where we always do," he said. "Toward the back on the right."

"I'll find you."

"Sue Jane still mad?"

"No. She's alright. But I don't have a date with Sue Jane."

"Really?" Billy looked a little surprised.

"I've got a date with Lannie Mae."

"No, you don't," Billy said in disbelief and disappointment.

"Oh, yes. It's a long story."

July 1960

"Does Toby know?"

"Not yet," I said.

Billy looked genuinely hurt that I had chosen to see Lannie Mae after what had happened to Toby, so I felt compelled to tell him the whole story.

Cars were lined up from the box office to the main highway. We must have sat in line for twenty minutes waiting to get in. We drove around searching for Billy's car. He was right where he said he would be. As we drove toward him, I was just finishing the story I was telling and Toby was laughing and beating the dashboard.

"So, this doesn't mean I wouldn't like to have her here at the Drive-In," I was saying, "'cause she's still the prettiest thing I've ever laid eyes on. It just means she deserves what's happenin' tonight. I knew when I got up Tuesday morning what I was goin' to do if I could and if I had the guts."

Billy had gotten out of his car and was standing beside it, clapping and smiling all over himself. "You did it!" he yelled. "You really did it."

Toby was still beating the dash and Billy was beating the hood of my car as I parked and reached for the speaker. Toby hollered at Billy, "We're gonna have a ball tonight while Lannie Mae Kiser's butt is sittin' at home, all dressed up and nowhere to go and nobody ringin' her doorbell!"

We all laughed. I did what I had to do and I was pleased. But I was not happy. I protected a friend and got even for him. But I probably lost an opportunity I could never retrieve now. By eight o'clock, she would realize what had happened and decide never to speak to me again. I had consciously closed a chapter in my life, and I had felt the book slam shut.

Piano Days

I drove by the old Twilight many years later when I was home and saw its empty marquee hanging in shambles. I turned around in the middle of the road and went back and drove in the old entrance. I had never done this in broad daylight. It all looked so different in the sun. I stopped at the box office sitting out there in the middle of cracked concrete and got out of the car. I tried the door and it was, surprisingly, open. I stepped into the little six by six cubicle and looked from a vantage point I had never experienced. All the families and lovers that have been looked at through these old windows. All the tickets pushed through this little slot. I walked out and read a sign hanging on the side where the showtimes used to hang. FLEA MARKET EVERY SUNDAY 1 P.M. No movies ever again.

I drove through the open gate and was weakened by the sight. There was the old concession stand that housed the restrooms and projection room, boarded up and still standing among weeds knee high. The speaker poles, minus the speakers, still stood in perfect rows like headstones in a military graveyard. Little monuments saluting the past that had drifted off somewhere in time. I turned to the screen. A giant with torn limbs. Weak with age and out of style. Huge squares, ripped and hanging from its front. Ignored and neglected after all the joy it brought to so many. What used to be a lively Saturday night meeting place, full of teenagers, car hopping, or making what they thought was love, was now still and silent. Not a whisper of a voice or a blast of a Hollywood gunshot. They were all gone. Martin and Lewis. Sandra Dee. Elvis. The Bowery Boys. There was so much to remember and so little to do about it.

Memories raced through my mind as I stood there among the dead and the gone. I thought about Sue Jane and Billy and Toby. I thought about Dagwood. I thought about Daddy.

July 1960

And, of course, I thought about Lannie Mae and how much I had loved her and how miserable I was that night sitting right back there, watching a double feature with Toby. But ole Toby, I loved him, too.

And then I had the strangest thought. I suddenly remembered that the first shot at Fort Sumter was fired on April 12, 1861, not April 9. I looked again at the ghosts surrounding me, and then I got back in my car and smiled, wondering to myself just how in the world Clifton Snyder will ever know now when it's spring.

It's clearer to me all the time, although my mother may disagree with me, that my uncle recalled the bulk of these memories years after they happened. If he had been writing them as a teen, there are numerous places where he could not have referred to the future and how the lessons had benefited him in other walks of life. Or he may have done rewrites later on that I wasn't aware of before I had the privilege of reading them. Or maybe he simply had insight beyond his years. Either way, I don't suppose it really matters. They were his words and his thoughts at whatever time in his young life he chose to commit them to paper. But Mom was relentless in trying to keep him interested in what she so badly wanted him to do. She called him and wrote him constantly his freshman year at college, urging him not to forsake his "chapters." I think, as the story has been related to me, that he ignored her completely until Christmas of '64, his sophomore year. When he came home for the holidays, among the packages he had for her to put under the family tree was a festively wrapped box containing two complete chapters that surprised her and pleased her to no end. I was only two years old at the time, but through what research I have been able to do all these years later, I believe those chapters to be the last two you just read here. (There was definitely a rewrite on chapter six when he visited the old deserted Drive-In years later.)

Mom's anticipations of regular mailings were not met with much satisfaction. As it turned out, it was only about fourteen months after that, during his senior year, when my uncle announced to the family that he was dropping out of college. This was a family scandal, and no one sided with him. My grandparents were incredulous, my parents were outdone, and all his friends were highly critical of what they called his impractical thinking. But it was the war. Vietnam was raging, and Uncle Be-Bop was watching the news every day and reading every story in the papers and hearing of old high school friends who went and never came

July 1960

back. I've been told that at one point, before he made his decision to quit college and enlist, he had served as a pallbearer once a month for a three-month stretch, carrying old friends his age through cemeteries to the sound of Taps. It was more than he could endure. He was safely on the sidelines and ashamed of himself for being there. Complacency was not a characteristic he wore well. He might have been scared but he wasn't afraid, and you have to feel both of those words sometime in your life to understand the difference.

In the spring of 1966, he was on a bus to go stand naked in line for his physical. He passed and went straight into basic training. In no time, the jungles he had been reading about and watching on the news were a daily habitat, and the blasts of the firepower that found relief in commercial breaks on the evening news never stopped in his ears. The sounds of war were incessant, and he hated every minute of it. But he was more pleased with himself being there and being miserable than being in a comfortable, clean dorm feeling guiltier with every passing day.

No one, not even my uncle, ever gave me the clear, blow-by-blow account of how it all happened. It was always told in the most general terms. Your uncle was shot. He was shot in the leg. Legs, actually. He'll be all right. He's coming home. Yes, he'll be in the hospital and probably for a long time. But he's coming home and he's going to be all right. My young mind and my mature mind have craved to know the details. What kind of fire got him? What was he doing when he first felt the shelling? Was there immediate and excruciating pain? How close was he to medical help? No one in the family would talk about it, but as I got older, I always had the hope that maybe he would find the right day to share some of this with me. I only wanted to know because I loved him and I wanted to be sure he hadn't suffered as much as I feared he had. That's all. But talking to him was not always an easy task.

His stateside destination was a VA hospital in Richmond. I have a dim, distant memory of the whole family gathering there the day he arrived. It was a sight not effortlessly erased from the mind of a preschool kid. He was wheeled in on a gurney, and as he passed us, lined up on the hospital walkway, he reached out and took my grandmother's hand. She walked with him, crying, to the entrance, holding his thin bandaged hand in both of hers until my grandfather made her let go so he could be carried through the door and to a room. He was there, in that one room, for over two years. We visited many times, but my memories were mostly of sitting in the back seat of my father's Pontiac, looking at comic books, while my mother went in to see my uncle. The most vivid memory was that she always came out sadder than she went in.

But it was there, inside those walls, that Mom continued her passion of keeping her brother's spirit alive and healthy. She insisted, even more fervently, that he write more chapters. She told him it would be good for his mind. For his attitude. For his health in general. He often resisted her with just a smile, but then, giving my mom the credit she's due, pages started arriving in the mail, and the contents of that little locked box in her bedroom closet began to grow.

Chapter Seven

October 1960

Memories are like old clothes. You go through them and save the ones you like, the ones that make you feel good, the ones that look the best on you, the ones that still have color and can give essence to what you want to be at the time. Then you discard what's left. The drab ones. The ones that have lost their usefulness. The ones that don't make you feel good anymore. Throw them away. Forget them. They never existed.

The past is easily controlled because of our freedom to pick and choose the good and the bad. The future is another story. The future we take as it comes. The good and the bad all mixed into one ball that flies across the plate in a blur, and we usually have one strike at it. The future gives us no time to lie about it. We have to deal with it fast and furiously every second of the day. We can dream about it and plan for it and pray over how it will be, but we can't see it coming until it's right on us. And usually, it's too late to duck.

It was ten minutes into second period on a Friday morning. I had a hall pass in my shirt pocket and was just rounding the corner by the science lab, heading for the library, when I heard a crash and saw a snake, amid large pieces of glass, rolling directly toward me. The smell that preceded it made me grab my nose even before I moved my feet to get out of the way. I could hear Toby laughing before I saw him. The odor of formaldehyde filled my nose, and I jumped back against the wall to put myself out of the stream pouring down the middle of the hallway. Toby grabbed my arm.

"Come on. Let's get out of here before somebody blames us," he said, already on the run.

We turned the corner and headed for the library at full trot. We laughed and looked back the whole way and never spoke a word until we were seated at the back table behind the reference books. We were working on an English project together and had been meeting there each morning all week.

"What happened?" I asked, bending low over the table.

"I was comin' down the hall," Toby said in a whisper, "and Victor Wormsley was comin' out of the science lab with this jar in his hand."

"Guano?" I asked.

"Yep. Victor 'Guano' Wormsley himself. Anyway, he had this jar in his hand and he was grinnin' and just as we both got to the door, he wound up and slung it as hard as he could and threw it down the hall, and boy! When it hit...well, you saw it. It spewed glass and formaldehyde all over the place."

"Guano Wormsley?" I asked again in disbelief.

"None other," Toby assured me.

"I saw it hit but I didn't see who threw it. But why Guano? Why would he do something like that?"

"I don't know," Toby said, shaking his head, "but it kinda makes me mad that I didn't think of it."

Victor "Guano" Wormsley was not popular with the boys at Jackson High. He was also not popular with the girls. Teachers hated him, and it was rumored a school bus driver once quit because Guano rode his bus. Guano had rust-colored hair and teeth. His skin drifted from a cloud-white complexion to something close to a rash. The only thing more breathtaking about him than his general appearance was the stench that walked ten feet ahead of him. Guano changed clothes only about twice a month. What you saw on Monday, you saw on Friday. Only the shiest girls and the most easily whipped boys sat anywhere close to him in class. People actually fought not to sit next to him. He looked mean, and I suppose he was. I can honestly say I never heard him say over two dozen words throughout our high school years. The most famous ones were uttered our freshman year in geography class. Guano would watch the clock like a death row inmate, and two minutes before the bell rang he would reach in his shirt pocket, shake out a Lucky, and put it in his mouth. With his eyes glued to the clock on the back wall, he'd wait for the blast of the bell so he could light up with no waste of seconds.

About the third day of school, Mr. Humes, the World G. teacher, walked back to Guano's desk, held out his hand, and said, "Give me the cigarettes, Victor."

Guano stared at him, slowly reached to his mouth, took the cigarette from between his lips, and laid it in Mr. Humes's outstretched hand.

"All of them," Mr. Humes said.

Guano didn't like it, but he reached under that month's sweater and came up with a near-full pack. Mr. Humes took them and walked back to his desk. He put them in a drawer and continued class. In about ninety seconds the bell released us for lunch, and Guano strode straight for the front of the room. Billy and I fiddled with our books so we could hang back and hear the inevitable exchange. What came was a punchline we would laugh at for years to come. Sometimes we'd say it with no relation to the subject at hand and just howl. It was one of our favorite real-life jokes.

Guano stood in front of Mr. Humes's desk, held out his hand, and said, "Hey, Teach. Gimme my cigs."

Even Mr. Humes laughed out loud and gave him his cigs.

In the back of the library, Toby and I were two pages into a biographical sketch of Walt Whitman when the intercom buzzed and the voice of Mr. Dressel, our principal, asked the librarian to call the office. Within the minute, she came to our table and asked for our names. We told her, a little scared and a lot curious, and she nodded and said, "I thought so. Mr. Dressel would like to see you both in the office. Come up to my desk and I'll write you a pass."

We gathered our papers in silence, trying to ignore the churning in our stomachs, and followed her past the walls of worn books. We waited while she scratched her name and the time of day on a pink slip and then headed, somewhat bewildered, to the office of our commander, Admiral Dressel—called this, of course, only to his back. It seems he had been a career man in the Marines and had come out after twenty years as a lance corporal. He pursued his educational career, which he had apparently started before his time of service, and had been the principal at our high school for seven or eight years before we entered ninth grade. Someone long before us had given him the nickname Admiral. Someone with enough military knowledge to know that the Marines were a branch of the Navy or someone with little enough knowledge to know there were no admirals in the Marines. I wondered often just which type of person named him. I also wondered if he knew what the students called him when he walked away from them. Sometimes I felt sorry for him. Sometimes I felt that he realized his inadequateness. Sometimes I felt the helplessness he felt in awkward situations. But most of the time I called him Admiral, just like everybody else.

We walked into the office of Mrs. Branscomb, the school secretary and always a pleasant sight. Her moods were all cheerful, she was always smiling, and she treated every student like a person with rights and feelings. She never talked to us condescendingly, and I often wished she had at least been a teacher if not the principal. She told us to take a seat and that Mr. Dressel would be with us momentarily.

Our denim had hardly touched the plastic green cover of the metal sofa when the Admiral himself walked up to us and pointed to his office and simply said, "In there." We followed and quietly sat and silently wondered exactly why he wanted to see us. I felt in my stomach it had something to do with The Snake, but I wasn't sure, as I had really done nothing wrong. And if Toby was telling me the truth, he hadn't either. The Admiral sat dramatically behind his desk and let the hush eat around the room. He looked at each of us with a slight, smug grin and then clasped his hands in a heavenly yet firm posture and said, "Tell me all about it, boys."

I felt Toby look at me for guidance. I looked at Mr. Dressel and asked, "Tell you about what?"

"Don't make this hard on yourselves, boys. Tell me what you know. Why you did it. Everything."

"Did what?" Toby asked.

"The snake!" he hollered. "Don't act like you don't know what I'm talking about. The snake!"

"You mean the snake in the jar that got busted in the hall this morning?" Toby asked.

"Yes. That's the snake I'm talking about. What other snake have you seen today?"

"We don't know much about it, Mr. Dressel. And we didn't bust it." I felt trapped and not sure why.

He stood and looked down at us. His shoulders were nearly as wide as his desk. His mouth was set in a stern pattern that varied from serious to only a sneer. He had several long strands of hair that he combed from one side of his head to the other, hoping to fool someone into thinking his pate was well covered. He was only fooling himself. He gave us his best I've-got-the-goods-on-you look and softly informed us, "You were both seen running from the scene. If you are not guilty, why were you running?"

This man was drunk on *Dragnet*. I could smell the cell block in his voice. I could see the badge on his chest. I was waiting for him to say, "Let's go downtown," when Toby said, "We were runnin', but we didn't throw it."

"Oh, someone threw it? You must have seen someone throw it if you know it was thrown. I never said it had been thrown. How did you know it was thrown?"

Toby turned slowly and gave me the same look he had given me that night from the front of the church just as they began speaking in tongues. I didn't want to know what he was going to do, so I started talking. I looked Joe Friday right in the tie and said in my most convincing voice, "Mr. Dressel, I saw the snake rollin' down the hall but didn't see how it got there. I jumped back to keep the formaldehyde off my shoes, and then Toby and I ran. I guess we ran because we knew there was goin' to be trouble. We weren't part of it so we just wanted to get out of there. That's all."

"Who threw it?" The Admiral asked.

"I didn't see anybody throw it, sir," I answered honestly but not convincingly.

"How about you?" he asked Toby. "Did you see anybody throw it?"

"I didn't throw it," Toby answered without answering.

"But you saw somebody. You both saw somebody. You both know who it was. And you both are going to tell me. You're going to sit right here until you tell me all you know. And you're going to get a zero in every class you miss until you do. Then you'll talk and you'll talk plenty."

A sudden shower of realization washed over me. This wasn't Joe Friday at all. This was Edward G. Robinson, Little Caesar himself. He glared at me and squinted and drilled the next question into my ears. "You know who did it, don't ya?"

My answer surprised even me. "Yes sir."

He jumped. "Who?"

I took a deep breath. "I had nothin' to do with it. It was none of my business and it wasn't me. That's all that matters. Who it was is none of my business, and I'm not goin' to say."

This infuriated the Admiral, and he chomped his imaginary cigar in two. "Don't tell me you won't. I say you will and you will. You'll sit here until you do. You can instruct your parents they are welcome to meet with me on Monday and we will discuss the matter at length. Until then, you will sit in this office indefinitely. You report here first thing Monday morning. No more classes for you."

He turned to Toby. "As for you, young man, I'll give you one more chance to come clean. Who threw the snake?"

Toby merely looked at the floor. He never answered him. The Admiral calmed and paled and spoke softly again. "Did you see Victor Wormsley anywhere near the scene?"

Toby looked up wild-eyed and angry. "Was it Guano who said he saw us runnin'?"

"Was it who?" Dressel asked, puzzled.

"Victor. Victor Wormsley. Is that who told you we were there?"

"It doesn't matter who told me what. But what did you call him?"

"Ah, it's just a nickname," Toby said offhandedly.

"I don't like nicknames," the Admiral said, gritting his teeth.

That answered a lot of my questions. I knew from the look on his face and the gravel in his voice that he knew about his nickname. He pursued this line of questioning to both Toby's and my surprise. The nickname issue really fired him up. "What did you call him?"

"Guano," Toby said rather sheepishly.

"And what exactly does that mean?" he pushed.

"It's just what everybody calls him. It's a nickname. Guano Wormsley."

It looked to me like the Admiral was badgering Toby for no reason. He was completely off the track of the snake and pounding Toby on a totally unrelated matter. Toby could only be pushed so far, and then his breaking point would come quickly. He was trying, but I knew if Joe Friday kept shining the lamp in his face, he would tell him the truth in certain and direct terms.

"You call this boy Guano. What does that mean?"

The light in his eyes was too bright and the heat was too intense. Toby was tired of playing his game. Consequences were of little consequence to him when he lost patience. When he finally didn't care, he was dangerous and a joy to behold. He was unpredictable in the most fascinating and entertaining way. He paused for a second, cocked his head to the side, looked the Admiral squarely in the eye, and said, "You don't know what that means?"

"No, I do not. What does it mean?"

"Well," Toby began, "you know that stuff in bird poop..."

"That's it! That's enough!" Dressel yelled and slammed his desk. "Young man, you have had it. You are also here indefinitely. Tell your parents you are only released when they meet with me personally. You both sit right here. You sit there"—

he pointed to me—"and you sit in there." He waved Toby to another partitioned cubicle. Then he stormed out and there we sat.

I couldn't see Toby except when he would lean around the door frame and talk to me. Most of the time we talked through the wall until Mrs. Branscomb would come back and tell us to be quiet. She was even nice about that. We had been there about thirty minutes when Toby leaned around the doorway and said, "Guano is here."

"Can you see him?" I asked.

"No, but I can smell him. He's somewhere within forty feet, I'd say."

Mrs. Branscomb had to come twice to calm us down over that one. I was still laughing when the bell rang for lunch. We were allowed twenty minutes in the lunchroom and then had to report back to the office for the rest of the day. The old leatherneck was sticking to his guns.

The three o'clock bell sounded, and as we walked out of the office and to our lockers, we saw Victor Wormsley still sitting in his cubicle and Dressel working at his desk. Neither one looked up at us, so I waved my hand in front of my nose at Guano and Toby saluted the Admiral. The weekend was afoot.

Saturday mornings in our little town were very much like Saturday mornings everywhere. Slow, late, and lazy. Our house never started to come alive until after eight thirty, which was two and a half hours later than on weekdays. By nine, there was the smell of pancakes and the sound of radio in the kitchen. Mighty Mouse still flew and sang on the television set in the living room even though no one was watching anymore. I liked having it on just for old times' sake. My dad was always outside.

I never knew what he was doing out there every Saturday morning, but he was never anywhere to be seen in the house. Mom hummed as she cooked. In all my years of trying to decipher, I never heard her hum a recognizable tune. They were just random notes. I can still hear them in my head, and it's my favorite melody to this day.

I had told my parents the night before about The Snake incident. My dad had simply said if I didn't do it, I shouldn't worry about it. But it stirred my mother to frustration.

"What do you mean, don't worry about it? If he's sitting in the office getting zeros for every class, someone's got to worry about it." She turned her attention to me. "You go to school Monday morning and to the office like you're supposed to. I'll be there and talk to your principal and we'll settle this matter once and for all." And that was really all that was said about The Snake. In our house, anyway.

The phone rang about ten. I answered it and it was Howard. He sounded unusual. He was very serious and to the point.

"Have you seen Bud?"

"When?" I asked.

"Anytime," Howard said back desperately.

"I saw him at school yesterday."

"No, I mean since then."

"No," I said. "I saw him about fifth period go by the office. Why, what's up?"

There was a pause I couldn't read. Finally, Howard said, "He's gone."

"What do you mean he's gone? Gone where?"

His voice was much lower and more worried now. "We don't know. He's missin'."

"Since when?" I asked, a little irritated. Could Howard just give me the whole story without me having to ask all these

October 1960

questions?

"Since yesterday at school, I reckon. I came on home like usual and he never did. I just thought he got detention hall or somethin' and would be home later. I went to town with Larry Harley and down to Dinkel's and all. We were just hangin' around. I got back about suppertime. Mama and Pop thought he was with me. This was like five o'clock. I went back to school to look for him, and then we went all over town and everything. We don't know where he's at."

I began to have the feeling that I was in a dream. Something unreal was happening to me. I was in a story I was actually watching on TV. I was in a news article in the paper. This was not real life. This was something that happened to other people. This was mysterious and dreadful. Interesting and fascinating, yes, but not fun at all. This was someone I knew personally who had been missing for about nineteen hours. I sat down on the floor because my knees and stomach couldn't support the standing position. I felt lightheaded. I wanted to know more but I couldn't think of a question.

Howard continued now without further prompting from me. "Pop has had the police out already this mornin'. They wouldn't start lookin' till this mornin'. I'm callin' everybody I can think of. Would you call Toby and Billy for me? See if they know anything?"

"Sure, I'll call them," I said, still in a daze. "I'll call you right back if they know anything."

Jayo answered the phone. He wanted to play the way I usually played with him when I called. I tried to get rid of him as quickly as possible. He finally called Billy to the phone.

"Hello."

"Billy, you're not goin' to believe this. Howard just called me and Bud is missin'."

"Missin'? Bud Spinner?"

"What other Bud do you know?" I asked, frustrated. "He's been gone since yesterday."

"Where do they think he is?" Billy asked stupidly.

This is the kind of unthinking question people ask when they are surprised with a fact. You tell someone you lost your ring and the first thing they ask is, "Where did you lose it?" You tell someone you lost your hat and they ask, "Where did you have it last?" If you knew these answers, the objects wouldn't be lost. So you tell someone that someone is missing and they ask, "Where do they think he is?" It's natural but stupid. Of course, I didn't say that to Billy because I think he was just as bothered by the whole thing as I was.

"They don't have any idea where he is. They have the police out lookin' for him now."

"Police? Boy, he is grass when they do find him. Big Bud is goin' to be hot."

"Yeah, if he's run off or somethin'. But what if...you know...it's somethin' else?"

"You mean like kidnapped or somethin' like that?" Billy was bravely putting my thoughts into words, and they were scaring me to death.

"Yeah," I said. "What if somebody took him?"

Billy thought about this for a while, and there was silence on the line as we both pondered what our next move or thought should be.

"Have you called Toby?"

"Not yet. Why?"

"I'll come up there and we'll go over to his house and tell him."

"Okay," I said. "I'll be ready in about ten minutes.

The weakness I felt initially had worn off a bit. I was still not accepting the reality of it all, but I was beginning to handle the anxiety a little better. This was like anything that happens out of the ordinary, allowing life to exist on nerve endings. Even a death—not a close family member, mind you, but someone you know such as a neighbor—might upset your routine, stretching and testing your emotions. Unusual occurrences can take you places you are not expecting to go. Something as simple as the electricity going out for an hour or a hurricane watch has a strange negative charm. I remember once, water getting into our basement two feet deep. Mom and Dad were exasperated, but we all got together and spent one whole night cleaning it out. There we were together, working in a muddy mess and eating a sandwich at one o'clock in the morning and laughing about the mud on Mom's nose and then finally going to bed at five thirty. Unusual things keep life on its toes.

Toby was in his backyard attempting to give the lawn its final mow of the season. His father had recently bought an item that was the talk of the neighborhood: a power mower that ran by itself. If you took your hands off the handle, it would keep going in a straight line. It was a futuristic sight, funny and potentially dangerous in the wrong hands. And, of course, Toby had a few ideas on how to make this work for him. As we were coming across the lawn, we saw his current attempt at harnessing labor power. He had tied a long rope on the handle grip and tied the other end around a tree. Then he let the mower go with the expectation of it circling the tree until it cleanly mowed the area while he lay under another tree and sipped Dr. Peppers. This piece of physics works only in the imagination of someone as impractical as Toby. The mower wound up on its side after a half circle. Toby spilled his drink and almost cut off two fingers trying to get the mower upright without turning off the engine. I pushed the metal strip against the spark plug and killed the roar, and Billy set it back on all four wheels. Toby was cussing his half-empty drink bottle, and I was glad we had walked up when we did.

"You should have known that wouldn't work. Why would you try somethin' that dumb?" I asked to no avail.

"I think I need a heavier rope," Toby reasoned.

"Forget it," I suggested. "Have you heard about Bud?"

"No. What's wrong? Is he dead?" Toby's question startled me.

"Why do you say that?" I asked weakly.

"When somebody says have you heard about so and so, it's usually somethin' bad. What happened to Bud?"

"He's gone," Billy joined in.

"Then he really is dead?" Toby asked. And I couldn't tell for sure if he was serious.

"No, Toby. He ain't dead!" I was getting angry. "At least, we don't know he is. He's just missin'. Disappeared. Gone."

"Ah, he's probably just down at Dinkel's," Toby offered as he checked the gas in the lawn mower.

"Hey, we're serious," Billy said. "He's been gone all night. Even Howard is worried. They got the police out."

"Police" can be a sobering word in almost any situation. Even to people who have never been in trouble with the law. When you say the police are involved, the song changes keys. This is the word that did it for Toby. Suddenly he became aware of the significance of the situation and why we were so somber and concerned. His verbal reaction didn't necessarily show it, but I do think he realized it.

"The police? Really? Well, with that many people lookin' for him they shouldn't have any trouble findin' him."

We sat around my house all Saturday afternoon

October 1960

wondering what the news was. We didn't want to call the Spinners and ask, and we didn't really want to go over there. I have always hated to go into some situation that may turn into an emotional scene. But our curiosity was growing and, to be honest, we were frightened. We could not think of any reason why Bud would run off. We speculated on every possible subject within our knowledge. We ruled out kidnapping because the Spinners didn't have the kind of money that would attract such a crime. We couldn't imagine Bud doing anything drastic without Howard knowing about it. Toby held out that Howard *did* know about it and was acting to cover up for Bud. We wanted to know more but didn't know how to find out. But that solution was about to be handed to us. My dad walked down the stairs and stopped in the living room where we were lounging. I looked up and saw he had changed from his outdoor Saturday clothes to khakis and a sport shirt.

"Do you boys want to go with me?" he asked.

"Where to?" I asked back.

"Over to Buddy Spinner's. I figure it's time to check on them and see if there's anything we can do."

We all looked at one another and agreed that, yes, we wanted to go.

Dad didn't know the Spinners all that well. He was mostly acquainted with them because of my friendship with the twins. But my dad was one of those who respected the old ways of community relationships. He visited homes of deceased neighbors and people he wasn't exceptionally close to. And when he offered to help, he really meant it. If he knew of someone who had an extended illness, Mom would bake a pie and he would take it over and stack wood for them or mow their grass or shovel their walk or do whatever was needed. So it wasn't unusual that he would stop by the Spinners' place and inquire as to what he could do to help. That's just the way he was.

Billy, Toby, and I hung back in the front yard while Dad knocked on the door. Howard answered and let him in, then came out to talk with us.

"Have you heard anything?" I asked quietly.

Howard was subdued. "Somebody thinks they saw him downtown last night. He had on a red shirt, and they saw somebody with a red shirt and blond hair downtown somewhere."

"Did you check the pool room?" Toby asked. "You know he always likes sneakin' in there."

"I don't know," Howard said. "I guess they checked all those places."

"Is your dad mad?" Billy asked.

"He was last night. But the later it got the more worried he got. He never went to bed. Today, he's just sittin' in there smokin' and lookin' at family picture albums. It's really weird in there."

"Don't you have *any* idea where your brother might be?" I asked suspiciously. I had seldom seen one of these boys without the other since we started grade school. They not only looked alike; they thought and acted alike. How could one do something this bizarre without the other one having some idea as to what was going on?

Howard just shook his head and I could see his eyes filling up. This was answer enough for me. I asked no more questions. Big Bud and my dad walked out of the house and onto the porch. Big Bud looked like the ashes of hell. Even worse than usual. He stared an empty stare at us but never completely focused on us. Dad was doing all the talking.

"You call Margaret or me if there is anything we can do. If you have to go anywhere, your boy there"—he indicated

October 1960

Howard—"is welcome to stay with us. Let me know as soon as you hear anything."

Big Bud nodded appreciatively and flipped a cigarette butt into the yard. Howard said goodbye to us, Toby stepped on the butt, and we all four got into the car.

Nothing much was said all the way home. When we got out, Toby and Billy went to their respective houses and Dad and I went in. I took a bath and started getting ready to go to the football game. I went in the living room about six thirty and found Dad in his chair reading the *TV Guide*. He looked up and said, "Of all the new batch of shows on this year, at least *Gunsmoke* is back."

"Can I have the keys because I kinda need the car tonight?"

"Tell me again," he said as he dug in his front pants pocket for the keys, "why are you going to Welton tonight?"

"Football game," I said.

"On a Saturday night?"

"It was supposed to be last night, but there was some sort of Fall Festival already scheduled on their field. Some kinda mix up. They made the announcement at school this week. So we're playin' them tonight."

"You be sure there's gas in the car. It's twenty miles over to Welton. And you be careful driving in town there. You're not used to their streets. You ever drive in Welton?"

"Once," I said. "I'll be alright."

"Pay attention to the road."

"Yes sir. By the way, what all happened over at the Spinners'? Did they have any news?"

"What did the boy tell you?" Dad often answered my questions with another question.

"Nothin'. He really doesn't know anything," I said

169

honestly.

"None of them do." He went back to reading the yellow pages in the back with all the news tidbits. "But something is fishy," he added.

I waited. He had more to say, and I waited to see if he was going to confide in me. He wasn't.

"What do you mean?" I asked finally.

"I don't know. The wife never came downstairs and Buddy never...I just don't know. We'll see in time." And that was it.

I told Mom goodbye as I went through the kitchen. She said to come straight home after the game. I said I would, and I was gone into the night to a new world of intrigue and adventure. Sounds serious, doesn't it?

Welton was a small town about the same size as our little town. Like ours, it had two movie theaters, a few national chain stores, a lot of local shops, and three or four lunch counters and restaurants in its seven-block stretch of commercial downtown. Unlike ours, it had a town square with the courthouse sitting smack in the middle. All around it was a Woolworth's, a McCrory's, a local furniture store, a jewelry store, a Greek-owned lunchroom with the skinniest hot dogs and the hottest chili a human tongue could endure, a shoe store with an x-ray machine so you could see how close your toes were to the ends of your shoes, and a number of clothing stores for men, women, and children. The Square was the place to be on Friday and Saturday nights in Welton. The traffic was heavy from eight till midnight. "Let's circle the Square," was the misnomer you could hear after any ballgame or early date. And sometimes even *before* a ballgame, because that was exactly where we were heading prior to kickoff just in case there was anything going on that we might want to see.

We, along with dozens of other slow-moving cars, "circled the Square" until shortage of time and boredom melted together and suggested we head for the football field. All the way to Welton, our conversation had been dominated by the activities of the last two days. We speculated some more on the possibilities of Bud's whereabouts and the reasons for his disappearance and filled Billy in on all the details of the Admiral, Guano, and The Snake. We were only half a mile from the field and less from the Square when we passed the sign that would change the course of our evening. It would lead us into new worlds of thought and excitement and give us cause to remember it for many years and nights to come. It would strike us as funny and leave us wondering. It would scare us and entertain us. It would give new dimension to our conversation, new color to the development of our character, and a good story to tell our proverbial grandchildren. It was a simple sign. It was not neon and it did not glow in any way. The attraction was in the simplicity of its lettering and the framing that encased it. On a wooden plaque, hanging by the side door to what was merely identified as CAFÉ, was painted an Ace of Hearts with the words "Madam Tiara" drawn in free style and outlined in red. Toby saw it first.

"Let's get our fortune told," Toby yelled and pointed.

"I've always wanted to do that," Billy said quietly and then grinned, looking suddenly ashamed of himself.

"Then let's do it," Toby encouraged. "Let's ask her where Bud is."

"Let's don't and say we did." That was my statement, and I sincerely felt it would be the final statement on the matter. After all, I was driving.

"Come on. You scared?" Toby pushed.

"Yeah, let's just say I'm scared," I answered, driving on by the place.

"Ah, come on. Let's go back," Toby whined.

We went to the game, but that did not end the conversation concerning Madam Tiara. The first quarter was slow and uneventful. The second quarter was a runaway, and by halftime they had us 17–0. On top of this, it seemed all the good-looking girls had dates. Football was losing its hold over us, and Toby took advantage of our growing disinterest as the Welton High band took the field and played "76 Trombones." He started pushing Madam Tiara again. Billy started agreeing with him, and I finally said if she were still open when we went back by, maybe, just maybe we'd stop. We left during the third quarter, and she was open.

We sat in the car under the Ace of Hearts and planned our next moves.

"I guess we just knock on the door and tell her what we want," Billy said.

"If we knock on the door," I said sarcastically, "she'll know what we want."

"You mean 'cause she can read our minds?" Toby asked excitedly.

"No. Because that's what she does," I answered logically. "If we wanted a hamburger, we wouldn't be knockin' on her door."

I wasn't sure if I was disgusted or scared or curious or ashamed or excited. I did know that deep down, somewhere in my untouched soul, I didn't want to know some of the things she might tell me. Even if I didn't believe her, I didn't want to have to make that decision. If she told me something good, it could be fun. But what if she told me something really bad?

October 1960

Should I believe her or...? Toby broke my train of thought.

"My granddaddy told me he went to a gypsy one time and she told him he was gonna have a wreck on his motorcycle. Two weeks later he did and it nearly killed him."

There was a long silence in the car. Billy finally turned in the seat and looked at Toby. I could see the doubt in his eyes, but when he spoke, I realized I had misread the doubt because he wasn't questioning the gypsy's prediction.

"Your granddaddy had a motorcycle?"

"Yeah. He's a really cool old guy," Toby said proudly.

"If we're goin', let's do it." I said, opening the car door and leading the way into the Valley of the Shadow of Death.

"You knock," Billy urged me when we got to the door.

"I ain't scared. I'll knock." Toby pushed by us.

When the door opened, Toby stepped quickly behind me and said, "Hi."

Standing before us was a small and very pretty woman of about forty years. She had beautiful black hair and dark skin that belied a definition of nationality. We weren't too adept at distinguishing races and nations, so she looked sort of Italian and Spanish to us. She spoke softly through a slight and unidentifiable accent and smiled sweetly with every word. "Hello, gentlemen. Won't you come in, please?"

We were simultaneously hypnotized by her looks and manner. We stepped into her room as if she had commanded us instead of merely inviting us. It was sparsely decorated and lighted only by one floor lamp. I was expecting a table with a crystal ball, but instead she directed us to a sofa. We sat deeply in it, all in a row. She sat across from us in a normal-looking straight-back chair. Her skirt was a little longer than what the girls were wearing that year and a little more sheer and silkier. It was very colorful. Red and green is all I can remember. Her blouse was white, and she wore some sort of patterned scarf around her neck. She, strangely, looked very modern, mysterious, and sexy at the same time. She spoke again in that same beautiful voice. "In what way can I be of help to you this evening?"

"Well," Billy started and faltered, "this is the first time we've ever been anyplace like this. I guess we want you to read our palms."

She smiled understandingly. "I can help you in a number of ways. I can read your palm. I can give you a minor psychic reading. I can give you an astrological reading, your horoscope, or I can give you a personality analysis. Each service is five dollars for each person." She had gone straight and quickly to the point.

"I don't know." Billy looked at me.

"I don't know," I added intellectually. "What's the best?" I asked the foreign lady like the true idiot I was.

She smiled again. She never laughed at us or became impatient with us. She was gentle and willing to explain everything we asked. She was the helpful saleslady when you were buying a Christmas present for your mother. The good teacher who was trying to make you understand how to diagram a sentence. She had plenty of time and was not offended by our lack of knowledge. "May I suggest a simple, general reading, as this is your first time? For fifteen dollars I will give you information and insight I think will be helpful to you in your future life. Maybe in the near future, maybe in the distant future. We all can face easier what we can easier see."

I actually heard Toby say "Wow" under his breath. I didn't look at him. Billy nudged me with his knee, as he was sitting between us, but I didn't look at him either. I just leaned forward and pulled my billfold out of my hip pocket. As I pulled out the five-dollar bill, Toby and Billy did the same. We all three reached to hand the money to her, but she gently waved us away and toward the table beside her. We got up and placed the three bills on the small end table and sat back down quickly and self-consciously.

Madam Tiara pulled her chair closer to the sofa and looked at us intently. Her gaze rested finally on Toby. "Young man, you appear to be susceptible to the power."

Toby took this as a compliment, even though I'm not sure he understood precisely what it meant. And maybe he should have. I really didn't know. But I do know it encouraged him to reply, "My granddaddy went to a gypsy once."

"I'm so glad," she replied, "but I'm not a gypsy, and your grandfather is no longer with you."

"No, he's not dead," Toby bristled.

"I didn't say he was dead." Madam held her own. "I said he is no longer with you."

Toby thought for a few seconds. "Hey, that's right. He used to live with us but he don't anymore." Then his eyes glazed over. She had him. He was a believer, and I knew anything else that might happen would have a positive effect on him. He really was "susceptible to the power" of suggestion.

She moved her attention down the sofa and concentrated on Billy. She looked at his hair. Curly and neat. His features. Billy was actually a very good-looking guy. He dressed well. He gave off a good impression. She inched forward in her chair and took his hand from his lap and held it and rubbed it. She closed her eyes and spoke as if she were speaking just to him. "Love is imminent. Affairs of the heart are open to you. But love is also hazardous if precautions are unchecked. Beware emotional infidelities. Give sparingly and take with vigilance. Ne cede malis."

I think she was finished with Billy, but I couldn't be sure. Toby interrupted just as the Latin ended. "Do me some more. Tell me somethin' else."

She looked at me, smiled, and moved back to Toby. She took his hand and held it in her lap. Her gaze rose to the darkness someplace above our heads. "You have heartbreak. But you will overcome and conquer fears and doubts and obstacles of confusion. Life will bloom and you will...wait!" She halted and a chill went through the room. Toby swallowed loud enough for me to hear it. She had *my* attention now. "There has been sickness in your family. Is that not right?"

"Yes ma'am, that's right," Toby answered weakly.

"That, too, will fade, and good health will prevail." She dropped his hand.

She moved toward me. It's difficult to say what she saw as she studied my face, my hair, my eyes, my clothes, and all the things she must have considered before speaking. We are never a good judge of how other people perceive us. So I just sat there and waited for her evaluation without any preparation for what might come. She took both my hands and held them in the folds of her skirt, rubbing the backs of them with her thumbs. If I hadn't been so frightened, I may have been aroused. Okay, I was both. The Madam did not close her eyes or look off into the darkness. She stared directly at my mouth. Some people do that. Some people look at your mouth when they talk to you instead of your eyes, as if they're watching your words fly into the air. There we sat, her reading my lips even though she was the only one talking. And she talked to me as if I were the only one in the room. "I portend fortune if fortitude perseveres. You are the master of your will. The augur to your fate. In love and out you will rive the spirits and hearts of those who touch you with affection and sweetness, but never with malice or intent.

October 1960

Experto Credite."

I was still aroused but no longer frightened because I had no idea in the name of Julius Caesar what she was talking about. I didn't know most of the words she used, and the ones I did know made no sense the way she used them. I have to admit, the Latin totally stumped me and left me scratching my head. I was ready to leave. Toby wasn't.

"Tell us where Bud is," he demanded, much to Tiara's confusion.

"I beg your pardon," she said as she turned toward Toby, still holding my hands.

"Bud. Our friend. He ran away yesterday. Or he's missin' anyway. We don't know what happened to him. Tell us where he is."

Toby never asked if she knew where he was. He simply demanded to know where he was. He already had complete faith in Madam Tiara's advertised powers. He was completely confident that the next words out of her thinly shaped lips would be an address or a description of Bud's present surroundings. He waited gullibly and hungrily. I can't say she never hesitated, but she used the pause with great conviction. She put both hands to her neck, one on each side, and bowed her head just slightly as if she were taking her own pulse. Then she spoke slowly in reverent tones. "Bud is peacefully under the shelter of safety. Comfort yourself and his family." She raised her head, looked each of us in the eye, and said, "Is there anything more?"

"Yeah. Yeah, there is." This was Toby again. "Who's gonna win the World Series?"

The Madam came back fast and without forethought. "Lay five to one on the Pirates." She scanned our faces once more and said, "Gentlemen, this session is over. Please come back anytime. I wish you well, and Godspeed to you."

She walked us to the door and stood in the open doorframe and watched us until we pulled out of the parking lot. She formed a striking figure in the light from the lamp behind her. Her silhouette is memorable to this day, and the attitude of her stance is unforgettable in my mind. And the fact that she wore no underwear was a topic we didn't avoid on the drive home.

Toby was the first to change the subject from Madam Tiara's body to her mind after we hit the highway. Her translucent predictions were of more interest to him than her transparent dress.

"Wow, man! That woman is a witch." Toby was hooked. "She knew my granddaddy wasn't dead. I mean, how could she have known that?"

"A lucky guess," I offered, watching the road while Toby sprawled over the back of the seat.

"No, it couldn't have been," he said. "I mean, most people's granddaddies are dead. She knew mine wasn't. And she knew about the illness in my family."

"Yeah," Billy said, "I wanted to ask you about that. What was that all about? Who's sick in your family?"

"My aunt," Toby answered in a tone that suggested we should know all about it.

"What's wrong with her?" I asked, looking at him in the rearview mirror.

He leaned over the back of the front seats so far, he was almost sitting between Billy and me. His manner was confidential. "My aunt has the flu. Aunt Petty? You know. My mother's sister? She called in sick yesterday. Didn't go to work.

October 1960

My mother went over there this morning to check on her."

I looked at Billy before I challenged this one. He looked at me, grinned, and then peered back out the window. I decided to field it myself. "Toby, I don't think having a twenty-four-hour bug is what she meant by an illness in the family."

"Why not?"

Toby could always ask simple questions that required complicated answers. I chose to ignore him for the moment and explore other matters on the table. I switched my attention to Billy. "Did you understand everything she said about you? Because I didn't get all of mine."

"Some of it," Billy claimed. "Let's write it down while it's fresh in our minds and see if any of it comes true."

"Good idea," Toby agreed and slapped the back of the seat.

"There should be a tablet and pencil in the glove compartment. My dad keeps a record of all his oil changes in there."

"Yours was somethin' about 'if you pretend to have fortune' or somethin' like that." Toby said to me.

"No, she said portend, not pretend," I corrected him. "I know that one. But there was plenty other stuff I didn't know. I think I can remember mine or at least most of it."

Billy wrote down all the points by the light of the dashboard as best as we could recall them. We tried to come up with what she actually said and what she meant, and he even wrote the Latin down phonetically so we could look it up later. We'd each had one year in Mr. Lassiter's class but couldn't agree on a sensible translation between us. We talked about the spookiness of it all. We wondered how long it might be before something would come true. And we even wondered where she came up with the stuff she said if she wasn't on the level. Toby didn't spend much time on this speculation because he was a believer.

"And how about that thing with Bud? What was it she said?" he asked from the back seat.

"Peacefully under the shelter of safety," I answered, almost sure it was verbatim. "Now Toby, that's so general it could mean anything."

"Yeah, and it could mean he's dead, too."

"Come on, Toby," Billy scolded. "That's a sick thing to say."

"Well, you don't know," he shot back. "And she does. I believe that. I mean, it's proof to me. She told me my aunt had the flu, didn't she?"

"No!" Billy jumped at him. "*She* said there was illness in the family. *You* said your aunt had the flu. See? That's how stuff like that gets started."

"Well, the one thing we didn't ask her that we should have asked her," I said, trying to bring the tone of the car back to normal, "was who won the football game and what the score was. 'Cause that's the first thing my mother's goin' to ask me when I walk in the door."

It was a typical Sunday afternoon of my teen years. I did my homework and then sat at the piano to work on a song. Mom had recently bought me a piano book called *50 Unchained Melodies*. My favorite was the one that gave the book its title. She bought me lots of songbooks through the years and lately had taken to buying showtunes, much to my dismay. Her pick of them all was "On the Street Where You Live" from the Broadway musical *My Fair Lady*. Vic Damone had a top ten record of it just a few years before, and she loved him. Me? I hated the song but I always played it for her because…well, she was my mother. I would never, ever play it for anyone else, and I used to complain when I had to play it for her. Then she would say, "But you play it so pretty," and what could I do? I'd play it. But only for her. The phone rang while I was working on a little intricate part with the left hand. Mom answered and said, "It's for you."

"Hello."

Howard was on the other end. "Bud's back," he said, almost in a whisper.

"He is?" I said happily. "Is he alright?"

"Yeah. He's fine. He's hungry."

"Where was he?" Now I was talking in a whisper.

"At Uncle Simon Lee's church. He's been livin' in the basement there since Friday night. Boy, is he hungry!"

"Why was he there? Why'd he run off?"

"I don't know. I gotta go. I just wanted to tell you. Bye."

I picked up Billy and Toby shortly after that and we rode around the Dairy Queen and ate ice cream and I told them about Bud.

"See!" Toby demanded. "See! Madam Tiara said 'under the peaceful shelter of safety.' He was under, in the basement, of the Shepherds of Peace Holiness Church. Peace. Peaceful. See! She was tellin' us where he was all along. If we had just thought about it, we could have found him last night."

"Toby, you were the one who said he might be dead after what she said last night. Now that he's alive, you think that's what she said. You see, she can mean anything you want her to mean." I sounded convincing to myself but not to Toby.

"Yeah, but what about Aunt Petty's flu and my granddaddy's wreck? She couldn't just be guessin' and hit all those things by accident. I tell you, she's a witch."

And maybe she was. We rode around town for about an

hour. I wanted to get home in time to see the *Ed Sullivan Show*. Roger Williams and Peter Nero were going to be on tonight playing dual pianos. I was suffering through that crazy mouse, Topo Gigio, when my dad came in from Deacon's Meeting at church. He and Mom talked for a long time in the kitchen, and when the show went off he called me to come out. Said he had something to tell me.

"You know that Bud came home this afternoon?"

"Yes sir. Howard called me. He didn't know much though."

Dad looked at Mom and then back at me and said, "No, he probably doesn't. And if he does, he probably won't tell you. But I thought you ought to know the truth about it being as how you're so close to them. If for no other reason, just so you don't say the wrong thing or ask the wrong question sometime."

I waited.

"I got this pretty straight tonight, but I don't want it goin' out of this kitchen.

I nodded.

"Seems Bud came home from school Friday afternoon and Buddy didn't know he was in the house. Buddy was on the phone with a woman he's been running with for some time now. Bud heard him on the phone, listened, and took off. It upset him and he just took off. I don't know if Buddy knew this for sure at the time or not, but I think he suspected it the way he was acting yesterday. So, anyway, the boy went to that holiness church where his uncle preaches and broke in the basement window and has been there since Friday night. Simon Lee found him this morning when he went to open up the church. Nobody had noticed him before, which is sort of strange because I think they have services there on Saturday nights."

"Yeah, I think they do." This was me.

"But anyway, for whatever reason, they didn't find him till this morning. Simon Lee brought him home after church. That's the first time he and Buddy have spoken in years. So maybe something good will come of it after all."

"I'm glad he's back." I was sincere. I really did feel better.

"Me, too," Mom added. "If you ever ran off like that, I don't know what I'd do. I'd wring your neck when you came back though, I do know that."

Dad was eating ice cream and Mom was drinking coffee. I took a cold chicken leg from a dish on the stove that was left over from dinner.

"Who was the woman?" I asked boldly.

Mom looked at me with mock, wide eyes. Dad never looked up from his bowl. "Why? Do you want to call her?" he asked.

"Maybe," I said. "I'm always on the lookout for new and wild women."

"You'd better be on the lookout for bed," my mother came back. "And don't forget, I'll be at school in the morning to talk to that principal of yours."

We all three watched *What's My Line?* and went to bed.

Toby and I went straight to the office as directed. Guano was already there. I fantasized that he may be clean on a Monday morning, but no such luck. Same stench, different sweater. Toby went for him immediately.

"Are you the one who told on us, Victor? Are you the one who said you saw us runnin' down the hall?"

"I didn't say nothin'," was Guano's sole response.

Toby was still trying to question Victor Wormsley when the Admiral came in.

"All right, men. Break it up. You three find a seat and get quiet. I'll be with you in a minute."

The halls had gotten still. School was in session. And Mr. Shilling, the Shop teacher, was the first cast member to arrive. We didn't know his importance in the matter at the time, but the Admiral did and he explained it to us shortly. Guano apparently excelled in Shop. He liked to build things and had gotten really good at it. Mr. Shilling had gained his respect and had taken him under his wing. So, sometime since Friday, Guano had gone to Mr. Shilling and confessed that he had thrown The Snake. We never learned the reason, but Mr. Shilling had contacted the Admiral over the weekend and was now here to support Guano.

"Victor will be suspended for two days, and that settles my dealings with him," the Admiral pronounced, then looked at Toby and me. "And even though that clears both of you of the actual crime, it still does not exonerate you of the insubordination you showed in this office Friday by not telling me all you knew about the situation when I demanded you to. You will still sit in this office, as I said you would, until I meet with your parents and inform them of your attitudes. So make yourselves comfortable. It's up to you and your parents as to how long you will be here."

"Sir, there's something I need to tell you before they come," Toby said earnestly, sincerity dripping from each word.

Now this is where my all-time favorite Toby story begins. He loved practical jokes even at the most impractical times. Some were cruel and some were harmful, but the one characteristic they all shared was that they were all funny. Age and authority played no role in his selection of victims. He created situations to suit his moment, and he enjoyed them no matter the consequences. I had a feel for what might be coming, only because I knew Toby so well. He had told me the first half on the way to school, but I think he wanted to surprise me with the second half. He knew it would entertain me more that way. In the car that morning, he'd told me that he had not told his parents anything about The Snake until Sunday night. He wasn't sure what their reaction might be, so by keeping it from them, he was assured it wouldn't interfere with his weekend. Just before bed Sunday night, he confided the truth in them and told them they were to come to school Monday morning for a meeting with the Admiral. His parents were the kindest, gentlest two people I've ever known in my life. According to Toby, this is how the conversation went:

"Now Toby, I don't think you should call him that. You call him Mr. Dressel. That's his name and I'm sure he's a very nice man." Mrs. Painter saw good in everyone.

"He wants both of you to come in the mornin'. You're off on Monday this week, ain't you, Daddy?"

"Yes, son, I'm off and we'll both be there. I do wish, though, you wouldn't always be getting into mischief. But we'll go see him. We'll talk to Mr. Dresser."

"Dressel, Daddy."

"And we'll work out something so you can get back in class. Are you keeping up your studies, Toby?"

"Yes, Mama. I'm doin' all right."

"You need to keep up your grades, son, so you can get a good job when you get out of school. You only have one more year after this one."

"What time should we be there, son?" Mr. Painter asked.

"Any time after school starts will be okay. But there's somethin' I need to tell you before you come in the mornin'. You see, Mr. Dressel was in the Marines, and I guess hearin' bombs and missiles and everything go off, it affected his hearing. He won't wear a hearin' aid, so when you talk to him, you have to talk really loud. As a matter of fact, you have to get up real close to his face when you talk to him and you have to holler. If you don't, he won't hear you and it embarrasses him to have to ask people to repeat what they said. So be sure to get really close to him and talk really loud. Just holler right in his face. It's the only way to communicate with him."

"Well, that poor man," Mr. Painter said. "We'll do that. We don't want him to feel uneasy about his hearing problem. We'll talk right up to him."

That's all I knew. When Toby said to Mr. Dressel, "Sir, there's somethin' I need to tell you before they come," the rest was new to me.

"What is it, Painter?" The Admiral was fingering some papers on his desk.

"Well, sir, it's about my parents. It's kinda embarrassing and I don't know how to say it, sir."

The Admiral looked up. There was concern in his eyes. I even heard it in his voice. "What is it, Toby?"

"Well, you see, sir, my parents have sort of a problem. Neither one of them hear very good at all. But they're both too proud to wear hearin' aids. So, when you talk to them, Mr. Dressel, you'll have to get up real close to them. Up in their face and actually holler at them. It's the only way they'll hear you, and it really makes them feel bad to have to ask people to repeat themselves. That's why I'm so loud, I guess. I have to holler all the time at home. And they talk so loud because they can't hear themselves and...well...sir, I hope you understand."

The Admiral was touched. "I do, Toby. I understand."

And I understood too. And I wanted to get out of there as fast as possible. I don't think I could have withstood the meeting that was about to take place. Toby never looked at me. He knew better. I stared at the floor until I heard the door to the outer office open, and I prayed it wasn't the Painters. My prayer was answered. It was Mom.

The Admiral invited Mom into his office and motioned for me to join them. He had just begun his story when I realized how angry my mother was. She interrupted him and said, "There is no need for you to tell me the entire rigamarole about that snake. My son has already told me. And he also told me he didn't throw it. So there is little more to say about it."

"Yes ma'am, we know he didn't do it," Dressel began, "but he refused to tell me who did it when I asked him."

"Good!" Mom said. "That means he's not a tattler. If I knew, I wouldn't tell you either. He knows how to mind his own knitting. You find who did it and punish him. As for my son, I want him back in all his classes immediately."

"Yes ma'am." The beaten Admiral looked at me and said, "Report to your first period class."

Mom turned and walked out, and I headed for the door that led to the hallway. I heard Mom speak to the Painters, who were coming in as she was going out. I went to my locker to get the book I needed for first period. Then I had to walk back by the office to get to the classroom. I was still three doors away from the door marked PRINCIPAL when I started hearing the shouts. They kept getting louder, and a few teachers began to come out in the hall to see what was going on. As I walked past the office door, I slowed down and took a chance on looking

Piano Days

in. I could see directly into the Admiral's glass cage, and I could see Mr. and Mrs. Painter and him standing in the middle of the floor, noses practically touching, yelling at the top of their voices. Toby saw me and, of course, grinned and waved. They never learned the truth about one another, and Toby was also back in class by the end of first period. Guano was back in school by Wednesday, and Jackson High went back to normal. And I had a new favorite Toby story.

In retrospect, it certainly was a full weekend. Bud never told us why he ran off and we never asked. Because we never asked, he probably figured out we already knew. His parents divorced as soon as he and Howard graduated, and I never did find out who the woman was. We kept our predictions from Madam Tiara and checked them often to see if anything was coming true. We even went back to see her just before Christmas, but some older woman was there who claimed she was Madam Tiara. We left without a reading, wondering how there could be two Tiaras. We looked up the Latin, just as I'm sure the Admiral looked up guano. They both amounted to about the same thing.

And the fact that Toby's instincts about the Madam were not entirely bogus and Billy's and mine were not entirely true is just another lesson in life. Because she did come through. We didn't lay the five to one as she suggested, but Bill Mazeroski did knock a home run in the bottom of the ninth, and the Pirates won the World Series!

———

October 1960

Throughout his college years, my uncle worked weekends and summers as a pianist for many different and varied orchestras and bands. Locally there in North Carolina, he worked beach clubs and played jazz and light rock. Sometimes he played dinner music in an upscale restaurant or a did a turn at a piano bar. He played organ and piano for at least three different churches in the area during those collegiate years and often traveled through the South and Midwest with an ensemble that provided the music for Broadway road shows. His talent at the keyboard was unlimited. He could finesse any style, any genre, with a skill that amazed every professional he was thrown in with. By the time he was only twenty-one, he had agents interested in promoting concert tours featuring him and record companies wanting to sign him for an album deal. I think this attention was what caused most of the shock that ran through the family and his network of friends when he decided to leave school and march off to war. Because in one swift move, he not only gave up a degree and a promising career but also gave up the piano and ended up with a life that held no music and none of the joy he had grown up cherishing.

After being shipped home on a stretcher from South Vietnam, my uncle found that the room in the Hunter Holmes McGuire VA Medical Center in Richmond was his small and only world. And it became smaller each day. There was healing, but it was slow. There were visitors to cheer him, but he didn't always allow them in. One bright light of hope kept him alive and gave him purpose and her name was Abby. Abby was a nurse in the Physical Therapy Department and was assigned to the wing of the hospital where he spent his days staring out over the parking lot and his nights listening to the radio. If not for her, he may not have been able to survive those twenty-six tortuous months. The physical, emotional, and mental pain robbed him of his desire to get better and stripped him of his sense of humor. Abby worked on the first three while Mom *felt if she could save the latter, she could have her brother back. With the prevailing will of God, both ladies succeeded.*

Practically every American was able to quote off the top of their heads that the Vietnam conflict—war—saw over 58,000 military deaths. But not everyone was aware of the 153,000-plus wounded who required hospital care. Rooms, units, and hallways were full, and Uncle Be-Bop was a statistic that drifted much too quickly from most folks' minds. Of course, he never left my mother's mind. She paired quickly with Aunt Abby (who was not yet my aunt), and they formed a team of strength that my poor uncle had no resistance against. Never had a chance. Abby was with him daily, falling in love with him, and Mom was back to her old tricks. She took him his portable typewriter and stacks of paper, along with a little speech about it being good therapy, and, surprisingly, he congenially agreed with her. In all reality, Abby probably had more to do with it than Mom, but you didn't hear that from me.

Where he picked up the story each time was his decision. A few pages came home after each visit until there was a complete chapter. He shared this conversation with me, many years later, that had taken place in his hospital room:

"Nurse Abby, give these papers to my sister the next time she comes to see me."

"Why can't you give them to her yourself?"

"Because she'll want to sit here and read them before she leaves."

"Just tell her not to." Abby picked up the finished pages and said, "Are you going to let me read these someday?"

"Someday."

"What's the big secret?" Abby laughed. "Do you confess somewhere in here to robbing a bank or blackmail or something?"

"I haven't really confessed anything in here so far, and maybe

October 1960

that's why I'm a little ashamed of what I've written all these years. To have lived as much as I have, I should have things I'm hiding. But I really don't. Or maybe I've just lost my conscience and I'm not really ashamed of anything anymore. Isn't there a medical term for that?"

"Oh, yes. But they lock people up for years with that."

"Nurse Abby, come back tonight, and I'll read them to you. One page at a time."

"Why would you want to do that?"

"Because I love you and I want you to know who I am."

This, Uncle Be-Bop confessed, is when he started getting better.

Chapter Eight

October, November, December 1961

Scenes and names fade. Accurate accounts of the way things seemed and the way they actually happened get clouded and hazy. Your attitude toward things back then gets mixed up with your attitudes toward those same things now, and it's hard to decipher what you were really thinking at the time. That teacher you look back on now and profess how special she was and what she meant to the direction of your life is, in reality, the same teacher you were laughing about and making fun of when you had her for English 101. It wasn't until ten years later that you evaluated and appreciated her effect on you. But now you tend to remember how exceptional she was in the classroom, which is totally inaccurate. Back then, all she was to you was five pages of homework each night and a grade.

People, places, and things (we were taught these were nouns and I guess they still are) all lost their true identity with time. The only things that hold true with the ages are feelings. You may forget the name of an old schoolmate, maybe their face, and exactly why you should remember them. You may forget the date something supposedly happened and how long ago it was and how important it was. And you may confuse where something took place. Was it in the cafeteria or third period history where Rudy Sanger threw up and they sprinkled that green stuff on the floor? Was it your sophomore or junior year when they announced over the intercom one Monday morning that Mr. McNally, the science teacher, had died over the weekend? Was it January or September? For these things we need some sort reference. But feelings you never forget. Walking into your first school dance. Kissing warm lips and a cold face in the front seat of a '58 Mercury. Summer nights at Dinkel's sitting on the drink box. Dancing with someone to "Stranger on the Shore" and knowing you may never dance with her again. Halloween parties. Thanksgiving breaks. The annual Friday night Christmas parade downtown, with all the stores open and holiday lights lining the streets. Little kids waiting for Santa, big kids looking for girls and boys, whichever the case may be, and parents freezing their noses to accommodate the occasion.

Feelings don't fade. They grow and grow until you can't contain them in the small heart you're born with, and then they burst open that heart and flood all over your life. And the fountain never ends. The feelings are always there, growing more sensitive as each year and each Christmas parade passes.

I dated about six or seven different girls throughout high school. There was Sue Jane, who should always be at the top of the list, and Lannie Mae, who I never know whether to list at all. But in between, for sure, there were some very sweet and definite memories. For me anyway. I don't know about the girls. Some relationships lasted for weeks, some for months, and some on and off for years.

Shirley Dunn was the memory of the moment. We met in the summer of '61 at a pool dance. Met isn't the right word because we had gone to high school together for three years but had hardly ever spoken to one another in the halls. But something was right with the stars that night, and we danced together and spent the summer together. We dated steadily and then erratically right up to the long Thanksgiving weekend. I

October, November, December 1961

can honestly say I don't recall a lot about our relationship. Just highlights. The night we met is still rather vivid, and the little ordeal during the girls' basketball season still pops in my mind from time to time. Maybe it's an interesting story even though it doesn't have a great deal of bearing on who I am or what I became. Or maybe it does. Maybe everything that ever happens to us, large or small, makes us who we are. And God, please, if I owe anything to Shirley, let me pay up now. I may not be able to afford the interest later.

Shirley was very athletic. She played basketball all four years at Jackson High and was a pillar of the team our senior year. I went to as many games as possible to please her during their September-October season. During one game toward the end of the season, Billy and I were joined on the bleachers by three girls from the opposing school. Their names were Tina, Tina, and Susan. If we ever knew all three last names, they are chewed up in the jaws of time now. Susan's last name was Colter. We had seen them at other Jackson vs. Bulvane events but had never exchanged a word with any of them.

"Both of you are named Tina?" I asked, a little amazed by the coincidence. Had they both been Mary or Betty I wouldn't have thought twice about it.

"Yes," one Tina said with a giggle. "We call her Tina and me Teeny just to tell us apart."

"All three of you seniors?" Billy asked.

"Yes, thank heaven." Susan sighed. "I couldn't take another year of this."

"Been a bad year?" I urged, trying to get the conversation her way.

"Just so much to do. Everything is geared toward getting ready for college. There's always something. I'm sick of college and I'm not even there yet."

Susan seemed the most sensible and the most talkative. She was also the prettiest. She had long blonde hair and a dimple in her chin and teeth that looked like they were fresh out of braces. She had the kind of face you caught yourself looking at after she quit talking. She smiled constantly.

Tina 1, or Teeny we'll call her, was short of stature with short auburn hair. Her lips were her most prominent feature. She chewed gum and her lower lip alternately. She was extremely attractive without being very pretty. Something about her made you want to take her to the drive-in from the first moment you saw her.

Tina 2, and she will remain Tina, had a cute and crooked nose, blue-black hair, beautiful legs, and enormous breasts. On the whole, the game on the bleachers took precedence over the game on the floor.

"Where you goin' to college?" I asked, just in case it was close.

"Dalewood. An all-girls' school. You heard of it?"

"I have. I know where it is."

"Where are you going?" she asked back.

"I don't know yet. I have my application in a couple of places, but I won't know anything until probably the first of the year."

"Once I get out of good ole Bulvane High, I ain't goin' to school anywhere," Tina informed us without being asked. "I'm gonna get a job in a bank or get married or somethin', but I'm not goin' to school anywhere."

"I am," Teeny with the lips informed us. I'm goin' to cosmopolitan school to be a hairdresser startin' in June, the day after graduation. What about you?" she asked Billy.

Billy and I exchanged a look over "cosmopolitan" before he answered. "I don't know yet. I haven't decided." And he really hadn't. He had a number of good options he talked to me about all the time.

Talk of our plans after and between schools led to talk of our plans after the school week and during the weekend. Phone numbers were asked for and given, and before we knew it, the game was over and I didn't know who won or what the score was.

We had been having too much fun and not watching the game as intently as Shirley wanted us to. She informed me of all this as soon as she opened the door of my car at the back of the gym where I was waiting with the motor and heater running.

"Who were your girlfriends up there on the bleachers?"

"They're not my girlfriends. They were just talkin' to us."

"Boy, were they ever. All through the game. I missed at least ten shots watchin' you up there. The coach was not too pleased with that."

I made my big mistake when I tried to change the subject. I added flame to an already simmering fire. "How many points did you make today?"

"If you'd been watchin' the game, you'd know how many. But no, you were all tied up with those sluts from Bulvane. I know about Susan Colter. Everybody knows about Susan Colter. And those other two looked like trash waitin' to be dumped. Do you know how embarrassed I was throughout that whole game? Every time I looked up there, you were just laughin' and they were hangin' on you…"

"They weren't hangin' on anybody!"

"Don't tell me. I've got two eyes. I know what I saw."

And Shirley proceeded to tell me what she saw and what she imagined she saw and what a heel I was. She cried and yelled and cried some more and suddenly demanded I stop the car in the middle of a country road about a mile from her house.

"Stop the car! Stop this car! Right this minute! Stop it!"

I hit the brakes just to shut her up. Before it came to a full stop, she had the door open and had jumped out and was running down the bank by the side of the road. I jumped out and called her a couple of times and ran a short distance to catch her. I halted my pursuit when I saw her disappear into a dying corn field. I went to the edge of it, but it was getting dark and she wouldn't answer me so I gave up and went home. I didn't call her and she didn't call me. We never spoke at school the rest of the week, and that Saturday night Billy and I took two of the bleacher girls to the movies. Susan and one of the Tinas. Shirley found out about it and took it rather seriously.

The following Monday was the last girls' basketball game. I was getting in my car after school, about to pull out, when one of the girls from the team, already in uniform, ran up to the window and motioned for me to roll it down. She was out of breath, wide-eyed and scared.

"Coach Hemmings needs to see you right away."

Coach Hemmings, whose first name was Laura, was a P.E. teacher and the girls' basketball coach.

"Coach Hemmings?" I wondered out loud. "What does she want with me?"

"She just said to come and try to catch you before you leave. I think it's somethin' to do with Shirley."

"What!" I said to no one in particular. "Don't tell me she's gonna get in the middle of this." Teachers knew their places, respected their students, and kept their distance in most instances, but coaches had a way of getting involved in their players' lives. They wanted to control everything about them. Studies, home life, romances. Everything. I never understood it.

"Where is she?" I asked the girl. I knew she was a freshman but didn't know her name. She looked awful cute in her little basketball suit.

"She's in her office at the gym," the girl answered.

She got in the car and we rode to the side door of the gym. She was nervous.

"Are you and Shirley still datin'?"

"Not right at the moment."

She looked around the car. "You got any cigarettes in here?"

I glanced over at her. "No. Why? Do you smoke?"

"Yeah. Filters."

"I see. No, I don't have any. I didn't think they let you smoke on the basketball team."

She jerked around in the seat and pulled back like she was going to hit me. "You're not gonna tell, are you? Come on, jerk! Coach Hemmings would kick me off the team, my mama would kick me outta the house, and my daddy would kick my butt all over the county. You're not gonna tell, are you?"

"Hey. No. Calm down. I'm not gonna tell anybody."

And thank the good Lord we were at the gym.

The little basketball suit led me to the door of a small office that overlooked the gym floor, as if I didn't know where Coach Hemmings's office was located. She knocked on the door and delivered me inside, then turned and glanced desperately at me as she left, as if to ask, just one more time, if I was going to tell on her for smoking. The door closed behind me and Miss Hemmings, in her gym shorts, sweatshirt, and whistle, offered me a seat. No, make that ordered me to sit in a chair in front of her desk. Her words were actually, "Sit down!"

Coach Laura was about twenty-eight years old, with short brown hair, glasses, beautiful skin, and long legs. Someone was always offering a tale about her sexual preferences, but she was too pretty for me to want to believe any of the rumors. I was still young and capable of ignoring things I didn't want to notice. It's a luxury of youth. One more thing I should add in describing her, she was *mad*.

"Do you know where Shirley Dunn is right this minute?"

"No ma'am, I don't."

"Do you care?"

"Yeah. I suppose. I suppose…I care."

She looked out the large plateglass window and down to the gym floor where her team and the opposition were warming up. "Do you know what this game means today?"

"It's the championship, isn't it? You have to win this one to go to district."

She turned back and glared at me. "You got that right, buster. We gotta win. And my best player, the player I've been nursing along for four years—four years, do you hear me? My best player is in the infirmary and it's twelve minutes till game time. The first crack I have ever had at district. The last chance I may have in years. And you're the little weasel who's going to keep me from having it."

"Wait a minute," I said, not knowing what I was going to say next.

"No, you wait a minute. Shirley Dunn is in the infirmary and may be in the hospital before this day is over and you're the reason. You! Men are garbage, every last one of you. Now get out of here. If you have any decency about you at all, you'll go check on her. It won't do me or the team any good at this point, but it will probably mean something to her."

"What's wrong with her?" I was puzzled and a little scared.

Miss Coach Laura Hemmings just stared at me without saying a word, and I became a lot scared. I started for the door and said, "I'll go check on her now."

"Yeah, you do that."

The infirmary was next to the principal's office, and no one was usually there this long after school. I knocked and Nurse Berry opened the door. She was a nice lady and she smiled at me and said, "Come in."

"I'm lookin' for Shirley Dunn. Is she in here?"

She dropped the cheeriness from her voice and said quietly, "Yes, she's in the back. I'll see if you can go in."

She disappeared, then came back and motioned me through a closed door. Shirley was lying on a cot in her basketball uniform with a sheet up to her waist. She had been crying and she looked very white. More than just pale. She was white all over her arms and hands and face and everything that I could see. I paused for a second and then asked the obvious. "What's wrong?"

"How did you know I was here?"

"Coach Hemmings told me. What happened?"

She began to sob and finally pushed the sheet down to her knees to reveal a large gauze bandage on the inside of her thigh, about three inches down from her torso. A little bit of blood was seeping through the center of the dressing. I said nothing. I just looked at her and waited for her to quit crying. She finally did.

"I've been so upset. I didn't know what I was doing. We dressed out during last period for the game, and after I dressed, I took a pair of scissors from the locker room and did this to my leg." Sobs took over again and she couldn't talk. I waited. When she stopped, I asked my question.

"Did you stab yourself?"

"No, silly. I didn't do anything that stupid. I just carved your initials in my leg. I went a little too deep, I reckon. Lost a lot of blood and they're afraid it might get infected. It hurts awful bad."

I began talking slowly and I think got louder with each word. "You carved my initials in your leg? Up there? How can you possibly explain that to your mother and father? What is wrong with you? Are you crazy?"

"Don't holler at me." She started to sob again.

No wonder Coach Hemmings was mad at me. Her parents would soon have a price on my head. This girl was coming unwound right in front of me. First the cornfield and now carving her leg with scissors. I talked her out of crying anymore just long enough for me to get out of there.

The game was played without Shirley and the district possibility was lost. I called her at home over the next few days to check on her, and she was back to school by Thursday. I avoided her there as much as I could because I didn't know how to handle the severity of the situation. I knew it was more than I could grasp or deal with but didn't know how to explain that to her. So I just made myself as scarce as possible. And on top of everything else, Billy and I had dates with the bleacher girls again on Saturday night. We were to go to a Halloween party.

Susan Colter called me just hours before the party and asked if I could dig up another body to bring along. "You see, Tina has been going with this guy for over a year now and he's joined the Coast Guard or something and she's not going to have a date. Could you bring somebody for her?"

"Sure. I know just the guy. They'll be perfect for each other." I started to tell her Tina would have to holler really loud at him all night, but I thought better of it. I hung up with her and picked up immediately with Toby.

"Let's go to a Halloween party."

"Where?"

"What do you care? I've already got you a date and you're gonna love her. Long hair and big blue eyes."

"How big?"

"You remember the movie *The Girl Can't Help It*?"

"Jayne Mansfield! Are you kiddin'?"

"Of course, I'm kiddin'. But close. Awful close."

"What time and do we have to dress up in silly costumes?" That was all Toby was concerned with.

"Eight o'clock and we're supposed to dress up but Billy and I are not goin' to."

"Who are ya'll takin'? Shirley and Patsy?"

"Ah, no. Susan Colter, and Billy's girl is named Tina and so is yours."

There was a relatively long pause on the other end of the line. When he finally spoke, he said, "Is this some kind of Halloween joke?"

"No. And that's April Fool's you're thinking about. I'll explain when I pick you up at a quarter till eight."

Maybe this is the place to say it. We were young and imperfect. Worse than some. Not as bad as others. Looking back on those wonderful and tender years, I can see some things that we did were crude, even rude, and yes, we bent some rules but never broke any laws. We walked up to the line more than once but seldom crossed it. We were boys, red-blooded and green. Adventurous and curious. We liked girls and girls liked us. Some decisions we had to make on the spur of the moment; some we fretted over for days. But everything we finally did, we lived with for a lifetime to come, and, to be honest, we had more good times than we had regrets. I don't know of any surviving adult who will admit to everything that has gone through their minds, or will confess to all the things they did and said when they were teenagers, or will own, without reservation, everything they wish they'd never done. Would I not change a thing? I won't go that far, but reflecting on all those sweet and youthful memories, there's some I wish I'd never done but a few I wish I'd done more. To intentionally repeat myself, we were young and imperfect, but we had fun.

The Halloween party was in the basement of the First Street Methodist Church. Everyone was in costume, young and old, except ole Larry, Curly, and Moe. At first, we felt rather stupid and conspicuous, but after studying some of the costumes around us and the way those disguises made the people under them act, we started feeling a little better, if not superior, about ourselves. We wouldn't have known any of the people there if they had taken off their masks, so we really felt doubly out of place with all the strangeness around us. We sat in a corner a lot and made fun a lot and looked at our watches a lot.

Our three dates were in costume when we picked them up at their front doors and were still in costume when we got in the car to leave the party. Susan was a witch with the traditional black garb, pointed hat, and craggy face. Curvaceous Tina 2 was a clown. Rubber ball on the nose, round red rouge marks on the cheeks, red fright wig, and one-piece orange suit with big green buttons down the front. And Toby was taken by her just the way I'd predicted. Billy's Teeny, Tina 1, was another story. She was a shoo-in for the most original costume but made Billy laugh every time he looked at her. She finally got disgusted with him and demanded he stop laughing at her. He never did and she got used to it. She was dressed as Jackie Kennedy, our illustrious First Lady. Two-piece suit, heels, a black wig in that famous coiffure, and a smile painted on with lipstick to make her mouth look wider. She was both pretty and eerie at the same time. It was like "The Three Stooges Meet Their Match."

We left the party at ten thirty and rode around, and they hung out the car windows and had fun with their outfits. They wanted to ride around the Dairy Queen and the Hamburger Shop and see and be seen. At eleven thirty Tina said she wanted to stop somewhere and try to buy some beer. Susan and Teeny said no and that if she did, they were going home. Then Susan said she wanted to go home and change clothes and Teeny and Tina said no and that if she did, *they* were going home. Finally, Teeny hit the jackpot. "Let's go home to my house. My parents are at an all-night Halloween party and won't be home until early in the morning."

Susan balked for just a second until Tina suggested, "Call your mother and tell her we're stayin' at Teeny's. She'll let you stay with no questions asked."

So over the river and through the woods to Teeny's house we go. We walked in the basement, the Witch, the Clown, Jackie, Larry, Curley, and me, and discovered a beautiful rec room complete with a pool table, a card table, a ping pong-table, and an upright piano. "Play something," Susan coaxed as soon as we cleared the door. Someone had apparently told her I played.

"Naw," I said. To play at someone's first urging always looked too anxious. To wait for a third nudge was sometimes too chancy, so when she pushed the second time with, "Come on, please," I said, "What do you want to hear?" and sat down on the stool.

She smiled that Ipana smile at me from under her Wicked Witch of the West hat, laid her dimpled chin on top of the piano in a most seductive way, and said, "Something appropriate."

I played "Bewitched, Bothered and Bewildered," and I think only she and Billy and I caught it.

"Let's shoot some pool," Toby said from somewhere behind me.

"I can't," Teeny said. "I don't know how to hold the pool pole. My uncle has tried to show me but I just can't get it."

"How about ping-pong?" Toby said, picking up a paddle.

"Ping-pong is such a sissy game," said Tina 2, Toby's date with the big blue eyes. "Let's play poker."

"What's your game?" Billy asked, picking up a deck of cards from the table and shuffling them. "Stud or draw? Don't tell me. I'll bet it's Dr. Pepper."

Susan was still staring at me and I was still giving Broadway a fit. "What's Dr. Pepper?" she asked me quietly. By this time, she was sitting on the piano stool with me.

I looked her in the face and kept playing. "Tens, twos, and fours are wild, but don't worry about it. We're not gonna play anyway." The pretty witch smiled back at me and we were in a world of our own.

Then the mood was eternally broken. The course of the night forever changed. The words that rang out and bounced off the cinder block walls rerouted the events I was beginning to feel inevitable about from my perch on half of that antique piano stool. Susan stiffened and turned her attention away from me for the first time since we had entered the basement. Billy quit shuffling the cards and Toby slammed a ping-pong ball that sailed by and narrowly missed my head. Tina 2, still

October, November, December 1961

in full circus regalia, had cast a spell and a challenge on the entire room with her loud and definite answer to Billy's question of "What's your game?" She had parked her orange-clad derriere on the corner of the pool table, her oversized clown shoes on a nearby chair, and stated, in no uncertain terms, her favorite game.

"Strip poker!"

Everyone laughed. And then coaxing and daring and pushing and giggling began, and before we knew it, all the girls were in different stages of agreement on the matter. Strangely enough, Larry and Curly and Moe said nothing. We couldn't quite believe what we were hearing. Toby was all smiles listening to the girls discuss it, but Billy and I were exchanging glances that said it was time to split up and get out of there. This was not something we had signed on for, and we both much preferred having dates with less of a party atmosphere. But then Tina shoved it over the limit. "Come on, girls. Chicken! Chicken! Chicken! It's 1961! Don't be a chicken! Chicken! Chicken!"

Within minutes, we were all seated in a circle around the card table. There they sat, Hazel, Bozo, and the First Lady. They wore their full costumes so they would have more to take off. And there we sat, the Kingston Trio in our street clothes, feeling more out of place than we had at the Halloween party at First Street Methodist.

While Billy shuffled the cards, his date Teeny spoke up. "I can't do this."

"Aw, for heaven's sake, Teeny. You can do it," Tina 2 said with her rubber ball nose still in place.

"No, I can't," Teeny protested. "I really can't. I can't play poker."

"Why?" Susan asked anxiously.

"I don't know how. I never could learn. I can't play pool and I can't play poker. I can't dance fast and I can't back a car up. I just can't play. I never can remember what beats what."

Tina 2 was losing patience. "Just what, then, do you know how to play?"

Teeny thought for a while and Susan rubbed my foot under the table with hers. Toby stared at and waited for Teeny to answer and Billy continued to shuffle. Her answer came as a shock to us all.

"*Authors.*"

"*Authors*? The card game *Authors* is the only thing you know how to play?" Tina asked sarcastically. "Come on, Teeny. Grow up! Strip *Authors*?!"

Billy and I looked at one another and shrugged, and I think we both felt the crisis was over. Then, much to my surprise, while everyone was laughing at "Strip *Authors*," Teeny, with the funny First Lady lips, got up and went to a cabinet and got a deck of *Authors*. She handed them to Billy, who riffled and shuffled them and slid them over to me to cut. I did and the game was on.

It may have been the most unusual evening I had ever spent up until that time. (I just paused as I was writing this and considered that it may be the most unusual evening I have spent up until *this* time.) Some people go through lifetimes of wild and daring adventures and never play a game of strip *Authors*. Susan was the first to lose and took off her Lone Ranger type mask. Tina 2, with the big fuzzy green buttons down her front, lost and took off the rubber ball nose. And little darling Teeny, suffering her first lost, believe it or not, took off her lipstick. Billy and I were untouched, uncomfortable, and underwhelmed. Toby was the same but wasn't taking it as well as we were. He proclaimed, "This game ain't fast enough for me,"

October, November, December 1961

and proceeded to take off his shirt and khakis, toss them on top of the piano, and show no discomfort at all walking across the room in his underwear to get a Pepsi from the refrigerator.

Washington Irving was the hot card for me. I won with him every time. My Washington Irvings over your Longfellows and that beats your Sir Walter Scotts. I had never enjoyed English Lit so much in my life. I was developing a new respect for the masters and promising myself I was going to read *House of Seven Gables* for the next six weeks' book report. Tina 2 lost her fright wig and was tickled to death. I think she was a little disappointed she wasn't losing faster. I didn't know how long this might go on or how long I even wanted it to. But that was soon not my worry and not my decision. It wasn't the car lights against the basement window curtains that startled me or the sound of the engine on the carport that made me stop and listen closer, because I wasn't used to the neighborhood sounds here and didn't know what was normal and what was not. It wasn't even the opening of the back door that caught my attention or the opening of the door leading down the basement steps from the kitchen, because I never heard any of those warning noises through the laughter and excitement that was taking place around the table. The first inkling I had that someone else was in the house was visual. I saw the white shoes coming down the stairs out of the corner of my eye. My exclamation was quiet and reserved. It was to myself and was not meant to admonish the others, as I realized it was much too late for that. It was merely an unconscious sigh of frustration and anxiety. It was an impulse utterance of the knowing dread that was about to come. What I said to myself was simply, "Here it comes."

The white of the shoes stretched up the leg and became white pants, then stretched farther up and became a white shirt.

What I learned later and what I started putting together at that instant helped me understand what was going on but did little toward making the situation any better. Susan had told me earlier on the phone that Tina's boyfriend had "joined the Coast Guard or something."

Beware when a woman sloughs off important information with "or something." "I think the dress only cost thirty dollars or something like that." This means it was on sale for $69.95. Or "It's only a hundred miles or something down there." This means where she wants to go is 210 miles and she knows you'll put up a howl if you know the whole truth. "He joined the Coast Guard or something" meant he's in the Naval Reserve and had a called meeting tonight and that's why Tina 2 didn't have a date at the last minute.

"All right, what is goin' on here?" was the loud, booming enquiry coming from the angry white suit standing on the third step, exploring the room.

Tina, clown girl extraordinaire, turned and jumped and said, "Dutch! What are you doin' here?"

Susan's hand gripped my arm as if for protection, and Teeny froze in her natural stupor. Billy and I watched the white suit closely to see what his next move was going to be. Toby turned to both of us and said in disbelief, "Dutch the sailor?" I never ceased to be amazed at his sense of humor in the face of danger.

"Just what kind of party is goin' on here, Tina?"

"Now, Dutch, honey, nothin' is goin' on here. Nothin' has happened here. Don't get excited now." Tina began nervously gathering up her belongings.

"Who are these three guys and what are they doin' here?" Dutch was a couple of years older than us and built like a six-foot block of wood. The muscles in his shoulders connected directly to his jaws, and the veins in his forehead were about to pop.

"Just friends of Susan's and Teeny's. How did you ever find me here, honey?" Tina was scrambling to find her purse while her silly shoes flapped on the tile floor. "I didn't know you were goin' to be through so early."

"Early?" Dutch roared. "Do you know it's one o'clock in the mornin'? Who are these ratbags and which one is with you?"

"None of them are with me, Dutch honey. I'm just playin' cards with them."

"What about that one sittin' there with no shirt on? What kinda card game is this?"

"It's nothin' to worry about, sweetie," Tina said as she took Dutch by the arm and tried to gear him up the steps. "What time was your meeting over, honey?"

"That don't matter. Is this the Halloween party you've been at all night?"

"Oh no. That was at a church. You should have seen the costumes there, honey. Teeny won the most original award. Let's go now, honey."

But Dutch was having none of it. He jerked his arm out of Tina's desperate grasp and walked down to the center of the room. He pointed and glared at us and growled, "I don't know who you three city boys are but I'd better never see any of you, ever again, anyplace. You understand me?" He was so mad his eyes were bulging and his lips were blue.

"Now, Dutch, honey," Tina said.

Billy and I just looked and listened. We were not frightened but were actually somewhat in sympathy with this poor guy. What an awkward situation he was in. His girlfriend had betrayed him right in front of all of us. He was not just angry but embarrassed, and he felt his manhood threatened if he didn't show some sort of gallant flare in the eyes of the girl of his dreams. But Toby felt none of what we were feeling. Of course, it was Toby's date he was dragging off into the night. And I could sense it. It was almost palpable, running between the three of us. We knew Toby was not going to sit still for all this the way Billy and I were and just wait for Dutch to run out of steam and exit up the steps. Toby got up slowly, while Tina was begging Dutch to leave with her, and walked across the room to the refrigerator again in just his boxer shorts. He passed deliberately between and dangerously close to the two standing lovers. He got another Pepsi and walked back and stood between Dutch and Bozo.

"And I'll tell you somethin' else, boy. I don't appreciate you walkin' around in front of my Tina in your underpants." But I could detect that a little of the fire was gone from Dutch's delivery. Adding humiliation to the list of things he was feeling, you couldn't ignore a more than slightly surprised look on his face at Toby's unconcerned attitude toward his rantings.

"Come on, Dutch, honey. Let's get outta here," said Tina with the sailor on her arm, and they started up the stairs.

Toby had not said a word, and Dutch was all smug and smiles as he looked back over his shoulder at us. You could see the self-contentment on his face at having backed down three guys and you could almost hear him relating it to his friends tomorrow at work. I knew it was all Toby could do to maintain himself and not smart off to him. Maybe he was feeling some sympathy for him after all. And maybe he would never have said a word, just stood there in his underwear and sipped his Pepsi, if Dutch had not turned around, pointed his finger directly at Toby, and said through clenched teeth, "I ain't forgettin' you, boy."

October, November, December 1961

Toby burped, wiped his mouth, and walked toward the steps, "That's the second time you've called me boy tonight. Don't make it three. And don't forget I kissed your girlfriend, Popeye!"

Tina 2 went through the motions of pushing Dutch up the steps but he didn't require much persuading. His confidence had been shaken and he never came back down.

The party was obviously over. I kissed Susan good night in the kitchen while Billy did the same to Teeny on the carport. Toby waited in the car for us, and we could hear him singing in the back seat even though all the windows were rolled up.

I'm Popeye the sailor man, I sail on a garbage can
I love to go swimmin' with 'em mermaid women
I'm Popeye the sailor man

I saw Shirley once or twice a week for the next few weeks, but our dating took on a causal air. Quite frankly, I was safraid to let her get too emotionally involved. She had scared me with the way she thought and acted. I didn't want any more of whatever she might have in mind. She said her leg was healing nicely and offered a number of times to show me, but I declined, and then her feelings hurt more than her thigh. She still walked a little funny and couldn't wear tight skirts or sit long in one position. Toby suggested I get her a woodcarving set for Christmas, but I was hoping I wouldn't have the obligation to make that decision. I was waiting for the right opportunity to ease out without having to worry about how she would react or retaliate against me or harm herself in the process.

She heard about the Halloween party from someplace. The one at the Methodist church, not the one in Teeny's basement. She said she didn't blame me for going, that it was her fault I went and that she would never drive me off again. She could talk so sane one minute and do something so irrational the next that she kept me off balance all the time. We were sitting in front of her house about five nights before Thanksgiving. I was about to get out of the car to walk her to the front door when she said, "Wait. I have something I want to talk to you about."

"Okay."

"This is kinda awkward. I don't know how to start." She was nervous and unconsciously running the zipper of her coat up and down, up and down. "You know Kenny Miles." It was more of a statement than a question.

"Yeah, I know him."

"He's a freshman at VPI this year and he's comin' home over the Thanksgiving break." She looked out the window on the passenger side and struggled with her words. "He called me a few weeks ago and wants to see me while he's home. I told him no, of course. That you and I were goin' steady. But I just wanted you to know that other people do find me interesting."

Kenny Miles. Yeah, I knew him and never liked him. Not until now, anyway. Here was my escape. Houdini couldn't ask for a better setup. Kenny was about to get him a Thanksgiving weekend date. Engraved and everything. But my expression never changed. "He wants you to go out with him?"

"Yes, he does. Do you find that hard to believe? That someone else might want to touch me even though you don't? You don't even like to talk to me anymore."

That look was coming back in her eyes, and I knew I had to move fast or she might chisel *her* name in *my* leg before the night was over. My words dripped with sincerity and understanding. "I can tell, by the way you talk, you want to go with him."

"No, I don't. I just wanted you to…"

"Yes, you do. And you'll never be satisfied if you don't."

"No, really, I don't want to…"

"Listen to me. I have a confession to make and I don't know how to start either. This is even harder for me to say than what you just said. You see, I still feel terrible about that Halloween party with Susan what's-her-name."

"Colter."

"Okay, but listen. I lay awake thinkin' about it and how rotten it was what I did to you and I haven't really found the right way to make it up to you. So, you can do this for me. You can get even for me. You can go out with Kenny Miles and that will even the score for the Halloween thing and I promise you, I think I'll feel better about it all and then maybe things can get back to normal with us."

"Do you mean this?" Shirley had mercifully stopped zipping her jacket and was looking deeply into my eyes.

"I really do, Shirley. Get even with me and help me feel better about myself. Things will be balanced then and we can start over with a clean and even slate."

We kissed and then walked to her front door. She clung to me and told me how wonderful I was, and then she went inside and turned off the porch light and I walked back to my car. I felt a little bad and a little good. It's hard to say for sure which I felt the most, but I knew I was doing what I had to do.

Friday night after Thanksgiving, Billy, Toby, and I waited up the road in Toby's car and watched Kenny Miles pick Shirley up at six thirty. We followed them through town at a safe distance and watched them park and head for the Empire Theater. We did the same. They were standing in the lobby buying popcorn when we walked up beside them and I was "surprised" and "shocked" at running into them. I started to speak but then something caught in my throat and I turned and walked over to a corner of the lobby, where Billy and Toby came to console me. Kenny and Shirley self-consciously paid and talked and pretended they had never seen me, then walked into the darkened theater. Shirley was watching me over her shoulder and Kenny was trying to avoid looking in my direction at all. We gave them time to get seated and then went down and sat two rows in front of them to be sure they saw us. When the movie, *Blue Hawaii*, was over (and I did a better job of acting that night than Elvis *or* Angela Lansbury), we left before the credits ended, again to make sure they saw us. Shirley called me the first thing Saturday morning.

"I'm sorry about last night."

"You're sorry? I had no idea I was goin' to run into you and Kenny at the movies. Why didn't you tell me that was where you were goin'? You really stuck me in the back this time, didn't you?"

"What do you mean?" Shirley said, near tears. "Why are you mad?"

"Hey, I just went to a party with Susan Colter. There were a hundred people there and we were never even in a car alone together. But you and Kenny had a real date. And you liked it, didn't you?"

"Well, I see you can remember her last name this time and, yes, I liked it." No tears in her tone now.

"Good. Then you can have him. Just remember, though, that it was you who went out on me. Not the other way around. This is not my fault."

"You said you didn't care. Do you remember that?" Shirley was getting hot now. Good! I wanted her to be mad at me.

October, November, December 1961

"No matter what I said, it was different when I saw you two together. So I hope you're happy." And I hung up on her.

Billy was sitting at our kitchen table eating cereal. He looked up when I put the phone back in the cradle and said, "I know you probably feel bad about that, but in the long run it was the best thing to do."

"Yeah, I know. I hope it works. I gotta admit she scares me."

"It'll all be okay," he reassured me as good friends do. "What do you have happenin' tonight?"

"Nothin'," I said. "How about you?"

I was sorry as soon as I asked because I remembered Patsy was on one of her sprees. She had kept Billy on an emotional roller coaster ever since they'd met. You never knew if things were on or off, hot or cold with them. Billy seemed to enjoy the good times and just waited out the bad times. Maybe that's why Shirley and that crazy look in her eyes scared me so much. I didn't want to fall victim to such a volatile and unpredictable personality the way Billy had. He handled it well but I didn't think I would. I knew Patsy was going to a Harvest Dance this weekend with some college guy from Welton. And I knew Billy didn't want to talk about it. I said what I thought was the right thing to say: "Looks like we're both in the same boat this weekend, buddy. You name it and we'll do it."

Billy closed the Cheerios box and went to the cabinet to put it away. He turned back to me and shook his finger at me and said, "You know, if we could scare one up, I'm in the mood for a good old-fashioned game of *Authors*."

Atta boy, Billy.

The annual Christmas parade marched and rode itself down Main Street the first Friday of every December. Football was over and basketball had not yet started and everybody went to the Christmas parade. I can see the street and smell the cold air and remember where certain people stood year after year, as if I had just driven home from there this minute. I can hear all the area high school bands playing "Rudolph, the Red-Nosed Reindeer" and "Here Comes Santa Claus" and hear the students and families of students clapping as their school marched by. I can see the majorettes. The junior majorette clubs, out of step and cold and looking lost with mothers walking beside them. Little girls, five and six years old. I can see homemade floats with nativity scenes and carolers and antique cars. Boy Scout troops and local clowns and horseback riders and firetrucks and, of course, Santa. And I can see Billy and Toby and me walking the sidewalks behind the people lined up waiting for the parade to begin. We are looking for people to talk to. Looking for girls to impress. Hoping someone is looking at us. We are young and cold and full of life. But mostly young. And Christmas is three weeks away.

Santa, the star of the show who always brought up the rear of the parade, was portrayed by the same local merchant for thirty-two years. He was a 230-pound barber who ran a shop in town all of his free life. About five years earlier, he had met with a most unusual and uncharacteristic fate. Being a quiet, law-abiding citizen, not to mention Santa Claus, the town was in shock over the event that kept him from his annual sleigh ride.

J.D. Garber, Barber, which is how his sign by the red and white pole read, and alias St. Nick once a year, cut hair from eight to seven o'clock six days a week. He opened earlier and closed later than all the other shops so he could get the trade. His light was on to catch men on the way to work or on the way home. He gave me and a lot of other boys in town our first haircuts. J.D. always kept a radio playing low on the little counter behind his single barber chair. Unlike the stereotyped barbers in movies and books, Mr. Garber had very little to say to his customers. He listened to the radio while he cut and, therefore, so did the man in his chair. It was always on the same station day after day. The dial never changed even though the station did many times over the years. He listened to the news, sports, and weather and whatever music they chose to play for him. And he listened intently to a popular local, weekly show on Saturday mornings at ten a.m. The show was the most talked about production on this hometown station. Each week you were invited to send in your name, phone number, and address on a post card to be put in the big revolving barrel and take a chance on your card being pulled as the winner of the week. Just before the drawing each Saturday morning, the faceless radio voice would announce how may dollars were in this week's jackpot. If they drew and called your number, all you had to do was tell them the amount of the jackpot and you won. Simple and easy. Unless you weren't listening and didn't know the amount. Then the money would grow and next week it would be maybe twenty dollars higher. Different amounts were added each week by the sponsor just to keep it interesting. So you had to listen every Saturday morning, without fail, to hear the amount before the suspenseful dialing began. If no one answered the phone, that, too, would trigger a new amount the next week.

People listened and talked about it and waited for that program every Saturday morning. Some folks won $20, $50, $100. The buildup was exciting. J.D. would stop trimming hair and stand with a comb in one hand and scissors in the other and look at the ceiling while the radio announcer slowly dialed. You could hear the numbers tumbling as the rotary clicked back in place with each digit. You could almost count, if you listened closely enough, and tell if it was close to your phone number. The bigger the pot, the greater the anticipation. And the biggest it ever got was what got J.D.

The sun was shining in the open door of the barber shop, and two men and a little boy were leafing through *Field and Stream* and *Look* magazines. A man was in the chair with a barber cloth fitted closely around his neck. The "Telephone Jackpot" theme music began and J.D. stopped clipping with his cold, manual clippers, stepped back, and turned the volume up.

And a good Saturday morning to every one of you out there in radioland. It's time for "Telephone Jackpot." Today the jackpot is at an all-time high. Today the jackpot is seven hundred and thirty-two dollars. Remember that figure now. Seven hundred and thirty-two dollars, because we are going to make that call right after this message from Faulkner's Furniture.

The barber shop hummed with excitement during the commercial, as did most every store and home in three towns and two counties.

We're back and you can hear the rustling of paper as Joe King, our station manager, reaches into the money barrel and draws the name of our possible winner today. Okay, Joe is handing me the card and it's a local number. And here we go! We're dialing the lucky phone number. (The sound of the dial and its return.) And now we'll see who will answer...oops, the line is busy. Sorry folks. No winner this week for the $732 jackpot. But we will be adding more money for the telephone jackpot, so be listening next Saturday morning at this same time. The number we were dialing this morning was that of the residence of J.D. Garber, 124 Key Street. But the line was busy. So better luck next time, Mr. J.D. Garber. Sorry you missed out on winning our biggest pot ever, $732.

October, November, December 1961

J.D. never finished the haircut. He laid his clippers down, took his apron off, put his hat on, walked out the door, went home, and shot his wife three times in the heart. The barbershop is now a taxi stand, J.D. is doing life in some faraway prison, and an overweight dentist, with an actual white beard, is Santa Claus.

The colored lights, stretched across the streets every ten feet and mingled with greenery, came on at precisely six thirty p.m. That meant the parade had started, and soon we would see the motorcycle cop lead it down Main and motion for all the little kids to stand back on the curb. The Christmas season had begun. The heavy shopping started after the parade, and all the stores would stay open till eight o'clock every weekday and Saturday night until the big day arrived. People would be in good moods who had not been in good moods since last Christmas. The old man who ran the news and magazine store on the corner and ran kids out daily for standing and reading comic books would now give those same kids candy canes when they came in the door. The sidewalk policemen on the downtown beat who wrote parking tickets hourly, all year long, would suspend the practice until December 26. Salvation Army ladies in long, dark blue coats would stand by a kettle and play Christmas records and ring a bell and thank everyone who dropped a dime through the screened cover. The openings on the screen were just big enough to get a coin through but not big enough to get a hand through. The whole town was consumed with reds and greens and good cheer and Tiny Tim attitudes. Mothers and fathers and daughters and sons would shop together and then shop separately, trying to surprise one another with gifts they hoped they'd like. People would end every casual greeting on the streets with "Merry Christmas." And the other person would nod and say, "Same to you."

I have always loved Christmas parades!

The parade itself was full of the cast of characters from my life. Jayo marched with the Cub Scout Den #6. They were all in full uniform, as directed by their Den Master C. M. "Sim" Wester, who marched along beside them. Each boy wore his bright blue shirt and matching pants, gold neckerchief with the Cub Scout scarf ring, and the funny little striped hat that looked something akin to an umpire's cap crossed with a beanie. Oh, they looked sharp when they got dressed back at the house, but by the time they put on their winter coats, earmuffs, gloves, and wool scarves, they looked like a group of any eight-year-old boys walking down the middle of the street, out of step and freezing. The uniforms were no longer anywhere to be seen. The only thing they all wore in common were red noses. But Jayo was proud and we clapped and cheered when he marched by.

The Spinner twins, Howard and Bud, were in the band. Howard played the trombone and Bud played the bass drum. They had been in every Christmas parade for the past four years. This would be their last as members of the Jackson High School Band. I wondered, as I watched them strut by playing "The Twelve Days of Christmas" in march time, if they felt any sadness over this passing. Would they be glad not to have to dress up in those funny green and white suits with the brushes on the shoulders and walk out in front of the whole town, playing Christmas carols out of tune and getting their fingertips nearly frostbitten every year? Or would they stand off next year, on the sidewalk with friends, and applaud the school colors and wish inside that they were still there, center stage, in the middle of Main Street amid all the excitement?

October, November, December 1961

With Bud and Howard, you never knew. I could ask them, but they would only answer the way they thought I expected them to.

Sue Jane was also in the band. She played first clarinet and was very, very good. She preferred the spring concert and the Christmas concert over any of the marching duties such as football games, pep rallies, and parades. She liked concentrating on the music alone, not having to watch the people on each side and trying to keep in step. And she hated the way the cold weather got all the instruments out of tune. She could hardly stand to play in this kind of weather and listen to the others around her. Those military turns at street corners were her most dreaded moves. The band members closer to the corner took shorter, slower steps while the ones farther away took increasingly larger and faster steps. This gave it that swing turn with everyone, supposedly, in line. Yeah, she hated that. And she hated getting her hands cold. It took her hours to get them warm.

That's how I first knew she was behind me. She slipped quietly up next to my back and stuck her hands in my coat pockets while I was watching the parade. As the participants toward the front of the procession came to the end of the line, they would disband and walk back up the sidewalks behind the spectators who were still watching the proceedings, then head to the mouth of the parade to their cars or try to find friends and family. Sue Jane found me. We had not dated since early last spring. We had broken up because…you know, I don't know the because. I never seemed to know or remember why Sue Jane and I were so off and on. It was never anything explosive. Never any anger. We would just go together for periods of time and then drift away from one another. Then some situation would throw us together and we were back as if nothing ever happened. Not at all like Billy and Patsy. Ours was never an emotional strain. We simply liked each other very much and were comfortable with one another. Or maybe it was something more because, as I felt her hands in my pockets and her cold face against the back of my neck, I couldn't for the life of me remember why I had ever let this girl get so far away. She whispered in my ear, "Don't turn around. Go ahead and watch the parade. I just want to get my hands warm."

I did turn my head a quarter of a turn, which is all you can turn your head. "You looked pretty out there," I said. "Are you sad that it's over?"

"Sort of. I cried before I left home. It's like it's the last Christmas parade ever."

"No, it isn't. Next year you'll be here. You'll just be standin' back here enjoyin' it instead of out there playin'."

"Next year. I don't even know where I'll be next year."

She sounded sad. I didn't say anything. I just put my hands in my pockets with hers and held them real tight. She whispered to me again, "Will you watch the Christmas parade with me next year?" Her lips were so close to my right ear, I could feel it getting warm from her breath. Another band marched by playing "White Christmas," and I could hear the sirens from the firetrucks getting closer, announcing that Santa was on his way. Sue Jane squeezed me gently, playfully, and meaningfully, all at the same time. The band stopped in front of us and marked time and played the last eight bars:

May your days be merry and bright and may all your Christmases be white

"Will you?" she asked again.

I turned that quarter turn again and said, "We'll watch it together and we'll always stand right here at this very spot." Then I kissed her over my shoulder right there in front of Santa

October, November, December 1961

Claus and everybody.

The sirens were on us and people were holding their ears. Little kids were screaming and Sue Jane was squeezing me again. And through all the noise and excitement and distractions and Christmas cheer, I think I heard her say, "I love you."

And that was the Christmas parade, as it was, in our little town. It wasn't always eventful but it was always special. It was a time for Snow Queens to wave at their domain, for merchants to make extra bucks off the shoppers, and for everyone to become a kid again for a few minutes and make memories to be cherished for years to come. That entire holiday period, from Halloween to Thanksgiving to Christmas, is special. Everyone is of the same mind during that period of time. It's as if the festivities of all three seasons are tied together, and as one ends the other picks up and it's a constant time of being with family and friends and doing out-of-the-ordinary things. Maybe 1961 was the first time I noticed all of this, but I've made a point to notice it a lot since.

As for Halloween, I still have never read *House of Seven Gables* and probably never will now. The title is intriguing, but like most things, it's probably more intriguing than what is inside. None of us ever again laid eyes on Dutch honey and Tina 2. Teeny wound up going to trade school but never did become "cosmopolitan." And Susan married well, as she well deserved. Such a pretty dimple.

And Thanksgiving, well, I've always felt terrible about what I did to Shirley. Some of the girls in her P.E. class told me later her leg healed up nicely by the first of the year. I never knew for sure until about three years later when I was home on spring break from college. It was my junior year. I ran into her in the dime store. We talked and she seemed to have stabilized considerably. We made a date for later in the week and went out to eat and then to a movie. The conversation eventually came around to the inevitable and she confided that the scars got more pronounced with time. She said the tanner she got in the sun, the whiter the initials got. Later that night I was able to attest to that fact. Yes, it had healed nicely and was very readable. And suddenly I was sort of proud of it. It had survived the years well and so had Shirley.

And for that wonderful Christmas season the year of '61, Sue Jane and I saw each other almost every night for the rest of the holidays and for quite a long time thereafter. That year we gave one another identical silver ID bracelets with our individual names engraved on the front. On the back of mine is *Love SJW 12/25/61*. I still have it. I hope she still has hers, too. I've often wanted to ask her but have never had the opportunity. I was there for Christmas the next year and we watched the parade together just like we promised. But then there were some changes in our lives, and a few years later I moved away and missed the next ten years in a row. But I always went to the one in the town wherever I was living and, in my mind, imagined I saw Sue Jane. I was home exactly ten years after that special parade, and I went with my wife and my mother and insisted we stand in front of Cohen's Furniture store. They both thought I was being silly for wanting to stand at a certain place, but I explained that it was where I stood so many times as a teen, so they laughed and gave in to my sentimentality. Some of the store fronts had changed and some of the store names had changed and the faces of the people in the parade had changed, but the parade had not. I watched everything with my eyes and my heart and searched constantly for someone who might look like Sue Jane. But no one came up and said, "Well, look who's here. It's great to see you. And this is your wife?" And no one was standing close by in the spot we had

October, November, December 1961

vowed to always share. And when the Jackson High School Band went by playing "Santa Claus Is Coming to Town," there was not a familiar clarinet player in the bunch. But when the little majorettes came by, out of step, cold and looking lost, I did see a mother walking along beside them who looked a little familiar. Just as she passed Cohen's Furniture store, she looked my way and our eyes met for just a second. She never lost her smile but she did lose her color, and then I couldn't see very well because cold weather sometimes makes my eyes water. But as she passed on by, I noticed she had on gloves, and I was glad because she always hated getting her hands cold.

With all my heart and soul, I love Christmas parades.

My uncle's health began to get better. After he left the hospital, a number of good things started to happen in his life. He and Abby got married, he took a job with a major publishing company in Chicago, and more days than not, he was able to walk without his canes. Yet sometimes when I saw him he leaned on them immensely, and then at other times he would be without them and seem to have no hint of even a limp. I questioned my mother about this seemingly unusual situation and she explained, as best you can to a child, that some days were just better than others. The neuropathy and pain would subside for months, allowing him to live a normal and active life. Then he would have flareups that would render him immobile without a support in each hand, and that could last for months also.

He and Abby lived in a Chicago suburb, and he commuted daily to the offices of Vandoran Publishing House. He was in charge of the arm of the company that secured publishing rights of old songs and compiled books of piano compositions and orchestra arrangements. He loved his work. It kept him in the music world without ever having to play a note. Vietnam—A Shau Valley, Tay Ninh Province—and the like robbed him of his passion and his talent that was such a second nature to him. Many of the people who worked under him on a daily basis had no idea of his proficiency at the keyboard. And Aunt Abby said he forbade her ever to give them a hint.

Once, when he came home for my grandfather's (his father's) birthday, an unthinking relative, his first cousin Laverne, suggested he play "Happy Birthday" on the piano as we all sang. She motioned to the old spinet that still sat in the living room at Grandad's and Grandma's house, the one he had learned his first notes on. I watched him closely to see his reaction and only detected a slight negative nod of his head. Her insistent nature would not accept such a subtle gesture, so she offered the suggestion a second time in a much louder voice. He walked over to the sofa on the far side of the room, sat down defiantly, and said, "Laverne, you play it."

"Me?" Laverne said with her hand to her chest. "You know I don't play."

"And neither do I," he said firmly with no smile in sight.

Grandma saved the day and the moment. She sat down on the bench, rolled a G chord, and played beautifully while we all sang "Happy Birthday." All except Uncle Be-Bop. When the song was finished and I turned to find him, I saw him in the kitchen getting a cup of coffee.

I was busy growing up and lost track of when the chapters would arrive at our house. I also lost track of when they quit coming. But as I got older, Mom would share the pages with me and we would discuss them, laugh about them, cry about them, and feel the times that were so sensitive and nostalgic to her little brother and the uncle I idolized. We were visiting them in Chicago when I was about the age he was in his stories. I asked him if he would show me something about the piano. He said, "Why now? Why didn't you take lessons when you were six or seven?"

"Just not interested, I guess. But now I am. Can't you show me something simple?"

"No," he said. "It's too late. That's something you have to do early on. You could never catch up."

"What do you mean catch up?"

"I mean you've lost too many years. What if you were just now learning to count? Or just now learning to ride a bicycle? You've lost all those learning years. To start now would be mechanical and deliberate and you never want that in music. You want it to come as naturally as hugging someone you love or holding your breath under water or scratching your head when you're thinking. Instinct. That's what you want. And if it's not instinct, it's not music.

Even when you're reading it off the page. I've seen you dribble a basketball through your legs from one hand to the other. You learned to do that in your learning years. I never did, can't now, and never will be able to. I have no instinct for it."

It took all the guts I could muster up to ask the next question. I knew it could make him angry and maybe end this beautiful conversation, but I took my chances and asked. "When was the last time you played?"

He looked at me for at least thirty seconds before saying a word. I couldn't figure if he was trying to think of a clever and off-putting answer or if he was trying to think of a way to politely tell me it was none of my business, because I knew it was something no one had ever asked him to reveal. It was one of those unapproachable family subjects. And when he answered, I was shocked.

"April 20th, 1966. A Wednesday. The night before I enlisted. I sat down in the living room and played, and I think I knew I would never do it again."

"Do you remember the song you played?"

This pause was much longer than the last one. But I waited and he finally said, "Yeah. I remember."

Chapter Nine

Spring/Summer 1962

Beginnings are easy. Endings are hard. Beginnings just happen without you ever knowing they're happening. You meet someone and a whole new chapter of your life may begin, but you don't know it has until it's ended. Movies are like that. Some begin slow. Some are silent with no dialogue for two or three minutes. Some start out with action. John Ford would start with the bad guys on horseback at full gallop while the opening credits were still rolling. Some even start at the end like *Written on the Wind*, *Double Indemnity*, and *Lydia*. Then they flash back to the beginning of the story. So beginnings are easy. You can begin something almost any way you want to and it'll be all right. You can start a friendship liking someone or not caring one way or the other about them, or you can start off disliking them intensely. This has happened to us all. And years later we laugh with that good friend and say, "You know, when we first met, I couldn't stand you."

But endings are different. Some things just end and we aren't aware they have until we look back and realize they're not there anymore. You talk about "we used to do this" and become mindful of just how long it's been since "we did this," and that's a chapter. Then you realize "we" is not even "we" anymore. That "we" haven't seen one another for years, and that's a book.

Then one day you come home from a wedding or a funeral or a graduation and sit down and begin to count the chapters, and you worry about how many more chapters there might be.

This is when you begin to cherish the ones you remember and savor the ones you still have. And all the things that were dear to you become dearer, and all the things you hated—you forget. Everyone in your past was your friend and all your enemies were comical villains and all your girlfriends were beautiful and all your fights were KOs and then the phone rings and it's for somebody else, and that's life!

Everyone at school started talking about The Prom by February, three months before it was to be. Who are you going to take? What are you going to wear? Where are you going to eat before the dance? Where will you go after the dance? Questions were running rampant and answers were running scarce. Some of the answers were assumed and foregone conclusions. Billy and Patsy were going together. Sue Jane and I were going together. The girls would wear strapless, pastel gowns with crinolines and Billy and I would wear white dinner jackets rented from the Men's Shoppe. (Billy threatened to rent a baby blue tuxedo but chickened out.) Before the dance we would eat at the Hearth Steak House and after the dance we would go to Sue Jane's house at one a.m. and have a record party the rest of the night. Other people weren't quite so sure. Toby wanted to go but didn't have a date by May eleventh and the dance was the eighteenth. Billy and I tried to help him be prepared for any situation.

"Just order a dinner jacket and pants and all and then they'll be there if you get a date," Billy advised him.

"But what if I don't? I still have to pay for it?"

"Well, yes," I said hesitantly, "but we'll do something. I'll call them and tell them you have strep throat and you're sick in bed. I'll wait and call just hours before the prom. Certainly, they won't have the nerve to charge you if you're sick."

"How much does it cost for one night?" Toby was considering it.

"Fifteen dollars and fifty cents. Thirteen dollars if you wear your own shoes." I had my order receipt in my billfold, so I knew what I was talking about.

"Man, that's a lot of money if they should make me pay for it and I can't use it."

"Yeah, but think how you'll feel if you don't have one and Maxine Hodge calls at the last minute and wants you to take her," Billy joked.

"Sure," Toby laughed. "The whole football team would have to have strep throat before Maxine Hodge got around to callin' me. I don't know, guys."

"Just order the coat and pants. The shirt and tie come with it. And the cummerbund." I was pushing.

"Is that the belt?"

"Yeah. And you can get by wearing your own black shoes. I mean, you're only a senior once. I hope. And this could be the big night. Do it!"

"Okay. Thirteen dollars. Do they have to measure me?"

"Well, yeah. Old man Seigel will measure you."

"I don't want that old man feelin' around on me now. I don't like him and he don't like me. He's run me out of there before when I was just walkin' around lookin' at clothes."

"He'll do that, but he's real nice when you're buyin' somethin'. Or rentin' somethin'. Billy and I will go with you."

"When?"

"It had better be right now," Billy popped in. "That's the only store in town that rents formal wear."

"All right, but if he tries to run me out of there again…"

"He's not goin' to run you out. We're goin' with you."

Piano Days

The Men's Shoppe was on Main Street, the same place it had been since two weeks after World War I ended. Cyrus Seigel, then a young man, had come from...New York? New Jersey? The Old Country? No one knew where exactly. But he had come with his bride and set up shop above a dress store owned by his...cousin? Brother? Brother-in-law? No one knew who exactly. He tailored and altered suits. When his relative down below died during the Depression, he took over the whole store and had been a fixture in the center of town ever since.

Old Cyrus had sold at least one suit to every man in town. He fitted me and sold me my first one when I was twelve years old. He had not kept up with the fashions as he should have, so members of the younger crowd weren't regulars. But whenever you were shopping for a sweater or jacket for someone at Christmas or looking for a dress shirt for yourself, you always had to look at the Men's Shoppe or you didn't feel you had searched thoroughly enough. Cyrus was white-haired and five-foot-three in full dress. His wife, Mrs. Seigel—and I defy anyone in town, young or old, then or now, to come up with her first name because she was Mrs. Seigel to everyone—would sit in the back of the store at a sewing machine and do alterations and talk out loud to herself. She was about two inches shorter than Cyrus, I think, as I only remember seeing her standing up once. She was standing at the front window watching it snow one day when I drove down Main Street. I assumed it was her, as I could only see a thatch of gray hair and a pair of glasses peeping over the window display. She may have been sitting or she may have been standing on something. Or it may have been a mop leaning against the wall. I really don't know and it really doesn't matter. She was short and about six degrees nuttier than old Cyrus. This is what mattered.

Spring/Summer 1962

The three of us walked in the Men's Shoppe after school and Mr. Seigel met us halfway down the aisle. He recognized me. "If you're comin' in after those cussed dinner clothes, I've told you I don't know how many times, they won't be here till the seventeenth."

"Yes sir, I know. And no sir, that's not why we're here."

"What you want, then?" He was such a sweet guy.

"My friend here wants to rent the same thing I got." I pointed to Toby, who was gritting his teeth and glaring down at the old man.

He looked up at Toby and said in his usual tone, "What you want formals for?"

"For the prom," Toby said politely.

Old Seigel grinned or sneered or something and asked confidentially, "You got a date?"

"Yes sir," Toby lied obediently.

"No, you don't," Cyrus Seigel said and then turned and walked to the back of the store.

We looked at one another and shared the silent question of "what do we do now?" I started toward the back where the counter and cash register were. "Mr. Seigel, he really would like to rent a dinner jacket."

Cyrus, from World War I, stood near a big roll of white, coarse wrapping paper at the end of the counter. He put his hand on it and smoothed out some wrinkles and looked up at me and said, "Listen, Frank's boy." He knew my daddy through the years and knew me to be Frank's boy and that's all he ever called me. "I didn't fall off the last freight through town. Does that fat boy have a date? Look at me. Does he have a date? Or is he placin' the order just in case? Do you hear me, mamma?" He was talking to his wife now. "Do you think the fat boy has a date, mamma? Be true now. Look at me, boy."

He was talking to me again.

Mamma kept sewing and I kept thinking. Do I lie now or lie later? I did offer to call with the strep throat story so the burden was mine. But how did he know? What made him think Toby didn't have a date? Was the old codger psychic like Madam Tiara, or had he been burnt before, maybe by other guys in other years who had tried to pull the same thing? But even so, how did he know for sure? No matter, it was my move. I turned and looked at Billy and Toby still standing at the front of the store and then back at ole Cyrus.

"It doesn't really matter, Mr. Seigel. You don't need a date this year to go to the prom. So it really don't matter."

"What's the boy's name?" he asked quietly.

"Toby. Toby Painter."

"TOBY!" the old man yelled. "Toby, come here."

Toby and Billy ambled through the store and stopped at the counter.

"Turn around, Toby. Turn all the way around, for criminy sake. Don't you know nothin'?"

Toby obliged, reluctantly.

We could hear Mrs. Seigel talking to her sewing machine but couldn't understand a word she was saying. Every time the foot pedal would stop you could hear her mumble, and then the roar and the squeak would drown her out again.

"Hold your arms out, Toby. How big's your neck?"

"I don't know."

"How big's your waist?"

"I don't know."

"You really don't know nothin', do you Toby?" The old man grinned for sure this time. He was having fun now. "I tell you what I'm gonna do. I'm gonna have you a nice suit here, Toby. Nice formal suit of clothes. The seventeenth. Three o'clock. You give me half now, I'll take a chance on you, Toby."

"Now?" I interrupted.

"Now." He looked at Toby. "Six-fifty. What you think, mamma?"

Mamma didn't think jack! She just kept sewing and talking. Toby reached in his pocket and handed Cyrus seven one-dollar bills. Cyrus rang it up and gave him back a fifty-cent piece.

"You gonna measure me?" Toby asked.

"Naw. I can tell what you need by just lookin'."

We walked the long center aisle to the front door. Ole Cyrus was only a few steps behind. He called to me just as Billy and Toby were going out the door.

"Frank's boy!"

I went back and waited for what he had to say.

"Frank's boy, hate me if I was wrong. But don't hate me if you came in here to stick me. That freight train ain't stopped here in years."

"The seventeenth. Three o'clock." It was all I could think to say.

By Monday morning, just four days before The Prom, the school was abuzz with news and speculation and misinformation about what all was taking place Friday night. Who was going with whom? Who didn't have a date yet? Where were the after-prom parties, and what was going to happen at them? Without competition, I would have to give the blue-ribbon award for Best Original Story to the one floating around about Maxine Hodge.

Maxine had gone quietly through the first year of high

school with us, basically unnoticed. She was a not-ugly girl but wasn't someone you had dreams about, either. She was quiet and pleasant and an above-average student and was clean and rather straight in body and mind. It wasn't until the fall that began our sophomore year that anyone noticed Maxine at all. Something had happened to her during the summer because when school opened that September, so did Maxine. Like a thirsty rose drinking in the sunshine. Her nonexistent breasts were now bulging and threatening her summer tops, and her bottom was threatening just about everyone in sight. She had, in the three short months since school let out, become a full-blown woman. Her face was prettier, her hair was longer, and her attitude was more aggressive. She was a different person and nobody minded one bit. Maxine seemed as pleasantly puzzled by her metamorphosis as everyone else. She struggled a little with it but then made a drastic decision in dealing with it. For the first time in her life, boys were pursuing her and she loved it. Unlike little girls with long curls and pug noses and fluttering eyes who, at six years old and in the first grade, know how to handle the boys by the second grade, beauty came on Maxine late and all of a sudden. She had no time to prepare for it or learn about it. One day she was the ugly duckling and the next she was the swan. And all the gander and wild ducks wanted her attention. They wanted to talk to her. Make her laugh. Touch her and make her cry. Take her to ballgames and dances and drive-ins and hilltops. And she wanted to go because she had never been before. And Maxine went, and a good time was had by all.

 The story went that in those last three years of high school, she had dated seven guys off the football team, four of the five starters on the basketball team, and the first and second basemen and the center fielder on the baseball team. Maxine really loved sports. The joke was she had played the back field, the infield, and the outfield. And the truth lay somewhere among the exaggerations, as it always does. Coach Denny from Welton High said of our poorly performing football team after beating us 36–0, "Maxine Hodge is the best athlete on their squad." So Maxine's fame was widespread, and her intentions for the junior/senior prom of 1962 were no less infamous. In all the gossip of who was coming with whom, the word was that "The Hodge" would be coming with Charlie Tillman of the football team *and* Cecil Doyle of the wrestling team. Maxine seemed proud, the boys seemed pleased, and I couldn't wait to see them dance.

Toby's fate for the big night was not as well planned. It was Tuesday afternoon and he still didn't have a date. He was getting worried. Not about the date but about the thirteen dollars.

"He's gonna make me pay it, ain't he?"

"Yeah, Toby, you might as well know the truth. He's gonna make you pay it." Billy was getting tired of playing with him and humoring him.

They were sitting in a booth at the Burger Barn, just a few doors up from the Men's Shoppe, sipping Cokes. For decades, this had been an after-school hangout for students at Jackson High. When we were in grade school, our school bus used to go past there every afternoon at three thirty and the little restaurant and sidewalk in front of it would be overflowing with high school kids. It looked so good to us out the bus window, so inviting, and we couldn't wait till we were old enough to go there after school every afternoon and drink Cokes and eat hamburgers and sit with girls and talk loud to other guys. There was a breakfast and lunch crowd of business men and women six days a week, but by the time school let out each weekday, it was all high school all the time. School banners and school colors draped the walls, and a large jukebox in the front corner played the hits of the day, one nickel at a time, while white bucks and saddle oxfords danced by the booths and between the tiny tables. Billy and Toby were there that Tuesday when Sue Jane and I found them.

"I might as well take him the rest of the money right now," Toby was saying as Sue Jane slid in the booth beside him and I slid in beside Billy.

"Hold your money, pal. Mighty Mouse is here. Tell him, Sue Jane." All eyes were on Sue Jane and her attention was all on Toby.

"Well, Toby, if you're still open for Friday night (she was so diplomatic), I know someone who would sure like to go to the prom with you. (And so sweet.) I know it's late and she'll certainly understand if you say no, but if you decide to take her, I just know you two will have a ball together." (This girl was good!)

"Who is it?" Toby asked, wasting no time.

"Do you remember Alice Lutz? She went through the sixth grade with us and then her mother and father sent her to a private girls' school up north."

"I remember her," Billy said. "Short girl, black hair, and she used to wear penny loafers with quarters in them."

"That's her," Sue Jane said excitedly, as if it were Billy she was getting the date for instead of Toby.

"She was in our room in the third grade for sure and maybe the fifth," I added, trying to encourage the situation.

"I don't remember her," Toby said honestly.

"Yes, you do," Billy insisted. "She always sat in the front and was the one who took names whenever Miss Markle left the room." We laughed while Toby just made a face.

"I still don't remember," he said. "But anyway, what's the story?"

"That's it," Sue Jane shrugged. "She just graduated from her school up there last week and she's home now. I see her every summer. We're not real close, but we always see one another or talk on the phone when she's home. And anyway, she'd just like to see everybody again. She'll know everybody there, practically. It'll sort of be like her prom, too, even though she hasn't been a part of the class since the sixth grade. Still, it'll be fun and she wants to do it."

"Does she want to go with me?"

Here's where Sue Jane's true sweetness and charm shone brightest.

"Do you want to go with *her*? That's the question, Toby. This is *your* choice." (Son of a gun, she was smarter than all of us!)

"Is she pretty?" Toby was serious now.

If Sue Jane had come back with one of those stock answers about Alice's personality and about how cute she was and how much fun she was, she would have lost him right there. But she never skipped a beat.

"Yes, she's pretty. Do you want to call her or do you want me to?"

"I'll call her. And thanks, Sue Jane," Toby said shyly. "You're a real friend."

Billy looked at her and winked his approval. I just looked at her. She could make my heart melt clear across a room.

Our little town didn't lack for a lot of things. We were small but we had all the stores we needed. Service stations. A couple of factories. Three theaters. Policemen. Old families. New families. Restaurants. A golf course. Lots of churches and schools. And even town characters. Looking back, I'd wager we even had more per capita than other towns our size. There was Tinsel Talley who had walked the streets and hitchhiked the local highways long before I can even remember. He shuffled along and talked to everyone he met. People took care of him with handouts and the kids all loved him, though some made fun of him behind his back. When I was old enough to realize Tinsel was mentally inefficient, I felt terrible about the amusement people had at his expense. I always made a point never to laugh at anything anyone said about him and even defended him a couple of times to other guys who couldn't understand why I was so sensitive about it. I guess I felt I had to be sensitive for Tinsel Talley because he wasn't able to be sensitive for himself.

And then there was Alto May. She was old and tall and built like a piece of string. She wore bright-colored scarves—purples, reds, and greens—around her head and two winter coats, simultaneously, year-round. She carried a shopping bag with her as surely and as constantly as if it were growing out of her arm. No one had ever seen her without a brown Baysinger's shopping bag hung over her left wrist. The legend was that Mr. Baysinger, who owned one of the two department stores in town, kept her supplied with bags and gave her money to live on. Rumor was she was his mother, his aunt, his ex-lover, his former Bible teacher, or an employee he'd fired thirty years prior for embezzling. Again, the truth may lie somewhere in between or thereabouts, but not necessarily. We just knew her as a crazy old lady who walked the streets as incessantly as the Pilgrim prayed, grunting to herself, picking up pieces of paper off the sidewalk, and staring at children as if they all were going to steal something from her. And all us kids firmly believed she carried a silver-handled pistol in one of those coat pockets. Some even swore they had seen it when the sun caught it as she stuffed more paper scraps in her clothes. I will not be the one to swear to any of this.

However, I can affirm to a personal contact with two of the most famous and lovable characters we were privileged to have among our citizenry—two middle-aged men with no known first names. If they had a family name, we didn't know that either. If they were brothers, that was never known. All anyone knew about them was that they were always together, one riding a bicycle and the other one walking beside him. And they were simply known as Spotlight and Speedy. The merchants in town took care of them by giving them money and clothes; the restaurants gave them food; and it's said a realty company provided them free shelter, but I never knew where.

Spotlight rode the bike and wore a captain's cap and raincoat while Speedy, in dress hat, tie, and a pencil-thin Clark Gable mustache, walked beside him every mile and year of the way. It never varied. Speedy never rode and Spotlight never walked. They made some income on their own by working gardens in the summer and firing furnaces for merchants and churches in the winter. It was often said they probably had a key to every store in town. They were honest, hard-working, and silent. I don't think I ever heard them speak a word to each other or anyone else. They were town characters only because of their unusual lifestyle, their unordinary mode of travel, and because they were simply, always there. I remember once when I was ten years old, I had walked my bike with a flat tire to the Esso station on the corner, bought a patch, and was wrestling with putting it on behind the two-bay garage. I was having no more luck then as I would probably have now, as I am not very handy around any kind of vehicle. I remember getting frustrated, cussing and kicking a stack of tires because I couldn't get the patch to hold. Suddenly, I felt someone standing behind me and I turned in all confidence that it was Mr. Shull, who owned the station. But it was Spotlight. I froze. I didn't know whether to be scared or thankful. I had no reason to be frightened of him except that he was so big and quiet and intimidating. In seconds, between scared and thankful, I settled on scared. And just as my decision was made, out of the corner of my eye I saw someone come around the corner of the garage. It was Speedy and he was opening a new pack of Phillip Morris as he walked. He stopped beside his cohort and just stood there and lighted one up. At this, Spotlight leaned down and, in about three fluid moves and thirty intense seconds, picked the bike up, patched the tire, rimmed it, and put the air hose to it.

When he finished, he just turned, got on his bike, and rode away. My mouth was already hanging open so it took little effort for me to yell after him, "Thanks! Thank you, Mr. Spot…Thank you, sir." But he was gone down the street with Speedy beside him and I don't think he ever heard me. Speedy never broke his gait, but he could walk as fast as Spotlight could pedal. And they were never one without the other.

My, how I miss the things I didn't even think I noticed.

"Did you call her?" I asked as we walked to first period Wednesday morning.

"Not yet. I'll call her tonight."

"Tonight will be just two days away. Why haven't you called her?"

"I'm gonna. I'm gonna," Toby said, slightly agitated at me. "She's already said she wants to go, ain't she? So what's the big deal?"

I stopped in the middle of the hall and people stumbled into us and around us. Toby stopped a couple of steps ahead and turned around. "What's wrong?" he asked.

"What's wrong with you?" I demanded. "What're you scared of? Why haven't you called her or let Sue Jane call her like she offered?"

Toby looked at the floor and then at the ceiling. "I don't know. What if she's...you know. What if she looks like Zelda on *Dobie Gillis*?"

"What if she looks like Maynard?" I reasoned. "It's better than blowin' thirteen bucks for nothin'. And anyway, I think Zelda is kinda cute."

"Okay," he agreed. "I'll call her tonight. But if she's got a goatee, I'm not gonna kiss her."

Wednesday night Alice Lutz was not at home. Toby was at my house until eleven p.m. and he tried every fifteen minutes. So, Thursday after school at three p.m., our white dinner jackets and black pants with the satin stripe down the legs and the stiff white shirts with French cuffs and skinny black bowties and black cummerbunds and black patent leather shoes (for Billy and me) were waiting for us. And Toby, just as Cyrus Seigel had predicted, had no date.

"What should I do? Should I get the suit or not?"

"You've already paid for half of it," Billy said.

"Yeah, but if I go in there today, it's gonna be six-fifty more and I may never use it."

"And if you don't go in there today and get it, you might find her tonight and she'll say, 'Sure. I'd love to go with you, Toby,' and then you're up the creek with no paddle." Billy had a good argument, but it was Toby's money.

"I could always come tomorrow and get it after I try to

find her tonight."

"No. I've got a better idea." I was driving and the driver's ideas always had precedence over the passengers' ideas. "Let's stop at the Burger Barn before we go to the Men's Shoppe, and you try her from the phone booth there. You might get lucky."

We did and he did and *everybody* was happy. We were merrily marching down the street toward our first formals. We all three had girls for tomorrow night and less than three weeks till graduation. Life could never be better than this.

"She said she remembered me and she really sounded excited about going." Toby was almost skipping.

"You'll probably remember her when you see her," Billy said.

"But I still wonder if she's pretty."

"Sue Jane said she was," I reminded him.

"Yeah, but girls don't think about what's pretty the way guys do. What a girl thinks is pretty in another girl usually just means…clean."

Billy and I were still laughing at this when we reached Seigel's front door. Toby could always say best what was on other people's minds.

Old Seigel was at the counter at the back of the store. He started talking as soon as we pushed open the heavy glass door. "Look, mamma. It's the three dummkopfs. And close the door, for the sake of Moses. It's not cows livin' in here. It's people."

"We're here to pick up our suits," I said, ignoring the insults.

"Suits! They're not suits. They're formals. You can't go to a dance in a suit. You wear a suit to funerals. Don't you know suits from formals? Mamma, they want their suits."

Mamma quit sewing and looked straight at me and said something that sounded like "that big ole truck what clean the streets are too loud." Then she resumed pumping and the roar of the Singer relegated her speech to a mere mumble again. Cyrus reached under the counter and pulled up three hanging bags of clothes. They were tagged with our individual names and neatly waiting on us.

"Who are the three lucky girls?" he asked, almost sounding genuinely interested.

"Well...," I started to answer.

"The three that turned you down. That's the three lucky ones." And then he laughed really big. He was enjoying his joke. "Did you hear that, mamma? The three that turned them down?" Mamma just pedaled on, and occasionally you could hear her still mumbling something about that truck.

We paid our money, my $15.50, Billy's $15.50 and Toby's $6.50. "Hey, you little dummkopfs," Cyrus hollered just as we got to the door to leave. "You have those back here by noon Saturday. And you bring 'em yourself. I don't want no mammas bringin' them in here or no sisters or daddies. You bring them in here yourself and I inspect 'em before you leave the store. You remember they're rentals, so I don't want no liquor spilled on them or no vomit down the front. They're not your clothes. Noon. I got to mail 'em out by three or they charge me another day."

It was unlike Toby not to reply to Mr. Seigel's rudeness, but I guess he was in such a glee it just didn't matter. We laughed all the way home. The "Three Dummkopfs" in search of life.

"Toby wants to go with one of us tonight," Billy said on the phone Friday afternoon.

"I'll take them. I don't mind."

"I don't either. I think he's kind of nervous about Alice and he wants one of us around."

"I'm closer," I said. "Why don't I pick him up, then Sue Jane, then Alice, and we'll meet you and Patsy at the Hearth? From there we can all go to the prom together."

And that's exactly how it happened. Right up till the last second Toby was still grilling Sue Jane for everything she knew about Alice, which wasn't much more than she had told him. Just as he was opening the car door to go up the walk to her house, he said, "Tell me one more time. Is she pretty?"

"If she's not," Sue Jane replied, "I'll dance every dance tonight with you myself."

But she only danced once with him out of friendship, because what he came back down the walk with was a dream in a pink strapless gown. She was short, as Billy remembered, with black hair that curled around her ears toward her face and the most hypnotizing set of white teeth in teenage captivity. Her smile was so big she could hardly close her lips over it. Her skin was dark and her eyes were so brown they looked black. She talked and said all the right things and laughed at all the right places and listened when other people talked and spread her attention around like a Washington socialite. The girls all loved her and we loved her and all the teachers at the dance loved her. She was the hit of the prom: hometown girl comes back from the big city. Ole Toby finally had himself a real girlfriend.

We ate at the Hearth and then headed for the gym and made our entrance and pretty much *promed* as we had expected. The big talk was whether Maxine had arrived yet with her multiple dates. Some thought it was just a gag, but we were there to see her make good on her promise. The doors flung open about eight thirty, after everyone else had arrived, and she came through them in a bright green, floor-length gown, with

Spring/Summer 1962

Charlie Tilman on one arm and Cecil Doyle on the other. They were all three grinning, just waiting for the flashbulbs to start popping. They sat at a table next to ours and she danced the first one with Charlie, the second one with Cecil, and the rest with a different guy every time. The boys were lining up and smiling while the girls were lining the walls and boiling. We watched it all from our front row seats and were thoroughly entertained by the sideshow atmosphere. Alice and Sue Jane teased Toby and me about taking our turns with her, but when they teased Billy, Patsy began to pout. So we happily danced with the ones we brought and took home the ones we danced with. And the junior/senior prom of 1962 was soon a beautiful memory.

On the way to Sue Jane's house, we talked about the night and the people, but mostly about graduation. That was the next big event. Alice had already had hers in Connecticut and told us stories about it and how it felt to have it all behind her. "You feel like a different person. I mean, you think about all those years of having to get up and be at school and homework and now, it's just, I mean, like a load lifted off you."

"That's what I'm gonna do," Toby said. "The day after graduation, I'm gonna sleep till four o'clock."

"I wish I could," Sue Jane said over the back of the front seat, "but I've got to be at work at nine o'clock. I've got a job this summer at Baysinger's."

"Seventeen more days," I said, driving and counting on my fingers. "I've been waiting on that day since the first grade."

We were pulling into Sue Jane's driveway and Billy and Patsy were behind us. It was nearly one a.m. and a few other couples were also starting to arrive. The Wimers had the house decorated for the after-prom party and were in their bedroom. The house was ours, and we were looking forward to this as much as we had the prom itself. We took off our coats and ties and shoes and danced to "What's Your Name?" and "Soldier Boy" and "I Can't Stop Loving You" and "Wonderland by Night" and dozens more I can hardly stand to listen to today. My ears want to but my heart can't take it. We ate and laughed and talked about life after graduation and what we were going to do that summer and then danced some more. It was about two fifteen when Toby pulled me off to a corner in the living room.

"Can I have your car keys? Alice has to go home."

"Already?" I questioned. We all had planned to stay till three.

"Yeah," Toby said, not too convincingly. "She has to be in. I'll take her home and then come back and get you."

"Okay," I said and handed him my keys.

We all said our good nights to Alice, they left, and the party continued. In no time it became three o'clock and couples started to leave before anyone mentioned anything else about Toby. "Where's lover boy and your car?" Billy asked as he was putting on his coat.

"I don't know. I figured he'd be back here by now."

Then it became three thirty, and Billy was still waiting to see if my car was coming and if I would have a way home. "Should we call?" Sue Jane asked.

"Who are we gonna call?" I asked back. "We can't call Alice's house at three thirty in the morning. Something must have happened."

"I've got to take Patsy home. Ride with me and we'll go by Alice's house and see if we can find them," Billy offered.

"As sure as I do that, he'll show up here while I'm gone. You take Patsy home and go look for him. I'll stay here in case he comes back before you do."

"Yes, whatever you do, take Patsy home first." This was Patsy talking. I couldn't tell if she was being sarcastic or bored. But then I always had trouble deciphering Patsy's true emotions.

By four o'clock, Sue Jane was getting nervous and I was getting scared. Her mom had come out once to gently inquire as to why I was still there. I stood at the picture window in their living room and watched the road for my car lights. I played all the old waiting games inside my head. *He just turned onto Kelton Drive at the stoplight. He's coming up over the hill by the grade school. He's turning at the bottom of the hill onto Princeton Street. He's coming down by Larry Harley's house and rounding the bend and I should see the car lights right...now!* But I didn't. I played that game half a dozen times. Sue Jane suggested calling the police. I was just about to ask to borrow her dad's station wagon to go look for Toby. Then I saw lights.

"Is that him?" Sue Jane asked over my shoulder.

"Naw. That's Billy, though. I can tell by the headlights. But maybe he knows somethin'."

He didn't. So I kissed Sue Jane good night and told her if Toby showed up to send him on to my house. We left and rode around until nearly five a.m. looking for Toby, my car, and his girlfriend. I ranged everything from anger to worry to panic and back to anger again. I think I had settled pretty well into anger by the time we called it a night and went home. Billy spent what was left of it with me and it must have been almost six when I heard something at my bedroom window. It was little pebbles hitting the panes ever so lightly. Billy and I both sat up in the slowly fading dark and I went across the room, opened the curtains, and raised the window. It was Toby standing in the yard. I half whispered for him to come to the back door. I let him in and we tiptoed through the house and back up to my room. His pant legs were muddy to his knees. His face defied description, but I'll try. Toby's brow showed worry but his mouth was grinning. His eyelids sagged from the lack of sleep but his eyes twinkled with excitement. His clothes were torn and grimy but he smelled of sweet perfume clear across the room. His appearance was as mixed as my emotions. And his story was as good as anything I'd ever heard before or since.

"Okay. Okay. I'm sorry. I know you're mad at me but I couldn't help it. I got back as fast as I could."

"Got back? Got back from where? Where have you been?" I demanded as Billy got up and turned the lamp on. We both sat on the bed while Toby sat on my desk chair and wiped the mud off his Sunday shoes and told us his story.

"Alice and I left the party and, well, she really didn't have to go home like I said she did. We were dancin' over there in the corner and things started gettin' hot, you know, and she wanted to leave. Well, I didn't want to come and tell you that Alice and I wanted your car to go park in, so I just said she had to go home. Anyway, we left and rode around for a few minutes and then rode out toward the Knoll. I didn't want to bring it up on the first date and all and I didn't have to. She brought it up. She asked if it was still up there and I said yeah, I guessed it was, and she said she had always wanted to go up there and so up we went."

Toby's grin began to grow at this point in the story.

"We hadn't hardly stopped till she was all over me. I mean, it was like she was some kind of wild woman or somethin'. She took my tie off of me and my coat and was all over me, guys. I'm tellin' you, she is somethin'."

Billy and I looked at one another and didn't even try to

conceal our amusement. Billy beat me to the question. "So?"

"I think I'm in love!" Toby yelled at the top of his voice, with his arms outstretched and his fists raised toward the ceiling.

"Shh," Billy and I both hushed him.

"You'll wake up the whole house," I warned.

Things gradually got back down to a giggle and a grin and Toby continued.

"I know this suit looks pretty bad?" Toby pointed to the inseam of his rented tuxedo trousers. "Ripped my pants at a couple different places. I'm tellin' you, guys, what a night!"

"What about the mud all over you?" I finally asked. "You didn't get out and roll in a puddle, did you?"

"Aw, no." Toby's face went solemn. "That's where all the trouble started. When we got ready to leave, you know, I went to start the car and the darn thing wouldn't fire."

"What!" This was me.

"It's okay. It's okay. Don't get excited. Everything is all right now, but the engine wouldn't turn over."

"Where is it now?" I asked, getting up to look out the window.

"It's all right, I told you. It's in front of your house. Everything's fine. But at the time it wasn't. So there we sat on top of the Knoll at three o'clock in the morning or somethin' like that, and nobody else up there and no car and the only way down was walk."

"You walked all the way down from the Knoll?" Billy asked in amazement.

"Both of us," Toby said, shaking his head. "And her in high heels and that gown and me in this monkey suit. And it was dark and mud puddles everywhere. It must be a mile and a half down that Knoll and brush and rock and all in that old dirt road. It was terrible."

"Go ahead," Billy urged.

"Okay. It was terrible. But finally, we made it down and got to the main highway. Then she said, Alice said, 'What are we gonna do now that we're down?' 'Cause there we stood, all scratched and muddy and my pants tore at every seam, standing along the highway in the middle of the night. Not a car in sight. Not one. Three thirty, four o'clock in the morning. And I was tired and she was pretty, even with her hair messed up and her dress all wrinkled and dirty, and I kissed her right there on the side of the road. And if I hadn't thought a car might come by, oh, man, she is somethin'. But then on the other hand, I *wanted* a car to come by, you know what I mean? But man, at three thirty, four o'clock in the morning, there just ain't much traffic."

"So what did you do?" Billy pushed him. We were both getting into this story, and I in particular wanted to get back to what happened to my car.

"Well, we were standing there on the side of the road, lookin' for headlights, when we heard somethin' comin' down the other side of the road. We couldn't see anything, but we heard somethin' and I couldn't tell what it was till it got right on us. And there, and I ain't lyin', guys, at three thirty, four o'clock in the morning, was Spotlight and Speedy. I couldn't believe what I was seein'. I started wavin' my arms and yellin' for them, and they stopped and I told them what had happened and that I couldn't get my car started. Excuse me, *your* car started"—Toby nodded toward me—"and that I needed to borrow their bicycle to go get help. With no questions asked, Spotlight just got off of it and leaned it toward me and went over and laid down in the grass on the bank, and Speedy went over and sat down beside him and smoked. Well, I didn't want to leave Alice out there sittin' on the side of the road with them in the middle of the night, so she and I got on the bike and headed for the Shell station. It was the only thing I could think of that was open all night. And here we come pullin' in the Shell station, me with a dinner jacket on and her with an evening gown, sittin' on the cross bar, both of us ridin' a bicycle."

We had held it long enough. It was time for a break, and we broke and laughed for at least ten minutes without stopping. I wanted to hear more, but what was the rush? We had all summer.

"Why didn't you call us from the Shell station?"

"At four o'clock in the morning? I was afraid to call Sue Jane's house at that time. I thought you might be gone and I'd wake everybody up. So we just told this old guy who was workin' there, if you wanna call it workin'. He was sittin' on a case of Quaker State oil readin' an *Adam* magazine, or lookin' at the pictures, I guess, and he never even got up when we told him what had happened. He said"—and Toby changed his voice when he quoted the Shell station man the way people do when they're telling a story about someone they don't particularly care for—"'I can't do you no good tonight. I'm here by myself and I don't get no help till seven o'clock. Maybe then when Nick comes in, he can go up there with you and see if he can jump it.' I wanted to slap him upside the head and say 'Jump this, Mack,' but I figured I'd better be nice to him. He was the only thing open. So anyway, we begged him to call Nick or somebody but he wouldn't. And then a pickup truck pulled in to the pumps with two old men in it, and when they got out to get some gas, I saw one of them was Wyler Pratt, my mailman."

"In the middle of the night?"

"They were goin' somewhere to pick apples or somethin',"

Toby continued, "and he asked me what I was doin' out at this hour and, I mean, what choice did I have. I told him. I had to. I told him we'd been to the prom and then we rode up to the Knoll to look at the view of the town from up there and my car wouldn't start and could he help me. He didn't say anything for a while. He just finished checkin' his oil while the man there at the station filled him up with gas. I figured maybe he hadn't heard, you know, hard of hearin' and all. But when he got through and paid the Shell man, he said, 'Hop in the back. We'll ride up there and take a look at it.' So here we go again, Alice and me all dressed up and this time ridin' in the back of a pickup. By this time, it had quit being all that funny and I was wishin' I was home in bed."

By this time, it had not quit being funny to Billy and me. As a matter of fact, it was getting better by the minute. We took another little break from the suspense and laughed for another ten minutes into our pillows.

"Well, he jumped it as soon as we got up there and it started right up. I thanked him and offered to pay him and he just shook his head and rolled up his jumper cables and stuffed them behind the seat in the cab of his truck. Alice had already gotten in the car 'cause it was gettin' cold up there. I stood at the back of the car, kinda hunched over to keep warm, and said thank you to him again while he was gettin' in his truck. He stood there for a few minutes and just looked all around like he was lookin' for somethin' in the top of the trees. Kept lookin' around real weird like. And then he said, 'Toby, you still readin' your Bible?' I said, 'Yes sir' and then I tried to change the subject really quick so I pointed to the car, and just to make conversation I said, 'It sounds like it's missin' a little under the hood.' And he said, 'Aw, no, son. Not in these woods. Not with your girlfriend in the car.'" Toby paused here for us to quit laughing again. "He looked all around one more time and said, 'I ain't been up here for years. Ain't much changed though 'cept the trees are taller. Road's just as rough and there's a few more lights down below. But it's still just as good as it was 'fore the war.'

"He got in his truck, pulled the door shut and started the engine, then looked out the window and said to me, 'You don't remember the war, do you, Toby?' I said, 'No sir, I don't.' And then he just pulled off and I got in the car and took Alice home."

"What about Spotlight and Speedy?" Billy asked.

"Oh, yeah." Toby laughed. "I forgot about them and I sort of forgot about them at the time, too. We were just comin' down the dirt road and gettin' ready to pull out on the highway when I saw Speedy in my headlights. He was standin' right in front of the car. Alice said, 'Oh, no, Toby! We forgot those two men. Where's their bicycle?' I told her it was still at the station and then I rolled down the window and asked Speedy where Spotlight was and he sort of motioned over in the weeds with his cigarette. I told him to come on and get in the car and I'd take 'im to the Shell station to get his bike. He disappeared in the dark for just a few seconds and then here he come with Spotlight behind him and they climbed in the backseat and away we went. Of course, Alice tried to talk to them and thank them for the bicycle and she rambled on and on and they ain't said nothin' yet. Not one word. We got to the station, they got out and got on their bike, Spotlight did, and Speedy took off down the street walkin' and they were gone. Then I took Alice home and here I am."

And there we were. The Three Dummkopfs at dawn. Wide awake and hungry. So we got up and dressed and by the time it was daylight, Daddy was awake. We told him we were going downtown to the Burger Barn to eat breakfast. It was so much fun to be young and irresponsible.

We were sitting in a booth eating pancakes. "What about your pants?" Billy asked Toby. "How are you gonna have them back to old man Seigel by noon lookin' like that?"

Toby looked at me. "Can your mom sew 'em up and maybe wash 'em?"

"Why my mom? What's wrong with yours?" I shot back.

"I don't really want to explain all this to my mother," Toby reasoned.

"And you think I wanna explain it to mine?"

But I did. Mom washed Toby's pants and shrunk them about two sizes. Then she sewed up all the rips she could that he had torn on Spotlight's bicycle while going to get jumper cables at the Shell station because my car had stalled on the Dairy Queen parking lot where he and Alice had stopped on the way home for a Coke. (That was the best I could come up with on quick notice.)

We were back at the Burger Barn at eleven forty-five, just a few doors away from the Men's Shoppe and certain and sure doom. Our three bags of rental clothes were hanging on the coat racks at the end of our booth, waiting to be returned and explained. Just who and how was still a topic of conversation.

"All three of us have to go in," I said. "He'll never notice the rips. She did a pretty good job of sewin' 'em up. And he can't tell they're shrunk."

"What about the smudges on the white coat we couldn't get off?" Toby asked. "Boy, he's gonna be hot about that."

"We have no choice," I said. "We gotta take the chance. We go in, keep him talkin', and get out fast."

"We've got seven minutes," Billy said. "He's probably standin' at the door waitin' on us."

"Let's go in and get it over with."

"Wait a minute," Toby stopped us. "When we lay 'em down on the counter, let me put mine down first. At least mine will be on the bottom, and if he looks at the first two, he might not take time to look at mine."

"That's it!" Billy nearly shouted.

"What?"

"What?"

"We wait outside till he has three or four customers in the store. We go in while he's busy and he won't have time to look at all three of them."

And that's exactly what the Brothers Dummkopf did. Two men looking and a man with his wife buying a suit was our signal to burst through the door at approximately twelve fifteen.

Cyrus was at the back of the store sticking pins in a man's armpit while the man held his hands over his head. He looked up and saw us clear the doorway and yelled, "You're fifteen minutes late, you little schnooks."

"Sorry, Mr. Seigel," I said, taking the lead. "We got held up in traffic."

"Yeah, sure. It's like 42nd Street out there." He waved me off impatiently and said, "Just put 'em on the counter and get outta here."

We obediently did as he commanded and left as quickly as possible. Mrs. Seigel was pumping and mumbling and ole Cyrus was saying something about "stupid kids today" to the couple he was selling the suit to. We walked out the door and then ran up the street and sang our praises to one another and patted our own backs. Then we went home and slept long and sweetly.

When I woke up, the house was dark except for the light from the TV set in the living room. Mom and Dad were watching *Perry Mason*, and she warmed up leftovers from supper for me, and I sprawled on the sofa and watched television with them and life was good.

We all passed our exams. We figured we would. We even wondered if anyone had ever gone right up to graduation and not passed a subject and found out the day before the commencement service that they were not going to be a part of the festivities. What a horrible situation that would be. I had never known of anyone, but Howard and Bud claimed they had an older cousin by about five years named Navie Arehart who didn't pass two exams and was called to the principal's office the very last day of school. At least Navie thought it was going to be the last day of school. He was told to turn his cap and gown back in and informed he would still be a senior next fall. Navie, being the size of most families of four, told the principal he wasn't turning them in, that if the principal wanted them, he could come to his house and get them. The principal, and this was not our principal or even our school, allegedly challenged Navie and refused to let him leave the office. Navie, already being an involuntary five-year student and having not much at all to lose, picked the principal up and threw him through the window. He landed on the hood of a '47 Plymouth and had to wear a back brace to baccalaureate service, and poor ole Navie was never heard from or seen by the senior class until his picture came out in the paper a few months later announcing that he had finished basic training and was reporting for duty at an Air Force base in Germany. If only our boy Navie had been a little more sensitive to the English language and joined the right branch, what a better all-around story this would have made. Navie is in the Navy would have had a nice ring to it.

"I got a D in Government."

"For the six weeks or on the exam?"

"For everything. D average for the whole year." To his credit or discredit, Toby seemed pleased enough.

"Well, that's passin' anyway."

"You don't hear me cryin', do you?"

"What'd you get in English?"

"C."

"Aw, you're in good shape. You got nothin' to worry about."

We got Toby through. His cap and gown were in the big flat box in the back seat of his car. He was ready for pomp and circumstance, having no idea what either was.

"Don't tell me," I challenged Billy. "You got straight A's in everything."

"No, not hardly," he said quietly and sort of self-consciously.

"What'd you get then?" I asked, knowing he wanted to tell me but never would if I didn't insist.

"One B. The rest were A's. You?"

"Two B's. The rest were A's."

We were sitting in the lunchroom for the last time. I wasn't eating. I was just looking around trying to see it all and take it all in someplace where I could keep it sealed up and the air couldn't touch it and spoil it and make it go away. I never thought I'd miss this old lunchroom. I'd hated the smell of it for four long years and now I was getting sentimental about it. I listened to the roar and tried for the first time in those four, now-gone years to decipher just what it was—that metallic din and constant indescribable noise that was always in the background and made you have to holler at the person sitting across the table from you. Voices, trays clanging, seats squeaking, footsteps on the tile floor, laughter, large spoons scraping metal trays, glasses breaking, and silverware being dropped in bins. I realized I may never hear all of this again, and a week ago I never thought I'd want to.

Howard and Bud joined us. They hadn't eaten lunch with us all this past year. All the more nostalgic that they should join us on the last day. But I could tell immediately they were sharing none of what I was feeling. To them, it was just another day and another lunch. Hot dogs, applesauce, and chocolate cake on a Friday.

"Did everybody pass?" Howard asked as he set his tray down and straddled the swingout stool. Not waiting for an answer, he continued, "Bud almost didn't."

"Aw, shut up," Bud chimed in. "I made it. That's all that matters."

"Hey," Howard said, leaning in toward the center of the table in a confidential hunch, "did you hear about Maxine?"

I rolled my eyes. "Not another Maxie Hodge dare. What's she gonna do now? Give the Admiral the bird when he hands her the diploma?"

"Hey, Admiral Byrd. I like that," Toby said, never looking up from his tray and never stopping eating.

"No, it's better than that." Howard grinned.

"She's gonna marry the track team at baccalaureate service Sunday afternoon," Billy guessed in jest.

"No," Howard teased. He looked directly at me and said, "Do you wanna guess again?"

Tired of the game, I said, "I don't know, Howard. Maybe she's goin' to strip in the parking lot graduation night or somethin'."

"Man, you're close," Bud said with a mouth full of cake.

"Yeah," Howard said. "The word is she's gonna come to graduation with nothin' on but her cap and gown. And knowin' Maxine, she's just liable to."

And so went the last day of school. The afternoon was spent in the gym rehearsing the weekend activities and walking through the final march in preparation for the real thing Monday night. All the seniors were in gleeful moods, talking to people they hadn't talked to their entire eleven years in school. (The eighth grade wouldn't be added until two years later.) Teachers joked with the problem students they had tried to ignore all these years and hugged their pets and wished them well. Pretty girls even joined in conversation with guys they had never looked at before, and the athletes came down from jock heaven and actually smiled and sometimes talked to some of their lessers. And, yes, Maxine Hodge was asked a number of times by a number of guys if what was going around was true. She just smiled and seductively said, "Que, Sera, Sera," courtesy of Doris Day.

After school, we all went to the Burger Barn and ate cheeseburgers and French fries and tried to hang on to something while letting it gently go. There was really nothing we could do to make the day more special than it had made itself. We laughed at things that weren't funny and made wide gestures and loud noises and acted our ages as if we knew we could never act them again. Of course, we didn't know. Not really. Someone put a nickel in the Wurlitzer and played "Roses Are Red," and I knew right then, for the first time, just how rough it was going to be. Billy and Patsy were in the booth behind us. Toby was across the table from me, Sue Jane was beside me, Bobby Vinton was writing in someone's yearbook on the jukebox, and my moods were changing faster than Superman's speeding bullet. Sue Jane looked me in the eye, squeezed my hand, and then whispered in my ear, "Let's go." And we did. We excused ourselves and said we'd see them all at the drive-in tonight and left. It was only four thirty in the bright, near summer afternoon, and we just drove, not directly, but eventually and deliberately to the top of the Knoll. And on the last day of school, we lay on the bank that overlooked our little town, the same bank generations had laid on, and looked at the white clouds and the swaying treetops that had grown taller with the years, and we kissed and clung to one another and loved one another.

We were happy in a way that we never were again.

Clothes come in style and then out and we all expect this. Coiffures change with the decades. Hair gets longer and skirts get shorter and vice versa, and automobile lines streamline and then round off. New inventions come on the market and new phrases sneak into our language. Change is accepted and rejected and grieved over. But what about the things that just go? They don't change into anything. They just disappear. These are the strangest.

I was born and grew up on the tail end of radio, but I remember some golden nights, lying on the floor in the near dark, the only light in the room being the green light from the dial of the floor model Crosley, and listening to "The Lone Ranger," "The Fat Man," and "Ozzie and Harriet." Radio mysteries are gone. Movie serials are gone. The fifteen chapters that were shown one a week before the Saturday morning double feature (double features are gone) that ended in a cliffhanger at the end of each episode are no more. Quicksand is gone. No kid today knows what quicksand is, and every kid when I was growing up feared it and thought there might be some down behind old man Tully's potato garden.

Gold teeth are gone. Out of style. They were weird but they had character and gave character. I wanted none for myself, but they were certainly an attention getter in their time. Goiters. You would see elderly women with goiters all the time. Thank God they are gone, and I guess that's due to medication and surgeries. But the fact remains that kids today wouldn't know a gold tooth from a goiter. Even flies are out of style. I guess, with air conditioning and windows being closed, flies just don't have as easy a life as they once did. A flyswatter is no longer a staple kitchen item, and you couldn't find a roll of flypaper if you were Vincent Price himself.

Pickup, backlot baseball games are gone. Organized little leagues took over and parents took all the fun out of the game. No more felt ball caps. Black tennis shoes. Those little paper cups that came to a point at the bottom and used to set in metal stands, and you were served Coke in them at a soda fountain. Sadie Hawkins Day. Shooting marbles in a dirt ring. The doctor coming to your house at night when someone was sick. The barber putting lather on the back of your neck and shaving you with a straight razor after you got a haircut. All gone. Never to return.

But of all the things that faded and left, the one passing I regret most is the ice cream truck. That small white van with the loud bell ringing would come down our street every Monday, Wednesday, and Friday evenings after supper between May 15 and September 1 without fail. And without fail, from the time I was four years old, I would run from the house or the backyard with a nickel in my hand. Sometimes I would stand up on the curb waiting for half an hour. Even as we got to be older kids, thirteen, fourteen, and on, we would wait till the smaller kids got theirs and then we'd get in line, too. I remember one summer night, Billy and Patsy and Sue Jane and I were riding around town and heard the bell as we passed through another neighborhood. We pulled over, laughing, and got out and stood behind the little boys and girls and bought ourselves some ice cream cones. It was fun till the end. But then the end did come.

It was in the paper that the ice cream man, we never knew his name, was retiring and selling his truck to a creamery chain and thereby discontinuing his route, his business, and an era. The last run, the newspaper article said, would be Monday, June 4. I remember reading it and thinking wouldn't it be great to buy a cone from him the last night ever. But I never thought about it again because I had more important and personal things to consider this particular week. I had to get ready for graduation and the big day was upon me.

The weight of what I had felt in the booth at the Burger Barn fell heavily on me an hour or so before graduation on Monday night. I was in my room all alone, dressing, and the window was open. I sat on the bed and looked out across the front lawn and at the houses along the street. I was looking at the same scene I had looked at for most of my life. Since the first grade, I had sat here and looked out this same window while I did my homework each night. Sometimes there was traffic in the street; sometimes it was quiet. Sometimes there was snow on the ground and the rooftops and people shoveling their cars out. Sometimes it was just getting dark and yellow lights were coming on in the houses and supper was cooking in every one of them. This was my view. My personal vantage point since I was six years old. I had learned to read and write

Spring/Summer 1962

and spell and add and subtract at this window. Multiplication tables. Long and short division. I had conjugated and memorized and recited here. I had erased holes in my papers, skipped pages, and copied inside jacket covers for book reports. I'd had the flu and the measles and chicken pox here. I'd looked out this window every morning for eleven years to check the weather before deciding what clothes to put on for school. And I had daydreamed through it every night when I was supposed to be doing my homework. And now I was supposed to be getting dressed for my final act of public education, the day I had dreamed of and prayed for and waited impatiently on all these years. Yet here I sat on the edge of the bed in my underwear and socks, looking out my window at my personal view of the world with tears in my eyes. It was over and I really didn't want it to be.

There was a knock on the door.

"Come in," I said, still looking out the window, not wanting anyone to see my red eyes. It was Mom and Dad, and she had a box in her hands.

"We got you something for graduation," she said sweetly, "and it just came. It was supposed to be here a week ago."

She handed me the box and I opened it. It was a dark blue gaberdine suit. I pulled it out and put the pants on, which were two inches too long. Then I put the coat on, and the sleeves were about an inch too long.

"Oh darn," she said. "You won't be able to wear it tonight."

"I told you he wouldn't be able to wear it tonight," Dad added. "I knew it was going to be too big."

"That's okay," I assured them. "I can get it fixed tomorrow. I already have something laid out to wear tonight anyway. But I really do like it. It's really sharp."

"Well, you get dressed now," Mom said as she left the room. "And don't make yourself late."

Dad stopped in the doorway. "Sorry about those sleeves and pants legs, son. I wanted you to have a new suit for tonight. It came from Seigel's and it just came in today. He said for you to bring it in first thing in the morning and Mrs. Seigel would have it ready for you for Sunday."

"That's okay. I've got my black one I'm gonna wear tonight. But thanks. I really do like it." And I really did.

"You okay, son?"

He must have noticed my red eyes. I just shook my head. I didn't want to risk speaking because I wasn't sure I could. He stood there for just a few more seconds as if he were about to say something else. But finally, he didn't. He just nodded and closed the door behind him. My dad always knew the right thing to do.

I was going across the lawn in my black suit and red tie and with my cap and tassel in my hand and my gown over my arm. I had just reached for the car door when I heard the bell. The ice cream truck had stopped in front of our house. The ice cream man, whose name I never knew, leaned out the window and waved and yelled, "Big night tonight. Congratulations!"

"Thanks," I yelled back.

He leaned his head back in the window and started to pull off. "Hey, wait a minute," I yelled after him.

He was pulling away from the curb with his little jingle music playing. "Hey, wait a minute," I hollered even louder. "I want a cone." But the bell and the music drowned me out. I ran toward the truck but he was already going down the street before I could reach him. And for the first time in years, there were no kids on the corner, so he didn't stop. He just kept on going to the next block.

Spring/Summer 1962

"Hey! Hey!" I yelled again. "I just wanted to buy one last cone!" And my voice was angry. Frustrated. I wanted to kick in the side of that little ice cream truck. I wanted to blame somebody. For what, I wasn't even sure. I was feeling too many emotions I didn't know how to deal with. Everything was changing and I couldn't change fast enough to keep up. Even the ice cream man had gone off and left me. Or had I gone off and left him?

My cap and gown were still in my hand and the ice cream truck was out of sight and I was late for the next chapter of my life.

It was a beautiful June evening, and the sun was still hot as we started to arrive and park behind the gym and gather in and around the Home Ec. building. The doors and windows were flung open and a roar of voices, and a herd of bodies donning gowns and waiting in line for the two mirrors to put caps on heads was the general excitement of the moment. Everyone looked hurried and a little scared. Nervous laughter dominated the big room that I never quite understood what took place in. Is this where they actually cooked and sewed? Senior teachers, Government and English, mixed and patrolled and chaperoned. Everyone was high spirited and happy. Someone grabbed my gown from the back and almost pulled me over. It was Bud.

"Have you seen her yet?" he whispered, almost to the point of inaudibility in the present roar.

"Seen who?" I asked honestly.

"Maxine! Have you seen her?"

"No, I haven't seen her," I answered again, honestly.

"Come on." He tugged my sleeve. "We want you to ask her."

"Me? Why do you want me to ask her?" My question was directed to Bud, but by the time I'd finished it, it was being asked of everyone who had gathered behind him. Howard. Larry Harley. And three or four other friends who hung around with them. They were lined up and grinning and waiting for me to fulfill their desires.

"Aw, get out of here, guys. Come on. Scatter. Move it. Move it."

This was not me. This was ole Toby, who had overheard the whole thing and had come to my rescue. He said what I probably wouldn't have said and made them desist and disperse. Billy was standing beside him, zipping up his gown.

"Those guys are nuts," Toby said. "Do they think you're gonna just go up and ask Maxine to lift her gown and let them look-see if she's tellin' the truth? They're nuts. If you're gonna ask her, just Billy and me are gonna be there. Let them hear about it."

I laughed, but I knew down deep he was serious. And if I decided to ask, I'd certainly make sure Toby didn't get left out.

A loud shrill blast split the noise and brought the room to silence in a hurry. Coach Lambert had actually blown a whistle to get everyone's attention. "The time is here." He offered his last and final command to us. "Line up!"

Everyone started moving in different directions. We looked like the marching band on the football field just before they spelled out JHS. Turmoil and deafening noise. Someone grabbed my gown again. This time I swung around ready to tell somebody off. It was Sue Jane. She grabbed both my hands and stood on her toes and kissed me on the cheek. "You still don't know who you're marching with or sitting with?"

"Not yet. I was just getting in line now to see."

When we rehearsed Friday, I had marched in double file

with Betty Marshall. We were lined up alphabetically and according to homerooms, due to some new experiment by orders of the Admiral. Three people had been absent Friday and it threw off our order, so I still didn't know for sure who I would walk with. It wouldn't be Sue Jane though. She would be next to the end no matter what.

"If it's Maxine Hodge, I'll brain you," she threatened.

"It can't possibly be Maxine," I assured her. "Twenty-five people would have to be absent before that would happen alphabetically. And anyway, she's not in my homeroom."

We laughed, and she wished me luck. I kissed her again just because I wanted to and we found our places in line.

There is something terribly sobering about that melody. It's a cross between a funeral lament and a movie theme. It's reverent and calming while also being stirring and upsetting. From the time it began, its effect took hold of the entire senior class, and we were all so quiet you could hear a cotton ball bounce as the line began to move slowly toward the old gymnasium. Mrs. Branscomb, who I would miss behind her desk in the office, stood at the door as we exited and smiled at each one of us, wished us luck, and made sure all our tassels were on the right side of our caps. It was at the door that we teamed up with our marching partner, and who of all people did mine turn out to be? Toby! We grinned and gulped at each other and then turned our heads straight ahead in seriousness and marched for the last time into the old gym door and down its middle aisle among the Samson metal foldup chairs, our shoes creaking on the high-glossed oak floor. It was our last moment of glory in front of our parents and friends at Jackson High. We filed in our row and waited for the nod from the stage, and then we were seated for the last time. Our end had commenced.

The speaker was our little town's mayor, who also owned a huge furniture store there. He started his speech off with a bang. Some short anecdotes I recognized as coming from a Bennet Cerf joke book. I decided from the time he started that I was going to try to listen to every word he said. I was not going to let my mind wander. I had made myself this promise for years in church, but it usually only lasted about three minutes. The next thing I knew, I'd be somewhere I'd been Saturday night or off in a fantasy fight over the affection of a current infatuation. I had watched old men and women who had sat there every Sunday morning and stared straight ahead into the preacher's eyes for as long as he wanted to talk. And they never squirmed. Never twitched. Never coughed until the organ began to play the introduction to the next hymn, and then everybody coughed at once whether they had to or not. Were they listening to each word and thought, or were they, in reality, somewhere in the depths of their heads, thinking about some love affair they'd had forty years ago? I guessed I would never know until I was them forty years from now. But tonight, I was changing. Tonight, I was listening and Mr. Mayor was telling us about Stick-to-itiveness. Perseverance. Dedication. Ambition. And then Toby passed me a note.

On the back of his program, above the list of graduates, he had scrawled, *Somebody keeps pushing their foot in my back. Who's sitting right behind me?*

I waited a few polite seconds and then casually leaned back and looked down past my right arm and saw a bare foot massaging Toby's lower back. I followed the foot up the leg with my eye and then up the gown until I was looking squarely into the face of the infamous Maxine. She winked at me and I turned back around and wrote on Toby's program, *Lady*

Godiva.

    Within two minutes, someone tapped me on the shoulder just as the mayor was pressing hard on the attributes of a college education. Maxine leaned into my ear and said, "My shoe is under your chair. Will you get it for me?"

    I did, and when I turned to pass it back to her, one quick rustling of her robe and one simultaneous shifting in her chair revealed to me the Great Maxine Hodge Graduation Mystery of 1962. Why she wanted to reveal it to me and no one else was another mystery that, believe me, I never attempted to solve. Because what I saw and what good ole Maxine showed me was a pair of bright red Bermuda shorts under her robe. I was a little startled, a little amused, and a little distracted for a moment and lost track of what the good mayor was preaching to us from the podium. All I could think of was that Toby and the Spinners and all the rest of them would never believe what I had witnessed and would never believe that Maxine, the Hodge, had the last laugh on the entire senior class. Another lesson in learning that no one and nothing is ever exactly as we think it is. She winked at me again, and this time I winked back.

    Then came the name calling. We stood and walked toward the stage in the order we were seated, and as I waited at the edge of the steps leading up to the center of attention, my stomach did a little flip and my eyes clouded up. A sudden horror came over me. I thought, what if I get sick and throw up just as they call my name? What if I stumble on my robe as I'm walking across the stage? What if they say someone else's name and I walk up anyway and everybody laughs? But nothing like that happened. They called my name, I walked gentlemanly to the center of the stage, shook hands with the Admiral with my right hand, and received my diploma with my left.

Piano Days

When I turned and faced the audience to walk back to my seat, my mother, my sister, and Sue Jane's mother were at the bottom of the steps and took my picture. I've seen it recently and it's a pretty silly picture, but it captured the moment and the memory as it was, and that is really all a picture is supposed to do, isn't it?

I switched my tassel as Mrs. Branscomb had remined me and went to my seat. It was all over but the shouting and the celebrating. I wasn't as happy as I thought I'd be when I imagined this a month ago. And I wasn't as sad as I thought I'd be a few hours ago. I was more nervous. That's it, I think. Nervous and a little scared. My stomach and nerves were jumping and I was perspiring more than usual and my smile was forced. I took the ribbon off the rolled-up piece of paper in my hand and looked at it. I read it but did not absorb it. I read it again and felt my breathing get quicker and harder. Then I heard them call out Sue Jane's name, and I looked up and watched her walk across the stage and down the steps. The two mothers and my sister snapped her picture, and as she turned to go in her row of seats, she looked for me and caught my eye. She calmed my stomach and soothed my nerves and I felt good again and glad the night was ahead of me. And then that music started again and the swell of emotions it carried started all over. Everything I'd felt coming in, I felt going out. The only new feeling I had came just before the nod for us all to rise and march out. I suddenly felt a bare foot slide under my bottom and nearly raise me off the chair. I never turned around to see who it was. I didn't have to.

We marched out in glee, back down the same aisle as graduates that we had marched down just a couple of hours ago as students. Our parents and friends and families were looking at us and taking our pictures, and we were self-consciously

Spring/Summer 1962

looking at them and at the floor and the ceiling and at each other. Toby was waving and making the most of the march as if he were in a Fourth of July parade. We were halfway down the aisle when someone grabbed my arm. Sue Jane had squeezed ahead of her row to join us. She fell between us, hooked her left arm around mine and her right arm around Toby's, and we marched jauntily and triumphantly to the door this way. Just as we reached the doorway, Billy was waiting for us, his cap already in his hand, and in the frame of the old gymnasium entrance, we all four embraced and someone took our picture. I've seen that one recently, too, but I don't want to talk about it.

The remainder of the night was special and sweet, memorable and emotional and very personal, as was the rest of that summer. We all did things together with the joy of being together but also with an underlying sadness in knowing that we were doing everything for the last time. We went to the Knoll and rode around Hamburger Hatch and went to the Twilight Drive-In and had record parties and stopped in at the Hop and played softball and swam and lay in the sun at the pool. We did all those things we had done for years every summer, but this summer we did them with a richness and a fever we had never known before. We were putting a cap on a final chapter. It wouldn't be one of those things that just ended and you didn't know it was coming. We knew it was coming and coming fast. And no matter how much we tried to cram into those three short months, this chapter would be over and a new page would start for each of us.

Toby was going to join the Marines. He had made his final decision two weeks after graduation. He had signed up and coincided his leaving with the leaving of those of us who were going to college. He was due at Camp Lejeune on September 5. Billy, never sure of just where he wanted to go to school and not sure of just what he wanted to do, had enrolled in a two-year business college a hundred miles away. Sue Jane was going to the University of Virginia, a dream she'd had all her life. And I was on my way south to North Carolina to give Chapel Hill a try. Howard and Bud had changed their minds every time we saw them. If they were talking to Billy, they were going to business school. If they were with Toby, it was the Marines. If with me, it was some as-of-yet-unheard-from college. So we all had our courses and direction. We played hard that summer at stalling them, and yet, when the end did come, I was sort of ready.

    I said goodbye to Sue Jane first. It was the night of September 4. I took her home and we sat in the car in front of her house. I don't know how many songs played on the radio while we sat there, but in my memory it was only one. "Stranger on the Shore" must have played for a half an hour. Mr. Acker Bilk, Sue Jane, and I. We told each other goodbye and promised things we had no way of knowing we could fulfill. We kissed and cuddled and made all the sounds of love because we really meant it. We would see one another at Thanksgiving, we promised, and write every week and love one another for the rest of our lives. And we did.

    I said goodbye to Toby next. He was sitting in front of my house in his car at midnight when I pulled in the driveway from taking Sue Jane home. We lay on the front lawn like we used to on so many summer nights before and talked. We talked until after one o'clock. We were also waiting on Billy, who never came. He was with Patsy, and we figured something came up or maybe she wouldn't let him come if she had gotten a hint that we were all meeting there after our dates.

"You scared?" Toby asked, looking at the stars.

"Scared? Scared of what?"

"You know. Just scared. Scared of what we might be or might not be. Scared of failin'. Scared of not makin' it. Scared of bein' poor. Failure is windin' up poorer than your parents and mine ain't really all that poor. They do all right, you know. What if I don't do as good. What if I can't even afford a television set for my family and the county has to pay for my kids to drink milk at school. Scared of all that stuff. You know what I mean?"

We lay a long time in silence, cars going by occasionally and the street light giving us just enough light that we could see each other's faces and just little enough light we couldn't see each other's eyes. We didn't talk for a long time. We just lay there with our minds racing and our hearts pounding and time blowing a soft breeze across the grass.

"Yeah, Toby, I'm scared. I used to be just scared of the dark. Now I'm scared of everything *but* the dark. I guess that's growin' up."

I said goodbye to Billy last. He never showed up that night, but he was knocking on our front door at eight o'clock the next morning. His mother and Jayo were in the car waiting on him, and he just stopped to tell me goodbye on his way to college.

"Hey, buddy, I'm sorry about last night."

"That's okay. We figured somethin' came up."

"Yeah," he said, laughing nervously. "The last night and all. I just couldn't get away from Patsy. She was cryin' and all. Toby gone?"

"Yeah, he was leavin' early on the train. Six o'clock, I think."

"Well, I gotta go, too. Mom's waitin' in the car for me. Gotta sign up or whatever you have to do up there, so I guess I'd better get goin'. I just wanted to stop by and say goodbye. When you comin' home?"

"I don't know," I said. "Thanksgiving, I guess. That's the plan now, anyway."

Then we did the strangest thing. We shook hands. My best friend and I shook hands. I don't think we ever shook hands before, and it was very awkward. Billy walked off the porch and I waved to his mother and Jayo from the steps.

He turned around halfway down the walk and said something back to me. I didn't understand what he said and I asked him, "What?" He said it again but I still didn't understand what he said. It was one of those moments where you don't want to ask for a third time, so I just sort of laughed and said, "Hey, take care now."

I watched him pull off, and I've regretted so many times I never knew what he said. To ask him later would have been foolish. But I've wondered so many times what it was, and I still wish today I'd asked him over again. It may have been important. Things we said to one another usually were. I wish I knew what the last line to that chapter was. Billy was always my best friend and I would miss him most.

I didn't leave until that afternoon. I did last-minute things. Ran some errands and told some aunts and uncles and cousins and my sister goodbye. For my final packing, I needed some underwear and socks, so I stopped by Seigel's Men's Shoppe to see what they had. I had been in there a couple of times that summer and he had never mentioned anything about the prom clothes. He had fitted and altered my graduation suit and never said the first thing out of the way. But today, he was there by himself. Mrs. Seigel was off somewhere else talking to herself, I suppose, and no other customer was in sight. He rang up my purchases and waited until I was halfway out the door and then called out, "Hey, Frank's boy."

I stopped and turned. "Yes sir?"

"Which one of you little nimrods took my niece to the prom dance?"

"I don't know your niece, Mr. Siegel."

"Yeah, yeah, you do. The Lutz girl. My wife's brother's girl. Owns the shoe store. You know."

"Alice Lutz? That's your niece?" I said, genuinely surprised.

"Yeah, that's my niece. Which one of you little mashers took her to the dance?"

"Well, Mr. Seigel"—I stalled, not knowing what he knew or why he was asking—"you see, it wasn't like there were dates and all. You know, just guys there and girls there and not really dates and paired off and all and…I don't know."

"Yeah, yeah, and Hitler's in heaven. You know which one of you it was. I heard it was one of youse." He paused here as if it were my turn to talk, but I had nothing to say so I passed. He picked it up again. "That girl was nothing but trouble for her mamma and poppa since grammar school. That's why they had to send her off to live with family up in Manchester. They couldn't handle her either. They caught her with every boy in New Hampshire. Then she finished school and they had to send her home. Then one of you boneheaded little mutts take her to the dance. Look at me, Frank's boy! Was it you?"

"No sir. It' wasn't me."

"That good-lookin' boy with the curly hair that comes in here with you?"

"Billy?"

"Yeah, that's it. Billy, you call him."

"No sir. He has a girlfriend of his own."

"Abraham and Moses! Don't tell me it was Tubby!"

"Toby," I corrected him.

"Yeah, yeah, Toby or Tubby or whatever his name is. The kid with the dirty tuxedo. It was *him*?"

I fought the urge to answer. But I was an adult now and I really didn't have to answer every question anybody asked me, so I just looked at him blankly and said nothing.

"No! Tell me it's not him. Not my niece. Not the fat boy. It's not kosher, the little dolt!"

I closed the door behind me and walked to my car and so badly wanted to tell Toby and Billy what had just happened. I was laughing out loud to myself and had nobody to share it with. For the first time in my life, I couldn't go home and call them and tell them word for word what old man Seigel had said and laugh about it for nights to come. For the first time in my life, I couldn't stop by their houses on the way home and go up to their rooms and lay on the bed and tell them about the look on his face and how he had called Toby Tubby. Then a flash went through me and for a moment I thought, that's okay. I'll tell them about it tonight at the drive-in.

And then I sat in my car and realized things had really changed and it was going to take some getting used to. Tonight, for the first time in our lives, we were going to spend the night in entirely different towns. There would be no drive-ins, no hanging around each other's houses after school, and no double dating and no meeting in my yard after we had taken the girls home. There would be no more football games and stopping in at Dinkel's. No haunted houses and jumping the fence at the fair. No more Friday nights. No more Saturday

Spring/Summer 1962

mornings.

    I started the car and was about to pull out of the parking space when a school bus went by. It was the first day of school. The first day I wouldn't be going, and I felt lost and empty as if I should be on it. It was an elementary school bus, but even at that, I felt I should be on there instead of behind it driving a car. I drove behind it for a few blocks and I could see three little boys at the back window looking out at me, the way there are always little boys looking out the back of a school bus. The one in the middle finally waved and I waved back. The little curly-haired one on the left just smiled at me. And the little chubby one on the right stuck his tongue out at me and made an obscene gesture with both hands. Then the light caught me and they pulled away and left me sitting there in the middle of the street all by myself.

———

Uncle Be-Bop was a personal hero to me but also a super folk hero. His stories transported me back to an era I never knew. A time years before I was even born. But he painted pictures in my mind of places and people I would love to have seen and known.

We visited him and Aunt Abby a number of times in Chicago, and when we did, he would take my brothers and me to concerts and plays. Once we went to McCormick Place to see Victor Borge. We all thought he was the funniest man we had ever seen, but my uncle loved the parts of the show where he would play the serious pieces. Probably no one else in the audience understood those moments better than he.

When they visited us, we would mostly talk and sometimes go to a local ballgame or restaurant. Once he and I just rode around town together. I was in my early twenties and I asked him to show me some of the places he had written about in his "chapters." He showed me where the Burger Barn had been on Main Street. It was now an antique store, open only on Fridays and Saturdays. The Twilight Drive-In was a strip mall with insurance and dentist offices. Some of these things I knew, but it was such a treat hearing the stories directly from him. Then he turned the tables on me and asked if I had ever been up to the Knoll. I told him I hadn't because the road had been blocked years ago. I told him the rumor was that it was completely overgrown and the only way to the top was to walk it, the way Toby had. But I told him I would gladly call the city powers-that-be and see if I could get permission to drive a Jeep up there if he wanted to go.

He just smiled at me and said, "Now why would I want to do fool thing like that?"

My mother honestly thought this was the last chapter he would ever write. She felt it was the perfect ending to his high school adventures, so she had all the pages bound and kept them on a shelf in her den. But some ten years after he wrote that last line about

Spring/Summer 1962

the school bus going off and leaving him in the middle of the street, Mom found an envelope with another chapter, titled "May 1976," in her mailbox one morning. After reading it, she knew this was truly the final chapter.

Chapter 10

May 1976

Bad news always comes at night. Some of the worst news I've ever received has come after dark and usually in the a.m. Bad accidents. Deaths in the family. Sickness. It's gotten to the point that my heart races when the phone rings after ten p.m. I rush to grab it, afraid to answer it, scared not to. A wrong number at one o'clock in the morning will get even the most apologetic person a tongue cussing on the other end. I don't sleep for hours afterward.

And that night, I hadn't slept for hours, day or night. I had just come home from a business trip, and it was after midnight when I walked in the door and set my suitcase down. In my work, I travel some. I see more airports, hotel rooms, and fleeting cities than I really want to. Just buildings and people doing the same things in different places. My flight had been the last one out of Minneapolis, and when I landed I didn't bother to call Abby from the airport to pick me up. I just grabbed a cab and was home in less than an hour. She was asleep, as I knew she would be, but she heard the cab door close and met me at the patio door in her sweatshirt and shorts. We sat at the kitchen table for nearly a half an hour, talked and drank hot tea, and then I asked her to run me a bath. That was unusual as I am a shower person. Showers are quicker and, I've always thought, cleaner. But that night I was tired and wanted to lounge in a tub and soak off the grime of travel. And that's where I was when the phone rang at ten minutes after one.

On the first ring, I froze and started to jump out of the

tub to pick it up in the bedroom, but I heard her say, "I'll get it." It rang once more and I could hear her say, "Hello." I sat as quietly as I could, trying to hear her words and her tone, my stomach jumping with the knowledge that it was not a wrong number I could vent my impatient anger on, but instead someone who had meant to dial our number at this time of the night. I wanted to know who and what it was, and yet I didn't. I waited as long as my nerves would allow and finally yelled, "Who is it? What's wrong?" Then I faintly heard her say, "I'll have him call you right back."

She walked in the bathroom and saw the question on my face and I saw the pain on hers. She didn't say anything until she sat down on the floor beside the tub and rubbed her hand lightly down the back of my head. I knew it was coming, I just didn't know what. I already felt sick. If I could put off knowing for another minute it would help. No, it would only make it worse. She looked sadly in my eyes and said, "Honey, that was your mother. Billy's dead."

The flight that always took two and a half hours felt like a blink and an eternity. Some phases whizzed by and others stood still forever. I sat in a window seat and watched the country below me. From the sky, it's always farmland, just the way you saw it in the geography books in school. Brown fields and green fields drawn in perfect rectangles with skinny, winding roads wrapping around them. I saw them without seeing them and saw people around me without being aware of them. I was only aware of my wife, who sat quietly beside me, knowing best when to talk to me and interceding with anyone else, such as stewardesses or too-talkative fellow passengers, who might try to strike up a friendly conversation. She had taken over since the phone call, just as she had taken care of me years ago in the

May 1976

hospital. She booked the flights, booked the rental car, and pushed me to call my mother back like she had promised her I would. I needed the push because, as sincerely as I wanted to know the details, I didn't want to hear them.

"Mom. It's me."

"Hi, son. Are you alright?"

"Yeah, I'm okay. Well, not really. What happened?"

"Did Abby tell you?"

"Well, not everything. Just that he was dead. She said to call you back and you could tell me all about it."

"I don't know all about it. I got a call tonight. I was already in bed. I had just turned off the television set. I watch the news every night before I go to sleep. Your father got me in the habit of that. He always had to see the news before he went to sleep. So I had just turned off the set when the phone rang and it was Esther Foley. She works with Ruth at the hospital and she had just gotten off her shift when the call came into the emergency room. So she stayed to be there with Ruth, who wasn't working tonight, thank the good Lord above. If she had been on duty when they brought him in, well, I'm just thankful she wasn't. Anyway, Esther called me and I called you and I'm dressed now and I've fixed some food. I was just waiting for you to call me back. I think I'm going to go over there now."

"But what happened, Mom? How did it happen?"

"Oh, didn't Abby tell you that?"

"Just that it was a car wreck. That's all."

"Well, son, that's about all we know, too. He was apparently by himself and he was out on the Old Seminary Road. You know how twisted and crooked that old road is. He must have been going awful fast, though. I'll know more after I see Ruth tonight. When are you coming?"

"As soon as I can. We'll be there by ten in the morning."

287

"Do you want me to meet you at the airport?"

"No. We'll rent a car."

"Now don't do that. I can drive over to the airport in thirty minutes and meet you."

"It's okay, Mom. I want to. We'll need a car once we're there. We'll come straight to the house."

"Okay," she conceded. "And son, try to get some sleep. I hated so much calling you and telling you this."

"It's okay, Mom. I'll see you in the morning."

I don't remember the plane landing. I was only suddenly aware of people in the aisle, and then I stood up and followed the herd and walked through the routine of baggage claim and car rental. I was next aware that we were on the road home. The road I had always been excited about and was now dreading like a ten-year-old in a dentist's waiting room. It was a sunny spring day. Just a week till Mother's Day. Trees and flowers were blooming and grass was growing again and it all seemed so unreal to me. It was as if I were looking at a picture of it all instead of actually being in it. I was the customer standing off looking at it in its frame and trying to decide if I liked it well enough to have it on my wall for the rest of my life. Did it make me happy? Sad? Did it make me want to be a part of it? Did it seem so real I could reach out and touch it? No. And I didn't want to buy it even for a few days. But for a few days it was mine, like it or not. I could see the city limits sign coming up on my right.

Mom was waiting on the front porch. She met us at the car and started to cry when she hugged me. And the tears weren't just for why I was there today. They were for a lot of things only she and I understood. For sadness that builds up through the

May 1976

years and for the passing of time that brings the changes in our lives. We held each other and never spoke. We didn't have to.

By the time the three of us got in the house, things were somewhat normal and she and Abby went to the kitchen to make coffee while I put the luggage upstairs in my old bedroom. Now, there's an experience. Coming back home and sleeping with your wife in the bedroom you grew up in. We had done it many times before on happier occasions, and I always found it funny and uncomfortable. Abby would say, "What's so funny?" as I lay there in the bed beside her, grinning. But who can explain such a feeling? You truly have the sense of being two different people at the same time, the boy you used to be in that room and the man you are today. It stretches the mind and makes the Trinity easier to understand for even the most skeptical.

But as I walked up the steps and into the room and looked around me, I realized it was not the same house. Not the house I knew as a child. It began to change that Tuesday afternoon back in '62 when I left to go to college. And it had changed even more when Daddy died nine years ago. It, like him, was not alive anymore. It was then that it transformed to the silent, still home of a widow lady. It was quiet from morning till dark. The only words spoken in it were the ones Mom spoke to herself or into the telephone. The furniture had not changed, mainly because she didn't want anything new and didn't need anything new. For whatever reason, it had not changed and therefore, the furniture was dead, too. The pictures on the walls and on the piano that used to change constantly whenever we took new ones or whenever my sister or I brought new school pictures home—they didn't change anymore. All those pictures we took every Easter Sunday in the yard and every Christmas morning by the tree—at some point all those photos stopped. All those photos died. The same ones that were there ten, fifteen years ago were still there. The one of Mom and me by the lilac bush beside the driveway when I was ten years old was still there. We had just gotten out of the car, coming home from church. She still had her Bible in her hand, and I had that defiant look of wanting to get away and change clothes. The one of Daddy leaning on the hood of that green '51 Fleetline Chevy. The one of both of them sitting on the couch that I took Christmas night 1956, and five minutes later dropped the brand-new camera and broke the back out of it. The one of Daddy and me with the bike he had just given me for my eighth birthday. He was sitting astride it, laughing, and I was standing beside him with my hand on his leg in complete awe. Not of the bike but of him.

And then there was the one of our 1961 softball team, the year we won the championship. It had been on the piano all these years, and my nephews had me tell them who each person was in the picture every time we all were there. The only thing new in the house in fifteen years was a picture of Abby in her bridal gown, sitting on the mantle in the living room.

I walked over to Mom and Dad's bedroom, now just hers, and felt the quietness and deadness of everything in it. The sun was shining too brightly through the curtains and everything was too neat and too perfect. You could tell nothing was ever disturbed or bothered or out of place. All the things that make a house alive were gone. And at twenty minutes after three on any given day, the time I used to come home from school and turn the radio and the TV on and turn the kitchen cabinets inside out, the same quiet would still be throughout the house as it was right now. And at five thirty, when Daddy used to come home from work and supper was cooking and stories were exchanged at the table, stories about school and work and

May 1976

the neighborhood, the same stillness and deafening lull would hang as thickly as the memories that were fighting to get out of these rooms. I wanted to sit down and cry for all these things and purge myself of my regrets and unfulfilled dreams, but there was no time for self-indulgence. I was home to bury a friend who needed burying, not to revive old memories that needed burying. I turned and headed down the stairs to join Mom and Abby for coffee, and just for a second, I thought I could hear Daddy's voice talking to them in the kitchen.

"When you and Abby are ready to go see Ruth, I'll go with you. I was up with her till after six this morning."

"How is she?"

"As well as can be expected. You know Ruth. She's strong."

"What about Jayo?"

"Well, Jayo took it pretty hard. He and his wife were there last night."

"His wife," I said, almost to myself. "Jayo married. Wow."

"Yes, they have a new little baby. A little girl."

"Is he living here?"

"No. I forget where they said he was living. Not far, though, I don't think. When do you want to go over there?"

I ignored her question because I was thinking about something else or maybe because I was trying to put off answering her and facing up to the duty I knew I had to perform. Abby laid her hand on my arm. This was her way of nudging me.

"Where's Toby?" I asked Mom.

"At home, I suppose. I haven't heard from him."

"I want to go see Toby first." This came out of my mouth before it even went through my brain.

"Before you go see Ruth?"

This was my mother's way of nudging me. I looked across the table at Abby. At the good and loyal wife who so effectively fended for me on the airplane but who was helpless in the face of my mother. She smiled back at me and sipped her coffee. The battleground was mine.

"I'll go later this afternoon to see Ruth," I said.

"Your father would have been the first one over there. He was always the first one when there was death in a family or a tragedy or sickness. He would want you to go over there now, and to tell you the truth, son, so do I."

"Well, Mom, I'll say one thing about you. You don't waste time being subtle."

"Old women have no time to waste. Go wash your face and we'll get ready to go."

I got obediently up from the table as if she had just told me it was time to go to bed or time to do my homework. Old habits die hard.

"You know, Mom, you really should get a dog or a cat so you'd have something to boss around when I'm not here."

"Oh, I've thought about it. But I wouldn't know how to act if it didn't talk back to me."

It was nearly one o'clock when Abby and Mom and I knocked on the Hudlow front door. A lady I had never seen before answered and informed us that the family was at the funeral home making arrangements. She invited us to come and wait or to return in about an hour. We opted to return.

The three of us rode out the Old Seminary Road, as morbid and it sounds, and saw where we thought the accident had happened. It always seems a little sick to visit the scene of a

May 1976

tragedy like that, but it's something we all do sooner or later. This proved to be a little too soon for me.

We arrived back at the Hudlow house shortly after two and found the living room and kitchen full of people I didn't know or recognize. Ruth, Billy's mom, was sitting in a high-back wing chair by the piano looking old and sad, as she had every right to. She was talking to people and trying to reason and listen and act as normal as possible. A state we have all been in at some time or another. A state that leaves you weak and with no memory of who you talked to or what was said. When the line around her cleared away, I went to her and knelt beside her chair, and she hugged me and held me and cried steadily until she was dry. Until there were just no more tears. I stayed there with her, saying private words to her until the sobs quieted and she was able to talk.

Finally, she said, "I'm so glad you're here. But you had so far to come."

"Ruth, you know I would have walked," I said in a shaky voice I didn't recognize as mine.

"I know. I know," she said softly. "Had you talked to him recently?"

"I talked to him on the phone a few weeks ago. He called to ask if I was coming home over Easter. I wasn't able to and I told him it would be this summer before I got back. I wish now I'd come at Easter."

"That's okay," she said, squeezing my hand. "We have no way of knowing these things. Have you seen Jay?"

As she asked me, I assumed from her reference that time and age had turned Jayo into Jay. So often those cute little nicknames we hang on our children don't wear well into and after the teenage years.

"No, I haven't. I'll go find him now. Mom and Abby are

here. They want to say something to you. I'll see you in a little bit."

I stood up and walked through the house looking for Jayo. Although I was always home a couple of times each year, it was difficult to keep up with the changes in everyone. I couldn't remember seeing Jayo since he was probably in high school. Now they tell me Jayo, Jay, has a baby girl. I stood by the piano and looked into the kitchen to try to spot someone that might be him. But what I spotted was my old nemesis, the picture of Billy's dad in front of the barracks in his uniform. The picture I had played cat and mouse with so many times, so many years ago. I didn't look at it long. It wasn't the day for it. Then I felt a huge hand on my shoulder and heard someone speak my name into the top of my head. I turned and looked up at Jayo. Little Jayo, who I used to hold down and tickle in the grass, was looking down at me from a vantage point I had never obtained. He must have been four inches taller than me, and on the end of that enormous frame sat a face I remembered as vividly as if it had been in last night's dream. The unruly hair, the round baby cheeks, the little smile that used to melt all the grownups and now probably had the same effect on women, they were all the same. They were just higher up.

"Thank you for comin', man."

"Hey…" I started to say something but wasn't sure what. "Let's go outside."

Jay and I walked out in the yard. We had been out in this yard a lot together. Billy and I taught him to play ball out here. We had made tents out here by hanging blankets over the clothesline, and we had all three mowed it many times on Saturday mornings so we could get through quicker and make it to the matinee. We sat down on a little brick wall around the flower bed that had been added since those days.

May 1976

"So, where's Billy's family?"

"At home, I guess. Patsy hasn't been here and she hasn't let the kids come yet. I guess we'll see them before the day's over. She was at the funeral parlor earlier helping with the arrangements."

"Helping?" I asked. "It's up to her to make them, isn't it?"

"You'd think," Jay said as he pulled a Merit Menthol out of his shirt pocket. He offered me one and I shook my head. I hadn't smoked a cigarette for years, but today would have been a good day to start again.

"How do Ruth and Patsy get along?"

"Mamma gets along with everybody. Patsy only talks to me when she has to. And she never lets those two kids come around. Only when Billy brings them by himself. That breaks Mamma's heart. Two grandchildren right here in the same town with her and she hardly ever gets to see them. Billy ever talk to you about her?"

"About Patsy? Oh, yeah. A lot. One time he'd be pouring out his heart about her and the next time he'd protect her. It was always that way, Jayo. Even before you remember much about it. Always."

We were quiet awhile. I just sat there on the little wall and looked out across that old familiar yard. I knew where all the dips were. The tree roots and all the good Easter egg hiding places. And I looked at this man sitting beside me. Had we ever been out here, just the two of us before? Had Jayo and I ever been here without Billy? Were we now? I could feel something. A chill? A presence? A hope? Or maybe I was just trying to scare myself. Maybe Jayo and I really were alone and just had nothing more to talk about.

We went back inside and I talked to familiar faces and met new ones. I hugged Jayo's wife and kissed his new baby. I talked some more with Ruth. Comforting things. Memories and things-happen-for-the-best kind of things. We'll-understand-it-better-by-and-by and all that stuff people say to each other when whatever they say isn't going to amount to a hill of nothing anyway. Someone we all loved was dead, and we were each searching for a way to cope with it.

After supper, I called Toby. I hadn't seen him since Christmas, and of all the people I knew I would have to see this week he was the one I most wanted to be with. He invited me over, but instead I suggested I pick him up so we could just ride around. I felt this was the best and most private way we could talk.

Toby was married to a girl named Linda whom I didn't know well. They had one daughter, Lindsay, and they lived in a brick rancher not far from where he had grown up. Toby had joined the Marines that September in '62 and wound up in Vietnam. When he came out, he went to work at GernTech, a factory where his daddy had worked for forty years. He was stable, reliable, respectable, and all the adjectives it takes to be a quiet member of a quiet, family community. Nam changed everyone who saw it, but I don't know if it was the war or the maturing that changed Toby. He was now a negative of himself growing up. He was subdued and restrained. He was uneasy in a crowd of more than two people. All of his corpulence had turned to muscle but had not diminished his size. He was physically hard and emotionally a melon in the hands of the two females in his life. He loved them both dearly, and as far as I knew, they returned the same love for him. And just knowing this brought a certain peace to me I can't explain.

Toby's 220 pounds on his five-foot ten-inch frame made him fold slightly to get in my rental Chevy Chevelle. His hair was still cut in the military style he had apparently gotten

May 1976

accustomed to in the service, and his clothes were nondescript of any decade or fashion. He had on khaki pants, a blue oxford cloth dress shirt open at the neck with the sleeves rolled up past his elbows, and loafers. He could be any man you met in the past thirty years.

He got in the car, reached over and hit me on the leg and said, "Let's ride." It was as if I had just let him out in front of his mom and dad's house last night at midnight and I was picking him up to go to school the next morning.

"How's the family?" I asked.

"Great! And yours? I see your mother from time to time. She looks great. Just like she always did."

"Yeah, she does, doesn't she? Have you been over to see Ruth?"

"Yes, I have," he said. "I went by there this morning before I went to work. She's pretty tore up."

"I was there this afternoon. Talked to Jayo."

"What did he have to say?"

"Just regular stuff. Why? What do you mean?"

"I just wondered what he was sayin' about it all," Toby answered rather mysteriously.

I was watching the road and then Toby. And then back and forth about three times, and I was sure there was something more to what he wasn't saying. An old tactic came back to me suddenly. Toby always reacted to me when I was firm and straightforward. I figured I'd see if the war had taken that out of him. "What is it, Toby? Something's up."

"No, nothin's up," he lied, looking out the windshield.

"Toby, it's me," I said and nothing more. He felt what I was feeling and then started talking.

"Did Jayo say anything at all to you about the wreck?"

"No, not really." I tried to remember.

"Then maybe he doesn't know. Maybe nobody knows. Maybe I don't even know, but here goes."

My stomach tightened the way it had when I was sitting in the tub last night wanting to know and not wanting to know at the same time. I braced myself and gripped the wheel a little tighter.

"There's somethin' awful fishy about that wreck," Toby started. "Billy was in that '58 MG of his and he treated it like a third child. He never took it out of the garage except in the summertime and then on just the prettiest days. Even if there were still mud puddles around a day or two after a rain, he wouldn't run it. Me and him were out one time last summer, comin' from a sale over at Bannerton, and a cloud came up and it started rainin' and he whipped in somebody's driveway and pulled under their carport and we sat there under their carport till the rain stopped. And we even had the top up. I asked him, I said, 'What if the people who live here come out?' and he said, 'I'll just tell 'em we pulled in here to get out of the rain.' He was silly about that thing. He washed it and polished it all the time."

"So, what's so fishy?" I was beginning to think Toby was overreacting.

"Well, to start with, I saw Billy Friday night at the shoppin' center. We just happened to bump into one another. We saw each other at least once a week. We did things together and kept up with each other's lives. But Friday night, I saw him in this little food court at the shoppin' center, sittin' at a table by himself, eatin' ice cream. I stopped and sat down and we talked. I tried to talk anyway. He didn't have much to say."

"Can you remember anything he said?" I was desperate now for some understanding of what exactly was bothering Toby.

May 1976

"He asked about you. Asked if I had talked to you, and I hadn't. Asked if I knew where you were this weekend. He knew you were travelin', I guess, but he wanted to know if I knew what towns or hotels, and I didn't."

Toby was making me feel worse by the second. Billy had apparently wanted to talk to me and I wasn't available.

"So we talked," Toby continued, "and then out of the clear blue sky, he said, 'Toby, do you think we'll have a fifteen-year class reunion next year?' and I said yeah, I guess we would and he said, 'Are you goin'?' and I said yeah I guess I will. Then I said, 'How about you? Are you goin'?' and he stood up and took a big drink out of his water glass and set it down on the table and said, 'Don't count on it.' Then he walked off and never said another word. That was the last thing he ever said to me."

People always make a big thing over the last thing people say to them. They always want it to sound more dramatic than it was, and they search for some hidden meaning in those final words. I had an aunt, my dad's oldest sister, who was widowed comparatively early in life and made us all suffer for it the rest of ours. She was full of stories about Uncle Arlie, whom I never knew, but to whom she accredited a tale of wisdom concerning every subject that ever came up. On final words, she loved to tell, teary-eyed, how he sat up in bed at exactly five o'clock on the same evening that Franklin Roosevelt died and said, "Is the raccoons loose tonight?" and then he rolled over and died, too. Oh, how she loved to tell that story, and I was a pretty big boy and had heard it a few dozen times before I the nerve to ask her exactly what it meant. I think she was waiting on that, because she took a deep sigh and discoursed for thirty minutes on how it was his way of wanting to hold on to the simple life he had lived with his hunting and his dogs and his love of the outdoors and the democratic way of life. I asked Daddy about it later, and he confided in me that he had never known Arlie to own a dog or a rifle or to vote and that he had no idea in heaven or hell what that thing about the raccoons was all about. But he did know that Uncle Arlie died with a high fever and that he was probably talking out of his head toward the end. So, being typically twelve years old, I asked, "Well, why does Aunt Tess tell that story then?" And Daddy said, "I think she had the same fever. It killed Arlie but she still has it." I just nodded in confusion, though I've laughed many times since then, remembering it.

But I wasn't laughing now, and I couldn't tell if Toby was making a statement about last words or was just sharing with me that those were Billy's last words to him. "What does that mean, Toby?" I asked just as I had asked Aunt Tess.

Toby waited a long time before he answered. It was as if he were planning the right words in his head to see if they were going to say what he wanted them to say. Then he finally decided to air them and take his chances. "It means," he started slowly, "that Billy knew Friday night what was goin' to happen Sunday night."

I felt reality fly out of my head again, and I looked for a stoplight so I could stop the car and try to regain my perspective and slow my heart down. What was Toby trying to tell me?

"Are you telling me he killed himself Sunday night?" The words left my stomach sick and weak.

"Look, buddy," Toby said to me in a big brother voice, "I've told you about the MG and how he felt about it. I've told you about how funny he was actin' and you know all the problems he had with Patsy. And on top of everything else, it started rainin' Sunday evenin' about six o'clock. Ask your mother. And it never stopped till after midnight. You can see for yourself.

May 1976

The shoulders of the road and the grass is still wet. I'm tellin' you it rained last night and he would not take that MG out in the rain unless he was planin' on runnin' off the road with it."

I remembered Ruth's yard and how wet Jayo's and my shoes were this afternoon. Toby was right. It had rained the night before, and it made no sense that Billy was out riding in the rain with the top down at eleven o'clock at night.

"He had the top down?" I asked to confirm my thoughts.

"Yes. Less protection. He had a Bonneville Pontiac and a Ford pickup in his garage he could have taken. But he wanted as little protection as possible. A sports car with the top down. That's almost like jumpin' off that bank headfirst. Nothin' to protect you. And rainin'. I'm tellin' you, buddy, there's no doubt in my mind. He killed himself on purpose as sure as if he put a 12-gauge shotgun in his mouth."

I wasn't sure I was hearing everything clearly. Toby seemed not only extremely sure of himself, but he seemed rational and reasonable and very matter of fact. I had to think all the possibilities through before I let myself settle on an opinion. I was just beginning to sort out the believable from the improbable when Toby interrupted.

"All that on top of the other that I'm sure you already know about."

"What other?" I asked wearily. "I don't know anything about any other."

"You know Billy was havin' an affair, don't you?"

I pulled off the road and into a small graveled parking lot beside a little fruit stand. It was closed and the area was deserted, which is what I was looking for. I just needed somewhere to sit and not drive for a few minutes.

"Toby, this is the first I've heard about any affair. Who was he having an affair with?"

"Now, that I can't tell you. He just told me about six months ago that he was seein' somebody, and he seemed really serious about her. But he never told me who. I just figured he had told you."

"Why would you think that? You saw him a lot more than I did."

"Yeah, that's true," Toby reasoned, "but even though I saw him a lot more, you and Billy were closer than me and him. And I just always figured if he told anybody, he told you."

"He never told me a thing. So let me think." I stalled and pondered. "How does all this come together? You think life and all the pressure just got too much for him and he ran off the road and killed himself? Does that sound logical?"

"No," Toby said seriously, "but suicide don't happen to people who are logical."

You can glean wisdom from the most surprising sources if you don't look too hard for it. We sat there in silence and looked out the windshield for a long time. All I could see was that old boarded-up fruit stand. We, Billy and Toby and I, had stopped right here one night and bought a watermelon and busted it in the driveway of a history teacher who had failed Toby the year before. We each paid for a third of it. Billy sat in the back seat and held it on his lap and I stopped the car, and Toby got out and threw it and watched it splatter all over the hardtop drive and all over him. An hour later we were still driving around and laughing about it while Toby was picking pieces of it out of his hair and off his clothes and eating them. We laughed so much that night and that summer. But the car was silent now and the fruit stand was closed, and Toby had grown up and gotten wisdom and Billy had killed himself. I turned the car around and pulled out on the highway and drove home.

May 1976

I slept that night in my old bedroom with Abby close beside me. I woke up every hour and looked at the clock and the ghosts. The ghosts weren't there to scare me. Just to remind me. The clock was there to scare me. And it still does.

I was shaving when the phone rang at ten minutes after nine. My mother came and said there was someone who wanted to speak to me.

"Who is it?"

"A Roger Candleman, I think he said."

Roger Candleman and I went to college together. Afterwards, he went to law school and got his degree and married a girl from Humboldt, another little town nearby. He and his wife lived there and he had a practice there. I was surprised to hear from him and could not imagine why he'd called unless he just wanted to offer condolences. But after about twenty seconds of amenities, I could tell by his demeanor that he was not calling to say hello.

"I need to see you immediately," he said in a business tone I had never heard from him.

"Before the day's over?" I asked, wondering how to schedule something into today's agenda that wasn't already there.

"Before the morning is over," he said firmly.

"Okay," I said and waited for more information.

"I have in my possession, from this morning's mail, a letter concerning you."

"You have a letter for me?" I asked, confused.

"Not *for* you," Roger said, "but concerning you."

"Who's it from?" I asked, wondering now how an old schoolmate-turned-lawyer was getting my mail.

"It's from Billy."

Silence.

Roger was the first to pick the conversation up again with, "I know that sounds odd, but…"

I interrupted his thought. "You have a letter there for me from Billy Hudlow in this morning's mail?" Now I was more incredulous than confused.

"Yes. It's postmarked Monday, yesterday, so I must assume it was mailed sometime Sunday and not processed until yesterday and it arrived this morning. I think it's important enough that we meet immediately and go over the contents."

"Which are?" I asked.

"Well, I can read it to you over the phone or I can just tell you what—"

"Just tell me," I demanded as I wiped the dried shaving cream off the side of my face. I wanted to know what was going on as quickly as possible.

"Well, you see," Roger began his story, "I've worked rather closely with Bill for quite some time. He not only was a client on a few personal matters, but we also shared clients and did a lot of work together. His CPA firm and my office. I drew up a will for him a couple of years ago, and I suppose he considered me his official legal representative. This letter this morning, though addressed to me, is clearly instructing you as to his personal wishes.

"He says he has a safety deposit box downtown at the North Sentry Security Bank, and in it he has left effects for your eyes only. Enclosed in this letter is a key that he instructs me to give to you. He also asks me to inform you that you are the executor of his estate, and I can assure you that's true as I drew up his will myself."

I was slow to react, as I was stunned by it all. "So he wants

May 1976

me to go into his lockbox and get something."

"That's right," Roger confirmed. "Now, finding this a little irregular, I would suggest we get whatever is in there as soon as possible in case it is something that may, shall we say, change the will or alter its original intent."

"Can something change a will besides another will?" I asked, having gotten most of my knowledge of the law from Erle Stanley Gardner and Raymond Burr.

"Yes. A dated letter in his own handwriting can. But let's not get ahead of ourselves. Let's just take it one step at a time."

"Okay," I agreed. "So what do I do next?"

"Meet me at North Sentry Security in thirty minutes. Do you know where it is?"

"I knew where it was about thirty years before you did."

"That's right," he said, laughing, "I forget this is home for you. Meet me there in the Trust Department. And also, he says here in the letter that you will need a password to enter the vault."

"A password?" I couldn't tell if he was kidding or not.

"Oh, yes. Most banks do that. They have a word or words on file written on a card by the person who rents the box. And they always ask for it and won't let anyone in who doesn't know it, short of a court order."

"Okay, so what was Billy's password?"

"It was two words, actually," Roger said. "*Piano Days*. I don't know what that means. Maybe it means something to you. But anyway, that's what it is. I'll see you in thirty minutes."

And he hung up.

Roger was waiting for me at the front door of the bank. We shook hands and smiled our way through the lobby and to the desk of the keeper of the vault. He, in his lawyer voice, informed her of the situation and explained what we planned to do. He showed her his power of attorney and the letter and the key. She seemed to understand and went to the files to check the password. She handed me the key and took one from the files just like it. Then she said, "I have to ask you the password and hear you speak it."

I looked at Roger. He nodded to me and I looked at her. "Piano Days," I said.

"Very well. Follow me," she said and we walked into the vault, the keeper and I.

There looked to be hundreds of boxes lining the walls inside this walk-in strongroom. She went to the one numbered 271 and put her key in one of its keyholes. She then took mine from my hand and put it in the second keyhole. She turned them and extracted a long metal box and told me to come with her. She led me to a small hallway area where there were three little cubicles with doors. Each cubicle was about the size of eight phone booths. There was a small desk and one straight-back chair. She opened one of the doors and went in and set the metal box on the desk and then came out and motioned me in. She smiled professionally and said, "Just let me know when you're finished."

I said, "Thank you," and went in and sat down. Roger stayed in the hall just outside the doorway. I closed the door and opened the box. I wasn't sure what to expect and didn't know how to prepare myself for what I might find. My imagination could have carried me away or I could have been curious and frightened by it all. But instead, I was just numb. I didn't allow my mind to anticipate. I simply opened the box and sat

May 1976

there and looked at its contents.

What I was looking at were three letter-sized envelopes. In the left-hand corner, where a return address would normally have been, was May 7, 1976 #1. The date was that of last Friday. The same thing was on the second envelope, except the date was followed by #2. On the third, the date and #3. On the front of each was my name. All of this was written in what I recognized as Billy's handwriting. Looking at all three, I reasoned I was to open them in chronological order as numbered. I did this. In #1 was a two-page letter:

Dear old and trusted friend,
I know you're reading this and wondering why. Well, buddy, I'm writing it and wondering why. Why a man can have so much and be so miserable. Why it takes so little to make some people happy and yet so much can make some people's lives unbearable.
I have two wonderful kids, Freddy and Teeter. It breaks my heart to just write their names. And I have the greatest mother who has ever lived. A brother who would die for me and a friend, you, who would try to talk me out of this if you had only known in time.
But all of this just doesn't outweigh the pain and misery I live with every day. I love a woman so much who doesn't care if I breathe or die. I lay in bed at night and my heart races like I just jogged twenty miles. I don't sleep. I've lost sixteen pounds in the last four months. And you know better than anybody that this has been going on for so many, many years. Some days she's the woman I need and want her to be. But it never lasts over two days at a time. Then she is either gone or so hateful to the kids and me that I can't stand to be in the same room with her, but yet, I always want to be.

You know what's funny, buddy? If I could do it all over, I wouldn't change anything but her heart.

Now I know you're thinking I'm a heel for leaving my kids in this situation, but I know what I'm doing. Her parents will take the kids and she'll let them. And they will be better off. I just couldn't be mother and father any longer. It was killing me and it wasn't fair to them.

Is there another woman? Of course, there's always another woman. But nothing could ever be done about that. You know Patsy. Even though she didn't want me, she would never let anybody else have me. So, no matter how much I loved the other woman it would never have worked out. But that's why I'm writing you letter number 3. You can show that to whoever you have to legally show it to without having to show this letter to anybody else. This letter, buddy, is just between you and me.

Envelope number 2 is just some things I found this week going through an old chest of mine. Thought you might get a bang out of seeing a couple of things, so I stuck them in there.

There is not another note. The thing everybody looks for when somebody takes ultimate control of their own life. And there won't be. This is it. The only one.

Mom will be fine. Kiss her and tell her my last thoughts were of her. Give Jayo any help he needs. He's a good boy. And see that Patsy's parents get Freddy and Teeter as I'm sure they will. I really like her mom and dad. I always have.

And you. Well, you were always my best friend. There's nothing I can say to you that we haven't said with our lives. I only ask that you forgive me. I'm not crazy. I just don't want to get up anymore.

I love you, buddy,
Billy
P.S. Tell ole Toby goodbye.

May 1976

I sat in that little room with my head in my hands and my eyes closed and felt everything Billy felt when he wrote those words. The pages hung from my fingers and finally dropped on the small writing desk. I couldn't cry. I couldn't breathe. And I couldn't think anymore. I was consumed with the anguish that must have eaten Billy up. The pain and the emotion. I felt so helpless that an old friend had suffered so much, so long, so alone.

I folded the letter and put it back in its envelope and reached for #2. When I opened it, little pieces of tablet paper fell out. I recognized this handwriting even quicker than I had the other. I was startled for a moment by this fact and suspicious of who might have written these notes, until I realized that what I was seeing was also Billy's writing, but from some fifteen years ago. A less mature scrawl. I picked up the papers and read the scribbling on them, and my mind froze with the memory that streaked through it. In his teenage hand, the tablet papers said:

> *portend   fortune   auger- rive the spirits*
> *fortitude   experto kray e te*
> *heartbreak   conquer fears and doubts*
> *sickness in the family*
> *love is imminent   affairs of the heart*
> *love is hazardous if not checked*
> *infidelity   nay kay de malice*
> *peacefully under the shelter of safety*

They were the pieces of paper from the glove compartment of Daddy's old '57 Chevy. Billy had written these notes by the lights of the dashboard the night we went to see the gypsy. The actual pieces of paper. The notes we made and later

309

tried to figure out. We had saved them and read them and reread them and waited to see if her predictions would come true. "Love is hazardous if not checked. Infidelity. Ne cede malis (yield not to misfortunes)." Maybe we didn't wait long enough.

There was something else in the envelope. It looked like a clipping from a newspaper. I unfolded it and after close inspection saw that it had been cut from our school newspaper, *The Campaigner.* The date on the border said May 1962. It was the last edition before our graduation. And on closer scrutiny, I saw that it was a poem I had written for that publication. He had saved it all these years and I had forgotten all about it. I smoothed it out on the desktop and read the words I had written fourteen years ago to the month.

SCHOOL YEARS

THE SCHOOL YEARS WE LOVED AND HATED SO LONG
WILL SOON BE A PART OF OUR PAST
THE MEMORIES WE MADE, WE WOULDN'T TRADE
FOR THEY WILL ALWAYS LAST

SOME TEACHERS WE LIKED, SOME TEACHERS WE LOATHED
AND SOME FELT THE SAME ABOUT US
FROM COACH LAMBERT'S P.E. TO MISS PECK'S WORLD G.
I WOULD GIVE THEM AN AVERAGE C+

SO MANY THINGS WE WILL LEAVE BEHIND
LIKE DANCES, PEP RALLYS AND CHEERS
THAT BASKETBALL SHOT, THAT HOMERUN WE GOT
THE LAUGHTER AND THE TEARS

I KNOW WE'LL MISS THE GOOD AND THE BAD
AND THE MEMORIES WE MADE EACH YEAR
THE SENIOR PLAYS, THE PIANO DAYS
AND THE FRIENDS WE HELD SO DEAR

May 1976

There was a knock on the door. They knocked four times before I was able or willing to answer. I finally cleared my throat and said, "Yes?"

The door opened and Roger stepped in. He had a concerned look on his face. "We need to go as soon as possible."

"I'm not through yet," I said, not caring why he had to go. "I have one more envelope."

Roger saw the redness in my eyes and the frustration on my face and decided to take charge of a quickly developing situation that I was unaware of. He spoke to me sharply and like a guardian. "Patsy and her lawyer just walked in the lobby of the bank. I don't know why they're here, but I would have to conjecture it's to find you. I don't know how they knew about you being here or if they know fully why you are, but we need to act fast."

"We're not doing anything illegal, are we?" I asked, not really caring at the moment if we were or not.

"No," Roger answered abruptly. "But if there is anything here she shouldn't see, well, she shouldn't see it. Is there something here she shouldn't see?"

"Yes," I said.

"Give it to me," Roger advised and took the three envelopes and put them in his inside jacket pocket. "Now if she asks you if you have anything, don't lie. Tell her you don't."

"What can she do?" I asked for Billy.

"Well, nothing. But let's not give them, her and her counsel, any ground to cause us undue problems. Leave the box and let's walk out the front door and play it by ear."

We did just that until we were stopped by Patsy in the center of the busy Tuesday morning lobby of the North Sentry Security Bank. She had on a black raincoat with a matching black, floppy brimmed rain hat and dark sunglasses. She looked like a female spy from a grade B foreign film or, at best, the woman in the old MUM commercials in the 1950s. Her lawyer looked like a piece of bacon with a cheap suit on. Or maybe I was just mad for Billy's sake and looking for a fight.

"What are you doing here?" she asked in a voice I had forgotten and with a tone I had forced out of my memory.

"I had business here this morning," I said softly, so as not to attract any more attention than had already been accomplished. "And how are you?" I said sarcastically.

"Not very well, thank you," she answered mockingly. "I just lost my husband and don't need the likes of you here nosing in our business. Now what were you doing back there? Did you get in his safety deposit box?"

"What I was doing, Patsy, was no business of yours. Let's not make a scene here, okay?"

"Did he leave you something back there? Did he leave you some sort of note or something? I demand to know what he left you, and if it was a note I demand to know what is in it!" She was raving.

So was I. "Shut up, Patsy."

"One minute here," the Strip of Bacon said as he stepped between his client and me. "I'm counsel for Mrs. Hudlow, and I'll not have you speak to her in those tones."

I stepped closer to the good counselor, as close as two humans can get without one putting the move on the other, and spoke as directly in his left ear as I could while holding his left forearm in my right hand. "Speak to me one more time and I will rip your tongue out of your mouth and stick it down your throat. And I'm not kidding."

He pulled back, white and short of breath. "I take that as a threat of bodily harm," he said, trembling.

"Good," I said. "That means you were paying attention."

May 1976

Roger stepped in and took me by the arm and started guiding me toward the door. I was feeling so many emotions I couldn't recognize them all. I was grieved and angry and guilty for starters. Grieved for an old and best friend. Angry at his wife who had pushed him to his present state and then brought a lawyer with her to aggravate an already sensitive situation. And guilty at having let that friend down when he most needed someone who loved him to listen to him and reason with him. Those mixtures of emotions are dangerous and can cause even the most even-tempered man to temporarily lose control. And I'm not all that even-tempered to start with.

Patsy's voice stopped me before I reached the door. "Was there anything in there to tell if it was suicide?"

I stopped and turned around and walked back to her. I stood for a second, looking into her face. Her features were still pretty, but there was a hard edge to them. That drain that takes over when there's too much turmoil going on inside. There were no laugh lines around the eyes or the mouth. No softness that most feminine features convey. Nothing vulnerable or giving or caring. Just a face that had potential to be pretty and attractive but could only give uncomfortable looks and stares and speak harsh words and make demands. I stared into eyes that went nowhere. "How do you want it, Patsy? Do you want to hear that it was suicide to relieve your own conscience? Or do you want to hear he killed himself so you can feel one last sense of power in knowing you had that kind of control over another human life to the very end? How do you want it?"

"I just want the truth," she said back to me, never flinching.

"The truth is he loved you more than anything else on earth ever since you were fifteen years old. That's the truth. But you've had the truth for years and never did anything with it, so how could it possibly make any difference to you now?"

This time I left. She and the Bacon were still standing in the lobby plotting new and devious plans, I'm sure. Roger walked me to the car. I thanked him and he handed me the envelopes from his coat pocket. We promised to talk before I left town. He went to his car and I sat in mine and opened #3.

May 7, 1976
To All It May Concern:
This letter is to advise the executor of my estate and my legal representative that this letter should become an addendum to my will, dated March 24, 1974, and should be honored accordingly.

In addition to provisions made in that will and before any of those provisions are made, I wish to leave $10,000 cash to Mrs. Lannie Mae Granetti, 2236 Pine Hills Drive, Jackson Falls, Virginia.

William T. Hudlow

Life is full of little surprises and shocks and traumas. Birth is the first one, and we spend most of our lives getting over that. Then the pains of growing up and suddenly the realization that we have grown up and still don't know everything we are supposed to know. That's the big surprise. That we never know what we should and what we thought we would by the age we are at the time. We're always reaching and learning something new. And here I sat in my rented Chevelle, in a cloudy spring mist, with my hands full of letters from a dead friend who was giving me one surprise, shock, and trauma after another.

I drove home, to my mother's house, and ate a late breakfast. Then I sat down in the den and looked through one of my old Jackson High annuals she still kept on the bookshelf. I

May 1976

looked up every name and picture I could remember. I read all the silly stuff in the back such as the "most likely" this and that and even read some of the embarrassing things people had signed in it. "To a great guy." "To a real special guy." "Remember the fun we had in History class." And all the stock things kids have been writing to each other for decades and maybe centuries. I finally laid it down and came back to the present. I put it back on the shelf where it belonged and proceeded to do what I knew must be done.

"Hello."
"Lannie, you probably don't know who this is and..."
"Yeah, I know who it is."
"Well, maybe you know why I'm calling, too."
"Yes. I know that, too."
She gave me no quarter. I think that means mercy or slack. John Wayne used to say it in the movies and it's the only place I ever heard it.
"Lannie, I need to talk to you, and I don't think we should talk over the phone." I waited but heard no response on the other end. Finally, I said, "Do you want me to come to your house?"
"No," she said politely but firmly. "I'll meet you at Roman's."
"I don't know where that is," I said, a little confused.
"It's a restaurant on Main Street where the Burger Barn used to be. You know where it is. I'll meet you there at four o'clock."
"Okay," I said, "and I'll..." But she had hung up.
I placed the receiver back in its cradle and tried to picture her wherever she was. I tried to picture how she might look

now. How she would dress. Where she lived and what her furniture was like. And as I took my hand off the phone and sat there staring into space, strange numbers popped into my brain and I had to smile at it all. I could still remember her old phone number. But that was at her mother's, another house and another time.

I walked in the old Burger Barn, now Roman's, and saw checkered tablecloths on little round tables and skinny-backed chairs where the booths with jukeboxes used to be. I saw low-slung brass lamps hanging where the old bright florescent fixtures used to glare down on us. Abstract paintings of I couldn't tell what were covering the spaces where giant menus used to hang and high school banners used to drape. The Carpenters were singing softly through speakers Chuck Berry used to boom through. Almost everything had changed. Almost. Something was the same but I couldn't tell what it was. I could sense it but I couldn't see it. I also couldn't see if anyone was sitting at the tables, so I stood at the door and soaked in the changes while my eyes adjusted to the dimly lit room. Then in the back, next to the wall, I saw a lone figure. The only person in the place. She had long blonde hair, and although I couldn't see her face clearly, I could see the smoke around her head and smell a strong scent of perfume as I walked closer. My mind was racing with what should be my opening words. When I opened my mouth, I still didn't know what I was going to say, so I just let my natural charm lead my silver tongue.

"Lannie Mae?" I asked more than greeted. But she said nothing. She just looked at me and confirmed the feeling I got from talking to her on the phone earlier. She was cold and hard and bitter and yes, changed. Time had puffed her eyes and given a sag to her cheeks and a sadness to her lips. Time had given her an air of detachment and mystery. She was not pretty

May 1976

anymore the way I had imagined her. All the things I remembered about her were no longer to be seen. No trace of her sweetness and gentleness. She looked tired and weary, like an entirely different woman. Oh, my soul! This *was* an entirely different woman. I took a step back and realized in embarrassment that I had no idea who this lady was.

I fumbled and moved away and found a table on the other side of the room and waited, uncomfortable and self-conscious. The woman in the long blond wig smiled, shifted in her chair, and blew smoke at me from twenty feet away. With my elbows on the table, I rubbed my forehead with both hands and sighed while I remembered when I could rub it with just one. I closed my eyes and wondered if I'd be bald in ten years. Fifteen? I could feel the waitress at the table, and without looking up I said, "Just coffee, please."

Then I felt the waitress sit down and heard her say, "Get it yourself." The waitress was, of course, Lannie Mae, and she was smiling. And the only thing that had changed about her was her dress. She was even prettier than her younger self as only women who are aware and caring get. She had a healthy and elegant glow about her. Her makeup was tasteful and appealing, and she reminded me of all the summers of my youth and all the people I used to know.

"You scared me," I said honestly.

"Scared you? Do I look that bad?" she joked and at the same time left open a canyon for a compliment.

I remembered why I was there, so I didn't bite for the obvious. She looked great and knew it and I knew it and it was unnecessary to discuss it further.

"It's just that I thought I was alone except for...oh, ah," I said facetiously as I saw the only other occupant coming toward us. "We're getting company."

Lannie Mae turned and looked casually at the blonde woman approaching who had been sitting, smoking at the back table when I came in. She turned back to me and said, "Oh, that's my mother. She works for me a couple of hours each evening."

A number of things puzzled me about her last sentence, and I didn't know where to start asking questions that would unravel it.

"That's your mother? I don't think I ever saw your mother."

"She comes and goes. Always has." Lannie Mae finished talking with her mother standing close beside us and hearing every word, but she talked as if she were nowhere around. "Two coffees," she ordered, and Mamma turned and trotted to the kitchen. She brought her attention back to me and said informatively, "This is my place. I've had it for about eighteen months. Mother always lived with us for about a year at a time. Then she'd pick up and leave. She's been doing that since I was seven years old. She still does it. So whenever she's back, I let her work here. She likes it and it makes me feel charitable."

"You bought this place?" I asked, rather impressed.

"You might say," she smiled. "My husband, his name was Roman, we had it together. And then we split up and I got the restaurant. Did you come to eat?"

I took this as my cue that the history lesson was over and it was time to get on with the business at hand. "I'm the executor of his estate," I said, using the euphemistic "his" instead of Billy's name. It was my way of being discreet or stupid. I hadn't decided which. "There was a letter in his lockbox and in it he mentioned you."

She really looked at me for the first time. "Then you know," she stated more than asked.

May 1976

"Well, if I were a TV private detective, I would act like I know a lot more than I do and try to entice you to tell me more. I'd say something like, 'If a married man leaves $10,000 to a woman that looks like you do, I'd have to be pretty thick not to figure it out.' And also, Toby told me."

"Toby." She laughed and shook her head. And then her eyes filled and she looked up in exasperation and took a deep breath. "What did Toby tell you?"

"All he could, which wasn't a lot. He knew there was an affair with someone but even he didn't know how serious it was."

"Not until the ten thousand dollars, uh?" she said sarcastically. "That's how men judge seriousness. Wow! Ten thousand dollars! He must have been serious about that broad." Her voice was angry. And then she cried. She had been wanting to, I think, and I guess I just gave her enough reason to go ahead and do it. And I was glad she did. She needed it and Billy certainly deserved it.

When she stopped, she wiped her eyes and looked in mine and said, "And I suppose you want to know all about it."

"No, Lannie. I don't need to know all about it. I just came to tell you that you have ten thousand dollars coming. I didn't want you to go through the hell you're going to have to go through tomorrow not knowing that one of his last efforts was to take care of you in some small way. It won't make you rich, but you'll know he did it at some risk to his reputation and the welfare of his children."

I don't think she heard any of this.

"I'm going to tell you about it anyway," she said. "What we had was not cheap. It was back alley only because it had to be. Only because of Patsy Shriner and the unholy hold she had on him."

"Hudlow," I said.

"What?" She sounded startled.

"Hudlow. Patsy Hudlow. Not Shriner."

She didn't hear that either. Or she didn't catch it. Or she just refused to acknowledge it.

"We were at a PTA meeting," she continued. "I was by myself and so was Billy. She never took any interest in anything those kids did. Never went to ballgames or school plays. Nothing. It was always Billy by himself. She reminds me so much of my mother, who still hasn't brought those coffees. And, of course, Roman never went anywhere with me. So, one night at a PTA meeting of all places, we just happened to sit together and talk. We had never talked before. Never the whole time we were in school. Just...never. And then we were both put on a sports booster committee of some sort and we had meetings every other Thursday night and from there it just happened. She kept him crazy all the time. One week they were all lovey-dovey and the next she was off somewhere and he was depressed, and then she was back and he was happy and then he was with me and he was scared and...oh, dear God. I don't know. But I'll tell you this. I didn't kill him if that's what you're thinking. It wasn't us that made him kill himself. It was us that kept him alive as long as he was. She did it. She killed him the same as if she'd run him off the road and threw a match on him. She killed him seventeen years ago."

I wanted to say something to mitigate the drama but I wasn't sure what might be appropriate, so I resisted and just sat there and sipped the coffee Mamma had finally brought.

"You've fixed this place up nice," I said. "Lots of memories in here."

She didn't hear any of this either.

"We talked about you," she said quietly. "He knew all

May 1976

about you and me. Teenage boys talk a lot, don't they?"

"Teenage boys would have nothing to talk about if it weren't for teenage girls," I philosophized. We both chuckled at this and drank some more coffee. "Lannie, nobody loved him more than I did. And I'm not going to sit here and defend Patsy Shriner to you…"

"Hudlow," she corrected. "Patsy Hudlow." She had heard after all. She always was one step ahead of me. She was still a year older and I thought that only made a difference in school.

"I'm not going to defend Patsy to you. I never liked her and I never thought she was good for him. And, yes, you're right. What happened out there on that road Sunday night has been inevitable ever since that night at the Hop when we were fifteen years old and he first danced with her. He was hopelessly and helplessly in love with her then and ever since. But he was never happy. Love doesn't always make us happy. People misconstrue this. Love can poison you and it poisoned Billy. And if you made him happy, even for just hours at a time, you have my gratitude. No one deserved being happy more than him. And no one will know about that letter but the ones who absolutely have to in order to execute it."

"I don't know why you feel about all this the way you do unless you really do understand," she said. "And I hope you do. I don't care who knows about that letter. I loved him and I'm glad someone else knows he loved me. And I don't want the money. I could use it, but I don't want it. Give it to his children. I already have what I want. I have someone who knows and understands the truth without judgment. Thank you."

I couldn't quit looking at her and remembering how pretty she used to be and how beautiful she was now. Her heart was always right. She never meant any harm to anyone. She was a victim. And I needed to leave.

"Are you going to the funeral?" I asked, more to break my own concentration than for a need to know.

"Can I? Should I?'

She wanted me to tell her. Like the little girl she still wanted to be, she needed guidance. This woman who hired and bossed her mother wanted permission from me to go to her lover's funeral.

"Yes, Lannie! Absolutely yes! It's at two o'clock. You can go with Abby and me. You can walk in with us and sit with us. You want me to come by and pick you up?"

She leaned across the table, kissed me on the cheek, and said, "No, that's all right. You just did."

Then she got up and walked to the back and disappeared into the kitchen.

I sat alone at the table for a few extra moments and strangely thought of my daddy, of Miss Kathleen Moyers and her son, Basil. Of all the people who struggle with life and the people who protect them and respect them as human beings no matter what other people think of them or say about them. And I felt a certain fullness for Lannie Mae and for Billy. Maybe I was off center in my feelings, but I don't think so. As a matter of fact, I think Daddy would have approved and maybe even been proud of me.

I took my time walking to the door. I looked around again at the old Burger Barn, and as I was reaching for the door handle I realized what it was that hadn't changed. The floor. It still had the same tiles. The same ceramic squares those boys and girls I used to know walked on and danced on and spilled Pepsi Cola on and put their feet on while they sat in the booths and held hands. You can change the atmosphere and the colors, but the foundation never changes. It's what makes us who we are and forever keeps us who we were.

May 1976

I'm glad she didn't change the floor, although it could use a little polish from time to time. But can't we all.

That All-American funeral home ritual, the night before the Big Funeral, is too much party for me. Family and friends sit around the wall in their Sunday best and cry into tissues with everyone who comes through the line. And the line usually winds clear through the funeral parlor hallway and into the parking lot and consists of everyone who was kin to, knew, or even heard of the deceased. And yes, while all of this is happening, the guest of honor is lying quietly in a corner, on display for everyone to file past and stare at one last time.

He's the one everybody is talking about, saying, "Looks so nice." "Looks so natural." "Looks so peaceful." "Looks like he's going to sit right up and speak to you." He's the one in the room receiving all the compliments and hearing none of them. He is kissed and touched and cried on and talked about and stared at and even avoided by some. But he's the catalyst this party revolves around. And he will stay until the very end. He'll never disappoint his guests, never offend the late-comers, never question the early-leavers, and never grimace at the ever-crescendoing noise. There is sadness and warmth and curiosity and reunion and excitement and dread and laughing and storytelling. Parents and grandparents carry babies against their shoulders and show them off to family members they haven't seen since the last gathering in this very same room. People introduce new in-laws and children to old men and women who are still trying to figure out which niece or nephew it was they were just talking to. After all the hugging and shaking hands and listening and tearing, you try to make your way to the line that is slowly filing past the supposed center of attention.

Piano Days

Totally strange and vaguely familiar faces stop you repeatedly and try to engage you in every form of conversation. Some, who are spiritually moved each time a death occurs in the family, want to be sure you're saved. At least one wants to tell you a dirty joke. There are always a few who knew your parents in early life, and you can always overhear completely unrelated conversations between men telling stories about something that happened at work that day.

Each person in line views the remains with an individual style. Some stop and look at every detail, appearing to want to hold this sight in their minds through eternity. Some just glance self-consciously, never allowing their feet to stop as they pass, fulfilling an obligation they're glad will soon be behind them. Some talk to the person beside them as they look because they feel uncomfortable being alone with their thoughts and their ever-still friend. Others hold on to someone or have someone hold on to them. Some cry openly. Some silently. Some touch. Some stroke. Some stay at least four feet away. And some don't look at all.

Much too soon or not soon enough, the line diminishes and it's your turn at stage center. And having observed all the styles of viewing, you still don't know which style you will emulate.

I stood watching the procession and talking to people and keeping an eye on Ruth and Jayo on the sofa by the coffin. Toby was with me most of the time, but I missed him for a minute. I looked around and found him coming toward me with his arm around someone. They both walked up to me and stopped and Toby said, "You know who this is?"

Don't you just love introductions like that? I looked closely at the man standing beside him, and what I saw was a full, brown, briary beard, shoulder-length, dirty-blond hair,

May 1976

blue jeans, a crew-neck sweater, a gray wool sport coat, and sneakers. Nothing in his dress or his manner suggested I knew who this friend of Toby's was, but on closer inspection, something about the eyes seemed familiar. Then he spoke.

"Man, you really don't know who I am."

Oh, good Lord, it was Howard! I grabbed him and hugged him and he hugged me.

"Howard, how are you?"

"Hey, man, I'm hangin'. And how are you and the good life?"

"Great. Just great," I said, looking at him in disbelief.

"This the good woman?" Howard asked me, glancing at Abby.

I introduced them and tried to explain in brief who Howard was.

"What are you doing now?" I asked him, really wanting to know.

"Well, you know. Just coolin' out right now. I'm between. But I'm kickin', you know. Just kickin'. Ain't that a bummer about Billy?"

"Yeah," I said, looking at Toby. "Yeah, it was pretty rough."

Howard rubbed himself, his face, his beard, then his chest with both hands and continued a flow of talk while my gaze bounced from Toby to Abby in wonder.

"You know what's a killer?" Howard was saying. "Of all of us that went to Nam, Billy's the first one to buy the ranch and he didn't even go. He was married and had a kid and all before he got out of that school where he was goin'. But ain't that a killer? Ole Toby here, and me, we got shot at every day in the jungle, eatin' those bananas and mud and Charlie's fire, and Billy bites it before us. That's the odds, you know. You check your perimeters and then just peel the blindfold off of lady justice. You know what I mean?" He hit me playfully on the arm and added, "I know you know what I mean."

I knew all too well what he meant. And I knew more about where he was in life from his nervous ramblings than I wanted to deal with at the moment.

"I think it's the dreams that bother me most," Howard continued. "I'm okay in the daylight but at night, it just keeps comin' after me. But hey, I guess I need to go see old Billy. Is that him over there?"

"Yeah, that's him over there in the corner," Toby said, sounding briefly like his old self.

"We'll catch up with you later." And Howard ambled off in his permanent daze to stand alone by the coffin for at least ten minutes.

Toby looked apologetic, but at the same time he couldn't resist a mischievous smile. "I'm sorry about that," he said more to Abby than me. "Some days he's better than that. His brain is just burnt up and some days he's okay and…well, I couldn't tell till he started talkin'. But I've seen him worse. A lot worse."

"What about Bud? I haven't seen him tonight," I said, still keeping an eye on Howard over by Billy.

"I don't expect you'll see Bud tonight *or* tomorrow," Toby answered.

"Is he the same way?" Abby asked. "Was he in Vietnam, too?"

"No. He joined up the same as Howard but he never got out of the States. He wound up at Fort Knox his whole hitch. Howard went over but Bud never did. He was in administration and got a desk job somewhere along the way."

"Did he stay in?" Abby followed up.

"No. He works at GernTech with me. Been there, oh,

May 1976

eight or nine years."

I watched Howard while Abby and Toby talked, and I studied his clothes and his movements and marveled at how so many of us guys who came back from Nam ended up looking so much like and dressing so much like the ones who protested us being over there in the first place. Life deals us ironies we can only puzzle over. It left us all with our quirks and pains. I didn't look a lot like Howard on the outside, but I had a certain, kindred feeling that we were more alike on the inside than most would imagine. It was my turn to play Quiz Toby. "Why won't I see Bud tonight or tomorrow?"

"Him and Billy fell out a few years ago and they ain't spoke for I don't know how long."

"What about?" I asked, still not looking at Toby but watching Howard across the room, rubbing himself and pacing in front of the body. He seemed in a world and in a misery of his own.

"Aw, you won't believe this," Toby began, "but Billy and Bud both got boys about the same age and they coached a Little League Baseball team together one summer. Billy took Bud's kid out of the game or Bud put somebody in for Billy's kid or somethin'. I don't exactly know what, but anyway, they fell out on the field and almost came to blows right there. I think the game was finally forfeited to the other team and they cussed each other and as far as I know, they ain't spoke to each other since. Bad blood between 'em for years."

Abby looked skeptical. "Over a game?" she asked.

"Yeah." Toby laughed. "Little League is serious business around here. It's been probably three years anyway. That's how serious."

I was still watching Howard. He finally walked away and out another door. He had apparently decided not to come back to say goodbye or had forgotten we were even there. And to be honest, I was relieved. The line was gone and no one was with Billy. I took this opportunity to see him alone.

I made my final approach to him very slowly. My eyes were fixed on his face and the unnatural look it was going to carry to eternity. The human secrets, the everyday problems, the triumphs, the failures. The obvious agonies. I looked at his suit and thought of the day he must have bought it and how he couldn't have known as he first lifted it off the rack that this would be his final suit forever and ever. The school ring on his finger that would mean nothing to his body now but could mean so much to his daughter or his son. His hair was combed too deliberately. No one combs your hair the way you comb it yourself.

Memories began to race through my mind. Things we'd done together. Things we'd said to one another. The last time we'd talked. The first time we'd met. And as one last, awkward gesture of friendship, I reached out to touch him. But just as my hand was about to rest on his fingers, I was stopped by a sudden chill as I realized the watch on his left wrist was running. He was dead and his watch was still running. Not knowing exactly what I was getting from this revelation, I pulled back my hand and took into consideration that my time was up. There were people behind me and it was 8:23 p.m. I knew this because I had just looked at Billy's watch.

Toby and I were to be pallbearers along with two cousins of Billy's I didn't know very well and two business associates I didn't know at all. So we knew our duties for tomorrow and our schedule, but still we stopped at Ruth's end of the sofa before we left to offer added condolences and see if anything

May 1976

further was needed from us.

"No, no. You both have been so good. Thank you so much for staying so long tonight." She took Toby's hand. "And Toby, how is your father?"

"Not too well," Toby answered sincerely. "He wasn't able to come tonight but he said to tell you he was thinking of you."

"That's so nice," Ruth said through eyes that could hardly see.

I squeezed her hand and leaned closer to her and made the offer she had probably heard at least a hundred times tonight. "If there is anything at all I can do, just let me know."

How many times have we all made that offer to grieving loved ones and how often have they answered, "No, there's nothing"? Almost always. Almost. But not tonight. Ruth looked at me through weak and tired eyes and said, "Yes, dear. There is something. Would you play for Billy tomorrow? You remember how he always loved for you to play for him. Would you?"

"Ruth, I don't know," I stumbled. "I don't know if I can." We make those offers and then, when someone actually takes us up on them and tells us what we can do for them, we try to get out of it. But my doubts were legitimate. And I was honest with her.

"I haven't touched the piano for ten years," I pleaded. "And I'll be honest with you, Ruth, even if I could still play something, I just don't know if I'd be able to get through it or not.'"

"I understand. I understand. Tomorrow is not going to easy for any of us. But I just had to ask. I know that horrible war took so much of your heart and soul, and I pray for you every morning when I have my devotions. So don't you feel bad."

"Well, I do feel bad. I feel like I'm letting you down, but..."

"That's okay, honey." She took my hand in both of hers. "You're not letting anybody down. I know what you've been through and I know better than anybody what you're going through with all this. Just don't you think about it again." And she stretched up from her seat and kissed my cheek and told me good night, the way she used to at bedtime when Billy and I were little boys and I'd spend the night at their house.

I walked past Patsy and stopped and talked to the two children and then left with Abby and my mother. The night wasn't over yet.

I dialed Bud's number. He knew it was me immediately and maybe even knew why I was calling. After all the helloes and how-are-yous and other pleasantries, I got straight to the point of the call.

"We missed you at the funeral home tonight."

"Yeah, I couldn't make it."

"You coming to the funeral tomorrow?"

"Gee, I don't know. I ain't asked off from work or anything, so probably not."

"Aw, come on, Bud. What's so hard about this? The man is dead and he was once a good friend of yours. What's so bad you can't even come to his funeral?"

"Look, pal," Bud was getting hot. "I ain't seen you for over five years and then just on the street one Christmas, and you come back here all high and mighty and want to get in my face and in the middle of my life? You don't know the half of it, so back off."

"Yeah, Bud, I know the half of it. I know all of it. You fell

May 1976

out over a little boys' baseball game for heaven's sake. And you haven't spoken to him for three years."

"Hey, don't put it all on me," Bud corrected me. "Don't say I haven't spoken to him in three years. He didn't speak to me either. So don't make him a saint just because he's dead."

I paused long enough to take a deep breath and look at the walls and the floor. Bud waited in silence as if he knew I needed a little time to ponder and come back from his last statement, which, of course, was true.

"Bud," I started slowly and quietly, "have you seen Patsy?"

"No. And if I never see her again it will be too soon. And don't tell me you've gone soft on her either. You never could stand her any better than the rest of us."

I tried to ignore his logic, although it was getting harder to do by the minute. Maybe Bud should be counseling me instead of me, the self-appointed, self-important third party, counseling him. One more try.

"How about the boy, Bud? Freddy. Have you seen him? You coached him and had some sort of influence on him. Don't you think you could be of some help to him today and in the future? More than I can, that's for sure. I hardly know the boy. But you know him well and God knows he's going to need some kind of man to talk to. We can't throw him to the wolves and Patsy for the rest of his life. We owe that to him no matter what you thought of Billy. And we both thought the same of him at one time. We both loved him. You just didn't like him for a while. But what is that really in the big scheme of things? For all the years of playing ball and riding bikes and going to school and all the stuff we did, it's the least you can do for the man's son."

It was Bud's turn to pause and he did it well. And when he came back his tone was not exactly what I expected or even hoped for, but it had mellowed. His voice was soft and no longer angry at Billy. It had found a new victim.

"Just what do you get out of this?"

"Out of what?" I asked in all sincerity.

"What does it matter to you if I go to Billy's funeral or not? What does it matter to you if I talk to Freddy? What do you gain here? Goin' back to whoever asked you to call me and sayin' you talked me into it? Do you get some kind of thrill out of that? Does that make you feel like a big man or somethin'? Just who are you in all this anyway?"

"Bud, I'm just an old friend who didn't come home often enough. And when I did, I tried too hard to make things the way they used to be and we both know that's impossible. So I tell you what. You do what you want, and I really don't care if you come to the funeral or not. I'm sorry I called and I'm sorry you still hold a grudge against a man who was troubled enough to kill himself."

And I hung up. I allowed myself a few minutes of reflection before I got up from the side of the bed where I was sitting in Mom's room. But only a few. There were too many other things to worry about right now.

I slept that night in my old room again with Abby close beside me. The ghosts were there but they didn't disturb me. I think they knew how tired I was in mind and body, and even ghosts need a rest from time to time.

Mom and Abby and I slept late Wednesday morning and ate breakfast together. We took our time and finally Abby got up from the table, cleared it, and said she was going upstairs to make some calls. I was reading the local morning paper, thin as it was, when I realized I was sitting at the table alone. I

May 1976

looked up and saw Mom standing at the kitchen counter, aimlessly stirring a cup of coffee and looking into it as if it held the secrets of a lost universe. I got up and went to her and put my hands on her shoulders. "You okay, Mom?"

"It just all seems so unfair. Billy was such a good boy. Your father thought so much of him. Of all your friends, Billy was his favorite."

"Yes, I know. Mine, too. And he always like Daddy so much, too."

"I remember how he used to come and help Frank with things after you left home. He'd come on Saturday morning in the fall and help him put the storm windows in. And then you'd look up and here he'd come with a load of wood. Whenever he got himself a load, he always got us some, too. And if it snowed, he would be over here and have the walk shoveled sometimes before we even got out of bed. He was such a good boy, and your daddy thought so much of him."

The comfort I first felt from this conversation faded quickly. Hearing my mother talk about these two people I loved so much was more than I was prepared to handle on this particular morning. But I could see she needed it and maybe I did, too.

"And you know when your father passed away," she continued, "Billy was the first one over here. He came and stayed with me till your sister got here. He never left me for a minute. He thought as much of Frank as Frank did of him. He told me that night how he had always looked up to Frank and how he was the father he never had and how Frank taught him so much by just being the man he was."

Again, I couldn't get the memory of the Basil Herb night out of my mind. Daddy did have a way of dealing with people that I would never master. I could only try and hope to come close.

"I tell you, son, it just isn't fair. Billy didn't deserve his fate."

Should I tell her what I knew or hold that secret in me forever? Didn't she warrant the truth? Someone who had known him since birth, had helped raise him and obviously loved him the way she did? Shouldn't she know the truth about his life and his death? I didn't know what I was going to do until I did it.

"Mom, you know it was no accident," I blurted out and waited for her reaction.

She turned slowly toward me and looked at me quizzically and said, "Of course I know it was no accident." And then she turned back to her coffee.

She never stopped surprising me, the things she knew. Then I remembered that night on the front porch when Daddy had said he couldn't think of anything Mom didn't know. He was right, as he usually was. I finished my cup in silence while Mom put some dishes in the washer and dusted the crumbs from the table.

"Mom, you ever thought of selling this place?"

"Never," she answered without pause.

"Ever thought of getting rid of some stuff you don't need? Furniture. That old piano. Getting a smaller place. Getting rid of some of the reminders."

She looked at me sweetly and honestly and with a finality I could not ignore. "There's nothing here I don't need. Furniture or reminders. They are all a part of my life and they'll never go anywhere until I do. Now, if that old piano is what you want…"

"No. I don't want that old piano," I said firmly. "I don't play anymore. It's no longer a part of my life."

"Good," she said. "I wasn't going to give it to you anyway.

May 1976

Now go on upstairs and start getting ready. It'll be time before you know it."

The funeral was at two, and by one the crowd was already gathering at Ruth's. Soon a procession of family and close friends was on its way to the church. Toby and I parked our cars behind the limousine carrying the immediate family. We then preceded them in and took our seats with the other active pallbearers. I could look across the aisle and see Ruth and Jayo and his wife and Patsy and the two children in one pew. They were all physically supporting one another and emotionally letting one another down. I endured the service by studying the backs of my hands and smelling the too-rich aroma of flowers. I tried not to think of things that would cause me to become consumed with the sadness that was so thickly floating in the air.

The minister was saying general things and reading standard verses from the book of Psalms and trying to evoke feelings for someone he hardly knew. And he was doing all of this from the pulpit of the First Faith Presbyterian Church where Billy and I had grown up and attended since birth. We had gone to Sunday school in the basement rooms since we could walk. We had acted up in the pews as children and first taken Communion from these very seats. We had even once stolen a hymnbook from the rack on the back of the pew so I could play a song for Billy that he wanted me to learn. It was number 97, "At the Cross."

> *At the cross, at the cross where I first saw the light*
> *And the burden of my heart rolled away*
> *It was there by faith, I received my sight*
> *And now I am happy all the day*

Billy loved that old hymn. And I played it for him one whole week and then we got to feeling guilty about stealing a songbook from the church, so we sneaked it back in under his coat the next Sunday morning and no one ever knew it was gone.

It was in these pews we would pass notes to one another written on the backs of our bulletins. It was, now that I think about it, maybe this very pew I was sitting in when old Mr. Oliver Rose leaned over one Sunday morning to put his head down for the morning prayer and cracked his forehead on the back of the pew in front of him. It rang out like a gunshot in a cellar and Billy and I saw it all. We shook our pew for the rest of the service, trying to stifle our laughter. Daddy kept shaking his head at us, attempting to scold us and quiet us, but then he finally started laughing, too, and the whole bench nearly walked off with the entire family. And Lord in heaven please help me, it was right up there in the choir loft, so many years ago, when during an anthem featuring "The Old Rugged Cross," Miss Tilly Thompson, who fancied herself the superior talent in all the choir, made her place in musical history. As the lead alto, she stepped forward to sing her solo on the third verse and began singing the alto part instead of the melody. Once started, she couldn't get off of it and sang the whole verse, harmony only. Billy and I rocked the seat pretty good that morning, too. But Rosalee Heavener, the organist and choir director, saw no humor whatsoever in it and scowled and scolded Miss Tilly with looks of scorn throughout it all.

God must have allowed these little things to happen to test our faith and sincerity, and I'm afraid we failed the test. I just hoped we weren't failing it now. Billy's test was over and maybe mine was just beginning. The organ was playing a series of hymns and the minister had already sat down. I supposed he

May 1976

was through. My mind had wandered so much I wasn't aware of everything that took place. Then I heard a rustling around me as the men from the funeral home came down the aisle and began readying the bier for moving. I looked at the row of Billy's family across the aisle again. His brother Jayo, six-foot-three, muscular and strong and something near jelly from the love and anguish he was feeling for his big brother. Patsy, who had never loved him the way she should have, but then we can't choose the people we love, can we? His children, who I really didn't know but who must have adored this man who was certainly a good father. Such a good friend had to be a loving and caring father. And his mother Ruth, who was like family to me. She was shaking with silent and ladylike sobs, a handkerchief nearly covering her face, unable to watch the men who were beginning to move her firstborn son away forever. And me, the old friend, who had offered to do anything that was needed of me and who refused the one and only thing that was asked of me. I never felt lower and guiltier in my life. The last thing on earth I was doing for Billy was letting his mother down. And suddenly I knew I couldn't live with myself if I didn't fulfill her wishes and do the one last thing we both knew Billy would want me to do.

As the other five pallbearers and I walked to the front of the church to escort the body on its final trip, I didn't stop where I was supposed to. I continued up the steps, across the altar, and to the grand piano by the organ. The organist stopped playing as if on cue and watched as I raised the cover on the keys and sat down. The church went quiet, the pallbearers turned to watch, and I could feel the eyes and confused attention of everyone there. But I really didn't care. I had something I needed to do for Ruth and one last thing I wanted to do for Billy.

As I had told her the day before, I hadn't played for years. And I honestly don't know how well I did or how long I played. I only remember I played "The End." And maybe I played it through twice. I don't know. But I played it for all the nights at the Hop and all the trips to the Knoll and to the Twilight Drive-In and all the memories we had made together. And I played for all the sheet music he had bought me over the years and all the hours, into the night, he had sat on the piano bench beside me and just watched while I played it again and again. And I played it for all the years I would have without him. Without a best friend who could understand things without you ever having to say them out loud.

I only became aware it was time to stop when I realized the backs of my hands were wet from the tears dripping off my face. Then I stopped. I had played what Billy wanted to hear and now I'd carry him where he wanted to go. There's not much more I remember and not much more I want to remember.

I walked out of the church behind him, and along with Toby and four other quiet men, I lifted him into the back of his ride.

One funeral is not enough. There has to be another one at the cemetery. More public grieving and then the meeting and hugging of everyone who came. I had kissed everyone I wanted to kiss the last few days and didn't have many words left I hadn't spoken. Old friends I hadn't seen since graduation and people from the town I wasn't expecting to see. Mr. Dinkel from the grocery store. Larry Harley. Howard in his same pair of jeans and sport coat. The only thing different today from last night was that his shoulder-length hair was in a ponytail. Leland

May 1976

Perry. Admiral Dressel. I looked for Bud but I never saw him. I suppose his heart wouldn't let him change his mind. I stood between Mom and Toby while Abby stood off to the side as she didn't know all these people. I shook hands with Simon Lee Spinner. I stooped and spoke to and patted the heads of children of friends who I still remembered as children themselves. Kitty Huntley and Allen Welcher were there with their respective husband and wife. And across the grassy cemetery, I saw Lannie Mae Kiser Granetti standing alone. I wanted to go to her and say something that would comfort us both, when an old, strong, and weathered hand belonging to Coach Lambert reached for me and held me too long. By the time I got away from him, Lannie Mae was gone.

 I looked at Toby and then back across the lawn and told him with my eyes I was going to find her when a younger and more tender hand reached for me and gently stretched her face toward mine and held me longer than the coach had.

 It was Sue Jane.

 She spoke comfortingly in my ear at the same distance she had once spoken passionately in it. Either way, her nearness and her words still took my breath away.

 "I'm so sorry. So very, very sorry," she said, and I could feel her heart breaking.

 We cried. And I held her. Not for who she was but for who she had been. She pulled back and looked at me and let me stare into the still sweetest face I've ever stared into since or before. All people are made in heaven and sent down for some reason, but Sue Jane must have dropped out of God's pocket. She never took her eyes off mine while she spoke.

 "I'm putting something in your coat pocket. Something I want you to have. I've had it all these years and now I want you to have it. Look at it later and always know I love you." And then she just walked away.

Someone else shook my hand then, but I don't remember who.

There were cakes and pies and family and fried chicken and roasts and friends and crying babies and bread puddings and loud voices and much too much festivity for me at Ruth's house after the funeral. I didn't stay long. I promised her I'd see her before I left the next day. I shook hands with Jayo, I should say Jay, hugged Toby, and walked with Mom and Abby to the car.

When we got to Mom's house and she and Abby got out, I was overcome with the feeling that I wasn't ready yet. "You both go on in," I said to Abby. "I feel like I just want to ride around a little bit by myself."

"Take your time, honey," she said and leaned back into the car and kissed me.

I pulled to the end of the driveway, and for the first time in my life I didn't know which way to turn because I didn't know where I was going. All the times before, if I were going to school or Billy's, I'd turn left. If I were going to the ball diamond or Toby's or town, I'd turn right. It didn't matter, so I went right. I rode by Miss Kathleen Moyers's house, and only the peeling paint told me any time had passed at all. She still taught in that front parlor and I was hoping to maybe see her smoking on the front porch, but I didn't. Then Dinkel's was on the right and I started to stop and get a Popsicle but decided I would on the way back from wherever I was going. There in the late, quiet afternoon, the First Faith Presbyterian Church sat in wait of some more middle-of-the-week activity. Maybe a ball practice later this evening. I'd come back by and watch awhile, maybe.

May 1976

I took a left and rode out by the fairgrounds that still carried the name but no longer harbored fairs or carnivals. A new site had been built on the outskirts of town, and the old grounds were nothing more than a practice field for the T-ball teams and soccer. The pool, where we all danced and swam and tanned our youth away, was still covered. It wouldn't open until Memorial Day if the old schedule still held, and it probably didn't. Coming back toward town, I slowed down at the sight that set my heart to racing. The National Guard Armory. "The Saturday Night Hop is on the air!" I reached for the radio and thought, "Wouldn't it be something if I could pick up the oldies station right now and hear 'Alley-Oop'?" But then I pulled my hand away for fear I might.

Main Street. Christmas parades and Friday night shopping. Saturday morning movies and Saturday night cruising. And on the right, Seigel's Men's Shoppe. But it wasn't there. Old Cyrus and Mrs. Seigel had died years ago within two weeks of one another, and in the windows, where ill-fitting suits on chipped mannequins used to be, afghans and rag dolls and hand-stitched pictures were on display. A sign hung above the door that read, *Connie's Craft Store*. Then there was Roman's/Burger Barn. A notice on the front door said *Closed. Open Tomorrow for Lunch*. Good. I was glad she had taken a timeout as a show of respect for Billy.

Then I rode out to the other end of town to the Shepherds of Peace Holiness Church. The front door was already open. It was Wednesday evening and services were not far off. The windows were all open, too, but I knew that wouldn't last for long. Hamburger Hatch, the old drive-around drive-in restaurant, still looked about the same except now you could go inside and eat, too. A big new room had been added, and cars were packed all around the building just like twenty years ago. Then suddenly, as if it had jumped out in the middle of the road, there was the giant and ever-looming Jackson High School. Rumor was that next year would be the last year for it. A new consolidated school was already under construction, and Jackson High would be a shell with broken windows and cold, empty halls in no time. I didn't linger long there. I kept riding till I saw the broken marquee of the Twilight Drive-In and the weeds and cracked pavement. And I began to wonder if there was any place in town I really wanted to go or if it wouldn't just be better to remember everything the way it was. People, places, and time.

I should have taken my own advice, because within the next twenty minutes, I found myself alone and on top of the Knoll. The sun was gone but daylight was still fighting to be seen, and I could see the beginnings of the night lights of town down below. It was cooler up there. Always was. About five or six degrees cooler. I walked around and looked and touched familiar places. The old tree trunk that had been on its side for over two decades and maybe longer was rotted and nearly gone. I walked over and looked at the muddy bank that had been such a beautiful bed of grass that afternoon, the last day of high school. I remembered the first time we had sneaked up here, Billy and Toby and I, in Ruth's car, and run from the drunks. I remembered the parking and the music and the youthful privacy. And then I looked at the treetops the way Wyler Pratt must have that night and knew for certain what he must have meant. Nothing much had changed except the trees were taller and there were more lights down below.

This was where I needed to be. This is where it needed to end. Because Billy Hudlow wasn't the only person who had died this week. So many people I had grown up with had also passed away. That boy who used to live in my house and in

May 1976

whose room I'd been sleeping these past two nights, he had passed away, too. They were all gone, and here was where I needed to leave them.

I walked slowly back to my car, and as I opened the door to get in, I reached in my coat pocket for the keys and discovered something there I had forgotten about. Sue Jane had put something in my pocket, and as I took it out I saw it was a sealed envelope with no writing on it. I opened it carefully and found a picture inside. And not just *a* picture. But *the* picture. The picture of Billy and Toby and Sue Jane and me graduation night in our caps and gowns, framed in the doorway of the old gymnasium, hugging each other.

I sat there in the front seat of my rented car and sobbed. And then I started the engine and drove down the rough, bumpy, rocky road of the Knoll for the last time.

I slept once more that night in my old room with Abby close beside me. And the same ghosts came to visit. They sang songs to me I hadn't heard in years. They showed me pictures and scenes I thought were buried with the ages. Faces that seldom crossed my conscious mind. Names that had been lost with time. And memories that in general I just didn't allow myself to remember anymore. And at precisely seven a.m., as clearly as I can hear summer thunder, I heard Daddy say, "Come on, son. Get up or you're going to miss the school bus."

I got up quietly, so as not to wake Abby, put on my robe, went downstairs, and sat at the kitchen table to drink coffee and wait on the bus with Daddy.

This was the last chapter my mother ever received in the mail.

Once upon a beautiful time, this man I admired and loved so much, had enjoyed life and all the bliss and happiness that comes with youth. But a savage war raided his heart and soul and left him with little of the joy he had known in his young life.

Uncle Be-Bop was not meant to live long. He died in 1996 at the age of fifty-one. He left behind a loving wife, Abby, a devoted sister and brother-in-law (my parents), and three nephews of whom I am one. His last and final wishes were that there would be no obituary, no mention of his cause of death, no funeral, no memorial service, and, above all, no music.

May he rest, in the name of Jesus, in eternal peace.

ACKNOWLEDGMENTS

So, my sons, Debo and Langdon, who have taken over managing my writing career these days, said, "It's time for another novel." I didn't readily agree and told them other ideas I had in mind for my next book. They listened quietly to my other ideas and then shook their heads and said, "No, it's been ten years since your last one and it's time for another novel." I not only gracefully acquiesced, I caved to their borderline elder abuse and began writing.

Our good and respected friends at Mercer University Press, Dr. Marc Jolley, Marsha Luttrell, and Mary Beth Kosowski were their usual professional, friendly, and personable selves and made the whole project just a complete delight. God bless these folks, every one! The entire publishing world could learn from them about how to treat and get along with people.

My usual thank-yous go to my wife Debbie, my good friend Charles Culbertson, and of course, Debo and Langdon who read every chapter as I wrote them and cheered me on. This was a very personal and love-driven book that took me sometimes to places I wasn't expecting to go. But I thank you, the reader, for taking the journey with me. I hope you met someone along the way you remembered, liked, loved, and won't forget anytime soon. And about that dedication. Harold and I wrote lots of songs together about these times and these kinds of lovable people. This was just one big Statler Brothers song without the music.

Yeah, Bro Harold would have loved it!

About the Author

Don Reid, lead singer for the Statler Brothers, is a three-time Grammy Award-winner with twenty-one gold and platinum albums. He is a member of the Country Music and Gospel Music Halls of Fame. As a songwriter, he holds twenty-one BMI (Broadcast Music Inc.) awards. Also a television writer, this is his eleventh book published since his retirement from the music industry. Don lives in his hometown of Staunton, Virginia, with his wife Debbie and their dog Lucy.